Elizabeth Jeffrey was born in Wivenhoe, a small waterfront town near Colchester, and has lived there all her life. She began writing short stories over thirty years ago, in between bringing up her three children and caring for an elderly parent. More than 100 of her stories went on to be published or broadcast; in 1976 she won a national short story competition and her success led her on to write full-length novels for both adults and children.

Elizabeth JEFFREY

Hannah Fox

piatkus

PIATKUS

First published in Great Britain in 1998 by Judy Piatkus Publisher Ltd
This paperback edition published in 2012 by Piatkus

A CIP catalogue record for this book
is available from the British Library.

ISBN 978-0-7499-5797-1

Typeset in Sabon by Hewer Text UK Ltd, Edinburgh
Printed and bound by Clays Ltd, St Ives plc

Papers used by Piatkus are from well-managed forests
and other responsible sources.

MIX
Paper from
responsible sources
FSC® C104740
www.fsc.org

Piatkus
An imprint of
Little, Brown Book Group
100 Victoria Embankment
London EC4Y 0DY

An Hachette UK Company
www.hachette.co.uk

www.piatkus.co.uk

To my family in Sheffield
with love and gratitude for
their help and encouragement

Chapter One

It was one of the hottest days of the summer. Hannah could feel the sweat trickling down her back as she waited impatiently with the other girls while Joe Woods parsimoniously portioned out the wages. It wasn't fair, she fumed. She had been the one who had run all the way to the cutlers with the finished knives and razors and all the way back with the money, yet she would be one of the last to be paid because she was the youngest – except for little Tilly, who was only fourteen, two years younger than Hannah, and not yet old enough to be trusted with the precious razors. Or the money.

At last it was her turn. She held out her hand, two fingers wrapped in bloodied rags.

'That'll learn thee to tek a bit more care 'andling t'stuff,' Joe said, pointing to them as he counted out her meagre share. 'I hope tha took care not to bloody t'razors.'

That was all he cared about, Hannah thought bitterly. She could have cut off her finger and he wouldn't have cared as long as there was no blood on the razors.

She followed the other girls down the three flights of dim, rickety stairs. At each landing there were other workshops, and the grinders, chasers and silversmiths were all putting away their tools for the weekend, their grinding wheels and hammers still and silent now. Her father was there, along with the other grinders, but she didn't wait for him. His first call would be to the beer house; the thirst of grinders was legendary.

She came out into the yard where a few brave blades of grass struggled up between the greasy cobbles. The tall tenement buildings surrounding it on three sides blocked out the blazing sun and the worst of its heat but the air was still hot, thick and stifling with the sulphurous fumes that rose from the forge as the forger threw a bucket of water on his fire to dowse it for the weekend.

Some of the other girls in the team of acid etchers who worked for Joe Woods stopped and hung about the yard, gossiping and waiting to flirt with the men as they came out. But Hannah didn't wait. She was in a hurry because she was late – nothing new for a Saturday when the week's work had to be finished and delivered before wages were paid – and Stanley would be waiting for her on the corner of Norfolk Street.

Ever since Hannah had begun work, two years ago, just before her fourteenth birthday, her young brother Stanley had met her every Saturday on her way home and she had filched a farthing from her wages to buy him a treat, a stick of candy or a liquorice strip. He was twelve years old, her only brother and her favourite.

She hurried along the crowded Sheffield streets, noisy with the clatter of clogs, horses' hooves and iron-shod cart wheels, a tall girl, striking rather than pretty, with long, nut-brown hair that was usually tied back with rag, a pale complexion and a wide, generous mouth. But it was her eyes that people noticed. They were green, with hazel, almost golden flecks in them when she was angry or excited.

Not that she was often excited. Hannah's life was nothing to get excited about. It was dull, hard and for the most part dirty. Only in her dreams did she rise above the daily grind, telling herself that there must be more to life than learning to be an acid etcher at Fletcher's Wheel, as the tall, drab tenement where she worked was called. Fletcher's Wheel, like any number of tenements in the courts off Arundel Street, housed some ten or a dozen workshops rented out to self-employed craftsmen in the cutlery and silverware industry. These men were known as 'Little Mesters', and they worked for a pittance in unspeakable conditions to produce the hand-crafted pocket-knives, razors and all manner of exquisite silver-ware, respected the world over because they bore the proud title 'Made in Sheffield'.

This fact cut no ice with Hannah. Two years of working for Joe Woods and his team, delivering finished work to one firm, fetching rough work from another, collecting dinners from the cook shop, watching the various processes attached to acid etching, learning the dangers of corrosive acids, getting used to handling knives and razors that would have your finger off if you didn't watch out, convinced her that she had been born to better things. Not that Joe Woods' hull, as each work-shop was known, was any worse than the rest. They were all filthy, the whitewash – bug-blinding as it was known – turned to a dirty, peeling grey, the windows so grimed with the smoke of the town that they hardly let in any light, the stairs narrow and rickety, the paintwork chipped and blackened.

It was amazing that such exquisite work should be turned out in such squalid surroundings. Hannah hated it. She envied her sister Mary, who had recently gone into service. Hannah would have liked that. But she didn't have a choice. When it was time for her to leave school Nat Fox, her father, had happened to see a notice, GIRL WANTED, chalked up on the wall near Joe Woods' acid etching workshop and with no thought of consulting her, decided that it would do for his eldest daughter.

She glanced down at her filthy, bloodied hands as she hurried along and tried to wipe the worst of the blood and grease off on to the ragged dress she wore for work, all the time craning her neck to look out for Stanley.

He saw her first because she was tall and he waved and began to weave his way through the crowd, shouting excitedly to her as he was jostled out into the gutter by a group of men straggling across the pavement and already halfway to being drunk.

'Look out, Stan!' she screamed, and stopped in her tracks, her hand to her mouth in horror as she saw what was about to happen, powerless to prevent it.

It was over in a flash. One of the men had staggered and knocked into Stan, pushing him off-balance so that he stumbled straight into the path of a horse and rider galloping by. The horseman lashed out furiously with his whip, knocking the boy down as the horse shied and kicked out. Then he galloped on, muttering and swearing, without so much as a backward glance.

Hannah began to push and elbow her way through the crowd that had gathered round Stanley, now lying unconscious and bleeding in the filth of the gutter.

'Let me through. He's my brother. Let me through,' she kept shouting.

'Aye. Let the lass through. He's Nat Fox's little lad an' she's his sister.'

'Did tha see who was ridin' t'horse? 'E was goin' as if all t'devils in 'ell were after 'im.'

'Ay. It were young Truswell. Cutler Truswell's son.'

'He might have stopped, to see if t'little lad was hurt.'

'Stop? Not 'im. He's a reet mad allick, is that one.'

'There were no need to lash out at t'lad that road. It weren't 'is fault.'

'Poor lad could have been killed.'

'Niver even looked back.'

'Aye. Well, 'e wouldn't, would 'e? Too bent on cuttin' a dash.'

All this Hannah heard without really registering as she fought her way through to Stanley, lying where he had been thrown, in the gutter, a spreading pool of blood staining the filth.

She smoothed his hair back and her hand came away sticky with blood.

'Oh, Stan, lad, what have they done to you?' she whispered, cradling his limp figure in her arms. He was pale as death, his eyes closed.

'D'you live far?' Someone touched her on the shoulder.

'Off Wicker Lane,' she said without turning. 'Number three Angel Court.'

'Give him here. I'll carry him back for you. He'll not weigh more than two penn'orth.'

'Thank you.' She stayed crouched, watching, as the young man lifted Stanley gently in his arms and straightened up. She recognised him at once. He was Reuben Bullinger, a grinder who worked in the next hull to her father. She got to her feet to follow him and out of the corner of her eye she noticed something glittering in the filth of the gutter. She bent and picked it up. It looked like a gold thimble. Then she realised that it was the ferrule from the young horseman's whip. 'By,' she whispered through gritted teeth, 'he must have struck our Stan with some force to knock the end off his whip. Strikes me he's the one who could do wi' horse whipping, lashin' out at a young lad like that just because he fell in his path.' She clenched her hand round the ferrule. 'By 'eck, if I could get my hands on him, boss's son or no boss's son I'd give him whip!' Still clutching the ferrule she hurried after Reuben.

Jane Fox finished suckling the baby and put her down in the box that served as her crib. She was her tenth child, a pretty little thing, four months old now and still healthy. Frances, they'd called her, Fanny for short. Jane touched the downy cheek. It didn't do to get too fond of babies, they had a habit of worming their way into your heart and then breaking it by dying. Jane knew this from bitter experience. Four of her children were already in the churchyard, three of them never even drawing breath and the fourth dying after a matter of weeks. But this one looked as if she'd hold on to life. Jane smiled down at her.

'You're a bonny lass, Fanny Fox, even if you have made your Dad mad by being another girl. But I don't care. You stay bonny, that's all I ask.'

She cocked her ear as she heard a commotion in the yard. Quickly, she straightened up and hurried to the door.

'Yes, that's the one.' Hannah was pointing to the open door. Then she saw Jane. 'Mam, it's our Stan. He's been knocked down. He's hurt bad. Mr Bullinger carried him all the way home for me.'

'Bring him in and lay him on the couch, there.' A quick anxious look at her son and Jane indicated the old horse-hair sofa with its stuffing hanging out. 'And thank you kindly for your trouble, Mr Bullinger. It was good of you to carry him home.'

Carefully, Reuben put the boy down. He didn't know much about these things but the lad looked pretty bad to him. 'Shall I fetch the doctor, Missus?' he asked Jane.

Jane shook her head. There was no money for doctors in the Fox household.

'Thanks all the same, but we'll manage for ourselves,' she said covering Stanley with a ragged blanket. 'Blood allus makes things look worse. Hannah, love, fetch water and a cloth.' She turned to the two little girls who had crowded round to look at their wounded brother. 'You little 'uns, off you go, out and play in the yard. Give the poor lad room to breathe.'

Hannah took a bowl and went out to the yard to the tap. Reuben followed her. He was a tall, thin man of about twenty-five with a pale, serious face. Although he was a grinder he didn't behave like the others, swearing and spending most of their hard-earned money in the beer house. He lived with his mother and attended the local Ebenezer Chapel, which forbade both swearing and drinking. Because of this he was 'different' and the other men at Fletcher's Wheel didn't know how to treat him so they left him alone, making fun of him behind his back.

'Thanks for fetching our Stanley back,' she said as she waited for the bowl to fill. 'It was good of you.'

'I hope he'll mend well. I shall pray for him.' He frowned. 'It looks bad, that cut on his head. Wants stitching. And I noticed as I carried him home there's a nasty cut on his shoulder where the whip caught him.'

She nodded and gave him a brief smile, anxious to be rid of him now that Stanley was safely home. 'We'll see to it. Any road, thank you.'

'You're cut, too.' He pointed to the bloody rags round her fingers.

'Oh, that's nowt. They'll soon mend.' She hurried back indoors with the bowl.

The house was only one room deep but it was on four floors counting the cellar, which was too wet and rat-ridden to be used for much except keeping the coal, when they had any. The living room, on a level with the yard, was spotlessly clean but sparsely furnished. A table, two benches, the sofa and a stickback elbow chair beside the fire was the sum total, with a rag rug at the hearth. A cupboard built in beside the chimney breast held what food and crockery there was. Upstairs there was a double bed shared by Nat and Jane and the latest baby while the three girls slept on the floor in the attic. Stanley came off

8

best because now he was growing up he slept on the sofa in the living room.

Nathaniel Fox had never over-provided for his family; his thirst took priority over their needs.

As Jane gently sponged Stanley's head Hannah told her how the accident had happened. There was an ugly gash above his temple and a long laceration stretching from his shoulder to his elbow. She pointed to the gash. 'I reckon that's where the horse kicked him,' she whispered. 'An' look, that's where the whip caught him.' Her voice rose. 'Oh, I could kill that . . .'

'That'll do, my girl. Carrying on like that won't do our Stan any good,' Jane cut in. 'But I reckon you're right. Looks as if that whip caught him across the face, an' all.' She bent and kissed her son. 'It were a cruel thing to do to you, lad,' she whispered. Then she continued cleaning him up.

Stanley never moved as she worked and his breathing was shallow.

'I should go for the doctor, like Mr Bullinger said,' Hannah said, hovering anxiously. 'He looks real bad.'

'Don't be daft. How would we pay a doctor?' Jane's voice was rough with worry because she knew Hannah was right.

'I'll pay.' Hannah had been saving for months for a pair of soft leather boots like she'd seen in the window of Cockagnes department store but Stan's well-being was more important than footwear, since she'd either worn clogs or gone barefoot for most of her life, anyway.

'Wha's to do, then?' Nat came in. He'd received a message while he was with his mates at the beer house

9

that his son had had his head kicked in. He didn't like his drinking interrupted but Stanley was his only son, so he'd finished his beer and come home. Now he stood looking down at the boy, swaying slightly.

'Wha's wrong wi' t' lad?' His speech was slurred as he tried to get his fuddled brain round the unaccustomed sight of Stanley lying still and pale, his face still streaked with traces of blood.

'He had an accident, Dad,' Hannah said. 'He got knocked down and kicked by a horse.'

'Whose bloody horse? I'll kick his bloody horse, whoever it was. I'll . . .'

'He needs a doctor. Have you brought any money home or have you already tipped it all down your neck?' Jane cut in, her voice harsh.

Nat stared at her owlishly. He wasn't used to being spoken to like that. He felt in his pocket and slapped sixpence down on the table. 'That's all tha's gettin', woman, now shut thee face.'

He turned back to Stanley, trying to clear the haze from his mind. The lad looked proper poorly and no mistake. He wished he hadn't paid Ma Ragley so much off the slate. She could have waited. Then they could have sent for the doctor. If only he'd known . . . But it wouldn't do to admit that to Jane. A man had his pride.

He sat down at the end of the sofa, his hand on Stanley's foot as if he could somehow pass life to him through the contact. Stanley was his pride and joy, his hope for the future. Stan was going to make a fortune and see his old dad right. And now he was hurt real bad and there was no money to send for the doctor.

10

He sniffed. It wasn't really his fault. If Jane didn't keep falling for babies she'd be able to work more and there wouldn't be so many mouths to feed. He'd only to throw his trousers on the bed and she was up the duff again. All girls, too. Except the one. And now Stanley was hurt and he'd no money for the doctor.

'It's all right. Hannah's gone for the doctor,' Jane said, weakening under his hang-dog expression. 'She's paying, too. She's a good lass, is Hannah.'

'Aye. She's a good lass.' He coughed, long and hard. Jane watched him, an extra knot of anxiety twisting in her chest. Grinder's asthma. He'd been lucky to reach the age of thirty-eight before it began to take its toll. Once it did there was no going back. No cure.

The doctor came back with Hannah. He put several stitches in Stanley's head and went away, taking Hannah's boot money with him. He hadn't even looked under the blanket to see if there were any further injuries.

'How did it happen? I want to know how it happened,' Nat kept repeating. He was still sitting at the foot of the sofa, holding on to Stanley's leg.

Hannah repeated what she had seen, leaving out the identity of the horseman and the fact that he had struck the boy with his whip.

'Who was riding t'bloody horse, then?' he demanded. 'Tell me who was riding t'bloody horse!'

Hannah shrugged and lowered her eyes. 'I didn't see. Anyway, what does it matter? It wasn't his fault. Stan fell in his path. He was pushed off the pavement.'

'Tha's a bloody liar, my girl. Tha did see. I can see it in tha face. Now, out with it. Who was it?'

'I – I'm not sure. I believe it might have been young Truswell.' She whispered the last word because she knew it would be like a red rag to a bull.

'By Christ I knew it!' He slapped his knee. 'T'bloody Truswells again! Allus t'bloody Truswells! By God, if that lad dies . . .'

Hannah held her breath. The Truswells were the biggest cutlers in the town, barring Wolstenholmes, and her father hated their very name. In fact, ever since she could remember Nat had held the Truswells responsible for every misfortune, big or small, that befell the Fox family. She could never discover exactly why this should be, except that when he was drunk, which was most of the time, Nathaniel waxed maudlin on the subject of some mythical fortune that should have come to the Foxes if they hadn't been cheated out of it by some member of the Truswell family. Just what this fortune was and how they had been cheated was never made clear; because when Nat was drunk he was practically incoherent and when he was sober even the mere whisper of the name Truswell was enough either to plunge him into black despair or to send him off on a tirade against fate, punctuating every other word with a blow in the direction of whichever child – or indeed Jane, his wife – happened to be within reach.

'Never mind t'Truswells!' Jane's voice cut across Hannah's thoughts. 'Stan's going to be all right, Nat. He'll not . . .' She couldn't even bring herself to say the word. She bent over and stroked his hair, still wet from where she had bathed it and sticking spikily up through the bandage the doctor had wound round his head. 'You'll be all right, won't you, lad? You're strong. You'll do.'

12

It was wishful thinking. Few children in Victorian Sheffield were healthy, let alone strong and Stanley was no exception. He was short for his age and his legs were rickety. But as if in answer his eyes fluttered open, then closed again.

'There! What did I tell you?' she said looking up happily.

Hannah, watching, felt in her pocket. The gold ferrule was still there. Her hand closed round it, giving her a warm, comforting feeling. Because here was something she could sell. And the money would provide endless delicacies to help Stanley's recovery and if in the end he had to go to hospital – she was still anxious about the cut on his head even though her mother didn't seem overconcerned – there would be money for that.

On the other hand – a sudden thought struck her – she could take it back to its rightful owner! And she could give him a piece of her mind with it! She'd let him know that just because his father owned Truswell's Cutlery Works it didn't give him the right to lash out with his whip at a young lad who had had the misfortune to fall under his horse. She'd let him see that the Foxes weren't a family to be trifled with.

Her mind made up, she went out to the pump and fetched water which she took down the steps to the cellar. There she stripped off and washed carefully, ignoring the rat that watched with interest from the far corner. Then she went up to the attic and put on the only dress she possessed apart from the one she worked in. It was a red gingham that had faded to an almost uniform pink and was a bit tight under the armpits so she had to be careful as she brushed her hair and tied it back.

'Where are you off to?' Her mother looked up from spreading bread and dripping for the children's tea, one eye still on Stanley.

Hannah tossed her head. 'I'm going to Cutwell Hall to see t'Truswells,' she said, without looking at her father, who was still sitting at the end of the sofa.

'Thee'll not go beggin' to t'bloody Truswells!' Nat sat bolt upright at the mention of the word Truswell.

Hannah looked at him coolly. 'Why not, Dad? You're always saying they owe us, so why shouldn't they pay for Stan to get well?'

'I'll not have thee beggin' favours.'

'I'll not *be* begging favours. But I'm going to tell them what happened an' if they like to give me summat to pay for the doctor I shan't refuse it.' She had thought it all out and was determined not to be put off. 'Fair's fair, after all's said and done.'

'Fair's fair!' he mimicked. 'Fair don't come into it. When's life ever been fair to me? I'm tellin' thee. Thee'll get nowhere. Thee don't know t'bloody Truswells like I do.'

'We'll see.'

'Tha'll *not* see! Tha's not goin'!' Nat thumped his fist down on the table.

Hannah's eyes flashed golden. 'I'm going! It's for our Stan an' I won't be put off.' Her mouth set in a hard line.

'Speak to me like that, my lass, an' I'll tek me belt off to thee.' His face darkening with rage Nat stood up and began to unbuckle it.

'My leg hurts.' A plaintive little cry came from the sofa.

14

Nat and Jane both turned to their son. Hannah watched as Jane uncovered Stanley. His leg was swollen and bruised but it didn't look too terrible.

She snatched the opportunity to slip away before her father got his belt off.

Chapter Two

Hannah set off. She wasn't altogether sure where Cutwell Hall was, except that it was on the edge of the town, out Endcliffe way, but she was sure she would be able to find it because the Truswells were sure to live in the biggest house.

She left the Wicker and crossed Lady's Bridge. The River Don ran sluggishly beneath, murky and stinking from the filth that found its way into it, partly from the smoke-blackened steel mills and wire works that lined its banks and partly from other unsavoury sources. But she didn't notice the smell as she hurried on; her thoughts were too full of what she would say to young Mr Truswell when she came face to face with him. He should be ashamed of himself, hitting a young lad so hard that the end came off his whip. Stanley could have died . . .

She hurried on, until she crossed the end of the road where her sister Mary worked. Halfway across she stopped in her tracks. Mary didn't know about Stan's accident. Perhaps she ought to be told. Just in case . . . It wouldn't take a minute.

Impatient at having to make a detour yet knowing it was the right thing to do, Hannah ran up the road to the house where Mary now lived. Mary hadn't long worked for the Brownings and all Hannah knew about them was that Mr Browning was a floor walker at Cockagnes, the big department store in Angel Street, and wore a frock coat. She hoped they wouldn't mind her calling on Mary.

She reached the house, in a neat-looking terrace, and went down the steps to the basement and knocked at the door.

Mary answered it. She looked very smart in a white starched apron over her black uniform dress, a cap with long tails perched on her curls. She scowled when she saw Hannah.

'Hannah! What's up wi' you? Can't you leave me alone five minutes? It's nobbut six weeks sin' I left home.'

'I've come to tell you about our Stan. I wouldn't have come, else,' Hannah said sharply.

'What about him, then?' Mary said impatiently, obviously with no intention of asking her in.

'He's had an accident. He were knocked down and kicked by a horse. He's hurt bad.'

Mary covered her mouth with her hand and her voice changed immediately. 'Oh, Annie! How bad is he?' Now she stood aside for Hannah to enter.

'Bad enough for t'doctor to come and stitch his head,' Hannah said bluntly.

Mary slumped down on a chair, still with her hand to her mouth. 'Is it . . . ? Will he . . . ?'

Briefly, Hannah told her what had happened, finishing, 'It were an accident. Our Stan was shoved into the road

17

by some fellas who'd had too much to drink. It wasn't his fault he fell near the horse and scared it.' Her expression hardened. 'But there weren't no call for young Mr Truswell to lash out at him the way he did.'

'Oh, my Lor'.' Mary's eyes closed as if to shut out the scene her imagination had conjured up.

'Do you want to run home and see your brother for yourself, Mary, lass?' Cook looked round from the depths of the rocking chair where she was resting her aching feet. 'I'm sure t'missus wouldn't mind.'

Mary hesitated. She didn't want to go home. She didn't want to go home ever again to squalid Angel Court – Angel Court, that was a laugh – where her father did nothing but work and drink his senses away and her mother slaved her fingers to the bone trying to keep the family decent and where the cradle never seemed to be empty. Here at the Brownings' she slept in a proper bed, in a room that was all her own. She'd discovered that there was a better life and she was determined never to be dragged back to the old one. She shook her head, half ashamed.

'No, better not. I've got to take t'missus her tea soon,' she mumbled. She turned to Hannah. 'But you'll let me know how he goes on, Annie, won't you? You can come any time,' she added eagerly, trying to make amends both for her lack of welcome and her reluctance to go back home. 'Can't she, Cook?'

'Aye, that she can. And welcome.' Cook smiled round her chair at Hannah.

'Don't forget to give our Stan my love.' Mary went over to the dresser. 'Oh, and you can take him . . .'

'I can't take him anything. I'm not going home just now,' Hannah said quickly, going to the door.

Mary looked round in surprise. 'Where are you off to, then?'

Hannah pulled back her shoulders. 'I'm going to have it out with young Mr Truswell at Cutwell Hall. Look.' She opened her palm and showed Mary the gold ferrule. 'This came off his whip when he lashed out at our Stan. That just shows how hard he hit him. Well, he can have it back and I'll give him a piece of my mind to go with it. Nobody treats my little brother like that an' gets away with it.'

Mary's eyes widened. Then she laughed. 'Don't be daft. You'll never get near him. Look at you. You haven't even got any shoes.'

Hannah didn't laugh. 'Maybe not,' she said grimly. 'But I've got this, haven't I!' She threw the gold ferrule up in the air and snatched it as it came down. 'And look, it's got his initials carved in it. TJT, so he can't pretend it isn't his.' She shook it in her fist. 'By, you just wait till I see him . . . !'

Mary watched her climb the steps to the road. 'Well, I wish you luck,' she called after her. 'But you're wasting your time, if you ask me. They'll never let you see him.' She turned back into the house, adding, 'But I wouldn't want to be in his shoes if she does. I know what my sister's like when she gets her dander up!'

Hannah continued on her way, out on to the long, long road, uphill nearly all the way that led to Endcliffe and hopefully to Cutwell Hall, where Sir Josiah Truswell and

19

his son lived. As she walked she thought about her younger sister.

She hoped Mary realised how lucky she was to be working in that lovely house. Hannah had only seen the kitchen but she had been impressed by all the china arrayed on the dresser, plates of all sizes, with big dishes and enormous oval platters all to match, and the rows of saucepans hanging along the wall near the big range and the polished copper jelly moulds displayed on the mantelpiece. She had never seen anything like it in all her life.

And Mary had looked so smart in her uniform. It suited her slim figure and pretty face. She had always been the 'lady' of the family, Hannah reflected. She had never liked scrubbing floors or helping with the little ones, preferring to play in the street or to hide away to sort out her treasures, such as they were, in the box she kept in the attic beside her bed. And Mary had never been the one that had had to stay at home from school, losing precious learning time when Mam was lying-in with yet another baby. That had always fallen to Hannah, being the eldest. Yet Mary had hated going to school. Hannah was the one who was desperate to learn.

Guiltily, Hannah pushed away the feeling of envy towards her younger sister, remembering that she had good reason to be grateful to Mary. Because Mary had helped her to fill in the schooling she had been forced to miss, albeit reluctantly. It had been real hard work, Hannah thought wryly, recalling how she had bullied her sister into helping her with her letters and numbers. In fact, in the end Hannah could read and write and do figure work better than Mary could by dint of practically teaching herself, sitting at the kitchen table when the others were in bed, nearly dropping from fatigue after a hard day's work at Fletcher's Wheel, laboriously scratching letters and numbers on the slate she had bought with the few precious coppers she could keep out of her earnings, and risking her father's wrath at wasting the candle when he came home drunk.

It was ironic that Mary, who had no ambition beyond marrying a nice young man who would provide her with a decent home, should have landed herself a job with prospects, whilst Hannah, who was ambitious, was stuck at Fletcher's Wheel. Her work was hard and filthy with not much chance in the way of furthering herself, because although there were many different processes to be gone through in the craft of acid etching Joe Woods made sure that each girl only knew her own process so that there was no competition between them. It could be deadly dull. Hannah would have liked to learn everything, to learn about the different acids that were used, to learn about different knives and razors and why some were marked on one side and not the other and some on both, but so far all she had done was run errands and stick on transfers ready for the etching process until her fingers bled. But her father wouldn't let her leave, saying he'd got her the job and she must stick with it, especially as Joe Woods didn't complain too much if she had to have time off to look after Mam when she was poorly.

She trudged on. The sun still beat down although it was now quite late in the afternoon. It shone brighter yet was less oppressive in the clearer air now that the road was rising out of the industrial smoke. She had never been

21

this far out of the town before; even the trams didn't come as far as this. She could see trees in the distance, and hills, too, all shades of green and brown and purple, with great rocky crags sticking up into the skyline. She thought she had never seen anything more beautiful and she held her breath in wonder at the scene. The houses were becoming bigger now, half hidden by trees and with wide stretches of moor between them. How rich the people must be to live in these houses, she thought, her feelings a mixture of admiration and awe.

Suddenly, the enormity of what she was planning to do hit her; her heart began to thump wildly and panic twisted her stomach into a tight, painful knot. She sat down in the heather at the side of the road and rubbed her sore feet. Mary was right, she realised. She would never be allowed to see young Mr Truswell, let alone speak to him. And as for giving him a piece of her mind! If she came face to face with him she'd be too tongue-tied to as much as open her mouth. She might as well turn back now, before she made a fool of herself.

Then she thought of Stanley, lying there looking so white and ill and she thought of the injustice of it all and her determination returned. She got to her feet and began to look for Cutwell Hall.

She had no trouble in finding it. Two large stone lions stood rampant on gateposts ten feet high, holding wrought-iron gates over which the words CUTWELL HALL arched in huge wrought-iron letters. The gates stood open to a long drive winding through parkland dotted with sheep. The house stood at the end of the drive, a square mansion built of stone, with a porticoed entrance and rows of long windows. With her heart in her mouth Hannah went through the gates and began the long walk towards the house, cooling her aching feet by walking on the soft grass at the side of the gravelled drive. As she walked she rehearsed what she would say when – if – she came face to face with the young man she had come all this way to see.

She must be polite. Polite but not grovelling. 'Sir, my brother fell under your horse's hooves this morning. It wasn't his fault, he was shov . . . knocked off the pavement. If you please, there was no call for you to lash out at him with your whip like you did. No, it's no good you denying it. Look, I've brought this back. It fell off the end of the whip. That just shows how hard you hit him.' Then she would tell him how bad Stan was and how they'd had to call the doctor and then the young master would offer her some money – quite a lot of money – and say he was very sorry and if there was anything else he could do . . .

Suddenly, she was aware of the noise of horses and the rumble of wheels. She turned round guiltily.

'Out o' t'way, thee've no business here. This is private land.' The coachman had his whip raised and she put up her hand to fend off the blow.

'Ay, I know that, Sir. But I have got business here, if you please. I've come to see . . .'

'Who is it, Maskell? What's the hold-up?' A lady in an enormous feathery hat poked her head out of the coach window. 'Oh, I see. Well, what are you doing, walking here, girl? Don't you realise this is private land?' Her voice was soft and gentle and not at all unkind.

Hannah instinctively dropped a curtsey. 'Begging your

23

pardon, m'Lady. I was hoping to see young Mr Truswell.'

'Were you, indeed! And for what purpose, may I ask?' As she spoke Lady Truswell looked Hannah's figure up and down and heaved a brief sigh of relief at what she saw, or rather didn't see.

Hannah didn't notice. This was not at all what she had planned; it had never occurred to her that she might encounter anyone other than young Mr Truswell, unless it was a servant who would be despatched to find him, and she was busy trying to work out how to deal with the situation. She stole a glance at Lady Truswell. Her dress was a beautiful blue with lace all down the front and the feathers that covered her enormous hat were exactly the same colour. And so were her eyes. Large, kind eyes in the most beautiful face Hannah had ever seen. She took a deep breath.

'Well, y'see, m'Lady, it were like this . . .' She told her story, exactly as it had happened, her concern mainly with her young brother who she feared was likely to die. As she finished she held out the gold ferrule.

'I picked this up. It were in t'gutter under where our Stan had fallen. I brought it back because it must have fallen off the whip when t'young master lashed out at our Stan in his temper. It just shows how hard he must have hit him.' Her voice began to rise. 'There weren't no call for him to hit our Stan like that, m'Lady. It were a cruel thing to do. After all, it weren't Stan's fault. He were pushed into t'road. He's only a little lad and not very strong. If you ask me, it's the wrong one as got the whipping.'

Suddenly appalled at the way she had let her own

temper run away with her Hannah stopped and bit her lip. She realised that with that little outburst she'd thrown away any hope she might have had of getting help from the Truswells.

'I'm sorry, m'Lady,' she said in a quieter voice. 'I shouldn't have said all that, even though it's true. Here' – she held out the ferrule again – 'you'd better have this back. I reckon it's worth a lot of money.'

Lady Truswell put out a gloved hand and took it daintily from Hannah's sweaty palm.

Hannah turned to go back the way she had come. Her mission had failed.

'Wait a minute,' Lady Truswell called. 'I haven't said you could go.' She gazed at Hannah. 'You weren't tempted to sell the ferrule, then? As you say, it's quite valuable.'

Hannah hesitated. 'I did think about it, m'Lady, but it weren't mine to sell, so I brought it back.'

Florence Truswell leaned forward and once more studied Hannah from head to foot.

'Have you come far?' she asked.

'From t'Wicker, m'Lady.'

'And without a hat, too!' She didn't appear to notice Hannah's lack of shoes. She smiled. Hannah thought she had never seen such a sweet smile. She couldn't understand it, after what had gone before.

'Are you hungry?'

Hannah hesitated. It was nothing new to be hungry. 'A bit, m'Lady.'

Lady Truswell nodded. 'Then go up to the house,' she said. 'The kitchens are at the back. I shall send word that you are to be given something to eat before you return home.'

Hannah's eyes widened and she dropped another curtsey. 'Oh, thank you, m'Lady.'

Florence Truswell leaned back in her seat. 'Drive on, Maskell.'

Hannah carried on up the drive and round to the kitchens at the back of the house. It was the biggest house she had ever seen; even the Queen didn't live in such a big house she was sure.

By the time she reached the kitchen door word had reached that she was to be fed and there was a plate of cold beef and bread and a glass of milk waiting for her on the end of the kitchen table. With several pairs of eyes watching her suspiciously she took it and went to sit on the doorstep in the sunshine where she felt less conspicuous. The sooner she could eat it and be gone the happier she would be. The whole afternoon's episode had been a disaster and her face flamed every time the enormity of what she had done, or had tried to do and failed, hit her. All she had wanted to do was to shame young Mr Truswell into giving her a bit of money to make Stan better. A tear trickled down her cheek and she brushed it away. Now she would have to go home and face the belting from her father without even the satisfaction of thinking it had been worth it.

She ate the food, wishing all the time she had some means of wrapping it up and taking it home for Stan because she had never tasted anything quite so delicious in the whole of her life. Then she got wearily up from the doorstep, dreading the long hot journey home with nothing to show for her stupidity, and put the plate and mug back on the end of the kitchen table.

'Thanks, it were a treat,' she said to nobody in particular. 'I'll be off now.'

'No, you won't,' a rather stern-looking woman in a black dress with a bunch of keys hanging from her belt said sharply. 'M'Lady gave orders you weren't to leave until she's seen you.' She swept Hannah with a look that said she couldn't think why before glancing at the enormous wall clock ticking away beside the range. 'It'll be about half an hour, I should think.'

'I'll go back and sit on t'step, then.'

Whatever could m'Lady want? Whatever it was Hannah didn't intend to wait to find out. She felt sick with fear and shame and the sooner she could get away from this place and try to forget she had ever been here the better. She sat down on the step for a moment and examined the blisters on her feet. There were people in and out of the house at the moment but as soon as things had quietened down and there was nobody about she would be off down that drive and you wouldn't see her backside for dust.

Meantime, it was pleasant sitting in the sunshine, looking out over the neatly laid-out kitchen garden to the trees and hills beyond. She had never realised such views existed. Her horizons were bounded by smoke-blackened buildings. And here everywhere was quiet and peaceful compared with the noise and bustle of the town; she could hear the birds singing and even the clatter of pots and pans coming from the kitchen behind her seemed restful. She leaned her head against the door post and closed her

27

eyes for a moment, savouring the fresh, clean air, gathering her strength to run as soon as the coast was clear.

Florence, Lady Truswell, went up to her room and rang for tea. Her husband, Sir Josiah, often joined her at this time for a quiet and private half hour. It was a time she looked forward to every day.

He arrived as Percy, the housemaid, came in with the tea tray.

'Has the girl been looked after, Percy?' she asked as she lifted the silver tea pot.

'Yes, m'Lady.' Percy bobbed.

'I wish to see her before she goes. I'll ring when I'm ready.'

'Yes, m'Lady.' Percy bobbed again, privately thinking m'Lady must be out of her mind.

'What girl, Florrie?' Sir Josiah made his ample frame comfortable in the armchair opposite his wife. Florence told him.

'Cheeky young puss!' he said angrily when she had finished. 'She's got a nerve! Why didn't you send her packing, my dear?'

'Precisely for that reason, Joe. Because she had nerve enough to come here. She felt an injustice had been done, yet she was honest enough to return Tom's gold ferrule.'

Josiah nodded. 'He'll be glad to get that back. His godfather gave him the whip and had his initials inscribed on the ferrule.'

'Keep to the point, Joe. I think you should speak to Tom. He had no call to whip the child.'

Sir Josiah sighed. 'I always seem to be "speaking" to

that young puppy for one reason or another. The sooner he's in the Army the better, if you ask me.'

'We won't discuss that now, Joe. You know my feelings on the subject. About the girl . . .'

'What girl? Oh, yes. Well, what about her?' He frowned. 'Why do you want to see her, Florrie?' he asked suspiciously.

Lady Florence poured her husband a second cup of tea and put an extra lump of sugar in it. 'I think I shall ask her if she would like to work here,' she said lightly, adding before he could control his dropped jaw enough to argue, 'After that unfortunate business with Becket, our daughter Sophie is without a maid. I think this young lass might do very well in her place.'

'But you don't know anything about her, Florrie!'

'What difference does that make? Becket came on Lady Grenville's recommendation and what happened? In less than six months she got herself pregnant and had to be dismissed.'

Sir Josiah blushed at his wife's forthrightness, too embarrassed to remind her that the girl couldn't have got pregnant on her own. And also remembering the scene he'd had with young Tom. He'd reminded him, yet again, that wild oats were sown outside the house, that was an unwritten law. It simply wasn't done to bed the servants, it upset the smooth running of the house.

'And what makes you think this lass won't do the same?' he asked, to cover his embarrassment.

'I liked the look of her. She's honest. She's open and what's more to the point, she clearly has no time for our son.'

Josiah cleared his throat uncomfortably. Florrie was more perceptive than he had given her credit for. 'Well, my dear, hiring servants is your domain. I can't say I think you're wise but if you're set on the idea . . .' He cleared his throat again, anxious to get back to his study and a calming cigar.

'I am, Joe. And if you've finished your tea, I shall ring and speak to her now.'

'She may not want to come,' he said hopefully as he got up and went to the door.

Lady Truswell smiled sweetly. 'We shall see, shan't we?'

Chapter Three

Hannah danced home. There was no other word for it. Her feet hardly touched the ground as she skipped along, twirling and swinging her arms. She could hardly believe her good fortune and she kept looking at the half sovereign in her hand. She was to work at Cutwell Hall, the most beautiful house in the world, *and* she had money to make Stanley better! Oh, wouldn't Mam and Dad be pleased! She could hardly wait to get home and tell them.

And to think she had so nearly missed the chance! If she hadn't fallen asleep on the doorstep in the sunshine she would have run home, forever more to be shamed by the memory of her rash behaviour and would never have known Lady Truswell's intentions.

As it was she had been terrified when the footman woke her and took her to Lady Truswell's sitting room. Lady Truswell's *sitting room*, surely the most beautiful room in the whole world, with its beautiful pink carpet, so soft to Hannah's bare feet, and its elegant, spindly furniture. But Lady Truswell had been so kind and gentle

31

and had even given her a half sovereign to pay for bananas and oranges for Stanley. Bananas and oranges, indeed. Some of that cold beef would have done him more good than bananas and oranges, Hannah considered. But then she had asked Hannah questions about her home and family and about her work and she had seemed so interested that Hannah hadn't been a bit shy in answering them. In fact, she had even been bold enough to say how much she hated sticking transfers on all day and how lucky her sister Mary was to be in service.

And then, to her amazement Lady Truswell, instead of sending her away, had asked if she would like to come and work at Cutwell Hall! As maid to her daughter, Miss Sophie! At that point Hannah was sure she must have died and gone to heaven! But it was all true and she was to start work on Monday. If her parents agreed.

That bit had been rather awkward. Lady Truswell had wanted to write them a note and Hannah had had to say quickly that there was no need, she would tell them. She didn't want to admit that neither Mam nor Dad could read.

She was so full of her wonderful news that she hardly noticed the atmosphere becoming thicker and more oppressive as she left the open countryside and came into the town with its jumble of steel works and factories, overshadowing the sunless tenements where the little mesters wrought their miracles in silver and the crowded courts where they and their families lived.

Over Lady's Bridge and into Wicker Lane and home.

It was dim inside the house because no sunlight penetrated Angel Court. She stepped inside and waited for her eyes to become accustomed to the lack of light. Then she saw her father, still sitting at the end of the couch, with his hand on Stanley's leg. He had fallen asleep with his mouth open and he was snoring loudly.

She nodded towards Stanley, raising her eyebrows questioningly.

'He's a mite better, I do believe,' Jane whispered. 'He took a sup of broth and said his head ached. Then he went off to sleep. But his leg is proper poorly. Your dad bound it up against t'broom handle to straighten it. I hope it'll be all right.'

Hannah looked. Blood was beginning to seep through the bandage round Stan's head but he was less pale now and his breathing was even and steady.

Satisfied he was no worse she could contain herself no longer. She held out her hand towards her mother. 'Lady Truswell gie me this for our Stan,' she said excitedly.

Jane looked at the half sovereign in Hannah's hand and then up at Hannah, a suspicious frown on her face. 'How did you come by this, my lass? An' where would t'likes o' you see such as Lady Truswell? I want t'truth, mind.'

'I'm telling the truth, Mam. I went there. I went to Cutwell Hall like I said I was going to. I was that mad with young Master Truswell for whipping our Stan that I went to see 'im and gie 'im a piece o' my mind. But m'Lady came along in her carriage and she stopped so I told her instead.'

'You never did!' Jane was shocked to the core.

'Yes, I did.' Hannah lifted her head proudly and her voice rose in her excitement. 'And she weren't mad at me. She ordered me to be fed an' I had cold beef and bread and a mug o' real milk, all creamy and white.' She rubbed her stomach at the memory. 'Ee, Mam, it were lovely.' She went on, 'An' then I was sent for to go up to m'Lady's room – ee, Mam, you should see that house. It's more like a palace – and she gie me this money for our Stan. An' what do you think, Mam? She said I'm to go there to work!'

'Go where?' Jane frowned. She was having difficulty in following Hannah's excited gabble.

'To Cutwell Hall, o' course.' She shook her head impatiently. 'As maid to m'Lady's daughter! Miss Sophie, her name is. What d'you think of that, Mam! An' I'm to start Monday an' I'm to be given two set of underclothes and two uniform dresses! And *shoes!* An' I'm to get three guineas a year besides. An' me keep! Jus' think of it, Mam. I'll never have to go to Fletcher's Wheel again because I'm to work at Cutwell Hall! An' it's the most beautiful place I've ever seen. An' Lady Truswell . . .'

'Tha can forget that. Tha's not workin' for t'bloody Truswells.' A growl came from the end of the couch.

Hannah turned to her father. 'But, Dad, look!' She held out her hand to show the half sovereign in it. 'Lady Truswell gie me this to make our Stan better.'

He waved it away. 'I'll have no charity from yon Truswells. Thee can tek it back.'

'But, Dad . . .'

'I'm tellin' thee, I'll have nowt to do wi' t'Truswells an' I'll not see thee havin' owt to do wi' 'em, neither.'

'But I'm to work there, Dad. Lady Truswell said so. I can't go against what she said,' Hannah pleaded desperately.

'I'm thee father.' He banged his chest. 'You'll not go against what *I* say. An' I say thee'll not go workin' for t'bloody Truswells. An' that's my last word.' He closed his eyes.

Hannah looked at her mother in dismay. Jane spread her hands. She knew better than to cross her husband.

Seeing she would get no help from her mother Hannah took her courage in both hands. 'What's wrong wi' t'Truswells, then, Dad?' she asked. 'You've always said you hated them but you've never said why.'

'I've said. A hundred times I've said,' Nat growled. 'T'Truswells swindled us out of what was rightly ours.' He warmed to his tale and flailed his arms in the general direction of Endcliffe. 'It's us as should be livin' in Cutwell bloody Hall, not them an' I'll not have thee bowin' and scrapin' to them up there when it's them up there as should be bowin' and scrapin' to us down here.'

'But what did they *do*, Dad? You've never said what they did,' she persisted. 'And if I'm not to go and work there I reckon I've a right to know.'

Nat got to his feet. 'Thee've a right to know nowt. Bloody nowt,' he shouted. He shook his fist at her and would have hit her if she hadn't stepped back.

'She has, Nat.' Jane could contain herself no longer. 'If you'll not let her tek a job as she's set her heart on it's only right as you should tell her why.'

'Because I bloody say so!' Nat thundered, turning on her.

'No, Nat, that'll not do,' Jane said quietly. 'All these years you've ranted and raved about the Truswells but you've never really said what they did to you.' She sighed.

35

'I guess they never did owt. It's just made you feel better to pretend to have somebody else to blame for the fact that your childer run barefoot with empty bellies.' She closed her eyes, knowing full well that she would have to pay for that statement later, but willing to risk it for Hannah's sake.

'You bloody . . .! Are you callin' me a bloody liar?' He raised his fist at his wife but she had prudently put the table between them before she spoke.

'I'm waiting to find out,' she said quietly. 'And don't raise your voice. You'll wake our Stanley.'

Hannah held her breath, looking from her mother to her father and then back again. She had never seen her mother stand up to her father like this before.

Nat came and sat at the table, leaning forward and resting his elbows on it. 'All right. I'll tell thee what t'bloody Truswells did,' he said belligerently. 'I'll tell thee this, an' all. If it hadn't been for them my father would have been a rich man and it'd have been us riding around Sheffield in a fancy carriage instead o' them.'

'Go on then, tell us,' Jane prompted. She'd heard this much so many times that she was unimpressed.

'Gie me time, woman. Gie me time.' He glared at her. Then his face hardened still further as he began his tale. 'My father, Stan Fox – we named our lad for him – were a silver chaser. He were a clever lad too, by all accounts, drawin' an' suchlike, tha knows. He had a pal, Abe Truswell. They'd allus been pals, more like brothers really, sin' they were brought up livin' in t'same court – somewhere at t'back o' Coal Pit Lane – an' they kept together even when they started work for Bob Cornthwaite.

36

He were a silver chaser with a workshop off Matilda Street.

'Well, t'two lads learned their trade from Bob, but by all accounts although they were both good craftsmen Stan had a flair for design that Abe lacked. And Stan could draw, too. He'd sketch his designs on owt he could lay his hand to, scraps o' card, bits o' wood, he'd even draw on t'wall if there was nowt else handy.' Nat got up and fetched his pipe. Then he lit it and got it drawing before he went on. 'That was his downfall. He should have teken more care of his drawings, but it all came so easy to him that I reckon he thought nowt of 'em.' His lip curled. 'But that bloody snake in the grass Abe Truswell knew they were worth a bit, 'specially when he found out that Marshams, the cutlers off Bridge Street, were looking for a new designer. But he didn't let on to Stan. Oh, no. Instead o' that t'crafty bugger helped himself to some of Stan's best work – he even traced t'ones off t'walls – and took 'em to Mr Marsham, passing 'em off as his own work.' Nat puffed on his pipe for several minutes, even now his eyes narrowed in hatred. Then he coughed long and hard before going on. 'Old Marsham was right teken with these designs and thinkin' they were Abe's own work he took him into t'firm straight away. Then, o' course, it weren't long afore Abe – Abraham now, if ye please – were all done up like a dog's dinner, wi' his top hat an' gold-topped cane an' walking out wi' Mr Marsham's daughter. T'next thing they were wed and he were a partner in t'firm. An' all in less than a twelvemonth! After old Marsham died t'firm were even renamed

Truswell's! An' he built that bloody great house, runnin' alive wi' servants and employed I dunno how many extra people on the firm.' Nat spat in the fireplace. 'An' it was all done wi' *my* father's designs.'

'Not just with your father's designs, surely, Dad. I think Abe Truswell must have been a good businessman to have built the business up to what it is now,' Hannah ventured.

'That's as maybe. But what I'm sayin' is, he'd never have got in there in t'first place if he hadn't pinched *my* father's designs, although nowt could ever be proved, o' course.' He shrugged and admitted, 'Wi' sketches layin' all over the bench who's to prove who did which?'

'So they could likely have been Abe's own designs anyway,' Jane suggested.

'No they couldn't! Abe hadn't the flair for drawin' that me dad had. The drawin's were me dad's. He told me so himself. Many an' many a time.' Nat glared at her, daring her to contradict him.

Jane and Hannah exchanged glances. Hannah sighed. 'Well, whatever the rights and wrongs of it, Dad, it's all in the past now. It's got nothing to do with me and I don't see there's any reason to let it blight my life.'

Nat stood up and leaned over towards her. 'It's blighted mine, by God. I should have been a rich man. *I* should be t'one living in t'big house, not bloody Abe Truswell's son. An' *I* should be riding around in a posh carriage, not him. It's *him* as should be coughin' his lungs up at Fletcher's Wheel, not me.' He jabbed his chest with the stem of his pipe to emphasise each word. 'No, by God. T'Truswell's have done enough damage to my family wi'out insultin' us by wantin' my daughter to go an' slave for 'em.' He sat down and began to cough again.

'But, Dad . . .' Hannah began.

He glared up at her, still coughing. 'I've tell't thee, I'll not have a daughter of mine work for that family!' he said between spasms. 'An' if tha goes there to work then tha'll be a traitor to thy family name and tha'll not be welcome under my roof. An' that's my last word on t'subject.' Exhausted, he leaned back and closed his eyes.

'But what about this?' Hannah held out her hand and noticed that she had unconsciously been clenching her hand so tightly that the imprint of the half guinea was impressed on her palm. 'It'll pay for t'doctor . . .'

Nat opened his eyes and leaned forward to snatch the coin. 'It'll pay for what I think fit.' He got up and went to the door. 'I need a breath o' fresh air,' he said and went off.

'You'll not get a lot o' that in Ma Ragley's beer house,' Jane remarked to his retreating back.

'Oh, Mam! He wouldn't spend that money on beer!' Hannah protested, shocked.

Jane shrugged. 'You'll see.'

Hannah sat down heavily. 'Why can't me dad see this is my chance to better myself? Why must he always rake up the past? What happened to my grandfather's got nowt to do with me, when all's said and done.'

'Your father can't see any further than the bottom of a beer mug,' Jane said. She leaned over and laid her hand on Hannah's arm. 'As I see it, he's got to have somebody to blame for his life an' he's got to have a dream of what it might have been like, if only . . .' She sighed. 'Me, I never expected much so I'm not disappointed with what

I've got.' Her eyes rested on Hannah and her gaze softened. 'You're a good lass, Hannah, and now you've got the chance to get out, to make summat of your life. You're lucky.'

Hannah shook her head, her expression tortured. 'But, Mam, don't you understand? I can't take it. I can't go to Cutwell Hall. Not after what he's said. Not if it means I won't be able to see you and Stan and the little ones.' She gazed affectionately at her brother, sleeping through the drama taking place around him. 'And I'd got such plans to help you all,' she said dreamily. 'Three guineas a year, I was to have. An' I wouldn't need it because I'd be fed and clothed so you could have it all . . . But it's no use. I couldn't go, not knowing I'd never see you again.'

Jane looked thoughtful. 'Maybe we could arrange something,' she said vaguely. 'You'd not be able to come home, of course, not after what your dad said.' She glanced round the dim, shabby room. 'But that wouldn't be much of a loss, would it?'

Hannah followed her gaze, then a vision of the beautiful house she had visited rose before her. She could live there. She could actually live at Cutwell Hall! It was a chance in a lifetime.

Her gaze rested on Stanley and once again her spirits wavered. How could she leave him? And what would her mother do without her if there should be another baby?

'Oh, Mam, I don't know what to do,' she whispered, tears running down her cheeks.

'You must decide for yourself,' Jane said. 'Sleep on it. You've got till Monday morning to make up your mind.' She couldn't bring herself to put pressure to bear on her eldest daughter. The truth was she dreaded the thought of Hannah leaving. Until now she hadn't realised just how much she depended on her, not just for help but for moral support. But it would never do to let the girl know this.

Hannah didn't sleep. In the small hours she heard her father stumble blindly up the stairs, too drunk now to worry whether his only son lived or died and she wondered bitterly how much of the half guinea was left. She hated her father; she hated the life his drinking had reduced his family to. Yet she could understand it. All the grinders drank, the dust they worked in covered them with yellow swarf and gave them a thirst. And the thirst kept them poor. It was no wonder he was bitter about the Truswells. She could understand that too, because she knew he was right about his father's exceptional flair for drawing and design. It was something she had inherited and she had often wondered where the gift came from. Now she knew.

Often times she had drawn pictures in the dust with a stick for the amusement of the other children, creating scenes with a few judicious sweeps of the stick that she knew instinctively where to place and sometimes she had surprised even herself with the intricate patterns her slate pencil had tracked when she was stuck for the answer to a sum.

For two nights she tossed and turned on the lumpy mattress, her thoughts returning to the biggest decision she had ever had to make. A decision that would determine the course of the rest of her life. How could she leave her mother, with young Stan so poorly? How could she abandon her whole family? Yet to escape from this squalor and to live in a place like Cutwell Hall was more than she'd ever dreamed of and it was a chance that would never come again. If she didn't take it she would end up like all the other girls she knew, married too young, with too many children and too little money.

She thumped her pillow. It was cruel and selfish of her father to force such a choice on her. Why should something that happened two generations ago be allowed to blight her life as he had allowed it to blight his? If he chose to blame the past for his condition in life then let him; why should she let history repeat itself? She could imagine sitting in squalor and saying to her own grandchildren, 'Ah, yes, my life would have been very different if I'd been allowed . . .'

No, it wasn't going to be like that for her. She wasn't going to live out her life dreaming of what might have been. She would take her destiny in her own hands. And if her father disowned her, well, somehow she would find a way to see Mam and the children.

At five o'clock on Monday morning she got up, hoping to steal away to Cutwell Hall without waking anybody, but her mother was already downstairs; she'd slept in the chair ever since Stanley's accident in case he should need anything in the night.

Jane opened her eyes and rubbed them. 'You've made up your mind then, lass. Are you off already?' she asked, sitting forward and Hannah could see the pain in them.

Hannah nodded, too full to speak.

'You'll come an' see us, won't you, Sis?' Stanley said. He'd heard the argument raging and it worried him. 'Never mind what me dad says, you'll come an' see us, won't you?'

She smoothed his hair. 'I'll try, lad.' She gave him a watery smile. 'You don't think I could go too long wi'out seein' your ugly little face, do you?'

'I'll come an' see you, too, Annie,' he said eagerly. 'When me leg's better.'

'We'll see,' Jane said. She pointed to the fireplace. 'Now, riddle t'fire and pull t'kettle forward. But don't make too much noise an' wake him. He'll raise hell if he knows you're going. He's already threatened to lock you in t'cellar if you try to go against him.' She looked up at the ceiling. 'Mind, you'd as easy wake the dead, the state he came home in last night again.' She got to her feet and began to busy herself with mugs. 'Now, you'll be sure and keep your eyes open and your mouth shut, my lass. You're a sight too . . .' she paused and sniffed loudly, then went on, 'You're a sight too quick-tempered, too fond of . . .'

'Oh, Mam!' Hannah flung herself in her mother's arms and began to sob. 'I'll miss you.'

Jane held her close, tears coursing down her own face. When she had herself sufficiently under control she pushed Hannah away.

'Now, come on, lass, mash the tea, then you must be on your way.' She brushed her hand across her eyes. 'I could do wi' a cup, meself.' She began to cut a slice of bread and spread it with dripping. 'You'll need this to help you on your way,' she said, trying to make her voice brisk and matter-of-fact.

'No. I'm not hungry.' Hannah dabbed her eyes with her dress. 'Anyway, they'll likely give me breakfast when I get there.'

They both looked up at the ceiling. There was a

creaking noise as Nat turned over in bed. Then they heard him lumber across the room and his step on the stair.

'Quick! Go! Before he gets down and locks you in t'cellar. He carried on so much I told him you'd decided not to go.' Jane pushed her towards the door. 'Good luck, lass. And God bless you.'

Half blinded by tears Hannah stumbled out of the door and hurried across the yard to begin her new life.

Chapter Four

It was not quite six o'clock as Hannah began the long walk to Endcliffe and Cutwell Hall. Already the town was showing signs of industry. Great chimneys on the steel works belched smoke and the first trams of the day, pulled by horses with jingling harnesses, carried workers in from the more outlying districts. A penny would have taken her a good part of her journey but Hannah had no money and anyway she wasn't anxious to arrive at her destination too early.

So she walked, shedding tears at parting from her mother and her brother and sisters, yet with an irrepressible flutter of excitement in her heart to think of the wonderful life she was going to. And the further along the road she got the clearer the air became and the more the flutters of excitement grew, until as she walked up the long drive to the big house and saw the green parkland with its grazing sheep stretching out all around her and the blue sky overhead she was ready to sing with happiness.

On her arrival she was immediately taken to the

housekeeper's room where Mrs White, the housekeeper, was waiting for her. There was a blue dress on a hanger, with a white starched apron hanging over it. A pile of underclothes with black stockings on top were folded on a nearby chair and under this stood a pair of shiny black shoes. On the hearthrug was a large hip bath.

'Tek your clothes off and get in t'bath. There's a jug of cold water there and the kettle's boiled,' Mrs White said, not unkindly. 'Mek sure you wash your hair, too. And when you've done you're to put these on. I shall be back in twenty minutes. Make sure you're properly dressed when I come.'

'Yes, M'm.' Nervously, Hannah dropped a curtsey.

Ada White smiled. 'You've no need to curtsey to me, lass. But shape yourse'n or you'll be late upstairs.' She left Hannah to the unaccustomed luxury of a warm bath and to struggle into the unfamiliar clothes.

When she came back she looked her up and down. 'You'll need to see Mrs Jenkins, that's m'Lady's seam-stress. She'll show you how to tek t'seams in. By gow, lass, tha's as far through as a fourpenny rabbit. But a few good meals'll put some flesh on thy bones, I'll warrant. Now, what about t'shoes?'

Hannah wiggled her toes. She'd never worn proper shoes before. She'd either gone barefoot or worn clogs and the shoes felt soft yet at the same time restricting. 'I think they're all right,' she said doubtfully.

Mrs White got down on to her knees and felt her toes. 'They're too small,' she announced. 'Wait a bit. I'll find another pair.' She went to a cupboard by the side of the fireplace. It looked full of shoes to Hannah. She rummaged around for several minutes, then handed out a pair that looked more worn.

'Try these,' she said. 'Ah, yes, they're better. Now, let's look at you.' She frowned. 'Your hair's still wet and it needs a good brush. You'd better see to it before you go upstairs. And when you've done it put this on.' She handed Hannah a hairbrush and a starched cap, smiling at her. 'Don't worry, lass, you'll soon get used to it.'

She watched while Hannah brushed the tangles out of her hair, nodding approvingly. 'That's better. Now put your cap on. No, more on the top of your head. Like this.' She straightened the cap then stood back. 'Now, you'll be working under Lizzie Wainwright to start with. She's m'Lady's maid. She's a bit of a tartar – thinks she's a cut above the rest – so you'll have to watch your step. But if you're in any way troubled you're to come and see me.' She smiled. 'I'm not one o' these dragon housekeepers. To my mind it's important you lasses have someone you can turn to if you think you've not been treated fair like. So remember that. Now, we'd better go and find Lizzie an' she'll tell you what your duties are.'

Mrs White took her through to the kitchen. A blonde girl, about the same height as Hannah herself, was waiting for her.

'Ah, just right. Miss Sophie's breakfast is nearly ready,' Lizzie said briskly. 'Vera's just making the toast and mashing the tea.' Lizzie looked Hannah up and down, then moved forward and pulled her cap a fraction further forward on her still damp hair. 'That's better.'

'Good. Then I'll leave Hannah with you and you can show her what she's to do.' Mrs White turned away and

Hannah heard her calling to Ruby the scullery maid to go to her room and empty the bath.

Lizzie indicated the breakfast tray that Vera had laid. 'You can carry it. And mind you don't drop it or spill the tea. If you spill owt you'll have to come back and get a clean tray cloth.'

She led the way from the servants' quarters up two flights of stairs and along a corridor to a door at the end. She went slowly, mindful of the fact that Hannah was carrying a heavy tray and wearing unfamiliar clothing.

When they reached the door Lizzie knocked and went in. 'Good morning, Miss Sophie. It's a grand day.' Hannah noticed that her voice had changed and taken on a more refined note as she spoke to her young mistress. She took the tray from Hannah. 'Pull back the curtains,' she hissed as she took it. 'A nice boiled egg . . .' Her voice reverted to its normal tones. 'Oh, Lawks, she's gone again!'

'Gone where?' Hannah said in alarm.

'Out riding, I 'spect. She's always going off at the crack of dawn on her flippin' horse.'

At that moment the door opened and a small, dark-haired girl came in wearing men's riding breeches. She threw her crop down on the bed. 'Ah, good. Breakfast. I'm starving. Help me off with my boots, Lizzie.'

Lizzie turned to Hannah. 'Help Miss Sophie off with her boots, Fox,' she said in her posh voice.

'Oh, who are you?' Sophie turned a bright gaze on Hannah. 'Ah, yes. I know. Mama said you'd be coming.' She smiled encouragingly. 'What's your first name, Fox?'

Hannah dipped a curtsey. 'Hannah, if you please, Miss.'

'Hannah. That's a nice name. Isn't it, Lizzie?'

48

'Indeed it is, Miss,' Lizzie said.

'Well, Hannah. You can help me off with my boots. They're a bit tight so you'll have to tug hard. That's it. Well done.' She waved Lizzie away. 'No, I'll change and put a respectable dress on after I've eaten my breakfast, Lizzie. You can take my boots down to the boot room to be cleaned.' She stretched luxuriously. 'Charlie rode well this morning. It's good to ride in the cool of the morning before the sun gets too hot. We went for miles, Charlie and me.'

'That's her horse,' Lizzie mouthed at Hannah, raising her eyes towards the ceiling.

'Do you ride, Hannah?' Sophie asked, energetically attacking her breakfast.

'Me? Oh no, Miss.' The mere idea made Hannah want to laugh.

'You should. It's great fun.' Sophie smiled at her and Hannah thought what a lovely smile she had and what a pretty girl she was.

'You heard what Miss Sophie said, Hannah. Take her boots down to the boot room,' Lizzie said, pointing to them.

Hannah picked them up from when they'd been kicked. 'Please, I don't know where the boot room is,' she reminded her.

'They'll tell you in the kitchen.' Lizzie turned away. 'Now, Miss Sophie, which dress would you like me to get out for you?' She glanced over her shoulder at Hannah. 'Don't be long, Hannah. I need to show you where everything is kept before I go back to m'Lady. And Miss Sophie's dress will need pressing before you help her to dress.'

Hannah left the room. She liked Miss Sophie and she looked forward to working for her but she wondered if she would ever manage to learn everything there was to know.

The days sped past. Everything at Cutwell Hall was so new and wonderful and she was kept so busy that Hannah hardly had time to think about her family, let alone weep for them.

Every morning when she woke in her narrow, comfortable bed and looked round the little room under the eaves she had to pinch herself to make sure it was not all a dream and that she would wake and find herself back home on the lumpy mattress that she shared with her little sisters, covered by bits of old blanket and coats. She could hardly believe she was actually living in this magnificent house, surrounded on all sides by beautiful furniture and exquisite china, the like of which she had never even known existed, not to mention the ornate silverware that had pride of place in glass cabinets in the hall because it was the hallmark of Sir Josiah's wealth. And it was not just the house that she found breath taking. Each time she passed a window she stopped for a moment to savour the neatly laid-out gardens and the rolling parkland; the different greens in the trees, dark, almost black firs against the blue skies, the paler beeches with their silver barks, the great spreading oaks and tall, majestic elms. In truth, she hadn't known so many different trees existed. Everywhere she looked there was colour and space; she could even see rock-strewn hills in the distance, shawled with purple heather, and she never tired of watching the changing shape of the clouds in the blue sky. But best of all she loved to watch the sun setting behind the hills, painting the sky with streaks of gold, purple and red. It was all so far removed from the dingy town centre she was used to, where sunlight rarely penetrated and even the colourful billboards were grimed with soot, that for Hannah coming to Cutwell Hall had been like stepping into fairyland.

Of course she was expected to work hard. Each day she was up at six, to clean and tidy Miss Sophie's private sitting room and make sure her clothes were laid out ready for her. Then it was time for breakfast, which she took with the other upstairs servants in a small room off the kitchen. After that it was time to wake Miss Sophie – if she wasn't already up and out riding – and take up her breakfast tray. When that was done it was downstairs again to fetch water for her toilet. Hannah had never seen so many stairs and corridors in all her life and it was a week before she felt she was even beginning to know her way about.

Miss Sophie was unfailingly kind to her, never complaining if she fumbled with hooks when she was helping her to dress or pulled her hair when she was trying to brush the tangles out.

'This is your first post as a lady's maid, isn't it, Hannah?' she asked, smiling at her reflection in the mirror over the dressing table.

'Yes, Miss.'

'And what did you do before this? Were you at school?'

'Oh no, Miss. I were workin' at Fletcher's Wheel. I were learnin' to be an acid etcher. You know, learnin' to etch t'marks on t'silverware, knives and suchlike.'

51

'Really? How interesting.' Miss Sophie sounded as if she really meant it. 'Did you enjoy it?'

'No, Miss. I didn't. It were dull, mucky work. I hated it.'

Miss Sophie laughed, a merry, tinkly sound. 'Well, don't take it out on me, Hannah. You're pulling my hair!'

'Oh, Miss. I'm real sorry.' Hannah was mortified.

'It's all right. I know you didn't mean to.' She waited till Hannah had finished pinning up her hair, then said, 'Has Mrs Jenkins sent back my rose taffeta? I was hoping to wear it when I go calling with Mama this afternoon.'

'No, Miss, not yet. I'll go down to Mrs Jenkins' room and fetch it. It only had a torn hem so it should be done.'

She sped off down to the seamstress' room, carefully keeping her eyes down until she reached the door to the servants' quarters. The rules at Cutwell Hall were not as stringent as they were in many big houses, where servants were required to stand still with their faces turned to the wall if a member of the family happened to approach. Here things were much more relaxed and it was only necessary to keep the eyes averted.

She was on her way back, with the rose taffeta over her arm when she found her way barred by a pair of shiny black boots. Without raising her eyes she bobbed a curtsey and with a murmured, 'I beg your pardon, Sir,' made to step to one side.

But as she stepped, so the boots moved again, barring her way.

'You're new here, aren't you?' It was a young man's voice. Mr Thomas.

'Yes, Sir.' This was the man who had hurt Stan. She didn't want to talk to him.

'Well, let's have a look at you.' He put his finger under her chin and tilted up her face. 'What's your name?'

'Hannah, Sir. Hannah Fox.'

'Look up, damn you. I want to see the colour of your eyes.'

Fleetingly, she looked up into his eyes. This was the first time she had come into contact with him and she had to admit he was the tallest and most handsome man she had ever seen in her life. His hair was black and curly and his face was ruddy with health and good living. He had fine, clear-cut features and a ready smile and brown, almost black eyes, that held more than a hint of mockery in them. All this she noticed in the split second before she lowered her eyes again.

'Green eyes,' he was saying thoughtfully. 'How unusual. Cats have green eyes. Are you like a cat, Hannah Fox?'

'I don't think so, Sir. Cats sleep half their lives away.' She wished he would move aside and let her pass.

'Cats purr when they're stroked,' he said softly.

'Yes, Sir. So I believe.' She bobbed another curtsey. 'Now, if you'll excuse me. Miss Sophie is waiting for her dress.'

'Ah, yes. We mustn't keep my little sister waiting, must we?' He stepped aside and she slipped past, her face flaming with fury and embarrassment. It was inevitable that working at Cutwell Hall she would eventually see something of young Thomas Truswell, she had known that from the beginning, but she hadn't expected him to notice her, let alone force her to speak to him.

But in those few moments she had seen that she had been right about him. He was conceited and arrogant.

Worse, she had the uncomfortable feeling that he had been laughing at her. Hannah Fox didn't like being laughed at, especially by the handsome and reckless young man who had injured her brother.

After she had been at Cutwell Hall a month Hannah was allowed out for the afternoon.

First she polished her shoes. Hannah was very proud of her shoes, since it was the only pair she had ever possessed. Then, as she had nothing else to wear she put on her black afternoon uniform and borrowed a hat from one of the house maids. When she was ready she looked at herself in one of the many mirrors that graced the house. She hardly looked the same girl that had crept up to Cutwell Hall only four weeks ago, with the gold ferrule clutched in her hand. Her figure had filled out as a result of good wholesome food and regular meals and her complexion now was clear as a ripe peach. Her hair shone with the brushing it received every night before she climbed into bed and was neatly tied back with a black ribbon. Wouldn't Mam be proud of her? she thought, delightedly. Then she sighed. She desperately wanted to see her mother and to find out how well Stanley had recovered from his accident but how could she risk going home? What if Dad was there?

She thought about nothing else as she walked the long road from Endcliffe towards the town. It would be so wonderful to see Mam and Stan and the little lasses again, but if Dad found out it wouldn't be just her that suffered, it would be Mam, too, for letting her into the house. In the end she decided that the safest place to go would be to the Brownings' house near Paradise Square where her sister Mary worked. That way she would hear all the news without running the risk of her father's wrath.

Mary's jaw dropped when she opened the door and saw her elder sister standing there looking clean and smart in her black afternoon dress and straw hat.

'You come into money or summat?' she asked rudely, looking Hannah up and down.

'No, I've changed my job. I'm in service now, like you.' Hannah tilted her chin up proudly.

'Hm. Well, you took your time coming back.' Mary covered her surprise with annoyance. 'How's our Stanley? I told you to let me know,' she said accusingly.

Hannah looked at her in amazement. 'But that's what I've come to ask you. Haven't you been home, Mary? Haven't you been to see our Stanley?'

'You ought to know I can't get away just as I like,' Mary said with a toss of her head. 'Any road, why haven't you come and told me about him? You know how I worry.'

'Can I come in? Then I'll tell you,' Hannah said. She stepped past Mary into the cool kitchen, which didn't seem half as impressive as the last time she had been there. In fact, compared with the kitchen at Cutwell Hall it was quite small and ill-equipped. She pointed to a glass jug on the table covered with a beaded muslin. 'I could just do with a glass of that lemonade,' she said. 'I'm parched. It's a long walk from Cutwell Hall.'

'Cutwell Hall!' Mary's eyes grew round. 'What were you doing at Cutwell Hall? That's where t'Truswells live, i'n't it?'

'An' that's where I work now.' Hannah smoothed her dress. She couldn't help feeling just a little bit smug.

'How did you manage that?' Mary poured the lemonade while she was speaking and gave it to Hannah. She waved impatiently towards a chair. 'Well, come on, sit down and tell me. It's Cook's afternoon off so we'll not be disturbed.' She sat down opposite Hannah and leaned forward, her elbows on the table.

Hannah sipped the cool drink and told Mary her story and of the choice she had had to make between home and Cutwell Hall.

'That weren't hard, I shouldn't think,' Mary said.

'It's all very well for you, you don't care about Mam and the children. You've no wish to go back home, have you?'

Mary shook her head. 'No. I'm glad to be out of it,' she admitted. 'I couldn't wait to get away an' I never want to go back. But I've been worried about our Stan, Annie, honest I have.' She looked at Hannah, willing her to understand.

Hannah finished her lemonade and got to her feet. 'Well, if you've not been home it looks as if I shall have to risk it, then. For I'll not go back without news of how our Stanley's doing.' She stared at her sister for a moment. Then she said with a sigh, 'I'm disappointed in you, Mary. I thought you cared about your only brother.'

'I do,' Mary insisted. 'An' I want you to come an' tell me how he is.'

'I'll not have time. Not today. It's a long walk back to Cutwell Hall and I mustn't be late back. You'd better make an effort and go and find out for yourself.'

'You don't understand, Annie,' Mary said on a whining note.

Hannah looked at her and Mary had the grace to look ashamed. 'Oh, yes I do, Mary,' she said, shaking her head. 'Oh, yes I do.'

Hannah left and hurried along the busy, grimy roads towards the Wicker. She had never before noticed just how dirty the streets were and how soot caked all the buildings. Even the colourful advertisements on the hoardings for such products as Bovril, Colman's Mustard and the Music Hall were torn and caked with grime. And the stink as she approached the River Don was appalling. She was amazed how she could have lived her life alongside such filth and never really noticed it.

She crossed Lady's Bridge. Her shoes were beginning to hurt a bit now because she'd walked such a long way but she was too proud of them to think of taking them off. When she got near Angel Court, the place she'd called home until a month ago, her step slowed. Supposing her father was home? She looked at the clock on the cab stand as she passed. It was nearly four o'clock; he wouldn't be there, he'd still be at work. Or he should be . . . Her jaw tightened. Now she'd come all this way she was not going back without seeing Mam and Stan.

Stanley was sitting on the doorstep, catching what little sunshine filtered through the smoke-laden air between the roof tops. There was an ugly curved scar running from between his eyes up to his hair. When he saw Hannah his face lit up.

'Mam! Mam! It's our Hannah. She's come back!' As he spoke Elsie and Maudie, her two little sisters, came

57

running across the yard. 'It's Hannah! It's our Hannah come back!'

'Hush, all of you.' Hannah tried to hug all of them at once. 'Don't shout. I'm not supposed to be here. If our Dad . . .'

'He's at work. He'll not be back while six.' Stanley reached for the crutch lying beside him and scrambled to his feet. 'Mam! Mam! It's our Hannah! She's come to see us!'

As he spoke his mother came to the door, her tired face lighting up as she saw her eldest daughter.

'Oh, it's lovely to see you, lass,' she said. She hugged Hannah, then held her at arm's length. 'My, you look bonny. And that smart I hardly reckernise you!' She looked furtively over Hannah's shoulder. 'But you shouldn't have come, lass, you know that, don't you. If he was to come home an' find you here . . .'

'I know, Mam, and I'll not stay long. But I had to come. I had to know about our Stan. I've worried about him, he was so poorly when I left.'

'Aye. But he's a lot better now.' Jane was still looking over Hannah's shoulder as she spoke.

'Aren't you going to ask me in, Mam? I've walked a long way, you know.'

'Well, just for a minute, then. But you mustn't stay, lass. You mustn't stay.'

Hannah stepped inside. The house smelled damp and fusty although it was as neat and clean as it had always been. She picked up the baby, crying in her crib.

'I think she's grown. She's a bonny lass.' She smiled down at the baby in her arms, then at all the faces round the table. 'Oh, it's so wonderful to see you all again. Now, tell me what you've been doing while I've been away, Elsie.'

Both the little girls tried to talk at once; they wanted to know what it was like in a big house and Hannah tried to tell them but it was all beyond their imagination.

'Are there 'osses up at Cutwell Hall, Annie?' Stan said when he could get a word in.

'Oh, yes.' She smiled at him. 'Farm horses and horses that are for riding – all sorts.'

He gave a sigh. 'I should like to work wi' 'osses, one day.'

Hannah ruffled his hair. 'Happen you will, lad. One day.'

Jane bit her lip. 'It's been lovely to see you, Hannah, but you ought to be going. You've been here nearly half an hour. If he was to come back . . .' She glanced anxiously out of the open door.

'Yes. You're right.' Hannah had sensed her mother's uneasiness ever since she had arrived. She laid the baby down and kissed each one in turn, tears coursing down her cheeks. Now it came to it she hated leaving them all, even to go back to her wonderful new life at Cutwell Hall. 'But I'll come and see you again . . .'

'No! Don't. He'll be sure to find out,' Jane said quickly. She shook her head. 'There'll be trouble enough as it is. Somebody's sure to have seen you and they'll tell him you've been here today.'

'I won't let him hit you, Mam,' Stan said stoutly. 'I've got my stick.' He waved his little crutch.

'He still needs that if he's going to walk far,' Jane

explained. 'His leg's not quite right. But it's better'n it was, in't it, lad?' She smiled at Stanley, at the same time giving Hannah a little push. 'Go on now, lass. If your dad were to leave work early . . .'

'If Dad were to leave work early he'd make straight for Ma Ragley's beer house,' Hannah said with a trace of bitterness. 'Unless he's changed in the last month.'

Jane sighed. 'No, lass, he hasn't changed. All the same . . .'

Hannah put her hand in her pocket and brought out her month's wages and laid them on the table. 'There, Mam. You can buy something for yourself and the little ones. And don't tell Dad! I don't want him tipping it down his neck.'

'Ee, lass. You shouldn't have.' Jane looked at it longingly. 'I can't tek it.' She pushed it back to Hannah.

Hannah took a shilling. 'There. Will that make you feel better, Mam? Now, don't argue, take it and put it away, quick, afore me dad comes.'

'Ee, you're a good lass, Hannah.' Jane took the money and hid it on the top shelf of the cupboard.

'I'll get some more to you when I can,' Hannah promised. Then she left, with Stanley and the two little girls accompanying her to the other side of Lady's Bridge. They would have gone further but she sent them back; Maudie's little legs would soon tire and neither Elsie nor Stanley could carry her far. She noticed that Stanley leaned quite heavily on his crutch although he didn't complain.

They all cried as they parted and Hannah's tears didn't cease until she was well on the way back to Cutwell Hall.

She was glad she had been to see her family and for her own part she would risk going again. But it was clear that it was her mother who would be the one to suffer and for that reason she knew she could never go back. The tears began to flow again and even the sight of the rolling hills and the beautiful house that she now called home couldn't raise her spirits.

Chapter Five

'Ee, thy 'Annah's a reet bonny lass now, i'n't she, Mr Fox? Quite the lady in 'er smart black dress an' shoes. None o' yer clogs now, for your 'Annah. Gone reet up in the world, by all accounts. She were 'ere nobbut an hour ago. Pity tha missed 'er, Mr Fox. Tha'd 'a bin reet set up to see 'er.'

Jane closed her eyes, wincing as she heard Maggie Dobbs from across the yard letting her malicious tongue run loose to Nat. Always a troublemaker, she was thoroughly enjoying giving him every last detail of Hannah's secret visit, how long she had stayed, how pleased the children had been to see her, how reluctant they had been to let her go again. The one thing she didn't know, so couldn't pass on, was that Hannah had left money for them.

But Nathaniel guessed. He came into the house, his face like thunder. 'Come on, where is it? How much did she leave? Crafty little bugger. Sneakin' back here while my back was turned.' He banged his fist on the table as he spoke.

Jane turned away. 'I don't know what you're on about,' she said, trying to sound unconcerned.

He caught her by the shoulder. 'You know very well what I'm on about, woman. Didn't I tell 'er if she went to them bloody Truswells she'd not be welcome back in my house? What do you mean by goin' against me an' letting her back through t' bloody door?' He slapped her across the face as he spoke.

She put her hand up to the spot. 'Hannah's still my daughter, Nat. I couldn't turn her away, not sin' she'd walked all this way to see us,' she pleaded. 'She'd only come back to see how Stanley was gettin' along, him bein' so poorly when she left. And the children were that pleased to see her, Nat. It didn't do no harm. She didn't stay long. She weren't here but half an hour.'

Nat remained unimpressed. 'An' that's half an hour too long. She's a bloody traitor. She's chucked her lot in wi' them Truswells, them as did my father down and crippled my son an' I'll not have her darken my door ever again. Now, where's the money she left?'

'It's Truswell money, don't forget,' Jane said bravely. 'It's them as pay her wages.'

'Shut up an' tell me where it is.' Nat gave her a blow that sent her reeling.

'If you're so sure she left money then you'd better find it for yourself.' Jane picked herself up and sat down, rubbing her arm where she had caught it on the edge of the table when she fell.

Furiously Nat began searching, sweeping everything off the mantelpiece on to the floor in his temper. When he started throwing what little china they possessed out of the cupboard and smashing it Jane got to her feet.

'Get out t'road. I'll give it thee,' she said with a sigh.

63

She reached up on to the top shelf of the cupboard and gave him half the money Hannah had left.

He snatched it and left the house.

After he had gone Jane called Stanley and gave him the rest of the money. 'Go down to Mrs Fowler's corner shop. Tell her this'll pay what I owe her and a bit to spare. Ask her to keep it by for me. It'll be safer in her keeping where he can't find it and tip it down his throat,' she added with a sigh.

Hannah didn't go home again, dearly though she would have loved to. She had seen Mrs Dobbs standing in her doorway as soon as she entered the yard and she guessed that the old busybody would waste no time in letting her father know of her visit. For her own part she would willingly have risked Nathaniel's wrath in order to see her family, but she knew it would be her mother who would be the one to suffer if she did and she couldn't bear the thought of that. So instead of going home she spent her free time walking in the park or on the hills, trying to puzzle out how she could send home more of the money she was saving.

Apart from this one nagging worry she was happier than she had ever been in her life. She loved the clean, fresh air and the wide open spaces, so different from the crowded, grimy town with its narrow streets and courts hemmed in by tall factories and steel works. As summer turned to autumn she was amazed and fascinated by the changing colours. Trees that were green one day turned to yellow and orange and fiery red almost overnight. The whole landscape seemed suddenly to have taken on a brilliant hue and she resolved to paint the changing scene with the paints she had found in the old nursery when she was up there with Sophie one day on one of Sophie's mad, 'turning-out' expeditions.

She soon grew very fond of her young mistress. Sophie was a girl of roughly her own age and she soon began to confide her secrets, mostly about the young man she met out riding early in the morning of whom she was sure her parents would not approve. She was a happy-go-lucky girl, who never scolded when Hannah hadn't pressed her dress or cleaned the mud off her riding costume, saying it was of no consequence and would do later. Soon the two girls were more like friends than servant and mistress and Sophie knew how things were at Hannah's home and although it was all quite beyond her imagination she sympathised and offered totally unsuitable ways of helping the situation.

In her free time Hannah roamed the hills beyond Cutwell Hall, carrying her paints and sketching pad, totally content with her own company. She was sitting by a little brook one sunny afternoon, painting the brambles on the opposite bank, where blackberries shone black and succulent in the sunlight and were reflected in the clear water below, when she heard the sound of a horse's hooves, muffled by the mossy grass. She sat quite still, hoping the rider, whoever it was, would pass without even realising she was there.

'Ah, it's little Miss Green Eyes! I thought I'd find you if I searched long enough.'

She sighed in exasperation. Thomas Truswell's voice was an unwelcome intrusion on her solitude. Often, far too often for it to be mere coincidence, she encountered him in the corridor near her mistress's room, and he would stop and tease her, which she hated. And sometimes when she had been walking out here on the hills she had seen him in the distance and had hidden so that he shouldn't see her, but she had been confident that he wouldn't find her tucked away in this remote spot.

With a sinking heart she scrambled to her feet and hid her pad behind her. 'I was only sitting here enjoying the view,' she said defensively. 'I wasn't doing any harm. Sir,' she added as an afterthought.

'I never supposed you might be.' He dismounted and came over to her and took the pad from where she was hiding it. 'Mm. You're very good. Quite an artist, in fact.' He handed it back to her. 'Do you always come here and paint in your free time?'

'Now and then.' She didn't want to talk to Thomas Truswell. She didn't like him.

'How much free time do you have, little Miss Green Eyes?'

'An afternoon a week, Sir.' She didn't look at him.

'Always a Thursday?'

'Mostly.' She was getting angry. He knew very well Thursday was her afternoon off.

'You mean to tell me my little sister can spare you for a whole afternoon?' She knew he was mocking her so she didn't answer.

'You're very serious, little Miss Green Eyes. Don't you ever smile?'

'Only when there's something to smile at, Sir.' She returned his gaze coolly.

'And there's nothing to smile at now?'

'Not that I can see, Sir.'

He coloured with annoyance. He was not used to being spoken to like that. And by a servant girl, too.

He took a step towards her. 'Then perhaps we'd better find something to make you smile, Hannah Fox.'

Before she realised what he was about he had seized her round the waist and his mouth came down hard on hers.

Furiously, she struggled free and wiped her mouth with the back of her hand.

'How dare you do that to me!' she spat. 'I'm not one of your fancy women.'

He grinned at her. He had enjoyed kissing her, the more so because she had resisted him. 'Your green eyes take on golden flecks when you're angry, Hannah Fox. Temper makes you quite beautiful.' He moved towards her again. 'Perhaps I should kiss you again.'

'If you try I shall take your whip to you like you took it to my little brother.' Quick as a flash she moved and picked up his crop where he had thrown it down.

He frowned. 'What on earth are you talking about?'

'You know very well what I'm talking about. You lashed out at Stanley with your whip when he stumbled out into the road near your horse. It were about three months ago. Near Arundel Street.'

'My dear girl, you don't expect me to remember that far back, do you?' He laughed uncomfortably.

'Well, I haven't forgotten. And nor has my brother. His leg is crippled, so he's not likely to, neither.' She examined

67

the ferrule on the end of the crop. 'I see you've got this put back. I picked it up in t'gutter when you'd gone.'

He had the grace to flush.

'Yes, I thought you'd remember in t'end,' she said grimly.

He reached into his pocket and brought out a sovereign. 'Here, give this to your brother and tell him I'm sorry,' he said, giving her a sheepish smile. 'It's true. I really am, you know.'

She pushed his hand away. 'Stanley doesn't need your charity, thank you all the same. And now, if you'll excuse me I'd like to get on with my painting.'

He gazed at her, nonplussed. He wasn't used to being treated in this way. In his experience young maidservants were flattered by his attentions and went out of their way to please him. He'd never known one to be so indifferent to his charm and he didn't like it. It was a blow to his ego. It was also a challenge.

He smiled his most disarming smile. 'Of course. I won't detain you any longer, Hannah Fox. I'm sorry if I intruded on your solitude. I promise it won't happen again.'

He inclined his head graciously, then turned and flung himself on his horse and cantered off.

After he had gone Hannah sat down and resumed her painting. But it wouldn't go right. She was furious with Tom Truswell for seeking her out, and even more furious because he had dared to kiss her. But at least now he knew that she wasn't impressed by his handsome features and dark brown eyes, nor the way he raised one eyebrow a little higher than the other when he smiled his crooked, lopsided smile. Thomas Truswell might be the most handsome man she had ever seen in her life but it cut no ice as far as she was concerned. She didn't like him. She didn't like him one little bit. And not only because he had been the cause of Stanley's accident, although that had gone a long way towards turning her against him. But he was so arrogant! He had really believed that she would be flattered because he had deigned to notice her.

At last, her thoughts too much in a turmoil to allow her to concentrate on her picture, she packed up her things and sat staring into the brook, watching the changing shape of the pebbles as the water rippled over them and going over and over in her mind the scene that had just taken place. At least she had the satisfaction of knowing that she had made it quite plain that she wasn't flattered and she didn't want his attention. And she was angry that he should have been the one to steal her first kiss. She had always dreamed of her first kiss being given willingly, gently, to the man she loved, not being taken roughly and without warning by a man she didn't even like. She could still feel the strength of his arms as he had pulled her to him and the unexpectedly smooth texture of his face against hers. Even now, the faint aroma of shaving cream and macassar oil seemed to linger on the air, rousing in her an unfamiliar, unsettling sensation. Irritated by the spoilt afternoon, she gathered up her things and set off back to the house.

When she arrived back at Cutwell Hall Ruby, the scullery maid, was just crossing the yard with potato peelings for the swill bucket. She beckoned urgently.

Hannah went across to her. 'What's the matter, Ruby?' she asked, mystified.

'Someone's here to see you.' Ruby spoke in a whisper, looking round furtively as she spoke.

'Me? Where? Who? I don't know anybody,' she said with a frown.

'A little lad. Walks wi' a crutch.'

'Stanley! My little brother! Surely he's not walked all this way!'

'I dunno about that. But when I saw him I knew from the look of him that Cook 'ud have nowt to do wi' him. He looked, well, you know, too raggedy-like, so I asked him his business an' he said he'd come to see his sister. An' t'osses. He was right keen on seein' t'osses.'

Hannah nodded. 'Yes, Stan loves horses.'

'Any road, I took him across to Archie Bingle in t'stables,' Ruby went on. 'Archie said he'd keep an eye on him till you got back.' She nodded towards the stable block.

'Thanks, Ruby. You're a real pal.' Hannah squeezed her arm and hurried across to the stable block.

Archie, the groom was in the tack room. He was a little man, bow-legged and gaitered, with a fringe of wiry grey hair sticking out from under a cap that hid a shiny bald dome. When he saw Hannah he grinned and nodded towards a pile of sacks in the corner where Stanley was lying curled up and fast asleep.

'Poor lad, 'e were reet done up by t'time 'e got 'ere,' he said. 'Told me 'e'd walked all t'way from t'Wicker. A tidy step, is that, specially with a gammy leg. No wonder 'e's whacked out.'

70

Hannah went over to where Stanley was lying and sat down beside him, stroking the hair back from his forehead. At her touch he opened his eyes.

'I got here, Sis,' he said, smiling up at her. 'I made up me mind I were comin' to see you an' I did. By 'eck, it's a long way, but I made it.'

'Oh, Stan. And with your bad leg, too.' She gave him a hug. 'But it's lovely to see you.'

He sat up and flexed his shoulder. 'Me leg's all right. It's just me arm's a bit sore from leanin' on t'crutch.' He looked round. 'By, this is some place, Annie, i'n't it? I never saw such a big house in all me life. An' all these gardens ... an' grass! An' all them sheep!' His eyes grew wider as he talked.

Hannah nodded and laughed. 'No, lad, neither did I.' She hugged him again. 'Oh, it's good to see you, Stan. Are you hungry?' She laughed again. 'Daft question. You're allus hungry. Wait here while I'll fetch you summat to eat.'

When she came back she was carrying a tray with cold meat pie and vegetables and a lump of treacle pudding. Stanley's eyes nearly popped out of his head as he attacked the wonderful feast and Hannah felt a pang of guilt at the thought that it was all left over from the midday meal and would have found its way into the swill bucket if she hadn't rescued it.

When he had cleared every morsel he wiped his mouth on his sleeve. 'By 'eck, that were good,' he said. 'I'm glad I came. An' that old man let me stroke t'osses. Some of 'em, any road. He said some of 'em was a bit too frisky wi' strangers.' He straightened his shoulders. 'But I shan't be a stranger if I keep comin'. T'old man said I could come any time.'

'He's not an old man. He's Archie Bingle, Stanley.'

'He's nice. He told me he had a little lad once-over. He said he'd have been about my age, but he had scarlet fever an' died when he were only four.'

'Oh, I didn't know that.'

'You didn't know this, neither, Annie.' Stanley squirmed with importance. 'You remember Mr Bullinger? Mr Reuben Bullinger? Him as carried me home that day when I was hurt, Mam said, although I didn't know much about it?'

Hannah nodded.

'Well, I often see him now. He works at Fletcher's Wheel near me dad. An' he talks to me and sometimes gie's me a ha'penny an' asks me how I'm doin'. An' he asked me if I'd like to run errands for his mam. They live at Balm Green, not far from Barker's Pool. I get paid for it, too. Mrs B. is real nice an' she often gie's me a bit o' bread an' drippin' when I go there, so I'm not so hungry when I get home.' He grinned up at her. 'She says it'll leave a bit more for t'others if I've been fed.'

She ruffled his hair. 'And how are the others, Stan?'

He shrugged. 'All right. They're all right.' He looked up at Hannah. 'Annie, why is me dad the way he is? Why does he drink an' swear an' spend all the money so there's none for us? An' why does he knock our mam about?'

'He's a grinder, lad. All the grinders drink. The dust gets in their lungs and gives them grinder's asthma. That's why he coughs a lot, too. The dust makes our dad thirsty and the drink makes him violent so he takes it out on our

72

mam. He doesn't hit you children, does he?' she asked anxiously.

Stanley shook his head. 'I look after t'little lasses an' keep 'em out of his way.' He paused, frowning. Then he said, 'Mr Bullinger doesn't drink. He never touches strong liquor. An' he doesn't swear, neither. Why can't me dad be like Mr Bullinger, Annie? He's a nice man.'

Hannah shook her head, sighing. 'I don't know, lad. It's just the way things are, I'm afraid.'

He reached for his crutch and stood up. 'I'd better be gettin' back. Mam'll be wonderin' where I've got to. But I'll come an' see you again, Annie. That man, Archie, he said I could. An' I like to see t'osses.'

'Wait a minute, Stan. Don't go yet. I've got something for you.' She left him and ran into the house, up the three flights of stairs to her room to fetch the little store of money she had saved for her mother. When she got back to Stanley she hardly had enough breath left to say goodbye to him.

'Now look after that bag and don't let me dad get his hands on it,' she said, still breathless. 'There's a lot of money there.'

'How much?'

'Nearly nine shillin's.'

'Cor!' He stuffed the bag inside his shirt. 'I'll look after it, don't you worry.'

She gave him a hug. 'An' here's a penny for yourself. You mind an' get the tram for part of the way back. It's too far for you to walk all the way.'

'Cor, thanks, Sis.'

'An' here you are, here's another penny. That's for the tram next time you come.'

She watched him limp off across the park, her heart full of love for him. When he got to the hole in the hedge that had given him entry he turned and raised his crutch to her. She waved back, her jaw set. If it hadn't been for Tom Truswell, Stanley wouldn't have to rely on a wooden crutch to help him along, she thought bitterly and her hatred for the young man increased.

Chapter Six

Young Thomas Truswell was not used to being thwarted in his conquests. He had never before in all his twenty years come across a girl who could resist him and it was something of a blow to his self-esteem to discover that Hannah Fox appeared immune to his charms. It was also a spur to his ardour and he became obsessed by her. He had imagined himself in love any number of times but never had he felt for any girl the burning desire that Hannah Fox roused in him and he began to pursue her with a dedication that would have done him credit had he put it to work on his father's business.

As for Hannah, she became quite adept at keeping out of his way and on the occasions when she couldn't avoid contact with him she maintained a wooden impassivity to his overtures.

'Tom! Haven't you anything better to do than lounge around in my room?' Sophie said petulantly, one rainy afternoon when she and Hannah were sorting through ribbons. 'I'm quite sure you're not interested in girls' fripperies.'

'Oh, I dunno. You make a pretty picture, the pair of you, sitting there with all your gewgaws around you.' He stared at Hannah with undisguised admiration. 'I could fetch my paints and paint you.' She lowered her head so that he shouldn't see the angry colour that flushed her cheeks, afraid he might think she was blushing with pleasure.

'You'll do nothing of the kind, Tom Truswell,' Sophie said. 'You spend far too much time in my room as it is. I don't know what's come over you, these days. You never used to be remotely interested in your little sister and although your attentions are flattering I wish you'd go away. Hannah and I have things to talk about that are not for your ears.'

Lazily, he got to his feet and stretched. 'Very well. I can see when I'm not wanted. Anyway, I suppose I really ought to go down to the factory and make learning noises.'

'I should think that's a very good idea, since it will fall to you to run the business when Papa dies.'

'Oh, the Guv'nor won't pop his clogs for a good many years yet, never fear.' He yawned widely. 'But I can take a hint,' he said good humouredly. 'I know where I'm not wanted.'

'Good.' Sophie turned away from him. 'Now, Hannah, do you think we could trim my yellow muslin with this green ribbon? Ah, that's better,' as the door closed behind Tom. 'I can't think what's come over him. He never used to seek my company out. He *must* be bored. It'll do him good to go down to the factory. I only wish I could learn about silverware. But it's not the done thing for ladies, is it?'

'No, not ladies of quality,' Hannah agreed, with a faint touch of sarcasm that was completely lost on her mistress.

Gradually, Tom's visits to his sister's apartments grew less. Hannah was relieved, although with the perverseness of human nature just a tiny bit disappointed. She disliked Tom Truswell, she didn't want him pursuing her, yet in her heart of hearts she had to admit that she had found his attentions flattering and it had even given her a vague sense of power to rebuff him.

But life was too rich and varied to worry too much about Tom Truswell. She loved her new life although she never forgot her family and she looked forward to her brother Stanley bringing news of them. Every few weeks, even in the worst of the winter, he made the long trip to Cutwell Hall, taking the tram for part of the journey as she had instructed. He always went to the stables to wait for her and he soon became great friends with Archie Bingle, who showed him how to polish the tackle and even allowed him to groom the more docile horses.

One day, when Hannah received the message that her brother had arrived, she found Stanley almost beside himself with excitement.

He was just finishing a large helping of suet pudding – he was becoming well-known among the kitchen staff and someone always made sure he was well fed – and he looked up, jam smearing his mouth, as she entered the tack room where he was sitting with Archie.

'What do you reckon, Annie?' he said, jumping up and giving her a jammy hug. 'The young gentleman's just been in and he saw me and asked who I was an' he said I could have a ride on Buttons over there when the weather's better!' He pointed to a stall in the corner where an elderly pony was quietly munching hay.

Hannah looked at Archie for confirmation.

'Ay, that's reet enough. That's what young Mester Thomas said. When t'weather's better, mind. T'ground's too hard wi' t'frost for a bit, but when it's warmer he'll happen be able to exercise Buttons a bit. Both Mester Thomas and Miss Sophie learned to ride on him so he'll come to no harm.'

'That's grand, lad.' Hannah sat down beside him on the pile of sacks. 'Now, how's Mam? And the girls? And little Fanny? Has she got over her croup?' she asked eagerly.

'Oh, they're all right. The young gentleman said...' Stanley was much more interested in his newfound friend than relating family matters to his sister so in the end she gave up and went to fetch the money she had saved for her mother. Could she have misjudged Thomas Truswell, she wondered as she gave the money to her brother and left him to talk horses with Archie Bingle, or was he just trying to make amends for the injury he had caused Stan?

Spring arrived with a pale green mist that spread itself over the trees and hedgerows, heralding the bursting buds of young leaves and catkins. Everywhere looked new and fresh and Hannah once again took to walking over the hills in the warm sunshine, looking for sheltered places where she could sit and paint.

One afternoon she found a delightful spot, a tree-lined

glade near a tiny waterfall. She sat down with her back against a tree and closed her eyes, listening to the splash of the water into the pool below and marvelling that such a little fall of water should make so much noise. It was her seventeenth birthday, the eighteenth of April. The sun was warm on her face and the thought came to her that she must be the luckiest girl in the world, to be living in the lap of luxury at Cutwell Hall, with access to this wonderful countryside, and furthermore to be paid money for it so that she could make life easier for her poverty-stricken family down in the town. She breathed a prayer of thankfulness at her good fortune.

'What a delightful picture. A charmingly pretty girl sitting by a waterfall. May I join you?'

She looked up and saw Thomas Truswell towering over her, his hand on the tree behind her. She tried to scramble to her feet, saying, 'I didn't hear you come. I'm sorry . . .'

He put his hand on her arm and sat down beside her. 'There's nothing to be sorry about. I came quietly because I didn't want to disturb you. You looked so tranquil, so contented. What were you thinking about, Hannah?'

She looked down at her hands, folded in her lap. 'I was thinking how lucky I was to be here,' she said. She lifted her head and looked round her. 'It's all so beautiful,' she breathed. 'I never realised . . .'

He nodded. 'It is indeed beautiful,' he said softly, but his gaze was on Hannah as he spoke.

She looked at him sharply. 'I should be going. Miss Sophie will be wanting me.' She got quickly to her feet and adjusted her hat.

He followed suit. 'It's Thursday. Your afternoon off to spend as you choose. My sister will have to fend for herself for a few hours.' He smiled down at her. 'Has your brother been out on Buttons yet?'

'Yes, once or twice. He was very thrilled,' she said warmly. Then she remembered it was Tom Truswell she was talking to and added formally, 'Thank you for suggesting it. It was very kind of you.' She turned away from him.

'Well, I thought it might help to make amends for the accident.' He walked round to her other side so she was again facing him and said earnestly, 'I very much regret that, you know, Hannah.'

She didn't speak so he went on, 'I know you'll never find it in your heart to forgive me for what happened to your brother, but has it ever occurred to you that if it hadn't been for the accident you would never have come near Cutwell Hall?' He smiled, his funny crooked smile, one eyebrow quirked as he asked the question. 'And you love it here, don't you?'

She nodded almost imperceptibly.

'Well, then, if you look at it like that, perhaps I deserve a little thanks as well as castigation. Do you think that might be so?' He watched as various expressions fleeted across her face. 'You hadn't thought of it like that, had you, Hannah?' he asked softly.

'No. I hadn't thought of it like that,' she admitted.

He took both her hands in his and drew her down to the mossy bank again.

'Well, then, can't we call a truce? We don't have to be enemies, Hannah, and I've already said that I'm willing to do anything I can for your brother. I can't say more than that, can I now?' He gazed at her, his head on one side, his funny, quizzical expression on his face. He looked down at her hands, still held firmly in his. 'I'm . . . I'm extremely fond of you, you know, Hannah,' he said quietly. 'I've never met anybody quite like you. Somebody I could talk to. Somebody I could confide in.'

She turned her head away and bit her lip. This was a new, gentle Thomas Truswell, someone she found it difficult to hate. But she must hate him; it was because of him that Stanley was crippled.

'Look at me, Hannah.' Gently, he put a hand up to her cheek and turned her to face him, tracing her ear with his finger in a way that sent a funny tingling sensation through her. 'If we could just meet here and talk now and again it would be such a comfort to me,' he said. Again he gave that funny little smile. 'I daresay you think that being the only son of a rich cutler I haven't a care in the world, but it isn't true, you know. I have worries. The only thing is, I have to keep them to myself. I don't have anyone I can talk to.'

Hannah summoned up the remnants of her antagonism. 'I'm afraid if you want advice as to how to pay your gambling debts you've come to the wrong person,' she said, trying to make her voice hard and failing miserably because he was looking straight into her eyes.

'That was unkind, Hannah, wasn't it?' he chided gently.

She gave a rueful smile. 'Yes. It was a bit,' she admitted.

He moved away from her. 'Do you intend to come here and paint?' he asked in a more matter-of-fact voice. 'It's a beautiful spot.'

'I might do. If I feel like it.' She was relieved yet at the same time a little disappointed that the conversation had moved to a more general footing. Somehow she had felt she was floundering, out of her depth, yet she didn't understand how or why.

'Well, suppose I come and talk to you sometimes while you're painting. That would be really nice, wouldn't it? At least, I should like it. I should like it very much.' He smiled at her. 'What do you say?'

She hesitated. There couldn't be any harm in that, could there? She felt a small flutter of excitement in her breast at the thought of secret meetings, secret but quite innocent meetings. She smiled at him. 'Yes. All right.'

Throughout the rest of the spring and into the summer she took her paints to the little glade every Thursday afternoon. Sometimes Tom came and sat with her and while she worked they talked. She told him about her life and he told her of his ambition to travel the world.

'What about your father's business?' she asked one day. 'Aren't you interested in that?'

He made a face. 'That's the trouble. I'm not really. But of course I shall be expected to take it over when he dies. That's why I want to travel. Before I'm forced to settle down. That is, unless . . .' He stood up and came and looked over her shoulder at what she had been painting.

'Unless what?'

'Unless I marry, of course,' he said lightly. 'My word, that's very good.' He put his hand on her arm and leaned forward to look more closely, his cheek next to hers. Then slowly he turned his head and almost invol- untarily she did the same. This time when he kissed her it was sweet and lingering and it was he that pulled away, not her.

'I'm sorry.' He turned his head a little. 'I shouldn't have done that. Please forgive me. I hope you won't . . .' He hesitated, then began again, 'I hope we can still be friends and that you'll still allow me to come and see you here. You see, I couldn't help myself. I've been watching you over these last months and I've longed to do just that.' He gave his funny little smile. 'That's why I've stayed away some weeks, because I couldn't trust myself . . . Do you miss me when I don't come, Hannah?'

She was still too shaken by her response to his kiss to lie. 'Yes, I do,' she whispered.

'I miss you, too.' He lifted a lock of her hair and then let it fall again. 'I've known a good number of girls, Hannah, but I've never known anyone quite like you.'

'I don't know what you mean.'

'I think you do, Hannah.' His hand crept round the back of her neck.

'I must be going.' Her voice sounded faint even to her own ears.

'In a minute.' Gently he turned her face to his and kissed her again, his mouth becoming more urgent as he felt her responding. He began to fiddle with the buttons of her bodice but she dashed his hand away.

'No!' she whispered fiercely, coming to her senses. 'Who do you think I am? One of your doxies, yours for the taking?' She scrambled to her feet, golden anger flashing in her eyes. 'I know your sort, you think you've only got to sweet talk a girl and you can do what you like. Well, you've picked the wrong one this time, Mr Truswell.

I'm a good girl and that's the way I intend to stay until the day I marry.'

He stood up, too. 'Oh, Hannah, I'm sorry.' His face broke into its lopsided smile. 'I always seem to be saying sorry to you, don't I? But I mean it. I got carried away. Don't you realise what you do to a chap's senses? I've never met anyone like you in my life before.' He turned away. 'But you're quite right. We . . . I've been playing with fire and it's got to stop before we both get burnt. I won't come here again.'

Before she could speak he was gone and a moment later she heard the beat of a horse's hooves thundering away into the distance.

Thomas Truswell was as good as his word. For several weeks Hannah spent her Thursday afternoons painting without any interruption. But the painting didn't go right and she realised with dismay that she wasn't concentrating because all the time her ears were straining for the sound of Midnight, Thomas' horse.

Yet she didn't want to see him. She promised herself that if he came she would send him away because she knew what he was like, even without listening to the gossip in the servants' hall. She congratulated herself time and time again on having been strong minded enough to rebuff his attentions. All the same she relived his kisses every night before she fell asleep and dreamed of what it would be like to be his wife. Which of course she could never be.

'You're pulling my hair, Hannah,' Miss Sophie complained.

'I'm sorry, Miss.' Hannah made an effort to be more gentle.

Sophie put her head on one side and gazed at her reflection in the mirror. 'Is something worrying you, Hannah? You're very short-tempered these days and I believe you've lost a bit of weight.'

'Nothing's the matter, Miss Sophie. I'm sorry if I'm short-tempered. I don't mean to be.'

'You need to find yourself a lover. Like me.' Sophie clasped her hands to her breast. 'Oh, you should see Freddie. He's so handsome . . .'

'You need to be careful, Miss Sophie. What would your father say if he knew?'

'He'd be furious.' Sophie threw back her head and laughed. 'But he'll never need to know because it's nothing serious. We just meet early in the morning. And talk. And sometimes he kisses me. That's all. After all, he's only a groom. I wouldn't ever want to *marry* him. It's just a bit of fun.'

'Does he realise that?' Hannah asked.

She shrugged. 'I don't know. I've never asked him.'

Just a bit of fun. The words rang in Hannah's ears. That was what Thomas had been having. Well, it was finished now and she was glad.

It was July and too hot to paint. It didn't matter. Since that day in early summer, that last afternoon Thomas had spent with her, she had done nothing worthwhile. Not, of course, that it had anything to do with Thomas Truswell's absence; she was glad he no longer came to spoil her solitude, she told herself firmly.

She laid down her paintbrush and went to the edge of the stream and dipped her hand in the water and splashed it on the back of her neck. It was icy cold even on such a brilliantly hot day and the cold water running down her back made her shiver deliciously. She gazed into the stream thinking how wonderful it would be to take off her shoes and stockings and dip her feet in the water. Hardly had the thought crossed her mind than she had slipped them off and slid her toes into the stream. It was breathtakingly cold but so refreshing that soon she was standing in the middle of the stream holding her skirts up to her knees as the water lapped her legs. Further downstream a little bird was energetically washing its feathers, the water splashing in all directions and as she watched it she laughed aloud at its antics.

After a while she climbed out of the water and turned to go back to the tree where she had left her shoes and stockings.

Thomas was sitting there, quietly chewing a piece of grass and watching her.

She put her hand up to her mouth. 'Oh, my! I didn't know you were there, Sir. I didn't hear you . . . Oh dear, I shouldn't have . . .'

'Shouldn't have what? Paddled in the stream? Nonsense. You made such a pretty picture.' His gaze was disconcertingly admiring.

'I . . .' She smoothed her dress down. Had he noticed her shoes and stockings? They were lying in the grass where she had thrown them, not far from where he was sitting. She could hardly ask him . . . Neither could she simply pick them up . . . She stood, very conscious of her bare feet peeping out from under her dress.

'To tell you the truth, I was passing on Midnight and I saw you there and couldn't resist stopping to watch you for a few moments. I hope you don't mind, Hannah.' He got to his feet. 'But I mustn't intrude on your solitude any longer. I'll go now.' He paused, waiting for her to say something. When she didn't he went on, 'How is your painting going? Have you finished it yet?'

She shook her head. 'No. It won't go right.'

He smiled his attractive, crooked smile. 'I wonder why. Could it be that you're missing our little conversations?' He sat down by the tree again. 'Come and sit down. We'll talk. Just for a minute.' His smile widened. 'It might help the painting.'

'I don't think it will.' Nevertheless she sat down, trying to hide her bare feet in the folds of her dress.

'What pretty feet you've got,' he remarked, openly staring at them. 'But aren't they a little cold?' He laid his hand on her ankle.

She knew she should pull her foot away but he held it firm and the touch of his hand was warm. Even as he moved it up to massage her calf she said nothing; he was looking at her in a way that seemed to melt her insides and sap all her will power.

'Your eyes have golden lights in them,' he whispered as he leaned forward and kissed her, brushing her lips like the touch of a butterfly wing. 'Don't you realise what you've done to me, Hannah? I've thought about you night and day,' he murmured. 'I stayed away from you as long as I could but today I couldn't stay away any longer. I knew you'd be here. And when I saw you standing in the stream . . . Oh, Hannah, my love. How can I live without you?' He gathered her in his arms and kissed her eyes, her lips, her throat. This time when he began to unbutton her bodice she had no will, no wish to stop him.

'I love you,' he murmured as he took her to heights she had never dreamed existed. 'Oh, my Hannah, I love you.'

Chapter Seven

Tom Truswell whistled as he went about his daily round. Life was good; his father had bought him a new hunter in return for a promise to put in an appearance at the cutlery works every morning, and he was enjoying an extraordinary run of good luck at the tables. So much so, in fact, that in the last three months he had managed to pay off nearly all his gambling debts.

Of course, it was all due to Hannah Fox. She was his talisman. In conquering her he could conquer anything. Anybody. And all it had taken was patience and a little ingenuity – neither of which attributes he possessed in great abundance as a rule – and of course, determination. It had been a stroke of genius on his part to suggest letting that young brother of hers – what was his name? Stanley – ride old Buttons. The youngster was obviously the light of her life and she considered that this made some kind of amends for the 'accident' as she called it, when the young puppy nearly unseated him. As far as Tom was concerned the little blighter had got no more than his deserts, frightening the horse like that, but he was careful never to point this out to Hannah; he didn't want to jeopardise his chances! Because from the moment he had set eyes on her unusual green eyes and pale, unsmiling face he had been attracted to her, and the fact that she had rebuffed him had made him all the more obsessed with her. Even the charms of little Kitty Braithwaite, his mistress of the past year or more, had palled beside the thought of possessing Hannah Fox and teaching her the new – to her – and wondrous delights of lovemaking.

Occasionally a small, unfamiliar, maggot of guilt nagged at the back of his mind. This made him feel uncomfortable; Tom was not given to feeling guilty over his conquests as a rule. But Hannah was so young, so innocent, so trusting. Yet why should she not be trusting? He had told her he loved her and meant it. He did love her and he proved it to her very thoroughly every Thursday afternoon by the stream.

Only for the past few weeks she had become a little difficult and it had taken a good deal of time and all his expertise to break down her resistance. He found this a bit tiresome, especially with the knowledge that Samson, the new hunter, was pawing the ground behind the trees, impatient to give him an exhilarating gallop.

'What's the matter, Hannah? Don't you love me?' he asked one afternoon, trying not to sound impatient as she resisted his efforts to get his hand inside her bodice as they lay together on the warm grass by the stream.

'It's not that,' she said trying to twist away from him. 'But it's all wrong, Tom. We shouldn't be doing this. What if . . . ?' She couldn't bring herself to even speak of the fear that she had lived with in the months since their love affair began.

'You worry too much.' He was hardly listening. He had managed to get three buttons undone and had glimpsed her white flesh. For the moment nothing else mattered.

She moved her head as his mouth tried to find hers. 'But what . . . ?'

'What do you think, you silly little goose? I'll be twenty-one next year so we can be married. Now keep still . . .'

Back in her room Hannah was furious with herself. She had vowed it would never happen again but it had. She had told herself over and over again that she was playing with fire, and each month she had waited for the sign that all was well, a painful knot of fear twisting in her stomach if it was as much as a day late.

Each Thursday night she told herself that Tom Truswell was not to be trusted and resolved never to go to the spot by the stream again. Yet the next week she had gone there, deluding herself that she was only going in the hope that she would once again spy the kingfisher she had once seen there. Of course he had found her, as she had known very well he would, and as soon as he began to kiss her she had been unable to resist him. She hated him. But more, she hated herself for the magnetic attraction of the man, his darkly handsome features, his tall, well-built body and his gentle, practised touch. Because in her heart she knew that his promise to marry her was hollow. Tom Truswell would never – could never – marry a servant. It was unthinkable. She remembered Miss Sophie's words – 'it's only a bit of fun'. Well, it wouldn't be fun for her if she got dismissed from Cutwell Hall, it would mean back to the dirt and grime of the town and a life that didn't bear thinking about.

She made up her mind once and for all. She would never go to the stream again. She was thankful she had come to her senses before it was too late.

For three weeks she stayed away although it took all her will power. She roamed the hills on her half day, carefully avoiding going anywhere where she thought he might be, taking her paints with her but never even unpacking them. Instead, she sat and stared out over the autumn landscape, relief that she had managed to put an end to the affair turning to sick fear as the days passed and she came to realise that she had left it too late.

She knew all the signs. She had seen her mother in the early stages of pregnancy too many times to be mistaken, although she suspected that in her case the terrible feeling of nausea that assailed her all the time was as much due to fear as to the pregnancy.

'You look a bit peaky, Hannah,' Miss Sophie said one morning as Hannah stood brushing her hair. 'Are you all right?'

'Just a bit tired, Miss,' Hannah replied, trying to smile. 'There, is that to your liking?'

Sophie turned her head this way and that and then shook it to make sure the pins were secure. 'Yes, it will do very well. I'm going riding with Tom this morning so I don't want it falling down round my ears.'

There was a knock at the door. 'Aren't you ready yet, Sis?' Tom poked his head round the door. 'Bingle's had the horses saddled up for ages.'

'I'm coming now.' She picked up her crop. 'I hope you'll soon feel better, Hannah. It's a good thing it's your half day. You don't look at all well.'

'Under the weather, are you, Hannah?' Tom said cheerfully. 'What you need is a bit of fresh air, if you ask me.' He gave her a knowing wink.

'I'll be all right, thank you, Sir.' Hannah felt the all too familiar leap of her heart at his presence but she looked away quickly and busied herself tidying the dressing table.

That afternoon, on one of those unusually warm and sunny days in October known as St Luke's Little Summer, she did go to the stream. Indeed, she had no energy or inclination to climb hills and it was quiet and peaceful at the stream so she could think and try to plan what she must do. There were things you could take, herbs and suchlike, but that would mean confiding in someone because she wasn't sure which ones were reliable. Some might only half do the job; she remembered her mother saying that poor silly Frankie Gipps, who made faces and couldn't walk, had been born like that as a result of his mother 'taking something' before he was born. She couldn't risk that.

She sat with her chin on her knees looking down into the stream. If only it was deeper she could walk into it until it covered her head. It would be quite a peaceful way to die. But at its deepest it would only cover her knees so that was no good. She could lie down in it and let it gently ripple over her . . . it would be so easy, so comforting and would put an end to all this anxiety and fear. It was tempting. She began to unbutton her shoes.

'I've missed you. Why haven't you been here? It's

weeks now.' Tom's voice was rough with annoyance because it was true. He had missed her.

She looked up with a start. She was surprised to see him; she thought he would have given up looking here for her by now. 'I don't know what to do. I'm having a baby and it's your fault. I never wanted . . .' Suddenly, her face crumpled and she burst into tears.

He got down beside her and took her in his arms. 'There, there,' he said, stroking her hair and staring into the distance. This was a dashed inconvenience. Only today his father had told him he'd made arrangements for him to tour Europe with the Carter-Bradshaws so that he could visit foreign silversmiths and bring back some new ideas. If the Guv'nor got wind of this there'd be hell to pay and probably he could kiss the idea of a European tour goodbye. Yet even as these thoughts went through his mind he was conscious of the smell of her hair and the soft warmth of her body against his and he instinctively held her closer and began to caress her.

'I told you we'd be married, didn't I?' he whispered against her ear. 'Next year. When I'm twenty-one.'

'What good's that? By that time I'll have been dismissed with a flea in my ear,' she protested, trying to struggle free.

'Then we'll have to elope.' He turned her face to his. He had missed her. God, how he'd missed her. He began to fumble with the hooks and eyes at the back of her dress. It was difficult with only one hand but he managed it.

'Elope? Where to?' She hardly noticed what he was doing she was so intent on what he had said.

'To Gretna Green, of course,' he laughed. He nuzzled

her neck. 'But you'll have to give me time to make the arrangements.'

'How long?'

'Oh, a couple of weeks, I should think.' He lowered her gently on to the soft grass. 'And then we'll be able to do this all the time,' he whispered in her ear.

Afterwards as she lay in the crook of his arm in the dappled shade of the big oak tree he said, 'Now we're engaged I must give you a ring, mustn't I?'

She smiled up at him. 'I'd like that. But I wouldn't be able to wear it, would I?'

'You could wear it round your neck. I should like to think of it nestling down there—' he put out his hand and traced her cleavage.

She gave him a playful slap. 'Now, don't start that again,' she giggled. But she didn't really mind. She felt almost light-headed with the great weight that had been lifted from her mind and she was blissfully happy. Her worries were at an end because Tom did really love her and intended to marry her.

Although her pregnancy made her feel deathly ill she was so happy that she sang about her work. After all, it was Tom's baby she was carrying under her heart so what did a little discomfort matter? She counted the days until the following Thursday when he had promised to give her a ring.

She knew she wouldn't believe she wasn't living in a dream until she actually had it on her finger. Or round her neck.

He was as good as his word and seemed as excited as she was as he slipped it on her finger. It was a pretty little ring, in an unusual setting of turquoise and pearls.

'I'll wear it on my finger now but I shall have to keep it on a ribbon round my neck when I'm at work,' she said, examining it closely. 'I've never seen anything so dainty in all my life. Oh, thank you, Tom.' She flung her arms round his neck and kissed him.

'By jove, that's the first time you've made the running,' Tom said, returning her embrace enthusiastically. 'Keep this up and you'll be the most jewel-laden little lady in the country!'

Back in her room Hannah looked for somewhere to hide her precious ring until she could find a piece of ribbon long enough to go round her neck. She debated whether to confide her secret to Miss Sophie but decided that the less her young mistress knew about the planned elopement the less likelihood there would be of her getting into trouble for aiding and abetting it. But the whole idea was so exciting that Hannah had difficulty in concentrating on her work and she forgot to sew the ruffles back on Sophie's ball dress ready for the Hunt Ball and had to stay up until two in the morning to do it.

The next morning she was busily pressing the gown when she was conscious of activity outside in the corridor. She put the iron back on the hearth and went to the door.

Lizzie Wainwright was flapping up and down. 'I don't know what she's done with it, I'm sure,' she was saying to Brown, the footman. 'I'm sure I saw it only the other day. I don't think it's right to ask Mrs White to search the servants' quarters. Not till m'Lady's quite sure she hasn't mislaid it somewhere.'

'Haven't you looked, then?' Brown asked. He wasn't really interested in women's trinkets.

'Looked! I've turned the place upside down and inside out. I don't know what she's done with it. But I can't believe . . .'

'If Sir Josiah's ordered a search, that's what'll have to be done.' He cut her short. He wasn't worried. He knew his quarters were safe.

'What's this all about?' Hannah asked.

'Oh, some trinket or other m'Lady's mislaid,' Brown said over his shoulder. 'She thinks it must have been stolen.'

'Mrs White's been told to search our rooms,' Lizzie said. She was clearly offended.

Brown shrugged. 'I can't see what all the fuss is about, meself. If you've nowt to hide you've nowt to worry about.'

'You wait till they come and turn your room over. See if you still say that,' Lizzie warned.

Hannah wasn't listening. All she could think of was what if they discovered her engagement ring? She had hidden it among her handkerchiefs until she could find a ribbon to hang it round her neck. But if someone found it she would have to confess and the plans for the elopement would come out and everything would be ruined and Tom would be furious. Even worse, she'd lose her place here at Cutwell Hall. She couldn't risk that. The safest thing would be to go and fetch the ring and keep it in her pocket until all the fuss had died down.

She hurried up to her room. Mrs White was there. She was just shutting the drawer that held Hannah's handkerchiefs. 'I think you'd better come with me, Hannah,' she said grimly. She held out her hand. In the palm was the pretty little turquoise and pearl ring.

97

'But that's mine!' Hannah protested, her eyes wide with a mixture of fury and guilt because her secret was out.

'Indeed? Well, you'd better come and tell her Ladyship that, because it looks very much like the one that's missing. Come along now.'

For the second time Hannah found herself in Lady Truswell's sitting room. Lady Truswell was sitting in an armchair by the hearth and Sir Josiah was standing with his back to the fire, warming his coat tails and stroking his whiskers with an immaculate white handkerchief.

'I'm afraid I've found the culprit, m'Lady,' Mrs White said, tightlipped. She handed the ring to her mistress.

Lady Truswell looked at it and then at Hannah. 'You, Hannah?' She said in surprise. She looked up at Mrs White. 'Thank, you, Mrs White. You may go.'

Ada White left. She was sorry it had been Hannah, she didn't look the sort to go stealing from her employer, but there was no getting away from it, the ring had been in amongst her things, and carefully hidden away at that. It just went to show that you could never tell from appearances.

Lady Truswell waited until Mrs White had closed the door behind her, then she said in a gentle voice, 'Why did you do it, Hannah? Aren't you happy here?'

Hannah looked from Lady Truswell to Sir Josiah and back. She felt trapped. What could she say? If she told the truth her secret engagement to Tom would be a secret no longer and there could be no elopement but if she said nothing she would be dismissed as a thief. Why, oh, why had Tom chosen a ring for her that was so like his mother's?

'Are you quite sure it's the right ring, m'Lady?' she asked timidly.

Sir Josiah snorted. 'The impertinence! The right ring, indeed!'

Lady Truswell looked again at the ring in her hand and then at Hannah. 'Yes, I'm quite sure, Hannah. Why do you ask? I hardly think there is another quite like it. It's an unusual setting of turquoise and pearls and I'd know it anywhere because it's one of my favourites.'

Hannah hung her head and said nothing. She didn't know what to say. She didn't know what to think.

Lady Truswell waited a few minutes. Then she said, 'Why did you take my ring, Hannah?'

Hannah's head shot up. 'I never took it, m'Lady.'

'Don't lie, girl. It was found among your things,' Sir Josiah snapped.

'Leave this to me, please, Joe,' Lady Truswell said quietly.

He turned away and began to pace up and down. 'I'll be glad to. You brought it on yourself, Flo. I said no good would come of it in the first place. You knew nothing about the wench . . .'

'Either sit down or leave the room, Joe. You know I can't stand you pacing up and down like that.' Lady Truswell's voice was sharp. Obediently, Sir Josiah sat down. 'Thank you, Joe. Now, Hannah. If you didn't steal my ring how did it come to be in your possession?'

'I don't think it can be the same ring, m'Lady,' Hannah said earnestly. 'Mine was given me.'

'By whom?' Lady Truswell smiled at her although she had never felt less like smiling in her whole life. She would rather the thief had been anyone but Hannah.

'I can't say.' Hannah stared at her feet.

'Pah!' came from the depths of the wing chair.

'Joe!'

'Sorry, m'dear.'

'You'll have to do better than that, Hannah, if you want to keep your position,' Lady Truswell said gently. 'Now, who gave you the ring? I want the truth, mind.'

Hannah twisted her hands together and was silent for a long time. 'It were Master Tom,' she said at last because she could see no other alternative. 'He give it me. We're engaged to be married, m'Lady. Only it's a secret. Nobody's supposed to know. He'll be reet put out when he knows I've told you.'

'I can imagine,' Lady Truswell said dryly.

Sir Josiah leaned forward. 'You surely don't *believe* such a cock and bull yarn, Flo,' he said incredulously, looking from his wife to Hannah and back again.

Florence nodded. 'Yes, Joe. As a matter of fact I do. Whatever Hannah Fox may or may not be I'd stake my life on her honesty. You remember how she brought back the ferrule off Tom's riding crop? She had no need to do that, she could have sold it for quite a sum of money.' She pinched her lip between her thumb and forefinger. 'The problem is, what's to be done about her.'

'Well, of course, she'll have to go. No question about that.' Sir Josiah heaved himself out of his chair. 'I'll have a word with young Tom when he gets back. See how far his story tallies with hers.'

'Don't be silly, Joe. Of course it won't. Do you think Tom is going to confess to stealing a ring from his mother to give to a servant girl?' She turned to Hannah and took a deep breath. 'Of course, there can be only one possible explanation for this mess. Hannah, are you with child?'

Hannah hung her head, flushing to the roots of her hair.

'Yes, I thought as much.' She looked up at her husband. 'And this is our son's gallant way of dealing with the situation, Joe.' She turned back to Hannah. 'I take it Tom is the father of your child?'

Hannah nodded.

'You can never be sure of that, not with servants,' Sir Josiah exploded.

Hannah raised her head and looked him straight in the eye. 'I'm a good girl, Sir Josiah. I'd never . . . I mean I wouldn't . . . I mean . . .'

'I know exactly what you mean, Hannah,' Lady Truswell said, 'and I believe you. But you must understand that you can't stay here. Not now. If it was just stealing the ring we could perhaps have . . .'

'But I *didn't* steal it, m'Lady. Master Tom gave it me,' Hannah interrupted indignantly.

'Yes, I realise that.' She waved her hand dismissively. 'But it isn't just that. It's . . . the other business.' She looked pointedly at Hannah's flat stomach.

Tears began to run down Hannah's cheeks. 'But we're going to be wed, Tom and me. He said so. When he was twenty-one, he said. But when I told him about the baby he said we'd elope. To Gretna Green.'

Sir Josiah looked up. 'When?' he asked with the merest hint of sarcasm. 'When was this elopement to take place?'

She shrugged. 'Soon. He'd got to make the arrangements. That's why he gave me the ring. To show he was serious.' She looked up eagerly as an idea struck her. 'Why don't you ask Master Tom, m'Lady? He'll tell you I'm speaking the truth. Ask him now.'

'I'm afraid that's not possible.' Lady Truswell shook her head. 'Tom has ridden over to stay with the Carter-Bradshaws for a few days to finalise the arrangements for his European tour. They're off the week after next.'

'But he can't be!' Hannah looked from Lady Truswell to Sir Josiah and back again. 'He said . . . He told me . . .' She stopped as the awful truth hit her. Tom Truswell had taken the ring from his mother's jewel box and given it to her as an 'engagement' present, knowing full well that she would be dismissed for stealing it, taking with her the consequences of his philandering. Oh, what a blind, stupid fool she had been for being taken in by him. She nodded, too weary and sick at heart to explain or argue further. 'I understand,' she said in a flat voice. She turned to leave the room and said in the same flat tone, 'I'll go and pack my things.'

'Wait.' Sir Josiah felt in his waistcoat pocket and pulled out five sovereigns.

'Take it, Hannah,' Lady Truswell said. 'It's little enough, God knows . . .' She bit her lip against the tears that threatened, tears of sympathy for the young girl who had shown such promise and spirit, tears of anger at her profligate son, tears of frustration that there was nothing she could do to mend the situation, even tears of guilt that it had been she herself that had brought Hannah to Cutwell Hall and this disastrous fate.

When the door had closed behind Hannah Sir Josiah began pacing up and down the room. Lady Truswell didn't even admonish him but sat staring out of the window.

'A damnable affair!' he snorted. 'I knew no good would come of it when you engaged the girl.'

'Don't blame Hannah for Tom's faults, Joe. I believe her when she says he led her astray with his false promises. He may be my son but I'm disgusted with him. He's totally irresponsible. It's not the first time he's got one of the servants into trouble, either, is it, Joe?'

Josiah shrugged and muttered. 'I warned him to sow his wild oats elsewhere, stupid young puppy. Well, he won't do it again.' He raised his voice. 'As soon as he gets home I shall give him a good thrashing and do what I've threatened to do, only you've always prevailed on me not to, Flo, but this is the last straw. I shall send Bingle over to fetch him from the Carter-Bradshaws. He'll find that he's not bound for any European tour! The young whelp is going in the Army. See if that'll make a man of him.'

Florence nodded. 'Yes, Joe. I have to admit you're right. I think that will be the best thing for him,' she agreed with a sigh.

Chapter Eight

Hannah dragged herself up to her room and stuffed her possessions into a straw bag, tears streaming down her cheeks. Then she took off her uniform and laid it carefully on the bed and put on the cheap green dress and coat she had bought in happier days from the catalogue that circulated the servants' quarters and a straw hat that Miss Sophie had discarded in her direction. She liked this outfit, it made her feel smart. But not now. Now she felt sick. Physically sick and sick at heart and she cursed herself for the stupid fool she had been, letting herself be taken in by Tom Truswell's glib tongue and empty promises. Deep down inside she had known she was playing with fire, yet she had been unable to resist him, because he had made her feel – she groped for the word – *important* to him and because she had fooled herself into believing that fairy tales did come true and that like Cinderella she would marry her prince.

Savagely, she thrust the last of her things into the bag and took a last look round her precious little room. How blind she had been to sacrifice all this for a few stolen hours by the stream; she could see now that she had been like putty in Tom Truswell's experienced hands, he had played her like a fish on the end of a line and she was furious at her own gullibility in allowing him to do it. She ought to have known better. She left the room, slamming the door behind her in her anger and frustration. *She ought to have known better.*

She leaned her back against the door for a few seconds, gathering together the tattered remnants of her dignity, then squaring her shoulders she walked down the stairs from the servants' quarters and, ignoring the back stairs, walked along the deeply carpeted corridor to the big sweeping front staircase where a huge crystal chandelier hung in the stairwell, suspended from the domed ceiling high above. Servants weren't allowed to use this staircase, but she was no longer a servant here so as far as she was concerned this rule didn't apply. She made her way slowly down the stairs with her head held high and across the vast black and white tiled hall, pausing before the glass case that held some of the exquisite silverware that bore the Truswell hallmark.

Her lip curled. So her father had been right after all in his hatred of the Truswells. They were not to be trusted. But an empire built on lies and deceit was like an idol with feet of clay. One day it would topple. And, she promised herself through gritted teeth, I shall be there to see it. One day it'll be me that has the upper hand, Tom Truswell. I don't know how, nor why, but one day you'll come grovelling to me. Then it'll be *my* turn.

'What are you doing? You know very well servants aren't allowed in this part of the house without good reason, Hannah Fox!' It was Baines, the butler, hurrying towards her as fast as his bad feet would allow.

She lifted her head. 'I'm not a servant here. Not any more. I'm leaving. And I'm going out through the front door.' Deliberately, she turned her back on him and walked across the hall and out of the great oaken door, the thud as it closed behind her putting a full stop to her life at Cutwell Hall and an end to her bravado as she faced the huge empty world beyond the safety of the big house.

What now?

She couldn't go home. Even her mother wouldn't give her house room now that she was about to bring shame on the family with a bastard child. A Truswell bastard, at that. So where could she go?

She walked slowly down the long drive and through the massive wrought-iron gates to begin the long trudge back to the town. All her spirit was gone now. She was terrified and had never felt so alone in the whole of her life. The only way she could cope was to think from minute to minute. She daren't let her thoughts stray towards the future because visions of what it might hold were too terrible even to contemplate. She pulled her coat more closely round her against a cold October wind that had sprung up. The first thing was to find somewhere to stay for a few days while she looked for work. Work! Perhaps Joe Woods would take her back. God! The thought of going back to that filthy hull and the boring, dirty work turned her stomach. But beggars couldn't be choosers and if he'd take her that's where she'd have to go. At least until . . . Her mind went blank. Don't think about that. Not yet. Somewhere to stay, that was the first thing.

The roads were becoming busier and noisier as she reached the outskirts of the town and soon she could smell the smoke from the factories and other unnameable aromas that were part of Sheffield life. They were smells she never used to notice when she lived among them, but after over a year of fresh Endcliffe air her nostrils were offended by the stench and her already delicate stomach heaved.

She plodded on until, almost without realising it, she found herself outside the Brownings' house, where her sister Mary lived and worked. She hesitated. Mary wouldn't be pleased to see her, she knew that, but where else could she go? And it would only be for a few days . . . She went down the steps and knocked on the door.

Mary answered it. She looked decidedly dishevelled. 'Oh, it's you,' she said, looking her up and down. 'What do you want? You can come in if you like, but I've not got time to stop and talk. I'm run off my feet.'

Hannah stepped over the threshold. It was comfortingly warm but the kitchen was in a mess with pots and pans and dishes strewn all over the place. Mary was in the throes of pastry-making, her hair escaping from her cap and with a streak of flour down the side of her face. 'Why?' Hannah asked. 'What's to do?'

'Cook's sister's poorly, so she's had to go and look after her children. Never mind me, here! Left me to do everything, she has. And to cap it all t'Master's boss is coming for dinner tonight. Goodness knows how I'm going to manage.' She went back to the table and picked up her rolling pin and began attacking the pastry.

Hannah took off her hat and coat and threw them over

the rocking chair. 'I'll lend you a hand if you like.' She began to roll up her sleeves.

Mary looked up. 'Why, is it your day off? You don't usually come here, these days. Not like you did at first. I thought perhaps we weren't posh enough for you now you're in wi' t'nobs up Endcliffe way.'

'I've had other things to do,' Hannah said enigmatically. 'And for your information, no, it isn't my day off. I've left Cutwell Hall.' She looked round. 'Now, is there an apron I can wear? And what do you want me to do?'

'You can peel t'tatties. They're out in t'scullery. Then you can wash all these pots. Why have you left Cutwell Hall?'

'I'll tell you later. Where's the saucepan?'

Helping Mary prepare for the dinner party restored some kind of normality to life and for a few hours Hannah managed to forget the mess her own life was in. As she went from the kitchen to the dining room on the floor above she reflected that the Brownings' house was very small and cramped compared with the luxury of Cutwell Hall but her life at the Hall enabled Hannah to add a few extra touches to the preparation of the meal and the laying of the table that impressed both Mary and her employer. Even Hannah herself was surprised at how much she had picked up in not much over a year in service, especially as most of her work had been above stairs. She couldn't help feeling a little smug and superior when she asked for the grape scissors to put on the fruit bowl and neither Mary nor Mrs Browning knew what she was talking about.

When the last of the guests had gone Mrs Browning

came down to the kitchen in her purple evening gown that to Hannah's critical eye had a touch too many ruffles and ribbons and wasn't quite the right colour for a woman with ginger hair.

'I must thank you both for making tonight such a success,' she said, beaming at them. 'I was really worried about it all, especially with Cook not being back from her sister's.' She sank down on the nearest chair. 'What a lucky thing it was that your sister arrived, Mary. I can't think how we'd have managed without her.' She turned to Hannah. 'I suppose you couldn't stay on here for a few days, Hannah? Until Cook gets back? Mary could do with an extra pair of hands . . .' Her voice trailed off and she looked doubtful. Alistair might not agree to that because the girl might want to stay on permanently and it might be difficult to get rid of her without upsetting her sister but paying three servants on his salary would be right out of the question. 'Only for a few days,' she repeated hopefully.

'I think I could manage that. I've got a few days free,' Hannah said, careful not to sound too eager, although in truth she could have hugged Mrs Browning.

'Good. That's settled, then. Your sister can share your room, can't she, Mary?' Mrs Browning smiled at Mary.

Mary was less enthusiastic. She didn't want Hannah upstaging her all the time like she had tonight, with her silly talk of 'grape scissors'. Whoever heard of such a thing! 'I suppose so,' she answered grudgingly.

'That's settled, then.' Mrs Browning yawned. 'Oh, I'm tired. It's such a strain entertaining one's superiors. I thought the Willoughbys would never go.' She glanced round the kitchen, still cluttered with dirty pots and pans

109

and the remains of the meal as she got up from her chair. 'Oh, leave the clearing up till the morning and get to bed, both of you. It's very late and you've worked extremely hard. Thank you, both. Oh'— she turned as she reached the door – 'just make sure all the lamps are out in the drawing room before you go up, will you?' She swept out, leaving behind a faint aroma of ashes of roses.

'Come on then, Annie, let's do as she says. I'll be glad and thankful to get the weight off my feet and I'm itching to know why you left Cutwell Hall. I thought you said it was such a wonderful place to work.'

'I'll tell you tomorrow. I'm too tired now.' Hannah followed Mary through the house to check the lamps and then up the narrow wooden stairs to the attic and the tiny room where Mary slept. Compared with Cutwell Hall the whole house seemed cramped and over-furnished and Mary's boxroom was a far cry from her own spacious room under the eaves. Again she cursed herself for being a stupid, gullible fool.

She crawled into Mary's narrow bed with her.

'Thanks, Annie,' came Mary's muffled voice. 'I don't know how I'd have managed if you hadn't come.'

Hannah realised what an effort it had cost her sister to say those words. She squeezed her. 'Glad I could help, love,' she said.

'Why did you come here?' Mary asked again, but she yawned as she spoke, obviously more than half asleep already.

'I'll tell you about it in t'morning.' She didn't even want to think about it now.

* * *

But as Hannah retched over the chamber pot the next morning there was no need to tell Mary anything.

'My God! So that's why you came!' She leaned up on one elbow and stared at Hannah. 'You've gone and got yourself in the family way! Well, you can't stay here and that's flat. If Mrs Browning was to find out she'd be spitting feathers.'

Hannah leaned against the side of the bed, exhausted. 'She won't find out if you don't tell her.' She wiped her mouth with the back of her hand. 'Not for a week or two, anyway. That'll give me time to sort something out.'

Mary sat up in bed and hugged her knees. 'Such as what?'

'I don't know.' She closed her eyes. 'I'll have to think.'

'Who was it? A stable boy? The boot boy? A quick fumble in the butler's pantry?' Mary's tone was scathing.

'Mind your own business.'

'My God, you're a fool, our Annie, getting yourself into trouble. I'd have thought you'd got more oil in your lamp. Our Dad'll have a duck fit when he finds out.'

'He won't find out. And if he did he'd only say it served me right for trusting t'Truswells.' Hannah got slowly to her feet. 'Come on, we'd better go downstairs and get the kitchen cleared up.'

Mary scrambled out of bed and got dressed. 'You won't be able to stay here long, you know. I couldn't have you staying here once it begins to show. I couldn't have Mrs Browning knowing my sister . . .' She broke off and for the first time a note of real concern crept into her voice. 'What will you *do*, Annie?

'I shall have to find a job. Perhaps Joe Woods will take me back . . .'

'But you hated working for Joe Woods!'

Hannah shrugged. 'Maybe it wasn't so bad.' She went on, 'And I'll have to find a room somewhere. Oh, I'll manage, you'll see. I've got a bit of money put by to tide me over.' She tossed her head. She sounded much more optimistic than she felt.

Mary's concern was short-lived. She didn't like the way Mrs Browning deferred to Hannah on matters of etiquette. And as if it mattered if the table napkins weren't folded into complicated fans. Bishops' mitres had always been good enough till Hannah arrived on the scene. She could see the drift of it all. If she wasn't careful she'd be out on her ear in favour of Hannah.

'If you don't shape yourself and get your life sorted I'm telling Mrs Browning you're in the family way,' she said as they got into bed two nights later. 'Not that I'll need to tell her before long; she'll be able to see for herself.'

Hannah put her hand on her swelling belly. 'I'll go tomorrow,' she promised. 'When I've helped with the laundry.'

'I can do the laundry on my own. You're only making excuses.' Mary could be cruel when she chose.

Nevertheless it was true and it was with reluctance the next morning that Hannah put on her hat and coat and made her way to Fletcher's Wheel to see Joe Woods. It was a cold, damp morning and the weather did nothing to lift her spirits as she made her way across Paradise Square, past St Peter's Church and into Fargate and from there through to Arundel Street. The streets were noisy and crowded with people hurrying about their business but she walked slowly. She didn't want to go back to work for Joe Woods. She had hated the work when she was there before and she saw no prospect of liking it any better now. But there was no other choice. Eventually she reached Fletcher's Wheel and turned into the dim yard with its worn, slimy cobbles and began to climb the rickety stairs.

As she passed the hull where her father worked she heard him coughing. She stopped. She couldn't come back here to work, not in the same building as him. He'd kill her when he saw the state she was in and realised what she'd done. And he would tell Mam.

Quietly, she went back down the stairs and re-crossed the yard, relief that she had a good excuse not to return mingled with anxiety as to what she should do next.

'Hannah! Haven't seen you for ages. What's up? Have you come for your dad?' It was little Tilly, the errand lass.

'Tilly! Don't tell me you're still running errands for Joe Woods?' Hannah countered.

'Aye. T'old skinflint'll not tek anyone else on, so I've still to do it. Shall I tell your dad . . . ?'

'No. I've not come to see me dad. I came looking for me old job back. But I've changed my mind.'

'Don't blame you. It's hell up there. But you're not looking for work, are you? I heard you were up at Cutwell Hall.'

Hannah nodded. 'I was. But I left.'

'Didn't you like it?'

'It was all right. But I want to be independent.' She gave Tilly a smile that was a bit too bright. 'So I'm looking for a job. And somewhere to live.'

'My auntie's got a room to let,' Tilly said importantly. 'My cousin Jack's gone to sea so she's got his room spare.'

'Where is it?'

'Baker's Hill. Bottom o' Norfolk Street. Number eight. D'you want me to put a word in for you?'

'No, I'll go and see her for meself.'

'Well, you can tell her it was me as told you. Mrs Walters, that's her name. Mrs Clara Walters.'

'I'll do that.' Hannah left her.

'Oh, she'll not be back while six tonight, 'cause she's working,' Tilly called.

'I'll go after six, then.'

Hannah went back to the Brownings' house. Mary was in the scullery, poking the clothes in the copper in the corner amid clouds of steam. She turned when she heard Hannah come in.

'Well?' she asked, tight-lipped, holding the copper stick like a weapon. 'When do you start?'

Hannah stared at her sister. She could see no vestige of compassion in her face at all. Mary wanted her out of the way and that was all she cared about. Hannah could walk the streets for all she would care.

'I'll go and pack my bag,' she said quietly.

'There's no need to be so hasty,' Mary called after her. 'I only asked when you'd be starting work. Where will you stay?'

'I've got a room.' Hannah prayed it might be true.

'Where? I'll come and see you.'

'Like you go and see Mam and the children?'

'That's different.'

'I don't see why.' Hannah didn't stop to argue further. She and Mary were poles apart even though they were still sisters. She knew that Mary didn't really care what happened to her, Hannah, and she wasn't sure that she cared any longer what happened to Mary. It was sad. 'You can say goodbye to Mrs Browning for me and thank her for letting me stay.'

'Wait a minute, I'll come and help you pack your things.' Mary began drying her hands, anxious to make amends for her former lack of charity.

'It's all right. I can manage for myself. You get on with your work.'

'Well, come and say goodbye to me.'

'I'll say it now. Goodbye, Mary. I'm sorry if I've been a nuisance to you.'

Hannah went upstairs, packed her bag and left.

She wandered the streets of the town all day, looking for work, but in a desultory fashion. She must work, she knew that, but she couldn't yet face condemning herself to the life she had known before and hated so much. Tomorrow, she thought. When I've got somewhere to live. Then I'll start looking in earnest.

She managed to contain herself until ten past six before presenting herself at number eight Baker's Hill. The front door opened on to the pavement and a small bird-like woman opened it in answer to her knock.

'I'm looking for Mrs Walters,' Hannah said uncertainly.

'Aye. I'm Mrs Walters. What can I do for you?'

'I heard you had a room for rent. Your niece, Tilly, told me if I came . . .' Her voice faded. Mrs Walters looked a bit fierce in spite of her small size.

'Aye. I've a room to spare till my son, Jack, gets back from sea. But my rooms don't come cheap.'

'I can pay,' Hannah said defensively. 'I'm not without money.'

115

Clara Walters looked her up and down swiftly. 'Honestly come by, I should hope. I'm particular who I let my rooms to. I'm a respectable widow and I'll have no hanky panky.' Her face softened. 'No, I can see you don't look that type. Come on in, love. I've just mashed the tea. I've not long been home and I'm fair clemmed.'

She stood aside for Hannah to enter. The room she stepped into was spotless, with not a thing out of place. A brilliantly polished copper kettle was singing on a kitchen range that shone with black lead. Three velvet cushions were placed with precision along the back of the horsehair sofa and a patchwork blanket was carefully draped over the back of the Windsor chair beside the hearth. Even the brass weights hanging from the clock on the wall sparkled in the lamplight. The table was covered with a crisp white cloth and laid with pretty matching china.

'I'll get another cup down,' Mrs Walters said, going to the cupboard beside the fireplace. 'Sit yourself down. I've got a nice bit of bacon for tea and you're welcome to share it. That way we'll get to know each other and see if we're suited.'

'Thank you.' Hannah sat down at the table while Mrs Walters busied herself with the tea.

'What pretty china,' she said as Mrs Walters handed her a plate with two generous slices of bacon on it.

'Yes. I like pretty things. Help yourself to bread. It's good. I make it myself.' She loaded her own plate, then said, 'Now, tell me about yourself. Why do you want a room? You look young to be all on your own.'

Hannah bit her lip. She hadn't reckoned on being

questioned like this so she hadn't got a plausible story ready. 'I'm going on eighteen,' she said with a lift of her chin.

'Been chucked out?'

'Not exactly. Well, yes, I suppose you could say that. My husband died and so I had to leave our lodgings.' It was the first thing she could think of.

Mrs Walters nodded towards Hannah's plate. 'Finish your tea and I'll show you the room.'

It was up under the eaves, quite small and very neat like the rest of the house.

'I like things nice,' Mrs Walters said proudly. 'Just because I work in muck I see no reason to live in it. I've a buffing shop on Pond Hill,' she added by way of explanation. 'Me and my lasses do work for all the big firms, Mappin and Webb, Wolstenholmes, Walker and Hall, Truswells.'

'Truswells?'

'Oh, aye, we're never short of work.'

They went back to the living room. 'One and six a week I'm charging,' Mrs Walters said in a voice that brooked no argument.

'It's not a very big room,' Hannah ventured boldly.

'It's still one and six. It's not a bad bargain because you'll get your keep thrown in.'

Hannah nodded. 'In that case I'll take it. Thank you.'

'The question is, will *I* take *you*.' Mrs Walters put her elbows on the table and gazed at Hannah. She had piercing grey eyes that missed nothing. 'Why do you want the room?' she asked again. 'And this time I want the truth.'

Chapter Nine

Hannah hesitated. She desperately wanted to stay; the room she had been shown was clean and neat and the house was cosy and warm. But she was in a cleft stick. If she told the truth she wouldn't be given the room but if she continued to lie she'd be found out, because her secret was not one that could be hidden for long. Either way she was damned. She might as well get up and go now.

But something in Mrs Walters' face, something behind those sharp, searching eyes, a compassion that had been completely lacking in her own sister, broke Hannah's defences and her eyes filled with tears.

'Come on, love. Tell me about it.' Clara Walters' voice was gentle.

Hannah sniffed, took a deep breath and told the whole story, from Stanley's accident through to her few days with her unwilling sister Mary. The only thing she didn't confess was the father of the child.

Mrs Walters listened in silence. It was impossible to

know what she was thinking. When Hannah finished speaking you could have heard a pin drop.

'How far gone are you?' she said at last.

Hannah shrugged helplessly. 'About three months, I think.'

'And you know who t'father is?'

Hannah looked up indignantly. 'Of course I do. There was only . . .'

Clara held up her hand to silence her. She'd found out all she needed to know. Dolly mops, they called them in some places. Servant girls used for the pleasures of the masters. Or their sons.

'He said we'd be wed,' Hannah murmured.

Clara nodded sagely. 'Aye, they all say that.' She was silent for some time, then she said, 'Well, I'm sorry, lass, you can't stay here. Not in your condition. I've got my good name to think of.' She paused for what seemed an age then went on, 'But I like you. I know you're honest. I'll tell you what. You can stay here while you find yourself somewhere else to live.'

The tears overflowed and coursed down Hannah's cheeks. She felt weak with relief. 'Oh, thank you, Mrs Walters. Thank you.'

'Only for a few days, mind,' Mrs Walters reminded her. 'So you'd better be sharp about getting yourself fixed up somewhere else.' She put her head on one side. 'And if I was you I'd buy myself a curtain ring.' She indicated her own wedding ring. 'Then you might get away with it when you try to pass yourself off as a widow.'

Hannah looked down at her ringless hand and flushed. 'Oh, yes. I didn't think . . . I'll have to look for work, too. I've got some money but it won't last for ever.'

Mrs Walters smiled and the smile softened her features and revealed the pretty girl she had once been. 'Ah, there I can help you. You can come and work for me. I could do with another lass in my shop. Do you know owt about buffing?'

'Not much. I worked for Joe Woods, once-over, acid etching at Fletcher's Wheel. That's how I knew your niece, Tilly. Before I went to Cutwell Hall, that was.'

'You'll learn. It's mucky work, but not so dangerous as acid etching. My shop's on Pond Hill, not far from t'Old Queen's Head. You can come with me and start tomorrow.' Her expression hardened. 'But don't expect any favours. When I'm at work I'm t'missus and don't you forget it.'

Clara Walters was a shrewd business woman. Her husband had died when Jack was only two and over the years she had worked and saved enough money to buy a derelict terraced house that she had turned into a buffing shop, letting the ground floor to a penknife maker and keeping the two top floors for her own use. She reasoned it was good to have a man about the place because he could look after the steam engine in the cellar that drove the belts to the buffing wheels. She employed between ten and a dozen girls in the buffing shop at any one time.

The house was in an alley off Pond Hill and Hannah followed Clara through a passageway to a cobbled yard and down several steps to the back door. The levels were such that the front door opened straight on to the alley but at the back the cellar was only half submerged and had once had the luxury of a six-paned window. Now half the panes had gone, replaced by bits of wood or cardboard but by the light that filtered through the grimy panes that remained she could see old boxes and biscuit tins piled high along the back wall and discarded buffs and dollies strewn around over the floor. In the corner there was a heap of coal to keep the engine fed. There was just room for the penknife maker's bench under the window and a backless chair for him to sit on.

Clara took Hannah up the two flights of ramshackle stairs to the workshop, where six girls were working at a long bench that ran the length of the wall under the window and handed her over to a woman called Sally. Hannah noticed that the floor was well-swept but there was a smell of oil and grease hanging in the air that made her delicate stomach heave. Everything seemed to be covered in black grime and her heart sank as she viewed the greasy-looking workbench where the girls in layers of filthy aprons over their buff brats, with red head-rags to protect their hair, were at work, their hands and arms already black from the mixture of sand and oil they were using to throw on the wheels as they worked. They all seemed happy enough at what they were doing, and were singing over the noise of the belt-driven spindles. But standing at a buffing wheel polishing silverware with a dirty mixture of sand and oil was a far cry from being a lady's maid with nothing more onerous to do than pressing a few ruffles. Hannah cursed her stupid infatuation with a man she'd known she couldn't trust, because she had thrown away the best chance – the only chance – she had ever had and had catapulated herself right back to where she had started. Only now she had the added shame and burden of pregnancy. She closed her eyes tightly against the ever-threatening tears.

'She's a good gaffer, is our Mrs Walters,' Sally was saying. 'She looks hard as nails but she'd not see any of us lasses want. Here's your buff brat.' She handed Hannah a white calico overall. 'I'll tie it at t'back for you. It's shaped this road so as you can slip it off quick if it gets caught up in t'spindle. And tie your hair up in this.' She gave her a red head-rag and another to put round her neck. 'Not that it makes much odds. T'bloody buffing muck'll get through owt.' Expertly, she pinned on a brown paper apron to absorb the oil, over which went another dirty-looking apron. 'There, you'll do,' Sally said, fastening the leather belt that held everything together. 'Now, you'd better work next to me, where I can keep an eye on you. You can start off wi' 'eelin' and pippin' this lot.' She heaved a pan of spoons and forks up on to the bench. 'See 'ere, you do it this road . . .' She showed Hannah how to buff the ends of the handles.

Hannah learned quickly. She was naturally dextrous and she had been used to concentrating and working fast at Joe Woods in order not to hold up the next process.

'Sally says you're doing all right,' Clara said at the end of the first week when she and Hannah were sitting over their Friday night tea of bloaters. 'That's good. I was afraid you might not keep up.' She picked a bone out of her teeth. 'But I'm afraid I meant what I said when you first came here, lass. You can't stay here with me. Not for long. I'll not have a bastard born in my house. Any road, my Jack'll be back before long. But I'll not be hasty. I'll give you another two weeks. But then you'll have to go,

even if it means sleeping in t'cellar at t'shop.' She eyed
Hannah up and down. 'Don't any of t'lasses on t'side
with you know of lodgings? Them lasses seem to have
their ear to t'ground over most things. One of them might
even take you in if you was to ask.'

Hannah made a pattern on the tablecloth with her
thumb nail. Then she looked up. 'I'll not ask, thanks all
the same. I'll find lodgings for myself. I've been too tired
all the week when I finished work to go out looking but
I'd made up my mind I'd go and see what there was
tonight, when I'd had my tea.'

Clara nodded approvingly. 'And while you're out you
can call in at t'market and get me half a stone of potatoes.
I'm right out.' She got up and began to clear the table.

Hannah went up to her room to fetch her coat and hat.
Then she slipped the curtain ring she had bought at Mrs
Walters' suggestion on to her finger. She wouldn't make
that mistake twice. She looked at herself in the mirror by
the light of the candle and adjusted her hat. She looked
smart enough anyway. She went downstairs.

Clara Walters' expression softened as she entered the
room again.

'Aye, lass, you look bonny enough.' She shook her head.
'I'm reet sorry I can't let you stay with me, but you must
understand I've got my reputation to think of.' She nodded
in the direction of Hannah's stomach. 'Any road, like I
said, my Jack'll be back next month so you'd have to go
then.' She pinched her lip between her thumb and forefinger. 'I've been thinking. Why don't you try Betty Hardcastle
off Exchange Street? She lets rooms. I don't know what
they're like, mind. But it wouldn't hurt to tek a look, would

it? And if she can't tek you she might know of someone who could. Number four Duke's Court, she lives.'

'Thanks. I'll go there first.'

Betty Hardcastle couldn't take her. She was glad. The court where she lived reminded her too much of the squalor of her own home. But by nine o'clock, when she had been passed from address to address, each one a little worse than the last, she realised she was in no position to be choosy.

'Tha can tek t'cellar,' a fat, blowsy woman in a dirty overall told her at last, leading her down slimy steps to the small, damp, evil-smelling room with a bed in one corner and a small table and chair in the other. Even by the kind light of a guttering candle it looked cheerless and bare. 'And mind tha keep tha's men friends quiet. I'll have no brawlin' outside my house.'

'I don't have men friends,' Hannah said indignantly. 'I'm a respectable working lass.'

'I don't know what tha's doin' in these parts, then,' the woman said with a smirk. She sniffed. 'Well, dost tha want it or not? Sixpence a week.'

Hannah sighed. It was a dreadful place but she was weary from searching and at least she would be able to tell Clara she'd found a room. Her only hope was that once she heard what it was like Clara would refuse to let her go there.

'I'll take it,' she said with a catch in her throat.

The woman held out her hand. 'A month's rent in advance. Two shillin'.'

'I'll bring it tomorrow,' Hannah said, hoping never to see the place again.

'It'll be gone tomorrow unless you pay up now.' The woman's fat face was like stone.

Hannah paid the two shillings and left. In renting that sordid little room she knew she had sunk as low as she could get.

As she passed the market hall on her way back she remembered Clara had asked her to buy potatoes. In spite of the hour the market was still thronged with noise and people, a good many the worse for drink, looking either for bargains or a good time by the light of the kerosene lamps. The atmosphere was warm after the cold night air and thick with the smell of the lamps, rotting vegetables and unwashed bodies.

She bought the potatoes and put them in the bag Clara had given her and wandered aimlessly through the market, fingering the cheap glass necklaces and gaudy china ornaments on the stalls as she went. It wasn't until she stepped outside again that she realised she'd left by a different door, on to an unfamiliar maze of narrow, unlit streets and ginnels.

She told herself that there was no need to be unduly concerned because she knew she couldn't be far from Baker's Hill. Nevertheless she pulled her coat more closely round her and quickened her step, glancing behind every now and then to make sure she wasn't being followed.

After several twists and turns she saw a street lamp glowing dimly ahead of her in the darkness but before she could reach the relative safety it offered she saw three shadowy figures turn into the ginnel ahead of her, one of which she was sure she recognised as the tall, spare figure of Reuben Bullinger.

'Mr Bullinger!' Relief flooded through her. She hadn't realised how nervous she had become.

But her words were lost in the noise of scuffling feet as the other two men rounded on him and began attacking him viciously. For a few seconds she watched, petrified, then, as they knocked Reuben Bullinger to the ground and began kicking him she ran forward and, swinging the bag of potatoes, caught one assailant a blow to the side of the head, which sent him reeling the length of the ginnel. Then, as the other man looked up to see what was happening, she brought the bag down on top of his head with all her strength. He toppled over, hitting his head against the wall with a dull thud. It was all over in a matter of seconds.

She bent over the figure lying on the ground. 'Oh, Mr Bullinger, are you hurt bad?' she asked anxiously, trying to help him to sit up.

'No, a bit bruised, that's all.' Wincing painfully, he allowed her to help him to his feet. He put his hand up to his head and it came away covered in blood. 'We'd better get out of here before they start again,' he said.

Hannah handed him a handkerchief. 'Don't worry, they'll not trouble you any more. Look, that one's out cold and the other one ran off.'

'Gone to get reinforcements, likely,' he muttered, dabbing the gash over his eye.

'Why should they do that? Why did they attack you?' They reached the lamp-lit street and with relief Hannah recognised it as Shude Hill. 'Come on, we're not far from where I'm lodging,' she went on, not waiting for his reply, 'it's just under the bridge and up Baker's Hill. I'll take you in and we can clean you up a bit before you go home. Mrs Walters won't mind, I'm sure. Now lean on me.'

'We'd better hurry,' he said anxiously, trying to look over his shoulder. 'They'll be back. I know they'll be back. They've got it in for me now, good and proper.'

'Don't talk. Just concentrate on walking. That's right. Come on, we're nearly there.' With Hannah's arm round him for support he staggered up the hill to Clara Walters' house.

'Oh, my Lord, what have we got here?' Clara said when she opened the door. She'd been having a quiet read by the fire, a luxury she allowed herself on Friday nights, and she wasn't best pleased to have her peace shattered, neither by her lodger, who was giving her conscience a hard time, nor by the bloodstained man at her side.

'Can I bring Mr Bullinger in and clean him up, Mrs Walters? He was being attacked in a ginnel and I managed to rescue him.'

'*You* rescued him?' Clara said, standing aside for them to enter. 'And how did you manage that, I'd like to know?' She bustled about filling a bowl with water from the kettle and finding rags. The man certainly looked as if he'd been roughed up. There was a bruise under one eye and a gash over the other, his coat was torn and muddied and he was holding his arm close to his ribs as if they were painful. 'Sit him down by the table there.'

Reuben sat down carefully. He ached in every bone in his body. Heaven knew what would have happened if Hannah Fox hadn't come along. He looked up at her. 'Yes, how did you manage to scare them off?' he asked.

'I hit them with the bag of potatoes. Oh, Lord!' She

clapped her hands over her mouth. 'I dropped them when I helped you up and I forgot to pick them up again. I'll have to go back . . .'

'Not tonight, you won't,' Clara said firmly. 'Not after what's happened. Any road, they'll be long gone. In someone else's cooking pot by now, I shouldn't wonder. You can get some more tomorrow.' She advanced on Reuben. 'Now, let's have a look at you.'

Half an hour later, his wounds cleaned and his bruises painted with arnica, Reuben sat with a cup of tea and an Eccles cake in his hand.

'My mother used to make these,' he said, taking a bite. 'I haven't had an Eccles cake sin' she . . .' he swallowed hard, 'sin' she was taken.'

'And when was that?' Hannah asked. She remembered Stanley telling her he ran errands for Mr Bullinger's mother but he'd never said she was dead.

'Eight weeks last Tuesday.' He sniffed and took another bite. 'By, this is good.'

'They're fresh. I made them before work only this morning,' Clara said. She studied the man at the table. 'I take it you lived with your mother, Mr Bullinger?'

'Aye, that's reet. Till she were taken.'

'So you've never been wed?'

A dull flush spread over his face. 'No, I've never seen the need.'

'What were you doing all this way from Balm Green?' Hannah asked, frowning. 'That's where you live, isn't it?'

'Aye, that's where I live.' He shrugged. 'I were out for a walk. The house gets lonely sometimes, now I'm on my own.'

'Funny place to go for a walk, at t'back o' market,' Clara said, busying herself with the teapot. 'I'd have thought you'd have stuck to streets that were well-lit, this time o' year. You get some funny people about, round them streets.'

He shrugged but made no answer.

She looked up, smiling. 'But happen you were meeting someone? A friend, happen?'

He shrugged again.

Clara pushed another cup of tea over to him. 'When you feel strong enough I'll go and ask my neighbour if he'll walk home with you, Mr Bullinger. He's a big man, he'll see you come to no harm.'

'Oh, that's very kind, but there's no need for that.' The look on Reuben's face was akin to alarm.

'Well, I don't think you're in a fit state to go alone.' She studied him for several minutes and Hannah got the impression that there was something about the man that Mrs Walters didn't like. 'Perhaps you'd like Hannah to come, too?'

'I wouldn't want to put anyone to any trouble . . .' Clearly he was happier with that.

'I'll go and have a word with Frank, next door. I shan't be a minute. Put your coat back on, Hannah.'

Reluctantly, Hannah shrugged her coat back on. She had no wish to go out into the cold night air again and she couldn't see why Frank from next door couldn't go on his own. But Mrs Walters was not a woman to argue with, so together with Frank from next door she walked to Balm Green with Reuben Bullinger. At his door he thanked them both.

'You did me a good turn once-over, when our Stanley had his accident. It was only right I should do the same for you,' Hannah said, brushing off his gratitude. 'Likely they'd have killed you, whoever they were, if I hadn't come along.'

He nodded. 'Aye. Likely they would.'

As they walked back to Baker's Hill Frank asked Hannah where Reuben had been attacked.

'Oh, aye,' he said sagely when she told him, 'that'd be about it. There's a pub near there where them sort hang out.'

'What sort?' she asked, puzzled. 'I don't know what you're on about.'

'I'm saying nowt. Ask Clara. Happen she'll know.' They walked the rest of the way in silence.

Clara was toasting her toes by the fire when Hannah got in.

'Come and sit down, lass, you look starved to death,' she said, indicating the chair opposite. Now,' she continued, when Hannah had made herself comfortable, 'did you find yourself a room?'

'A room?' The business with Reuben Bullinger had pushed it out of her mind. The memory was not a pleasant one. 'Yes,' she said briefly, 'I found a room.'

'With Betty Hardcastle?'

'No.' She didn't want to talk about the damp and, she suspected, bug-ridden cellar that was to be her home. To prevent further questions she repeated her conversation with Frank. 'What did he mean, "where them sort hang out"? You find men spoiling for a fight at any pub you care to mention so I don't know what he was on about. Do you?'

Clara sat staring into the fire. 'Oh, aye. I know what he was on about, all right.'

'Well, aren't you going to tell me?'

She pursed her lips. 'Frank thinks like I do. Yon Mr Bullinger's a Nancy-boy. You know what a Nancy-boy is, don't you? A pansy?'

Hannah nodded uncertainly. She'd heard talk in the servants' quarters at Cutwell Hall but she hadn't totally understood what it was all about.

'A Nancy-boy is a man who likes to go with men instead of with women,' Clara spat the words out distastefully. 'Like Frank said, there's a pub not far from the market where them sort go – on the quiet, mind you – they'd get put in prison if they were found out. And quite right, too, if you ask me.' She nodded. 'Oh, aye, it all fits. He lost his mother not long since, so he was lonely and went looking for a bit of company. And comfort, too, I daresay.' She paused, then went on, 'I thought when I first saw him there was something . . . I couldn't quite put my finger on what. But it all fits. That's why your friend Mr Bullinger got himself beaten up. No doubt about that. And that's why he didn't want to walk home alone with Frank – not that Frank would have anything to do with that sort of thing. Frank's a proper man. But he was afraid someone might see and think . . .' She gave a disapproving shudder.

Hannah listened to this tirade in silence. Then she said, 'I noticed when I worked for Joe Woods that Mr Bullinger wasn't like the other men,' she said thoughtfully. 'He never, ever swore, for one thing. And kept himself to himself. I thought it was because he belonged to that church, what's it called? The Ebenezer Church.'

'Happen that was part of it. But not all,' Clara said. 'By, he'll have to watch out now they know for sure what he's like. News like that spreads like wildfire and they'll make his life hell. I wouldn't want to be in his shoes. Real men don't like Nancy-boys.' She stood up. 'Well, I'm for bed. I've to be up early in t'morning, and so have you.' Her expression softened. 'I'm glad you've got yourself fixed up, lass. It pains me to be hard on you, but I've my reputation to think of, and my Jack'll be back before long.'

Hannah went up to her neat little attic room. It was a far cry from the dank, bug-ridden cellar that would be her home from now on. But it was Jack's room and Jack would be home soon. If she'd heard that once she'd heard it twenty times and she was beginning to hate Mrs Walters' son Jack. Her thoughts turned to Reuben Bullinger. She felt more warmth towards him than she did towards the mythical Jack in spite of Mrs Walters' harsh words. He seemed such a gentle, harmless man and he'd been the one who'd carried Stanley all the way home after the accident. Nobody else had offered to do that. She was sure he wasn't a bad man.

Chapter Ten

When Hannah finally slept it was to dream about the horrible little room that was soon to be her home. But Mr Bullinger was there, too, sitting at the grubby table in the corner and she had the impression that he was hiding from something. Or somebody.

'You can't stay here,' she found herself saying, over and over again. 'You can't stay here. This room's wanted for Jack, Mrs Walters' son. He'll soon be back from sea. You can't stay here. We can't stay here. I can't stay here. Oh, God, I can't stay here!' She woke herself up shouting the words, tears streaming down her face. Quickly she fumbled for matches and lit the candle beside the bed to shut out the vision of that vile cellar and convince herself that it had all been a dreadful dream.

Calmer, she lay staring up at the ceiling. It was no use, she couldn't go to live in that dreadful place, even though she had already handed over two precious shillings. She was used to poverty, God knew, but not the level of filth and squalor of that cellar. Apart from the damp and the bugs it stank of drains. And worse. Somehow she must find an alternative. She blew the candle out and turned over and tried to sleep again. But sleep eluded her as her mind went over and over the events of the last evening, the tramping from place to place looking for a room, each one more squalid than the last, and then rescuing poor Reuben Bullinger from being kicked half to death. She dreaded to think what might have happened to him if she hadn't come along as she did. Poor man. What he needed was someone to look after him.

Suddenly, an idea came to her. She sat straight up in bed. It was so simple, such a perfect solution to everything . . .

She thought about it all day Saturday while she was at work and when she got home and helped Mrs Walters with the washing she was still turning it over in her mind. Of course, he might not agree, but supposing he did, was it what she really wanted?

After they had finished their dinner on Sunday Mrs Walters said, 'I usually go and see my sister on Sunday afternoons. Why don't you go and see yours? Tell her you've found yourself a room?'

'I don't think I'd be very welcome,' Hannah said. 'We didn't part on very good terms.' She looked up. 'Would it be a very forward thing if I were to go along to Balm Green and see if Mr Bullinger's recovered, Mrs Walters?'

Clara gave a disapproving sniff and shrugged. 'No, I wouldn't say as how it would be exactly *forward*, if you don't mind associating with such as him, that is. Myself, I wouldn't go within a mile of the man. Not now I know what he's like. But you must suit yourself.' She gathered up her things, then paused. 'If you go you can take him that last Eccles cake since he seemed so set on them. I shall be back at tea time. You can have t'table laid. There's muffins and a seed cake.'

After Mrs Walters had gone Hannah sat staring into the fire for a long time, trying to make up her mind what to do. Then she got up and put on her hat and coat. She was only going to ask if he had recovered. Surely, there was no harm in that.

Reuben Bullinger was clearly surprised to see her. He still moved stiffly and his eye had turned a dull purple.

'I've come to see if you're all right now,' she said awkwardly. 'And Mrs Walters sent you this Eccles cake, seeing as how you liked them and there was one left in the tin.' She thrust it out to him.

He took it gravely. 'That was very kind. Thank you.' He stood aside. 'Will you step in for a minute?'

'I will, thank you.'

There was an awkward silence as they both stood just inside the door. Then, since there seemed to be no alternative, he said, albeit reluctantly, 'May I offer you a cup of tea? I was just going to mash.'

'I wouldn't say no. It's a long old drag up from Baker's Hill.' She unbuttoned her coat and sat down in the low, padded chair beside the fire and gazed round whilst Reuben warmed the china teapot with water from the kettle on the hob. The room was over-furnished and full of little knick-knacks, all lovingly dusted. Under the window stood a file cutter's stiddy with the chisels and hammers all carefully laid out ready for use.

Hannah watched him as he made the tea. He was rather a stern-looking man, fine featured and with a long,

135

thin face. A shock of black hair made his complexion look even paler than it was. She noticed that some of his movements, particularly the way he moved his hands, were delicate, not quite what might have been expected of a man who spent his days in the filth of a grinding hull. Everything about him and the house was spotlessly neat and clean.

Oblivious of the fact that she had been scrutinising him he looked up. 'Sugar, Miss Fox?'

'No thanks. Just milk.' As he handed her the tea she noticed that the china was thin, with a pattern of roses round the rim.

'What pretty cups,' she remarked.

'Aye. They're Mam's best. It's not often they're used.' He examined his own cup. 'Mam had good taste. She liked pretty things.' He nodded toward the stiddy under the window. 'She was a file cutter. That's where she worked. I can see her now, sitting there, tapping away. I've kept everything just as it was.' He gave a satisfied nod. 'I see no reason to move any of her things.' His face took on an almost dreamy look. 'That stiddy's been under that window ever since I can remember. She took up file cutting again after me dad died, when I were nobbut three year old. Day after day she'd sit there, tap, tap, tapping away. Do you know she could cut over two hundred teeth a minute? And on some files there were over a hundred teeth to the inch.' He shook his head. 'But it got to her in the end. I wanted her to give up when her hand and wrist got all twisted from the constant tapping of the hammer. "I can look after you," I said. "I'm working and earning decent money." But she wouldn't have it. She was proud

136

of her skills and I guess she'd done it for so long she couldn't give up.' He took several sips of his tea. 'She had to in the end, of course, when she got poorly. They say it's something to do with the lead block used for cutting the file on. I don't see how, myself, but they seem to think it's the dust from the lead that does it. Gets into the system and poisons. Any road, I nursed her till she died.' He brushed the back of his hand across his eyes. 'I did all I could for her. Well, it was only right. She'd always looked after me, so when it came to it I looked after her. My mother was a good woman, Miss Fox. A good woman.'

'I'm sure she was, Mr Bullinger,' Hannah said.

There was silence between them for several minutes. Then he said, 'Another cup of tea, Miss Fox?'

'Yes. Thank you.'

He poured it out and handed it to her. 'It was kind of you to come and ask after me, Miss Fox,' he said, changing the subject. 'I'm all right now, except the ribs are still a bit tender.'

'And your eye.' She nodded at it.

'Oh, that. Yes.' He fingered it nervously.

'I wouldn't go that way again, if I was you, Mr Bullinger,' she said. 'By all accounts it's a pretty rough area round the back of the Market.' She hesitated. 'A bit dangerous for a certain sort of people to venture, if you take my meaning.'

He flushed to the roots of his hair but made no answer.

She took several sips of tea and then placed her cup very carefully on its saucer. 'What you need is a wife, Mr Bullinger,' she said without looking up. She hoped he couldn't see her heart hammering in her breast.

137

'I have no wish for a wife, Miss Fox,' he replied stiffly. 'I'm perfectly content as I am.'

'You need a wife and a child,' she went on as if he hadn't spoken. 'Then people might realise they'd made a mistake in thinking you were – something you weren't, in a manner of speaking.'

'I don't know what you're talking about. Anyway, you're mistaken. I could never marry.' He was beginning to sound agitated. 'In any case, I've never met anyone who . . .'

'You've met me.' Now her heart was pounding enough to suffocate at her own audacity.

He stared at her and a look almost of distaste flitted across his face. It was so brief that she wasn't even sure it had been there at all. He shook his head. 'You don't know what you're saying. I'm afraid, flattered though I am, that it's quite out of the question, Miss Fox,' he said, running his hand through his hair. 'I've already told you I have no need of a wife. I am perfectly happy as I am.'

She took a deep breath. 'I must beg to argue with you, Mr Bullinger,' she said quietly. 'After what happened to you the night before last a wife is *exactly* what you are in need of.' She paused. 'You don't want to risk being beaten up every time you step outside the door, do you?' He didn't answer, so she went on, 'You are a marked man, Mr Bullinger. The only thing that will save you is a wife and child. Perfect proof that you are not what men thought you were.' She realised as she finished speaking that her fingernails had drawn blood in the palms of her hands.

He frowned. 'I can't imagine why you are offering to

make this sacrifice on my account, Miss Fox. Obviously, it is not through affection. But whatever your reason, you're wasting your time. I could never give you a child.' He gave an almost imperceptible shudder at the thought.

'I wouldn't expect you to. I am already carrying a child,' she said quietly.

His jaw dropped open and he stared at her. 'But you're not . . .'

'No, I'm not married.' Her mouth twisted wryly. 'Now you can see why I am prepared to make this *sacrifice* as you call it.' She shook her head. 'Believe me, this bargain wouldn't be entirely one-sided, Mr Bullinger. You need a family to preserve your good name, but no more than I need a husband to give my child a name.'

He got up and began prowling round the table in the middle of the room like a trapped animal.

She watched him. 'Do you ever have nightmares about being found out and put in prison, Mr Bullinger?' she asked. She knew she was being cruel but it was cruelty born of desperation.

'I don't . . . It's not like that . . . you don't understand,' he snapped, sitting down in the chair opposite her and putting his head in his hands.

'Maybe those men who beat you up didn't understand, either, Mr Bullinger. But it didn't stop them attacking you. And now they've attacked you once, what's to stop them doing it again? They might even come looking for you.' She leaned forward in her chair. 'But if they realise they'd made a mistake . . . That you weren't what they thought you were . . . That you were only in that area because you'd lost your way . . . That in fact you'd got a wife and would soon have a child . . . That would stop them, wouldn't it?' She leaned back in her chair and ran her hand across her eyes. 'I'm sorry, Mr Bullinger. You must think I'm trying to blackmail you and I suppose I am, in a way. To tell you the truth, I'm desperate. As I've already told you, I'm pregnant. The father isn't prepared to marry me, I've been turned out of the house where I was in service and I've nowhere to go except a filthy cellar.'

His head shot up. 'How can you tell me such a pack of lies? You're living with Mrs Walters,' he said. 'You made the mistake of taking me there last night. Remember? So that story won't wash.'

She closed her eyes against threatening tears. 'I've got to leave. She won't let me stay. Her son will be home soon, she says. Whether that's true or not I don't know. But I do know she won't have a bastard born in her house, so I've got to leave. I've found myself a room but it's disgusting.' She shuddered and the tears spilled over. 'I'll kill myself rather than go there.' She was silent for several minutes, then she said, her voice flat, 'When the idea came to me it seemed that it would get us both out of a hole. It would give you a wife and child, so no one could accuse you of not being – normal – and it would give me a place to live and a name for my child.' Her mouth twisted. '"For our mutual comfort and benefit", doesn't it say in the prayer book?'

'I'd rather you didn't quote from the prayer book. Not in a situation like this.' He passed his hand over his face. 'I don't know, Miss Fox. Marriage is a big step. There's a lot to be thought about.' He leaned back in his chair and closed his eyes and heaved a great sigh. 'Oh, what a mess!

140

I only went to that place because I was lonely,' he said, more to himself than her. 'God knows, I'd never been anywhere like that before. But since Mam died it's been so empty and quiet here.' A tear trickled down his cheek. 'I miss her so much, especially in the evenings. It got so I couldn't stand it any longer. I only went there for a bit of company, a bit of comfort.' His voice dropped. 'I thought I might find a friend . . .' He shook his head and said, his voice barely above a whisper, 'Mam had no idea . . . She'd be horrified if she knew.' Suddenly, he put his head in his hands and began to sob. 'I'm so ashamed . . . But it was only because I miss her so.'

Hannah stared at this big man, his horny hands with their long, sensitive fingers pressed to his face, crying like a child. This was the man she had seen sitting astride the horsing in his workshop, sharpening long, evil-looking blades and covered in the thick yellow swarf that kept the big grinding wheel cool and trapped the worst of the dust as he ground the lethal-looking knives to a fine edge.

She leaned forward and put her cup back on the tray. Suddenly, she realised how her suggestion must look to this man, who was, after all, almost a complete stranger and she was appalled at her own temerity. 'I'm sorry, Mr Bullinger. I can see now that I should never have come,' she said quickly. 'I don't know what came over me, speaking to you like that. You're quite right, of course it would never do. You've got enough troubles of your own without taking mine on, too. I'm intruding.' She got up and hurriedly buttoned her coat, anxious to be gone.

'No, wait.' He straightened his shoulders and took a spotless handkerchief out of his pocket and blew his nose.

'I'm sorry,' he said, once more in command of himself. 'I'm afraid it comes over me sometimes, but I'm all right now.' He stared into the fire. 'It would be nice to have a bit of company in the evenings,' he mused. 'And I'm very fond of children.' He looked up. 'But you do realise that marriage is for a long time, Miss Fox? Till death us do part? Have you thought of that?'

She nodded.

'And of course, there would be no question of sharing . . .' He looked away again. 'You could have my mother's room. It's a nice room. Would that suit?'

She nodded again, her own eyes now filling with tears of relief. 'That would suit very well, Mr Bullinger. Thank you. I'm very grateful.'

He got to his feet. 'Thank *you*, Miss Fox. I realise you are right. I, too have cause to be grateful,' he said gravely.

'Will you make arrangements for the wedding, Mr Bullinger . . .' she hesitated, 'Reuben?'

'Yes. I'll do that, Miss . . . Hannah.' He held out his hand and she shook it gravely.

Hannah Fox and Reuben Bullinger were married at eight o'clock in the morning on a dark, foggy day in early December. She was three and a half months pregnant, a fact not lost on the half drunken priest and his dusty-looking verger, whose palms had been generously crossed to perform and witness the ceremony.

It had taken a certain amount of persuasion to get Mrs Walters to act as a second witness, not because she was perjuring herself in swearing that Hannah was twenty-one when she was, in fact not yet eighteen, but rather because she was uncertain of the wisdom of the union.

142

'But those sort of men don't get married!' she had exploded, horrified, when Hannah told her of her intention to marry Reuben.

Hannah had turned an innocent gaze on her. 'What sort of men, Mrs Walters?'

'But I thought he was . . . ? Well, you know.' She'd looked puzzled. 'After all, wasn't that why he was beaten up the other night?'

Hannah had shrugged. 'Perhaps he was mistaken for someone else. People do make mistakes.'

'You mean, he's not . . . like that? Are you quite sure? I mean, you must admit he looks a bit . . . well, effeminate.' Clara had given her a searching gaze. 'And how can you tell? After all, you hardly know the man! Oh, lass, are you sure you know what you're doing?'

'Perfectly sure. Reuben and I will do very well together,' Hannah had replied with more confidence than she felt.

She'd frowned. 'Well, I must have misjudged him, that's all I can say.' Her face had cleared and she'd put her hand on Hannah's arm, although she couldn't quite bring herself to smile. 'If you're quite sure this is what you want, lass, all I can say is, I'll come and see you wed and I hope you'll be very happy together.'

'Thank you, Mrs Walters.'

Happy? Hannah mulled the word over in her mind. She was being given a roof over her head and a name for her child. Surely, it would be too much to expect happiness as well?

143

Chapter Eleven

After the wedding Reuben left his new bride at the steps of the church and went home. There he took off his Sunday suit and put on his working clothes and went to work. He was not entirely happy at having been married in an Anglican church but he had feared the minister at his own church might have asked searching questions which he was not prepared to answer. Now it was too late, he was wed and there was nothing the Reverend Enoch Partridge could do about it.

And Hannah had been quite right in her assumptions. Except for going to work he had indeed been afraid to venture off his own doorstep after what had happened that night she had rescued him. He had committed an offence – well, he hadn't actually committed the offence as it happened but, God help him, the intention had been there and it would have been a small point if it had come to a court of law – for which the penalty was imprisonment. He went cold at the thought. But now he was safe. He was married and soon to become a father so no accusation would hold up in court or anywhere else. He smiled a little. He thought he might like to be a father. It was something he had never ever imagined could happen.

As for Hannah, as she parted from her new husband and hurried back to Clara's to change and collect her few possessions, she felt an overwhelming relief in the knowledge that she was now a respectable married woman.

'You're late. Where've you been?' Sally asked disapprovingly when she arrived a little breathlessly at the buffing shop to start work. 'Look at the time! Missus'll stop you a half if she finds out. Mind you,' she added with a shrug, 'she were late herse'n so she's got no call to complain.'

'Then don't tell her I'm late.' As if she didn't already know! 'I'll make it up, don't worry.' Her fingers fumbled as she donned her buff brat and tied on the layers of protective aprons and she kept stealing a glance at the ring on her finger, the real wedding ring now, the one that had belonged to Reuben's mother, not the curtain ring she had bought to hide her shame. She hoped the other lasses wouldn't notice the difference. It was unlikely; they were far too busy at their buffing wheels. They worked piece work which didn't allow much time for gazing around. She picked up a handful of apostle spoons from the box and began work. Two of the buffer lasses had been to the music hall the night before, paying threepence to sit in the gallery, and they were singing some of the songs they had learned. Soon she joined in with the others, singing, 'Shall I be an angel, Daddy?', 'Don't go down the mine, Dad,' and 'Father, dear father, come home with me now,' with all the appropriate pathos and a few extra swoops and warbles thrown in for good measure. As she

145

started on the second gross of apostle spoons she couldn't help reflecting that it was a strange but not uncheerful way to spend her wedding day.

At six o'clock when the day's work was done Hannah hung back so that the other girls shouldn't see her leave with her bag.

Clara, always the last to leave, followed her down the stairs.

'I hope you've done the right thing, lass,' she said, laying a hand on Hannah's shoulder. 'God knows, I'd have chosen different for you. My Jack, now . . .'

'I'll be fine, Mrs Walters. Don't worry about me.' She knew Jack's name would never have been mentioned if she hadn't been safely married and out of harm's way. 'I'll see you in t'morning.' She buttoned her coat tightly against the cold night air and hurried along the dimly lit streets, her mouth dry with apprehension. Had she indeed done the right thing in marrying this man whom she hardly knew? How did he feel about it? How would she face him if he was home first? On the other hand, if she was first, what should she do? Go inside or stand at the door waiting for him to arrive? And ought she to buy pies from the pie-man on the corner for their tea?

She reached Barker's Pool and her step slowed as she crossed Pool Square to Balm Green and the neat house in Orchard Court. If it hadn't been that there was no alternative she wasn't sure that she could have gone on, especially when she saw that the lamp had already been lit in Reuben's house. She went and tapped tentatively on the door. He opened it quickly.

'There's no need for you to knock, Hannah. This is your

146

home now,' he said, standing aside for her to enter. 'The door's never locked so you'll not need a key.' He went over to the kitchen range where the fire was burning brightly and the kettle was singing on the hob. 'I allus wash myself down in the cellar when I get home from work. I daresay you'll like to do the same. There's a candle on the side there to light your way and you can take hot water with you, sin' it's so raw cold. Nay, wait a minute. I'll carry it down for you. I don't want you falling.'

'Thank you, Reuben.' She followed him down the spiral stairs to the cellar, where he poured the hot water into a bowl and left her. Unlike the cellar at her old home it was clean and dry and looked as if it had been freshly whitewashed. The bowl stood on a scrubbed table and there was a folded towel beside it. Reuben's swarf-stained trousers and shirt were folded and laid on a backless chair nearby and coal was stored in a boarded-off corner opposite. There was even a mirror hanging over the shelf where the candle and Reuben's shaving tackle stood, and a leather razor strop hung on a hook underneath. Two tin baths stood one inside the other next to an iron mangle beside the brick-built copper.

When Hannah had washed off the filth of the buffing shop and put on her clean dress she made her way up the stairs again. Reuben had laid the table and was putting meat pies out. 'I got them from the pie-seller on the corner,' he said.

'I nearly bought some, too,' she admitted. 'But I wasn't sure . . .'

'There's no need. I've allus shopped sin' Mam took poorly,' he said. 'Sometimes I get chitterlings from the butcher's on Barker's Pool. They do a good brawn, too.' He spooned potatoes on to her plate and poured gravy over.

'I'll get some chitterlings tomorrow,' she promised.

'There's no need.'

'I'd like to.'

She drew her chair up to the table. There was a sense of unreality as she sat opposite this man who was her husband, eating the meal he had provided, in the intimacy of the crowded little room that seemed to exude his mother's presence from every corner. She wondered if Mrs Bullinger would have approved of this strange union. She fancied not.

After the meal he cleared the table and went down to the cellar to wash up, declining her offer of help and making her feel even more like a visitor.

When he came back he put the china carefully away and sat down in the tall, unpadded stick-back armchair beside the fire and indicated that she should take the low, padded chair opposite. 'That were Mam's chair but you can use it. We allus used to sit like this of an evening,' he said, picking up his Bible. 'I used to read to her most nights. Would you like me to read to you from the Good Book, Hannah?'

'I . . . if that's what you'd like to do, Reuben, I've no objections,' she replied. She didn't know much about the Bible. As far as she could remember there had never been a Bible at home, not that anyone could have read it if there had been. And the Bible readings at the daily prayers at Cutwell Hall had been executed either at a fast gabble if Sir Josiah read them or in a slow, halting monotone that made little sense if Brown, the footman, had to do it.

Reuben began to read. He read fluently and well and Hannah's eyes opened wide as he read expressively from the Old Testament, passages chosen to tell of a vengeful God, a God who promised that the sins of the fathers should be visited on the sons, a hard, unforgiving God. She was relieved when with reverence he finally closed the book for the night.

'We'll read some more tomorrow night,' he said, bowing his head. 'God forgive us, we need always to be reminded what sinners we are.' He raised his eyes to look at her and his gaze was tormented. 'I hope you go down on your knees and pray for forgiveness for your sins every night, Hannah.' To her relief he went on, without giving her time to answer, 'We are all sinners. Every one of us.' His voice dropped. 'And me more than most.'

He got to his feet and put the Bible back on the shelf. 'I don't keep late hours, Hannah. If you're ready I'll show you to your room. It was Mam's room so I'd be obliged if you wouldn't disturb her things.'

'Very well, Reuben.' She followed him up the winding stairs to his mother's room, where he gave her a candle and placed a chaste kiss on her cheek then continued up to his attic under the eaves.

She sat down on the iron double bed and made a space among the knick-knacks to put the candle on the little table beside it. She looked round. The chest of drawers was the same, with every inch of the top covered, a china dressing-table set, a brush and comb, two clothes brushes and so many ornaments that there was no room at all to adjust the swing mirror in the middle. Round the walls, nestled among the roses that rioted over the wallpaper, were numerous embroidered samplers bearing religious texts, the largest of these being over the head of the bed and stating ominously in large letters, THE ONE ABOVE SEES ALL. Hannah found them oppressive and decided that since Reuben was unlikely to enter the bedroom she could safely remove them and hide them in the chest of drawers.

Carefully, so as not to disturb her husband in the room above, she stood on a chair and took them all down. But when she opened the drawers she found every one full of clothes belonging to Reuben's mother, all carefully preserved in camphor. She opened the chest at the foot of the bed. More clothes. More camphor. She sat back on her heels and looked round. What a strange way to spend a wedding night, she mused, sleeping alone in the room that was kept as a shrine to her husband's mother. She didn't know whether to laugh or cry. Then her innate common sense surfaced and she told herself she had known that this was how it would be so she had no cause to complain. After all, she had a comfortable home and her child would be born inside wedlock. More than that she had no right to expect. She propped the samplers against the wall, undressed and laid her clothes on the wicker chair by the window, got into bed and blew out the candle. She snuggled under the patchwork quilt and her last thought before she fell asleep was that the bed was the biggest and most comfortable she had ever slept in.

In the days that followed Hannah found that her new home was indeed comfortable, to the point of stifling. As she had observed on her first visit Reuben's living room was fussy and over-furnished; now she had time to notice the details, the piece of dark green tasselled velvet draped round the mantelpiece, the tasselled velvet tablecloth and chair seats. Even the velvet curtains that hung behind the lace ones at the window were tasselled and there were tassels on the runner that graced the walnut chiffonier opposite the door. And there were ornaments on every surface, glass vases, an epergne, china dogs, fairings and in pride of place on the mantelpiece a marble striking clock with golden cherubs standing guard. The walls, too, were crowded with pictures, mostly of a religious nature, almost covering the busy floral wallpaper. Only the file-maker's stiddy that stood under the window with its neat array of tools was without ornamentation.

After a week, in which instead of beginning to feel more at home she progressed from feeling like a guest to feeling like an interloper, Hannah decided she must speak to Reuben. She waited until the supper things were cleared away and he had washed them up and put them carefully in the cupboard beside the fireplace, then she said, 'Just a minute, Reuben. I want to talk to you before you get your Bible out.'

He turned and looked at her in surprise, the Bible already in his hand. 'Well?' he asked.

'We're wed now, Reuben,' she began, 'I'm your wife. You've no need to treat me like a visitor and wait on me hand and foot. You should let me help. I've watched. I know where the pots are kept and it's time I took my turn.'

He put the Bible back in its place and came and sat opposite to her at the table. 'Yes, well, I was just giving you time to get used to being here,' he replied, running his long fingers through his hair in embarrassment. 'Any

151

road, it's no trouble to me. I've been used to looking after things sin' Mam took poorly.'

'Well, I'm not poorly so I don't want you waiting on me. And another thing. If you remember, that first evening – on our wedding day – I said I'd buy chitterlings for supper the next day. I did, but they're still on the plate on the shelf at the cellar head. You've bought the supper every night and cooked it. It's not right. I want to do my share and it's only right I should pay my way. I've not wed you to be a burden.'

'You're not a burden. I'm not short of a copper, Hannah. I can afford . . .'

'I'm not short, neither, Reuben. Wait a minute and I'll show you.' She went upstairs and came down again with a cheap leather purse which she emptied on to the table. Four sovereigns rolled out and Reuben's eyes widened in horror as he looked from the coins on the table to Hannah and back again.

'Where did you get all that?'

'I was given it, if you must know.'

He stared at her and his lip curled. 'Given it? There's only one way you could have got that much money,' he said, his voice barely above a whisper. 'You're a whore! God help me, I've married a whore!' He covered his face with his hands and began to rock back and forth.

'I am *not* a whore! How dare you accuse me of that!' Hannah shouted at him but he wasn't listening.

'Why didn't I think!' he moaned. 'Why didn't I realise what you were when you told me you were with child!'

'I guess it didn't occur to you because you were too wrapped up in your own troubles,' Hannah reminded him, her voice heavy with sarcasm.

He pushed the money over to her. 'Well, you can get out. Now! Right this minute! And tek your filthy money with you.'

Carefully, Hannah replaced the money in the purse. Of course, she should have realised what it would look like to him, seeing riches like that emptied on to the table. How else would a girl in her position be expected to be in possession of so much money. She took a deep breath to cool her own temper.

'I can understand why you should think ill of me, Reuben,' she said, keeping her voice level with difficulty, 'But you're wrong. I'm not a bad lass. I've never sold myself. Nor ever would,' she said quietly. 'Oh, I've been foolish, that I'll not deny. I was in service and foolish enough to think the man I loved, the man who promised to marry me, would honour his promise. But instead of that, when I told him I was carrying his child he got me dismissed from my post.'

Reuben looked at her for the first time, his expression suspicious. 'Are you telling me the truth?'

She spread her hands. 'Oh, Reuben, do I look like a woman of the streets?' She nodded towards the gold glint ing in the light of the oil lamp and her mouth twisted. 'And if I was and could earn money like that do you think I'd spend my days in a filthy buffing shop for the few shillings a week I get paid?'

He wasn't convinced. 'Then where did all this money come from? Your lover? If he gave it you it amounts to the same thing, you're still a . . .'

'No, it didn't come from my lover,' she said quickly. 'He was too clever for that. When I told him I was pregnant he gave me a ring and said we were engaged. But he said it was a secret and I must keep it hidden until he had made arrangements for us to elope. What I couldn't know was that the ring he gave me was one he had stolen from his mother. When she realised it was missing all the maids' rooms were searched and it was found hidden among my things.' She shrugged. 'Naturally, I was accused of stealing it and had to be sacked.'

He digested this for some time, then said, 'You still haven't explained how you came by the money.' He nodded towards it.

She stared at it for a moment, then looked up at Reuben. 'Sir Josiah Truswell knew what his son was like. He knew Master Thomas was a womaniser. And Lady Truswell believed my story.' She spread her hands.

His eyes widened. 'The Truswells!'

She nodded. 'That's where I was in service. At Cutwell Hall.' She went on, 'But what could they do? They couldn't let it be known that their son had not only put a servant in the family way, but had got her branded as a thief to save his own skin. So there was no alternative, I had be dismissed. And that's where the money came from, Reuben. Sir Josiah Truswell gave it to me to preserve his son's good name, because he knew I'd been unfairly treated.' She lowered her head. 'I've never told another living soul who the father of my child is, but you're my husband so I guess you're entitled to know.' She paused and then looked up at him. 'I'm sorry, Reuben, I should have told you all this before.'

He was silent for such a long time that she added earnestly, 'I swear it's the truth I've told you.' She looked round to the shelf where the Bible was kept. 'I'll swear it on the Bible if you like.'

He took a deep breath. 'There'll be no need for that, Hannah. I believe you.' He cleared his throat and said awkwardly, 'I realise I owe you an apology. I should never have accused you as I did, may God forgive me.'

She shook her head in a weary gesture. 'It's all right, Reuben. I didn't think at the time but I can see how it must have appeared to you. You weren't to know.'

He nodded towards the money. 'You'd better put that away somewhere safe. What do you intend to do with it, may I ask?'

Her eyes narrowed. 'I've had to spend a bit of it, there were five sovereigns once-over, but now I'm in work I'll make it up again and then I shall add to it as I can, ready for when I have my own business.'

'Business? What sort of business?' he asked, raising his eyebrows.

'I don't know yet.' She nodded at him. 'You're a Little Mester, aren't you, self-employed and working in your own workshop? Well, one day p'raps I'll be a Little Missus. Who knows? But I'll tell you this for nowt.' Her voice hardened as she swept the coins back into the purse. 'I'm not slaving the rest of my life away in a buffing shop. I'll show t'bloody Truswells, especially Master bloody Thomas Truswell, what I'm made of. They'll not ride rough-shod over me and get away with it like they did my grandfather.'

'That's enough filthy language!' Reuben got to his feet and his chair fell back with a crash. 'I'll not have words like that spoken in my mother's house, Hannah,' he said sternly. 'I can understand you have strong feelings about what happened to you but goodness me, Mam would turn in her grave to hear such language and I won't have it under her roof.' He was lighting a candle as he spoke.

She sighed. 'I'm sorry, Reuben. I didn't mean to swear.' She banged her fist down on the table. 'But I get that mad when I think of t'Truswells.'

'That's no excuse. Come with me.' He picked up the candle and grabbed her hand and dragged her down to the cellar. There he took a bar of soap and before she realised what he was about he had shoved it as far as he could into her mouth. 'Language like that has to be washed out with soap and water,' he said fiercely. His voice rose as he forced a mug of water between her clenched teeth. 'Now, swill your mouth till it froths. Go on. Do as I say.'

He held her head over the bowl.

'I shall be sick.' She cried with a mouthful of froth, trying all the time to twist away. But the more she struggled the tighter he held her. Not until he was satisfied that he had made his point did he release her. 'That's better. Now we'll have no more filthy language in my mother's house, Hannah. Remember that.' He handed her a towel and smiled at her to show that she was forgiven.

She didn't smile back. She ignored the towel and wiped her mouth with the back of her hand. 'Don't you ever treat me like that again, Reuben Bullinger,' she warned, her voice a vicious whisper. 'And it's time you faced up to the fact that this is not your mother's house any more. It's yours.' Her voice rose. 'Your mother is dead, Reuben. She's *dead*, do you hear me? Keeping her house as a shrine won't bring her back.' She turned and went up the stairs to her bedroom and slammed the door.

Inside, she systematically emptied Mrs Bullinger's clothes out of every drawer and piled them in a heap in the corner. There would be plenty of poor women who would be glad of good clothing. Then she put her own things away. There weren't enough to fill more than one drawer so she put the samplers in another. Finally, she swept all the ornaments and knick-knacks into the chest at the foot of the bed and banged it shut. At least she had exorcised Mrs Bullinger's ghost from one room, she thought with satisfaction. She realised she would have to tread more carefully with the rest of the house.

The row, if such it could be called, between them seemed to clear the air and they settled into a more companionable way of living. Each morning they left for their respective work places at the same time but as she was usually the first to arrive home at night she had time to wash the grime of the buffing shop off in the cellar and begin preparations for the evening meal before he came back. She was glad that, unlike her own father, he never sat down at the table until he too had cleaned himself up and changed out of his swarf-stained working clothes.

After they had eaten and he had read aloud a passage from the Bible he would light his pipe and sit by the fire reading religious tracts given to him by the Reverend Enoch Partridge whilst she busied herself stitching for the coming baby.

At weekends Reuben seemed to spend most of his time at his church, the Ebenezer Chapel nearly a three-mile walk away. He never suggested that she should accompany him and she never asked to. It seemed that the arrangement suited them both very well because she didn't want to go and she suspected Reuben had never even told the Reverend Partridge that he was married so it would be something of an embarrassment to suddenly turn up with an obviously pregnant wife.

Hannah used her Saturday afternoons and a good part of Sunday to clean the house, which, although he didn't approve of any work being done on the Lord's Day, Reuben didn't actually forbid her to do. After all, cleanliness was next to Godliness and the work had to be done at some time, so as long as he didn't actually see her scrubbing floors and cleaning windows he was glad to see the fruits of her labour and to know that the shrine to his mother was being kept in pristine condition. One thing that puzzled and amused Hannah was that he didn't appear to notice that the ornaments that jostled for space on the chiffonier were gradually thinning out. She was removing them, just one at a time, moving the others so that the space left wouldn't be noticeable and putting them into the chest upstairs with the ones from the bedroom.

She always found time on Sunday mornings for a chat with Maggie Lewis, an elderly widow living in the cottage opposite. She was a big woman with a big heart who, although she had no children of her own had delivered hundreds in her time. And if there was sickness Maggie was there with advice and a pair of willing hands to help. They became friendly when they met at the tap in the middle of the yard and Maggie would make a pot of tea for them to share.

'You helped nurse Reuben's mother while she was poorly?' Hannah asked, sipping the welcome mug of tea after whitening the step.

'Only at t'last, when he couldn't manage by himself. Very private people, they were, didn't encourage neighbouring. But you'll know that. You must have known her.'

Hannah fell straight into the trap. 'No, I never met her.'

Maggie looked at her oddly but made no further comment. She went on, 'Well, I will say this for Reuben. He looked after his old mam champion, even after she were bedridden. Worked his fingers to the bone for her, he did. Mind, she were a reet tartar. Would have everything just so and he couldn't move wi'out she was calling to him, wanting this or that, asking where he was going and when he'd be back. Ruled him wi' a rod of iron, she did.'

'Still does, it seems,' Hannah murmured into her mug.

Maggie didn't hear. She smiled at Hannah. 'Any road, I'm glad t'lad's wed.' She eyed Hannah's figure. 'But you say you never met Mrs Bullinger?'

Hannah shook her head. 'No. Never.'

She raised her eyebrows. 'She didn't know quite as much about her Reuben as she thought then, did she? When's it due?'

'Late spring, I think.' Hannah didn't think it necessary to enlighten her further.

'Well, lass, I'll be here when you need me.'

159

Chapter Twelve

It was two days before Christmas when Hannah's brother Stanley paid them a visit.

Hannah and Reuben were just sitting down to a supper of hot pies which Reuben had bought from the pie-seller on the corner on his way home from work when they heard the tapping of a crutch on the cobbles followed by a tentative knock at the door.

Reuben went to open it.

'Hullo, Mr Bullinger, I've come to see . . .' Stan's jaw dropped and his words tailed away as he saw his sister sitting at the table. 'Annie! What's to do? What're you doing here?' Reuben stood aside for him to come in and he snatched off his cap and went straight over and gave her a hug. 'Ee, Annie, I'm reet glad to see you. I've been that bothered about you. I went all the way up to the Hall, twice, but they wouldn't let me in. They wouldn't have nowt to do with me, not even Archie Bingle, him as had said I could help him wi' t'osses. What d'you think of that?' Without giving her a chance to answer he went on, 'I

160

couldn't understand it, Annie, not after they'd allus been so nice to me, an' all. They just said you weren't there any more but they wouldn't say where you'd gone, so I didn't know where to look for you. I even went to see our Mary but she's gone all toffee-nosed, she didn't want nowt to do wi' me. Ee, I've been that scared. I thought you must be dead!' He gave her another hug, tears streaming down his face. 'Ooh, Annie, I'm that glad I've found you.' He straightened up and dashed his hand across his eyes.

'Hang on a minute, lad,' Reuben said when he could get a word in. He handed him a penny. 'First things first. Nip down to the pie-seller and get yourself a pie. You look clemmed half to death. Your sister'll tell you all about it when you get back.'

'Ee, thanks, Mr Bullinger.'

Five minutes later Stan was sitting at the table with them, trying to eat his pie and at the same time tell them his own story. His father could no longer work because his cough hardly left him any breath and Stan was now apprenticed to a penknife maker in the Wicker.

'I mostly do odd jobs and run errands but Sam says if I shape up he'll learn me all he knows. He's a gradely chap, is Sam.' Stan's eyes were alight with enthusiasm. 'Sam does everything, makes his own blanks, does his own tempering, hardening, filing, assembling – he says he'll learn me how to do all that.' He took a great bite out of his pie. 'He made a penknife with forty-eight blades once-over,' he said, spraying crumbs over the table in his eagerness to tell them everything at once.

Hannah nodded approvingly. 'I'm glad you'll have a trade to your fingertips, lad,' she said.

He grinned proudly. 'Any road, that's why I haven't been to see Mrs Bullinger lately. On account of I've been at work.' He paused with the pie halfway to his mouth again and looked round. 'Where is she? Has she teken to her bed? I knew she was poorly. Is that why you're here, Annie?'

Hannah shook her head.

'My mother died two – aye, near on three months ago, Stan,' Reuben said sadly. 'Your sister Hannah and me's wed.' With those words a note of pride had crept into his voice.

Hannah nodded. 'Just over three weeks since,' she said with a smile.

'By Gow! You two's wed! Well, fancy that! I never knew you were even courtin'.' Stan chewed on his pie for several minutes, looking from one to the other and back again. 'I'm reet sorry Mrs Bullinger's gone,' he said at last. 'She were a lovely lady.' He drew the back of his hand across his mouth as the last of the pie disappeared. 'But I'm glad you're here, Annie. I'll be able to come and see you. If Mr Bullinger doesn't mind,' he added quickly, glancing at Reuben.

'You'll always be welcome, lad,' Reuben said. 'If for no other reason than you were the apple of my mother's eye.'

'He's your brother-in-law now, Stan,' Hannah said, her eyes twinkling. 'You don't need to call him Mr Bullinger. You can call him Reuben.'

'By 'eck! I'll never be able to do that, Mr – Reuben.'

Hannah burst out laughing and even Reuben looked pleased.

'There you are. You can. See?' Hannah said. She leaned

forward and rested her arms on the table. 'Now. Tell me, Stan. How's our mam?' she asked. 'And the girls? And how does Mam manage, with Dad not at work?'

'I give her what I earn and she gets a bit from rough scrubbing. But it's hard, Annie, 'specially with the baby an' all.' Stan frowned as he spoke.

'But little Fanny's not a baby. She must be nearly three,' Hannah protested.

'Aye, she is, but we've got little Agnes now. She's nobbut three month old. She's bonny. Our Elsie and Maudie tek turns to stay off school to look after her and Fanny when Mam's at work. Can I have that piece of bread, Annie?'

Hannah pushed the crust over to him absentmindedly as she digested the news of her family. Those poor little girls. It was their turn to miss precious schooling now. Things were going from bad to worse, there was no doubt about that.

'If I give you some money will you make sure Dad doesn't get his hands on it, Stan?' she asked.

'Oh, aye, I will that,' he nodded vigorously.

'Does he still drink as much?'

'No. Some days he hasn't the breath to get to t'beer house. Then I have to fetch it for him and he swears at me 'cos I don't bring him enough. But I'm not strappin' beer for him, if he can't pay he'll have to go wi'out.' He finished the crust and looked round to see if there was anything else. 'I don't know which is worst, when he goes there and gets drunk and loses his rag, or when he loses his rag because he can't get there.' He shrugged. 'Either way there's no living with him.' He began to chew on the crust

163

off the new loaf Hannah had cut for him. 'But I think I'd rather see him in a temper than when he sits in the corner and cries, though,' he said thoughtfully. 'At least he's a man when he's mad.'

'Does he still go on about the Truswells, then?'

'Oh, aye. Only now they've teken his favourite child away from him, as well as everything else they're s'posed to have done.' He grinned. 'That's you, Annie. Did you know you were his favourite child?'

'I never was when I was at home, but they say absence makes the heart grow fonder,' Hannah laughed. 'But it was always you, Stan, as I remember it. You were going to make his fortune for him.'

'He might have made it for himself if he hadn't tipped it all down his neck,' Stan said bitterly. He shook his head soberly. 'I'm never going to spend my money on beer like me dad. If I ever have any to spend, that is,' he added with a sigh.

Hannah ruffled his hair. 'Finish your crust while I fetch you a few coppers for Mam, lad.' She went upstairs to her room and took out one of the gold sovereigns Sir Josiah Truswell had given her. For a moment she stared at it, then put it back. A sovereign would arouse her mother's suspicions and that would never do. She counted out five shillings for her mother and sixpence for Stan and took them downstairs. It was a full week's wages but she didn't begrudge a penny of it.

'There, at least you'll all be able to have a decent Christmas dinner,' she said as she handed him the money.

'Aw, thanks, Annie,' he said, grabbing it gratefully. He gave her a slightly puzzled look as he pocketed it.

'Annie? How come you're . . .' he nodded towards her thickening waist '. . . like that if you've only been wed three weeks?'

She gave him a cuff that was only part playful. 'Ask no questions and you'll get no lies told you.'

He shrugged. 'Aw reet, don't get shirty. I only asked. When's it due?'

'End of May, I think. Or beginning of June.'

He grinned. 'I'll be an uncle, won't I?'

'That's right.'

'By! Just wait till I tell our mam!' He looked a bit anxious. 'I can tell her, can't I, Annie?'

Hannah hesitated. 'Yes, you can tell her.' She hesitated again. 'But don't tell her I've only been wed three weeks.'

'And can I come and see you again?' He looked from Hannah to Reuben.

'You're always welcome here, lad, I've told you that before,' Reuben said. 'Mam used to set great store by you coming to see her and running her errands and I'll not turn you away now she's gone.'

'And I'll need you to come and tell me about the family,' Hannah added.

'Perhaps you should go and see your mother now you're not working for Truswells,' Reuben said after Stan had left. 'I don't like to think of you estranged from your mother, Hannah. Mothers can be such a comfort.'

'I'll not go yet. Me Dad's not daft. Do you think he'll not put two and two together and make five? He'll know why I left Truswells and wed you so quick and that'll make him madder than ever. No, I'll wait till after the baby's born before I go.'

'You know best, Hannah,' he sighed as he reached the Bible from the shelf. 'But it's sad.'

'Oh, aye, it's sad, reet enough,' Hannah agreed bitterly.

Hannah didn't enjoy working at the buffing shop; as far as she was concerned it was a means to an end, although what that end might be she had as yet no idea. But she appreciated her good fortune in having been taken on by Clara Walters and it was not in Hannah's nature to give less than her best, whatever she did.

For her part Clara watched her with approval, noticing that she was not only quick but careful and dextrous in everything she did.

'That's good, but mind and watch how the others work when you've a minute spare,' she said after the first few days. 'The big firms can take on folk who only do the one process but I never know what might come my way and I'll not turn work down so I need lasses who can turn their hand to whatever needs to be done. This is only a small shop but I've a good bunch of lasses here. They work well for me because they know I'll see them all right when they're in trouble.' She pointed to the girl at the end of the bench. 'That's Marjorie. She's really a rougher, that's getting rid of the dents and marks in the silverware, and Alice next to her does most of the insiding, polishing the insides of the bowls of spoons, although both of them'll turn their hands to graining and edging if needs be. But Sally there does most of the graining, that's buffing between the prongs of the forks.' She pointed to the girl that had taken Hannah under her wing on her first day. 'Aye, all the lasses have their speciality but, like I say, they'll turn their hand to anything. Except Grace, of course. She works upstairs in t'attic on her own, finishing. She does nowt else. She works with a swansdown wheel and jeweller's rouge, and wouldn't soil her hands with buffer's sand! Not that finishing work is all that clean! Mind, some say it's more healthy working with the sand; the rouge can get on your chest and make you consumptive. You'll need to wait till she's in a good mood if you want to watch her at work, she's a bit prickly. Older than the rest of the lasses, she is, and doesn't mix much but she's a lovely worker.'

Hannah was intrigued but she waited until the pans of work came in from Mappin and Webb and saw that on the top were some carefully wrapped silver salvers.

'They've to go up to Grace,' Sally said, setting them to one side as she gave out the work to the others.

'I'll take them up to her,' Hannah volunteered.

'You're welcome,' Polly said with relief. As errand lass it was usually her job. 'You want to watch out. She'll bite your head off as soon as look at you.'

'Then I'll not stay long, will I?' Hannah smiled. She took the parcel of work up the narrow stairs to the attic, puffing a little by the time she reached the top. Grace was already at work on a silver asparagus dish.

'You're new,' she said without looking up.

'Yes, I am. Where do you want these putting?'

'Put 'em on t'side.' She gave a barely perceptible nod towards the bench beside her. She finished the asparagus dish, examined it carefully and then laid it carefully down. She looked up. 'Well, what's tha staring at? Has tha nowt else to do?'

'I was just watching you at work.' She went to pick up the dish Grace had just put down.

'Don't touch it!' Grace's voice was sharp. 'I don't want tha dirty fingers marking my work. Any road, it's too hot to touch.' She held up her hand, the fingers wrapped in rags. 'Why dost think I wrap these round my fingers? It's not just the buffers as get friction burns, tha knows. Now, get downstairs and leave me to get on.' She leaned over and unwrapped a salver and began to examine it.

Hannah went downstairs. There was something about the salver that didn't look right to her. The handles looked far too heavy for the delicate beading round the edge, to her way of thinking. But it had come from Mappin and Webb so it must be all right.

The weeks passed quickly. She learned to make her own buffs with bull-neck leather; she learned the different kinds of wheels that were used for different processes; salt and mustard spoons needed a much smaller buff than dessert spoons, some were only half an inch. Too, there were different buffs for different tasks; mops, dollies, felts, leathers, she wondered if she would ever learn them all. She watched Marjorie 'rozzling', melting resin in an old saucepan to dribble over the leather buff. When it set it gave the leather the hard glazed edge needed for roughing. Another of Polly's tasks was running out for more rozzle.

Sometimes Hannah's back ached, sometimes her ankles swelled through standing at the bench all day but she never complained because she was anxious to stay at work for as long as she could.

Reuben never questioned this; after all his mother had worked for as long as he could remember, tapping away on the stiddy that still stood memorial to her in the window, so it was no more than he expected. He had worked out carefully the cost of rent and food and coal and at Hannah's suggestion they paid half each, Reuben carefully counting out the money on Saturday nights and putting it in a purse kept behind the clock on the mantelpiece. He kept a careful account of what was spent and knew exactly what should be left at the end of the week. Sometimes Hannah had to surreptitiously add a few coppers of her own to the communal pot to make it balance because her idea of housekeeping was not quite as rigid – or parsimonious – as Reuben's. Even so, and with giving Stan a few coppers every time he called, she was managing to save a shilling or two each week.

Sometimes she reflected that she was little more than a lodger in Reuben's house even though they were married. She felt tolerated rather than welcome, but that was hardly surprising. Given the circumstances of their marriage she felt she had no right to complain.

Each evening they ate their evening meal in silence after he had bowed his head and thanked his Maker, and then however tired he was from his day's work he would take down his old, well-thumbed Bible and read aloud from it, always, it seemed, passages that fed his deep-rooted sense of guilt and sin. It didn't help that his voice was naturally rather slow and lugubrious. Occasionally, although she tried very hard not to, Hannah found herself dropping off.

He'd been reading a particularly wrathful passage from the Old Testament one night while she stitched for the coming baby to keep herself awake.

As he closed the book he let out a great sigh and shook

169

his head. 'I shall never go to heaven,' he said wretchedly. 'I'm far too wicked and sinful.'

She looked up. 'How can you say that, Reuben? You're not a wicked man,' she said indignantly. 'Look at all the good things you do. You go to church at least three times every Sunday. And look how hard you work. Sometimes when you come in at night you're quite worn out. And I know you never leave until you're satisfied with your day's work. You take great pride in what you do, don't you?'

He looked at her in surprise. 'Of course I do. I grind butchers' knives. How could they stand repeated sharpening if I didn't grind them well to begin with? I couldn't hold my head up if I turned out shoddy work. But that doesn't absolve me from sin.'

She tried again. 'You cared for your mother all those years . . .'

'But that was my duty, Hannah. There was no special merit in that. In any case, Mam looked after me for far longer than I looked after her.'

She was silent for a few minutes. 'Well, you never go down to the beer house. You never get drunk like most of the grinders I've known.'

'To tell the truth I don't care for the taste of beer.'

'You married me, Reuben,' she said with a hint of impatience. 'Don't you think that was charitable? I really don't know what I would have done if you hadn't agreed to that. And you're very good to me. You never complain at the way I must have disrupted your life.'

He flushed. 'The marriage was as much for my convenience as yours,' he pointed out.

She nodded. 'I know.' She took a deep breath. 'Reuben, I don't think you should feel so guilty about . . .' she hesitated, 'the way you are. It's not your fault. We can none of us help the way God made us.'

'You're wrong, Hannah,' he said firmly. 'I am an abomination in the sight of the Lord.' He reached again for his Bible. 'I'll read you where it says . . .'

She quickly gathered up her things. 'No thank you, Reuben. I don't want to hear. Surely, if God loves us, *all* of us, then he loves us however we are made and whatever we do. After all, he made us the way we are.' She gazed at him for a moment, wondering if she had said too much.

'We are all sinners. You should come with me to church and hear what the Reverend Enoch has to say. He knows. And he says we were all born in sin and unless we repent we shall die in sin.'

'Oh, I'm sure you repent, Reuben,' she said with a sigh. Then she said, 'Why do you always read the Old Testament, Reuben? Why don't you read the New? It's all about Jesus, and he says God is Love and he loves us whatever we are and whatever we do. I know that's right because I've read it in your Bible when you weren't here. I like that. I like reading about Jesus. You should try it some time.' She stood up. 'And now I'm going to bed. Goodnight, Reuben.'

'Goodnight.' He was still staring after her as she went to the stairs.

Spring came to the town but the only visible signs were that people no longer hurried about blue-nosed and

171

huddled into their rags against the cold and that flower-sellers began optimistically offering daffodils and violets for sale. There was no let-up in the smoke from the factories and steel works; it lay like a blanket over the seven hills, hiding whatever sun there might be.

Hannah dragged herself home from work one evening at the end of May. The warmer weather was making her feel tired and her back ached even more than usual. She knew that her time must be getting near and she had been careful to put enough money aside so that she could still contribute her share to the running of the house while she couldn't work. She was anxious not to be a burden to Reuben and she worried about how he would react to a baby in the house, disturbing the order and tranquility he had always been used to.

Suddenly, she realised that the ache in her back was more than an ache, it was a definite pain. She stopped until it had gone, rubbing the place where it had struck, then walked on slowly up the hill, pausing each time as another one washed over her.

She had just reached Orchard Court when a searing pain brought her to her knees, making her cry out. She managed to drag herself to the door and open it before another hit her and she fell inside.

Reuben was already home, frying bloaters. He rushed over to her, his face a mask of fear.

She clutched his hand. 'Fetch Maggie,' she moaned. 'I need Maggie.'

'It's all right, love, Maggie's here,' her neighbour's motherly voice came from behind her. 'I saw you from across the yard and I could see what was up. Coom on,

172

let's get you up the stairs. You can lend a hand, Reuben, when you've teken them bloaters off. By, they smell good, an' all.'

The next hours were a blur of pain. Hannah saw Maggie's face floating above hers, talking to her and smiling encouragingly but she couldn't respond; her world was too full of agony. She heard footsteps, voices, men's voices, then a man in a black coat was bending over her. An undertaker. Ah, so that was it, she was dead and this was the hell Reuben was always talking about. One long, agonising pain. No wonder he lived in such fear of it. It hadn't worried her before. She'd always thought death was peaceful but this wasn't peaceful, this was tearing her body apart.

Suddenly, the pain was gone and she felt nothing but a weak exhaustion. Then she heard a cry. A lusty infant cry. She opened her eyes to the familiar surroundings of her bedroom.

'It's a boy. You've got a son.' Maggie was grinning at her.

She had often wondered how she would feel when the baby growing inside her was born, the baby conceived in such trust and love that had ended in such bitter betrayal. The baby whose conception had pitchforked her from a life of luxury and clean, fresh air back to the filth and stench of the town and work in a grubby buffing shop. Often, when she had been feeling particularly tired, trudging home in the depths of the winter, she had resented the burden she was carrying, a burden that she knew would remain with her for the rest of her life. Unless it was born dead. She wouldn't care if it was. She knew she could never love it.

Maggie placed the blanket-clad bundle in her arms and she gazed at the little puckered face, the tuft of black hair, the long fingers with even now perfectly formed fingernails. As she looked the baby opened his eyes. They were dark brown, almost black eyes and they seemed to gaze back at her, vulnerable and completely trusting. At that moment a surge of love such as she had never known in her life before welled up inside her. 'My son,' she whispered. 'My little son.'

Chapter Thirteen

It was a full twenty-four hours before Maggie finally managed to persuade Reuben to visit Hannah and the baby. At first he said he wouldn't disturb Hannah. He was sure she needed to sleep. Then there was no time because he had to go to work. But when he arrived home after his day's work and had cleaned himself up there was no longer any excuse. Maggie had made a stew and when she suggested that he should take Hannah's up to her he realised he could put it off no longer without it looking very odd.

'I've never known a father so backward in going to see his first-born,' she said, handing him the tray with a grin. 'Usually they can't wait to see the fruit of their loins.'

Reuben flushed to the roots of his hair and hurried up the stairs.

'I'll wager you'll not be so backward when it comes to getting back into Hannah's bed!' she said under her breath to his retreating back.

Hannah was lying propped up on the pillows, her brown hair lying over her shoulder in a thick chestnut plait. The baby was lying beside her in a drawer taken out of the chest of drawers and lined with a piece of blanket. It was the first time since their marriage that he had been in the room and it took all his courage to enter it.

'Maggie sent me up with your dinner,' he said awkwardly, hovering in the doorway.

She smiled at him. 'Thanks, Reuben. Bring it over, then. I must say it smells good.'

He glanced at her quickly, out of the corner of his eye, then away. 'You're looking very well, Hannah,' he mumbled as he set the tray down.

'Aye. I'm feeling very well. I ought to, lying here being waited on hand and foot. I feel a right fraud.'

Now he did stare at her, open-mouthed as he straightened up. 'But I thought . . . well, I mean, aren't you ill?'

'No, of course I'm not ill, Reuben, I'm as fit as a flea. But I've got to rest for a few days, Maggie says.' She attacked her dinner. 'Mm, this is lovely.'

'Good.' He turned to go.

'Don't you want to see the baby?' Her voice dropped to a stage whisper. 'You're supposed to show a little interest. He's supposed to be your son, remember.'

'Aye. Yes.' He came round the bed and looked down into the drawer where the baby was sleeping. He had never had anything to do with little children and had never before in his life seen a new-born baby and he wasn't really interested.

But to his surprise he was enchanted, struck by the sheer perfection of the baby; the little round head, the perfectly formed nose and little button mouth, the fingers, that even in sleep flexed and then relaxed, showing the lines of tiny knuckles. Everything was there, in miniature, in the sleeping child, even the sweep of tiny eyelashes on the cheek. Tentatively, he put out a finger and touched the downy head. Then he looked up at Hannah. 'By, he's bonny,' he whispered, his eyes moist. Then, as if it was almost wrung from him, 'Oh, dear Lord, I only wish he *were* mine.'

'He is yours, Reuben,' she said gently. 'It's only you and me as'll ever need to know different.'

He remained looking down at the baby for several minutes. Then he looked up at Hannah. 'Can I come and see him again?'

'Course you can. It'll look odd if you don't. Come whenever you like.' She finished her meal and put the tray away from her. 'What shall we call him, Reuben? Have you got a favourite name?'

Reuben flushed with pleasure at being allowed to choose the baby's name. 'My father's name was Joseph,' he said at last. 'I don't remember him, he died when I was nobbut a little lad but Mam always told me he was a fine man. Would that be a suitable name for t'little lad?'

'Joseph. That's a good name. I like it,' Hannah nodded. 'Joseph it shall be.' She leaned over to the baby. 'Joseph Bullinger. Yes, it'll do very well.'

Reuben picked up the tray and turned to go. Then he stopped and gazed round the room, frowning, as if noticing it for the first time. 'This doesn't look like Mam's room any more. What have you done to it?' he asked. To Hannah's relief he sounded puzzled more than annoyed.

'It isn't your mother's room any more, Reuben. It's my room now,' Hannah answered firmly.

'But I asked you not to change anything. What have

you done with her samplers? They were all round the wall. Texts and that . . .' His voice trailed off.

'I've put them in that drawer. I couldn't be doing with them, to tell you the truth. They stifled me.' She watched for his reaction but he said nothing so she continued, 'I've put all her ornaments away, too. They're in the chest at the foot of the bed, if you're wondering what I've done with them.'

'Oh, dear. You shouldn't have done that, Hannah. I asked you not to. What about her clothes?' He was beginning to look distressed.

'They're gone. I gave them away. Some poor soul who hadn't a rag to her back'll be wearing them now. Surely you don't begrudge that, Reuben. I'm sure your mother wouldn't.' She didn't feel the need to enlighten him as to how she had smuggled them over to Maggie's house when he was out for Maggie to dispose of as she thought fit.

He nodded. 'No, I suppose not.' He stared round the room as if he couldn't quite take in what had happened to it.

Hannah waited a minute, then she said, 'Your mother died in this bed, didn't she, Reuben?'

He nodded. 'Aye, she did. She went quiet and peaceful at the last.'

'Well, look at it this way. Now, less than a year later, a new life has been born in this same bed. Life goes on, Reuben. We must look forward, not back.'

He nodded again. 'Aye, I daresay you're right, Hannah.' But he still didn't seem as if he could take it in and he never spoke of it again so she didn't know his real feelings. Sometimes, as she lay in the big bed with little Joseph, she wondered if Reuben was biding his time,

178

waiting for her to get up so that he could come in and put the room – as he would see it – 'to rights' again, hanging all the samplers back and setting out all the ornaments again. She was prepared to do battle if he did.

It was a week before Maggie allowed Hannah downstairs. In that time she looked after her like a mother.

'You need a bit of a rest, love. Likely as soon as you're on your feet again you'll be like all the others, itching to get back to work.'

'Yes, I'll need to get back as soon as I can. I can't expect Reuben . . .' She bit her lip and gazed at the baby at her breast. Maggie was a good friend but even she didn't know the true circumstances of Hannah and Reuben's married life and Hannah had no intention of enlightening her. She looked up. 'But I'll not go back till I've found someone to look after Joseph. It'll take a bit of time, I daresay. I couldn't let him go to just anyone.' She shook her head. 'Sally, a lass I work with, leaves her little one with a woman in Pond Street. It's handy for work, but the place is bug-ridden and I know from what Sally says that the woman doesn't look after the children properly. I couldn't let Joseph go anywhere like that. I couldn't let him go to someone who wouldn't care for him right, Maggie.'

'Will you let me have him? I'd like that,' Maggie said quickly. She had obviously already thought it out. 'You can pay me a few coppers a week and I'll see he comes to no harm. He'll be no trouble to me.' She grinned. 'And I can bring him along to you at work when he's hungry. It's handy, you working so close to the Old Queen's Head, I can nip in there for a drop of porter while you feed him. I like a drop o' porter.' She saw the expression of alarm that crossed Hannah's face. 'Oh, you've no need to worry, I never tek more than half a pint.'

Hannah smiled. 'You seem to have it all worked out, Maggie.'

'Oh, aye. I could see it coming, love, couldn't I? I knew you'd be looking for someone so I've had time to think about it. To tell the truth it'd suit me very well. It's time I stopped being at everybody's beck and call. I'm not as young as I was.' She shrugged. 'Any road, I'm thinking of tekin' a lodger. My brother, he lives in London, knows of a young man in the silver trade who'll be coming this way and wanting somewhere to live. I'm thinking I might offer him a place with me. Albert says he's a likely enough lad, clean habits and tidy with it.' She nodded. 'I've got a bit o' brass put by and wi' what I earn looking after him and minding the baby I could manage a treat, wi'out being called at all hours to look after other folks.'

'Oh, Maggie, would you take him? I know you'd look after him,' Hannah said eagerly. 'And it'd be right handy. All I'd have to do is pop him across the yard in the morning and fetch him back at night.' She cleared her throat. 'Of course, I'll have to ask Reuben if he agrees,' she added, remembering that appearances had to be kept up.

'He'll not say no. He's known me sin' he was knee-high to a grasshopper, so he'll not mind trusting his son to me,' Maggie said confidently. 'Now, let's have you out of bed for an hour. And tomorrow you can venture downstairs. Reuben's got a surprise down there for you.'

It was indeed a surprise. As soon as she set foot in the living room Hannah saw that Mrs Bullinger's file-maker's stiddy with all its tools had gone from pride of place under the window and in its place was a wooden cradle.

'He made it for the baby,' Maggie said, smiling broadly. 'He spent till all hours every night when he got home from work down in the cellar fashioning it. I wonder you didn't hear him banging. He said he'd not have his son sleeping in a drawer, he'd to have a proper cradle. Bonny, i'n't it? Look, it rocks an' all.' She pushed it gently with her foot.

'It's beautiful,' Hannah breathed. She laid the baby in it and gave it a little push. It was perfectly balanced and rocked rhythmically to and fro for several minutes before needing another push.

'He's reet handy, that man o' yours,' Maggie said admiringly. She cocked an ear. 'Ah, here he comes, home from work, so I'll be off. I've left the pan on t'hob with your dinner in. He'll dish it when he's ready. And kettle's boiled ready to mash the tea.'

They were like a family, a real family, Hannah thought as she and Reuben sat at the table eating the stew Maggie had cooked, with the baby sleeping in the cradle nearby. Only it wasn't real. It could never be real while she slept in the big bed and Reuben slept in the attic. She watched him surreptitiously. He was a not a bad-looking man, although slightly lantern-jawed, with thick black hair over a rather sallow complexion. His mouth, hard and thin-lipped, bespoke a sternness that was belied by his soft, vulnerable brown eyes. She knew he was a man driven by shame and guilt yet he had been for the most part considerate and kind to her in spite of the fact that she had almost blackmailed him into a marriage that was totally against his nature.

181

But he had the right to share her bed if he wished. At that thought a small frisson of excitement ran through her and then died. He had never shown the least desire to do that and she realised with a tinge of disappointment that he was never likely to.

'It's a lovely cradle, Reuben,' she said, smiling at him. 'Thank you for making it.'

He nodded gravely. 'I'm glad you like it, Hannah. It didn't seem right for the lad to sleep in a drawer.'

'A good many do that, Reuben.'

'Maybe. But since I've got the health and strength to fashion something better I'll not have my son lying in a drawer.' His tone brooked no argument. Not that Hannah wanted to argue; she was glad he was taking his role as father so seriously.

'What have you done with your mother's stiddy?' she asked tentatively.

'I've put it away. I thought over your words, Hannah, about life going on, and I knew you were right.' He nodded towards the cradle and gave a ghost of a smile. 'She'd have been reet set up to know there was a cradle there in its place.'

After the meal was finished and cleared away he took down the Bible and began to read from it while she, hardly listening, suckled the child, absent mindedly wishing he wouldn't continually punish himself by choosing passages that concentrated on sin and guilt. Suddenly, she looked up. 'Why don't you read that bit that says, Blessed are the poor in heart, Blessed are the meek, Blessed are those that travail and are heavy laden. I like that bit, it's comforting. What does travail mean, exactly, Reuben?'

182

'It means work hard.'

'Well, you work hard.' She sighed. 'And you're certainly heavy laden.'

'What do you mean?' He stared at her, his face like granite.

She had been going to say with guilt but her courage failed her. Instead, she grinned and said, 'With a wife and child, of course.'

'Don't be flippant, Hannah, when you speak about the Good Book.' He slammed it shut and sat staring down at it for several minutes. 'The child ought to be baptised,' he said at last. 'If he dies unbaptised he'll die with all his sins unforgiven.'

Hannah looked up, alarmed. 'Don't say things like that, Reuben. Joseph isn't going to die. He's a healthy baby.' She uncovered the baby. 'Look how bonny he is. And any road, what sins? He's not old enough to have any sins, bless him.' She dropped a kiss on the baby's head.

'We are none of us without sin,' Reuben said sternly.

'Joseph is and I won't have you say otherwise,' she argued, gathering him to her.

'He was conceived in sin.'

Her head shot up and she stared in disbelief at her husband. 'That wasn't his fault,' she protested hotly. 'That was *my* sin. It doesn't make him a sinner!'

'The sins of the fathers shall be visited upon the sons. He must be baptised.'

'He's not old enough to be taken to church.'

'I have no wish to take him to church. I shall baptise him myself. Here. Now.' His face was like thunder.

While Hannah watched, speechless with surprise, he

got up and fetched a small basin and poured water into it from the bucket that stood by the door covered with a cloth. Then he fetched a prayer book and took the child from her. 'I baptise thee, Joseph. In the name of the Father, the Son and the Holy Ghost.' He made the sign of the cross on the baby's forehead, then handed him back to her and sank down into his chair.

'There. It's done. He's safe now.' Reuben leaned back and closed his eyes.

It had only taken a minute but taken by surprise Joseph had begun to scream lustily. Hannah rocked him in her arms, staring from Reuben to the baby and back again. Sometimes, when it came to his religion, she was a little afraid of her husband and couldn't help wondering if he was quite sane.

When Joseph was barely a fortnight old she put on her shawl, tucked the end of it into her belt to make a little nest for him and set off to see her mother. Lying in bed she had thought about it long and hard; her father had said she would never be welcome in his house again, but that was because she had gone to work for the Truswells. Now, she had nothing to do with the Truswells; she was a respectable married woman with a child of her own so he had no reason not to welcome her. And it had been too long since she saw her mother and sisters. She could only hope her father's illness had mellowed him and that he would at least tolerate if not be glad to see her.

It was a forlorn hope. When she arrived she saw that the room hadn't altered much. The horsehair sofa was still there and still spilling its stuffing, the oilcloth that covered the table had lost most of its pattern and was worn through to the backing on the corners. Her father was sitting in the stickback elbow chair by the embers of the fire. He looked grey and shrunken, all his strength taken with his efforts to struggle for breath. But as soon as he saw her his face darkened and he would have thrown her out bodily if he had had the strength to get up out of his chair. As it was he had to make do with cursing her in the hoarse whisper which was all the voice grinder's asthma had left him.

She ignored him and sat down at the table, loosening the shawl a little from the baby.

'Christ!' he wheezed when he saw Joseph. 'Tha's a brazen bitch! How dare tha come here and flaunt tha shame?' He stopped to heave some more air into his lungs and then went on vindictively. 'You'll get no help from us. I knew t'bloody Truswells 'ud ruin thee. I told tha so, but tha wouldn't listen.' He struggled round in his chair as far as he could so that his back was half to her.

She didn't reply to him, but said, 'Here, Elsie, take this and go and get your dad a pint of beer from Ma Ragley's.' She handed her sister, who had been sitting on the step and nursing the baby while she watched the little ones play in the yard, a threepenny bit. 'And you can get some sweets for you and the little ones with the change.'

Elsie laid Agnes back in her crib and ran off while Maudie, a pale and skinny eight-year-old, ran after her, begging to be taken, too, leaving Fanny to sit happily in the yard eating the dirt.

Hannah settled herself more comfortably in her chair. 'Now,' she said, 'for your information, Dad, I don't work

185

at Cutwell Hall any longer. I'm wed, so there's no call for you to stop me coming home.'

She saw him stiffen with surprise and he turned his head but not his body. 'Wed? Who to?'

'Reuben Bullinger. Him as worked in the next hull to you. Him as carried our Stan home when he was knocked down.'

'How long sin'?'

'Long enough.'

He digested this with a fit of coughing and wheezing that left him breathless and purple in the face, a purple that quickly faded to a deathly pallor as he fell back in his chair, completely exhausted.

Elsie returned and put the beer down near him. As soon as he could summon the strength he picked it up and drank it down in one draught. Then he wiped the froth from the stubble on his chin with the back of his hand and lay back again.

'Where's Mam?' Hannah asked.

'Working to keep food in the children's bellies while I rot here wi' nowt to do but sit an' wait to die,' he panted. He glared at her. 'An' if tha hadn't been so bloody headstrong, tha'd still have been here, helpin' to keep things goin', instead of goin' off an' gettin' these'n wed. It's a struggle for tha mam, I can tell thee that, sin' I've not worked.'

'It was a struggle when you did work, Dad,' Hannah said, biting her lip before she said more. After all, he was a sick man.

There was a commotion in the yard and her mother came in wreathed in smiles.

'Annie! The lasses said you were here but I didn't believe

them.' She gave her a hug and a kiss. 'Oh, lass, it's that good to see you.' She peeped at Joseph, lying in Hannah's arms. 'And the bairn, too. He's a bonny lad. Stan told me he was on the way. I'm that glad you've brought him to show us.' She went over and put a few more coals on the fire and pulled the kettle forward on the hob. 'I'll mash some tea.'

While she bustled about, ignoring her husband in the corner, Hannah watched her. She looked tired and her face was lined, yet she had lost the downtrodden manner that Hannah remembered and looked almost contented.

She poured Hannah's tea and one for herself. 'He'll not want one. Look, he's gone to sleep,' she said, looking at Nat over her shoulder.

'I sent the girls to get him some beer.'

'Aye, he'll like that better. He never was one for tea.'

'He's bad, Mam,' Hannah whispered.

Jane shrugged. 'We knew it'd get him in the end.' She smiled, a wicked little grin that lit up her face. 'At least I know where he is all t'time now,' she said. 'And I can do as I like 'cause he's not got the strength to knock me about.' She sighed. 'But there'll be no more bairns from him.' She shook her head. 'I don't know whether to be sorry or glad about that. I love bairns.' Then her face cleared again. 'But I'll have the grandchildren. You'll bring them to see me, won't you, lass?'

Hannah got up and laid Joseph in her arms.

'Ah. My first grandchild.' Jane dropped a kiss on his head. 'And a bonny lad at that.'

Hannah smiled at her mother. Now was not the time to tell her that as far as she was concerned Joseph was likely to be the last as well as the first.

Chapter Fourteen

Joseph was just three weeks old when Hannah returned to the buffing shop on Pond Hill. This was much longer than most of the women took off when they were confined but in truth Hannah had thoroughly enjoyed staying at home with her little son and although she felt perfectly fit and strong she had not been at all anxious to return to the dirt and grime of the buffing shop. It was only because her savings were beginning to dwindle and she was determined not to be a drain on Reuben that she had decided she had been away long enough. And she was lucky in that Maggie had offered to look after Joseph. Hannah knew that her neighbour loved him and would care for him as well as she would herself.

And so she had given him an extra cuddle and handed him over into Maggie's capable hands before making her way, on a June day that promised oppressive heat, along streets noisy with the bustle of hurrying workers, back to the squalor of Clara Walters' buffing shop.

Less than a year ago, she reflected morosely as she

dodged across the road narrowly avoiding a brewer's dray from one direction and a horse-drawn tram from the other, less than a year ago I was working in that big house, more as a companion than a servant to Miss Sophie, and I could walk outside whenever I liked and see blue skies and trees bursting into leaf. At this time of year I could watch the sheep with their lambs frisking in the park and breathe air that was fresh and clean. And through my own stupid fault I threw it all away to come back to this. Her eyes filled with angry tears.

Then a vision of Joseph, with his dark downy hair and his huge brown eyes rose before her and she felt a pang of guilt. Poor lamb. It wasn't his fault. He didn't ask to be born.

She reached Pond Hill and heaved a sigh of resignation as she mounted the rotting wooden staircase. I know I'll never get another chance to better myself like that, she thought dejectedly, but if I do I'll not throw it away for any sweet-talking man like I did last time. I'll not be made a fool of again. Not by anybody.

She reached the buffing shop, tied on her buff brat and red head-rag, then pinned on the layers of paper aprons before taking her place on 't'side' as the bench that held the buffing wheels was known.

'Cat got your tongue? You don't seem very cheerful. Aren't you glad to be back wi' us?' Marjorie asked. She was a scrawny, sharp-tongued woman of thirty-five who looked fifty, with grey hair and bad teeth. She made no secret of the fact that she didn't like Hannah. 'Sally here only took three days when she had her Gladys.'

'Only 'cause I couldn't afford to stay away longer,' Sally said with a laugh.

'Aye. An' I was back on t'side wi'in forty-eight hours wi' my last three. Three weeks you've been gone! You must be made o' brass.'

'I 'spect she had comperlications,' Polly the errand girl said sagely. It was a word she had heard her mother use with regard to childbirth and she liked the sound of it although she had no idea what it meant. 'Did you have comperlications, Hannah?'

Hannah couldn't help smiling. 'No. I just liked being at home with Joseph,' she answered truthfully.

'You wait till you get eight of 'em, like me. You'll be bloody glad to get away from t'brats,' Marjorie sneered. She looked in the pan of work beside her. 'Oh, no! Bloody mustard spoons. I hate bloody mustard spoons. Fiddly soddin' things.' She grabbed a handful and threw them back in the pan again.

'Well, you'll not get paid for standing and looking at them,' Sally reminded her sharply.

Nothing changed, Hannah thought sadly as she threw a handful of sand on the wheel and settled to her own work.

Halfway through the morning Clara Walters came in looking hot and flustered. She flung off her hat and coat and sat down heavily on a backless chair by the fireplace, rubbing her side.

'What's up, Mrs Walters?' Sally asked. 'Got that stitch again?'

'Aye. I've been hurrying, to work off my temper,' Clara said, pursing her lips. 'I've been to Truswells. By 'eck they're a mingy lot, there. They want the work done yesterday but they're worst payers of the lot. They queried

190

the price of last lot of fish servers we did for them. I even went to see young Mr Truswell and he said, "Well, Mrs Walters, you know Hatty Beedle would have done them for fourpence a gross less than you've charged,"' she mimicked his voice. 'So I said, let Hatty Beedle do 'em next time, then. I'm not having my lasses working for nowt. Fish servers is quality work.'

'Them weren't quality work! It were like workin' on old bedsteads, any road, from what I recall,' Sally said.

There was a chorus of agreement from the other girls. 'Aye, Truswells work's not what it was.'

'Then Hatty Beedle'll be the best place for him,' Clara said cattily. 'Half her buffer lasses can't tell the difference between quality work and old fire grates, from what I can make out. All they think about is getting t'job done fast. I told him, my lasses are good workers, they turn out a first-class job and I'll not have them working for less than reasonable rates.' She shook her head. 'That young Mr Truswell hasn't his father's flair for t'business. He'll price himself out o' t'market. That's what he'll do, you mark my words. Folk'll not pay high prices for rubbish.' She paused for breath and rubbed her side again.

'Do you mean Mr Tom Truswell?' Hannah asked idly. For some reason her heart had begun to thump uncomfortably at the mention of his name.

'Aye, that's right.'

'But I thought he was in the Army.'

Clara snorted. 'Aye, he was, but it didn't suit him – well, it wouldn't, would it, not if he had to knuckle down and do as he was told – so he got his father to buy him out.' She stared into the empty grate. 'Funny how these things happen, though. In the end it turned out to be all for the best, because not long after Mr Tom got out of the Army his father had a stroke so he's had to take over running the business.' She shook her head again. 'But by 'eck, he's got a helluva lot to learn before he'll stand in his father's shoes.'

'Is his father still alive, then?' Hannah asked, trying not to sound too interested. But she was sad at the thought of the old man dying; he wasn't a bad man and he had been kind to her.

'Oh, yes, I believe so. Can't get down to t'works yet, though.' She made a face. 'He'll see a difference when he does! By 'eck he will!'

'Here's a cup of tea, Mrs Walters. Polly's just mashed.' Sally handed her a cup. 'We're not bothered about t'Truswells,' she said comfortingly, taking a sip of her own. 'We can do wi'out their work. Dixons and Mappins keep us busy enough.'

'Aye, while they prosper we'll not be short of work,' Clara agreed.

Thoughtfully, Hannah examined the bowl of a beautifully chased soup ladle. It was not the first time she had heard Clara complain about Truswells.

At the end of the day Hannah hurried home, anxious to see her little son. Maggie had brought Joseph in to her at dinner time and she had fed him while she ate her bread and cheese but all the same it had seemed a long day.

To her surprise Reuben was already home and had put vegetables on to cook. He had also fetched the baby from Maggie and was dandling him awkwardly on his knee, trying to stop his screams.

'Maggie said she gave him some pap earlier,' he said above the noise, 'but I reckon the poor lad's hungry again.'

Hannah took him and unbuttoned her dress to feed him. 'You're home early, Reuben,' she said.

'Well, I left a bit soon so as I could get t'supper on. I thought you'd be a bit wearied after your day's work.'

'Thanks.' She never ceased to be surprised at her husband, whether it be his little acts of kindness or his sudden fits of fanatical religious fervour. But all in all, she decided, life with Reuben was better than she had dared to hope, as long as she was happy for them to live in a relationship that was lacking any warmth or demonstrable affection.

'You'll soon have to start him on tatties and gravy if he goes on this road,' Reuben said, trying not to look at the guzzling baby. 'He's allus hungry.' The sight of Hannah's white breast embarrassed him although she was quite oblivious to this fact. Suckling her child was as natural to Hannah as feeding herself.

Reuben began to lay the table for their meal. 'Oh, by the way, Maggie's lodger's arrived,' he said.

'Oh, aye. What's he like?' Hannah, still busy with the baby, didn't look up.

'Looks a decent enough chap. Tallish. Fair hair. Come to work for Dixons, Maggie said. I didn't see him to speak to.'

'What's his name?'

Reuben frowned in concentration. 'James? Jenkins? Jarvis. That's right, Jarvis. Peter Jarvis. I believe Maggie said he's a silver chaser by trade.'

'I don't suppose we shall see much of him.' Hannah finished feeding the baby and laid him in his cradle. 'And our little lad won't worry him because when he's with Maggie Mr Jarvis will be at work, for the most part.'

Reuben straightened up in the act of putting the plates on the table. 'I like that, Hannah.'

She looked up. 'Like what?'

'*Our* little lad.' He gave a ghost of a smile and Hannah realised with something of a shock how seldom Reuben smiled.

'Well, you're already more of a father to him than my father has ever been to any of his children,' she said.

He nodded gravely. 'Aye, well he's a gradely little lad. Any dad 'ud be proud of him.'

The weeks and months sped past. Hannah had settled back at work, taking her place 'on t'side' with the other girls, learning all the different processes; which buffs were used for which job and how to change them, how to soften the new dollies with half a brick, how to rozzle the buff to give it a hard edge; she even learned to mend the belt that went up to the ceiling round the big drive shaft when it broke.

If Grace, the silver finisher, was in a good mood she would sometimes allow Hannah up into the attic to watch her at work, hunched over the spindles, coughing from the fine dust of the jeweller's rouge spinning off the swansdown wheel that gave the work a bright mirror-like finish, but more often she would wave her away, saying, 'Bugger off an' mind tha own business. Tha can do tha's work and leave me to do mine.'

But Hannah respected her. Her harsh tone belied the gentle, almost reverend way she handled the burnished silverware.

At home, Joseph thrived. He was a happy child, safe in the knowledge that he was loved both by his parents and by Maggie. Occasionally, when Hannah took him across the yard in the morning, Maggie's lodger would be at the tap in the yard, or just going out of the door and he would smile and say good morning, but he was a shy man and never stopped to talk.

'Aye, he keeps himself to himself, does Mr Jarvis,' Maggie nodded when Hannah remarked on this. 'But he keeps his room tidy and pays his rent on time so I've no complaints.' Her voice lowered, although Peter Jarvis had already gone to work. 'Does some lovely drawings, designs and that. Pictures, too. You should see them. Sometimes he works at home, you see.'

'Oh, dear. I hope Joseph doesn't disturb him,' Hannah said anxiously.

'No. He likes the little lad. Says he's a lively little chap. Any road, he mostly works up in his room.'

The next time Hannah saw Peter Jarvis at the tap she made a point of going out to fetch water herself.

'Maggie tells me you sometimes work at home, Mr Jarvis,' she said as he stood back to let her fill her bucket. 'I hope my little son doesn't disturb you when he's with Maggie.'

Peter Jarvis looked surprised. 'Oh, no. No, indeed. He makes very little noise, Mrs Bullinger, I assure you.' He gave a small, nervous smile and ran his hand through his fair, wiry hair in a strangely boyish gesture. 'I'm afraid I wouldn't hear him if he did cry when I'm working on a design. I get quite lost in my work.'

'Oh, that's all right, then.' Hannah said, relieved. 'I wouldn't want Joseph to be a nuisance.' She turned off the tap and bent to pick up the bucket.

'Allow me.' He picked it up and carried it across the yard and put it down on her step for her. 'He's a lively little chap,' he said with a smile. 'I'm growing quite fond of him.' He hesitated. 'He reminds me of . . . a little lad I once knew.'

'Thank you, Mr Jarvis.' She smiled at him and went indoors, not quite sure whether she was thanking him for carrying the water or for thinking that Joseph was a lively little chap.

Reuben had been standing at the window watching and he turned to her, his face like a thundercloud. 'I saw you, running out there the minute you saw Maggie's lodger at the tap. I'm telling you, I'll have none of that, Hannah. You're my wife, and I'll thank you to remember it and not go chasing after other men.'

Her jaw dropped in amazement. 'I only went out to ask him if Joseph disturbed his work, Reuben. There was no harm in that, was there?'

'Maybe not. But you were talking to him for some time.'

'Mr Jarvis was only saying what a lively little chap Joseph was. He said he reminded him of a little lad he once knew.'

Reuben sniffed. 'Well, just remember what I've said and don't try to get too friendly, that's all.' He went off to work, leaving her staring after him in perplexity. She wondered if she would ever really know this man, her husband in name only yet who couldn't bear it if she so much as looked at another man.

One afternoon when Hannah had been back at work some eighteen months Clara called her into her office. They all called it the office but in reality it was no more than the tiny back bedroom of the house, big enough for a table and two chairs and a cupboard under the window.

As Hannah walked in Clara was blowing her nose. It was obvious she had been crying.

'What's up, Clara? Is something wrong?' Gradually, almost without either of them realising it, Hannah had slipped into calling her boss by her Christian name although none of the other girls, most of whom had worked there much longer, did.

'Aye. There's summat wrong, all right, lass. I've had a telegram from the shipping company my son Jack works for.' She nodded towards the buff envelope on the table in front of her. 'Didn't you see the lad bring it up?'

Hannah shook her head. 'No. I've been doing those soup spoons. They're tricky. I must have been concentrating on that.'

Clara nodded and her eyes filled with tears again. 'I allus knew it'd come one day,' she said with a sniff. 'Ever since he went to sea I've known this would happen.' She looked up, her face agonised. 'He's been lost at sea. My Jack's been lost at sea. Washed overboard in a storm in the Bay of Biscay.' She pushed the telegram over to Hannah. The words were brief but final.

'Oh, Clara, love. I'm sorry.' The words sounded hollow

197

and inadequate. She went round the table and laid an arm round Clara's shoulders.

Clara leaned against her and put her hand up to hold Hannah's. 'That lad was my life. He was all I'd got. All I lived for after his father died,' she said. 'I never wanted him to go to sea. Oh, I could have stopped him, I know he'd have listened to me, but he was so mad keen to go I couldn't bring myself to say anything to him.' She was quiet for some time, then she said, 'I've always known in my bones that it would end this road, but it doesn't make it any easier to bear.'

Hannah gave her shoulders a squeeze. 'I'll go and mash some tea. You just sit here quiet. I won't be long.'

When she got back Clara had pulled herself together and was taking a spoonful of white liquid.

'It's only bismuth,' she said, with an attempt at a smile. She rubbed her stomach. 'I get terrible indigestion these days. I think it's the worry. I'm a terrible old worrit. I worry about Jack . . .' She gave a deep sigh. 'Well, I won't have him to worrit about any more, will I?' She sniffed loudly and made an obvious effort to pull herself together. 'And I worry about the work.' She waved her hand. 'Being in charge of all this lot takes it's toll. Knowing you lasses all depend on me for bread. Being a Little Missus isn't all honey, you know.'

Hannah looked surprised. 'Well, I don't see you need to worry about your buffer lasses, Clara. They all work hard and they're all willing to turn their hands to whatever comes along. They'll not let you down.'

'Yes, I know that. That's why I worry. I mustn't let *them* down.' Clara sipped her tea. 'Ah, this is just what I need.' When she'd finished it she said, 'I think I'll go home in a minute, Hannah. I'll not be much use here for the rest of the day. I know I can trust you to look after things till I come back tomorrow.'

'But surely you won't be in tomorrow? You'll need a few days to get over . . .' She nodded towards the telegram on the table.

'No. I'll be best working. After all, what have I got to stay at home for? I can't even give the lad a decent burial so I haven't got that to keep me busy.' She sighed and got up wearily from her chair. 'It doesn't seem right, somehow, not having a funeral to arrange. You need a funeral to make it real. To say goodbye, if you know what I mean.' She shrugged on her coat and put on her hat. 'You'd best go back on t'side. Tell the lasses what's happened. Tell them I'm away home.'

'I'll do that. And you're not to worry about a thing.'

Thoughtfully, Hannah went back to the buffing shop. The lasses were all subdued when she told them Clara's sad news.

'Aye, she allus set great store by her Jack,' Marjorie said, shaking her head morosely. 'It's allus a mistake to set too much store. 'Specially when there's only the one.'

'He was a gradely lad, too. I saw him several times when he was home. All weather-beaten from the sea,' Sally said. 'Quite fancied him myself, I did. I used to ask him when he was going to come home and stay. He only laughed and said who'd want to come back to Sheffield smoke when they could breathe good fresh salty sea air. I said I didn't know sin' I'd never breathed fresh salty sea air.' She laughed. 'Didn't sound healthy to me, all that

199

water, and damp air gettin' to your insides, tell the truth, but he seemed to think it was good for him. Poor Mrs Walters. He were all she'd got.'

'She's got us.' Polly looked up from stoking the fire. 'We're her family now.'

'That's true enough,' Marjorie agreed, adding with a rare burst of generosity, 'She's allus looked after us. Now we'll look after her.'

They were a good bunch of lasses, Hannah reflected as she went back to her work on the bench. She was finished the soup spoons and started on a batch of forks, changing to a buff that looked like a very thin leather wheel. It was strange, she mused, ever since the first day she had worked there Clara had always treated her differently to the other buffer lasses. And what was even stranger was the fact that they had accepted this without question. Even Sally, who had appeared to be in charge when Hannah had first arrived, seemed to defer to her now.

Suddenly, her thoughts were shattered by a scream from Marjorie. 'Me hand! Oh, Christ! Me hand!' The protective finger rag she was wearing had got caught up in the spindle of the buffing wheel and was winding itself round it, dragging her hand with it.

Quick as a flash, Sally, who was working beside her, switched off the driving belt and while Hannah rushed to hold the half-fainting Marjorie up, carefully began to cut away the rag to free her hand, which was bleeding and already beginning to swell. 'Get the smelling bottle from my bag, somebody,' Hannah called, as Marjorie began to buckle at the knees.

Polly rummaged in the bag and handed it to Hannah.

200

'Lucky she didn't lose her finger. I've seen fingers torn right off when the rag's caught,' Sally murmured as gently she cut away the last of the rag and freed Marjorie's hand.

Hannah helped Marjorie to the chair by the fire and wiped away the blood to try and examine the damaged hand. 'Looks bad. She ought to see a doctor,' she said.

'Don't be daft. Where would I get t'brass to pay a doctor?' Marjorie whispered weakly. 'It'll be all right. I'll just wrap a rag round it and carry on.'

'You'll do nowt of t'sort,' Hannah said firmly. She turned to Sally. 'Where's the nearest doctor?'

'There's one at t'back o' Sycamore Street,' Sally said. 'Shall I fetch him?'

Hannah looked at Marjorie, still almost fainting. She was in no fit state to walk even that far, although it would be cheaper than calling him out. She nodded. 'Yes, fetch him. And tell him to be sharp. We don't want Marjorie losing her finger.'

'But I've not got the brass to pay,' Marjorie insisted anxiously.

Hannah patted her good hand. 'Don't worry about it. Some of us can spare a copper for that.'

'You're bloody lucky, then,' she whispered, her head lolling back against the wall. 'Wi' my man out drinking every night I've scarce the brass to feed the children.' She sat up. 'I can't be off work. I can't afford to lose time.' She looked down at her hand, swathed now in clean rag. 'I promised our Henry he should have the boots he saw going cheap in the snob shop. I've been saving for weeks. I'll not be able to get them for him if I don't work.' Tears trickled down her cheeks.

The doctor came, put two stitches in the finger and splinted it. 'You'll not work for a month,' he said. 'Not with that hand.'

Hannah paid the doctor out of her own pocket and after he had gone went back upstairs. Clara wasn't here to make the decisions, and none of the other lasses were capable, judging from the wailing and crying that was going on in the buffing shop, so she would have to.

'It's not as bad as all that,' she said cheerfully.

Six tear-stained faces turned towards her in amazement. 'How can you say that, Hannah?' Sally asked. 'You heard what Marjorie said.'

'Yes, I did. Well, there's no reason why she can't still work. She can sweep the floor and keep the place tidy. After a bit she'll be able to mash the tea, too, I shouldn't wonder.'

'But that's all Polly's job,' Marjorie pointed out, unwilling to return to menial work.

'I know. Well, it's time Polly tried her hand on t'side for a bit. And it'll give Marjorie summat to do so that she can still draw her money.' She turned to Marjorie. 'Don't worry. You'll still get paid the same rate, I know Mrs Walters won't object when I explain what's happened.'

Marjorie's shoulders sagged with relief. 'Thanks, Hannah,' she said, 'you're a grand lass.'

It was the first kind word Marjorie had spoken to her.

Chapter Fifteen

The incident with Marjorie set Hannah thinking. There ought to be some money, just a copper or two, set aside each week in case any of the lasses were injured. Injuries were not uncommon in the buffing shop although mostly the girls simply bandaged the wound, put on a glove and carried on working. But sometimes, as in Marjorie's case, it was more serious, in which case families could be in dire straits.

When Clara had been back at work a few days Hannah spoke to her about it. Surprisingly, Clara was unsympathetic.

'It's up to them to make their own arrangements,' she said. 'I'm not running a rest home here, you know.'

'I realise that, Clara. But surely, a copper or two a week wouldn't break the bank?' She bit her lip. 'I paid for the doctor to see Marjorie out of my own pocket. Not that I minded,' she added quickly. 'But if there had been an accident fund it could have come out of that.'

'Then you were a fool,' was all Clara said. 'Do it once, they'll expect it again.' She rifled through some papers on her desk. 'And you were very hasty in letting Marjorie work on with that hand. She'll not pull her weight and I can't afford to pay people full rate for sweeping up and mashing tea. Any road, that's young Polly's job and putting her on t'side instead of Marjorie'll mean work'll get behind because Marjorie's quick and Polly's still learning.'

Hannah sighed. 'I'll make sure the work doesn't get behind, even if I have to stay late and do it myself, Clara,' she said. 'I thought I was acting as you would have done. I know you like to keep a happy workshop. I'm sorry if I stepped out of line. But I know Marjorie finds life difficult at home. And her husband's no help at all. She reminds me of my own mother when I was little, the way she has to struggle to make ends meet.'

'She's no worse off than the rest,' Clara said. She rubbed her side and made a face. 'Oh, I'm sorry, lass. I'm a bit tetchy this morning. I was up all night with indigestion.'

'You should see a doctor. It's getting worse, isn't it?'

'It was the upset of my Jack dying like that. I'm sure that's what set it off again.' She gave a ghost of a smile. 'All the same I meant what I said. I'm running a business here, not a Christmas club. Remember that and you won't go far wrong.'

Hannah opened her mouth to argue, then thought better of it and said instead, 'I'd better get back on t'side.' She got up from her chair and went to the door.

'No, wait a minute. I've got something I want to say to you.' Clara waved her back to the chair. 'I've been thinking, Hannah. Some of the bosses have been a bit difficult lately when I've gone for work. They've allus driven a hard bargain but it's getting worse. Maybe it's time you took over that part of the business. They might look more kindly on a pretty face.'

Hannah gasped. 'But I couldn't do that! I wouldn't know what to say!'

'Of course you won't, till I tell you.' Clara said impatiently. 'But you'll soon learn. I'll take you with me a few times and you'll see. These bosses all need handling differently. Some of them, the older ones, started out as tradesmen, found a partner who'd got a bit o' brass and gradually built the business up. They know what it's all about, right from the bottom. Not that that makes them any keener to part with their brass,' she added acidly, 'but at least they know what's involved in making a knife. Not like the ones who've inherited from their fathers. They've no idea what it's like to sweat on a bench; mostly they've been born with a silver spoon, so they don't care either. They've never been inside a buffing shop or a grinder's hull; they wouldn't soil their hands wi' owt like that.'

'You don't like the bosses, I can tell that,' Hannah remarked.

Clara shrugged. 'I've got no feeling either way. I need them and they need the likes of me, that's all there is to it. And they're all alike in wanting t'job done yesterday for next to nowt. They'll tell you they can get work done a penny or tuppence a gross cheaper somewhere else, and it's true, they probably can. But my claim is that we never, ever turn out shoddy work and we turn our hands to anything. And we deliver on time. That's most important. We deliver on time.'

Hannah shook her head. 'They wouldn't take any

notice of me, Clara. You're the Missus. It's your job to see the bosses. They know you and you know them. You enjoy it, you've told me so before. Your Jack dying like that . . .'

'My Jack's got nowt to do wi' it. I'd already had this in mind before I heard about him, Hannah.' She eyed her up and down. 'You're a smart-looking lass, even in your buff brat. I reckon you'll do very well. Anyway, think on what I've said. It'd mean an extra shilling in your pay packet,' she added as an afterthought.

Hannah still looked doubtful. 'If you're quite sure it's what you want I don't need to "think on", Clara. I'd like to do it. And it's not just the money, either. But are you quite sure . . . ?'

'Yes. My mind's made up. Now I know you're happy about it we'll start on Monday.' She smiled. 'But come in looking a bit smarter, won't you? You can't go sitting in a boss's office like that, it wouldn't look right.'

Hannah gazed out of the window, thoughts tumbling over themselves in her mind. What would Sally and the other lasses say when she told them what Mrs Walters wanted her to do? She hadn't been there as long as most of them so would it cause ill-feeling? And why was Clara prepared to pay her an extra shilling a week when she wouldn't spare a few coppers for an accident fund? It didn't make sense. But she desperately wanted to do it. It was a chance to get out of a buff brat and away from the filth of the buffing shop. A chance to better herself. *Another* chance, a small voice inside her said. But this time she wouldn't throw it away.

She hurried home, eager to tell Reuben the good news

but he wasn't there. Then she remembered, it was Friday and he would be collecting fish and chips for tea. So she cleaned herself up and went across to fetch Joseph.

He was walking now, a serious-looking toddler with a shock of dark hair and dark brown, almost black eyes. They were the one thing that reminded Hannah of his natural father. He toddled to the door to greet her, holding a piece of paper with a crude picture of a house on it. He thrust it into her hand proudly.

'Mr Jarvis has been helping him to draw,' Maggie said in explanation. She laughed. 'He says the lad's got the gift but I can't see where, myself.' Her voice dropped conspiratorially. 'He held his hand with the pencil all the time.'

Hannah picked Joseph up and kissed him. 'I think it's a lovely house, darling. You're a clever boy. I hope you thanked Mr Jarvis for helping you.'

'Of course you thanked Uncle Jarvis, didn't you, lamb?' Maggie tousled his hair affectionately. 'They get on like house on fire, those two.'

Hannah took Joseph home and together they propped the picture up on the mantelpiece.

'There, now when Papa comes home he'll see it,' she said.

As soon as Joseph had begun to form words Reuben had elected to be called Papa by him. Hannah had never been quite sure why and he had offered no explanation, other than that it was easier for him to say.

She laid the table, made up the fire and began helping Joseph to build a train with the wooden blocks Reuben had fashioned and painted for him while they waited for his return.

As soon as he heard Reuben's step on the cobbles Joseph scrambled to his feet and ran to him.

'Papa, look.' He caught his hand and dragged him over to the picture.

Reuben picked him up so that they could both look at it. 'That's gradely, lad. That's a real bonny house. Did you do it?' he asked. 'You're a clever lad if you did.'

'Maggie said Mr Jarvis helped him,' Hannah said, clearing away the last of the building bricks and standing up.

Reuben's face darkened. 'Has that lodger of hers got nowt else to do but play with the lad, then? I thought he was supposed to be such a busy man.'

'He works at home on his designs sometimes.' Hannah was busy with the plates so she didn't see Reuben's expression.

'How do you know that?'

She looked up in some surprise. 'Why, Maggie told me, of course.'

'Well, then, he'd do better to work at them than spend his time playing all day with our lad,' he said shortly.

'Oh, Reuben. He only spent a few minutes, you can see that from the drawing.' She burst out laughing. 'I do believe you're jealous, Reuben! I'm sure there's no need to be. Mr Jarvis was only being friendly.'

'Aye, well, maybe it's a friendship we can do without.' He attacked his tea without saying another word and silence reigned until he reached down the Bible from its shelf.

This was nothing unusual. The ritual was always the same. The meal was always taken in silence because since

Joseph had been old enough to take his meals with them Reuben had made it a rule – with which Hannah complied although she didn't agree – that there should be no talking at the meal table. After the table was cleared and Joseph was ready for bed Hannah took him on her knee and sat quietly cuddling him while Reuben read the passage from the Bible. He read in a droning voice and Joseph was usually asleep by the time it was finished. It was only with a great effort that Hannah kept her own eyelids from drooping. She didn't want to listen to the passages that Reuben picked out to read over and over again about an angry, judgemental God; she wished he would read some of Jesus' words, that spoke of love and compassion. Sometimes, when Reuben wasn't there, she would take down the Bible and read Joseph the story of the Good Samaritan, or the feeding of the five thousand, stories Reuben never chose. It was as if he must always punish and judge himself through what he read. Hannah found this very sad.

When he finished reading Reuben closed the book reverently and laid it back on the shelf. This was the sign for Hannah to take Joseph upstairs and tuck him into his cot at the foot of her bed. She got to her feet reluctantly. She loved to hold her sleepy little son and was always sorry when it was time to lay him down.

Tonight, after she had tucked him up she took her best shoes from under the bed and carried them downstairs to clean them, ready for the morning.

'What are you doing with your best shoes?' Reuben asked when he saw them. 'Do they need mending already? I'll do them when I put new soles on my boots.'

'No. I'm going to clean them. Mrs Walters asked me to go to work looking smart on Monday.'

He frowned. 'I hope you'll not go messing up your best clothes in you buffing shop, Hannah.'

'No, of course not.' Her eyes began to sparkle. 'I was waiting till Joseph was in bed before I told you, Reuben, but what do you think? Mrs Walters wants me to go with her when she goes to visit the Cutlery Works – you know, she goes and talks to the bosses from time to time to make sure she doesn't get fobbed off with all the rough work.' She spoke eagerly, her words tumbling over themselves in her excitement. 'And I'm to get an extra shilling a week for doing it!'

'Indeed? And what part will you have to play in all this?' Reuben's face was stony. 'I can't believe she's willing to pay you an extra shilling a week simply to trail round behind her.'

Hannah laughed. 'No, of course not.' She thought for a minute and then said soberly, 'Well, yes, I suppose that's what I'll do at first. I'll not learn, otherwise, will I? She says I've to watch her and see what she does. Then if she can't go some time I'll know what to do.' She looked over to him. 'Surely, there's nowt wrong with that, is there, Reuben?'

'I suppose not,' he said with a heavy sigh. 'But I'm not happy about you parading yourself in front of other men.'

Hannah's eyes widened in amazement. '*Parading myself.* Reuben, what are you talking about? This is *business.* I'll not be paying social calls.'

'I'm still not happy about it. Of course, I won't *forbid* you to do this . . .'

210

Her lips formed a thin line and her green eyes flashed dangerously with gold as her temper rose. 'No, and you'd better not try, Reuben. This is a chance for me to do better for myself. I've never intended to work in a buffing shop for the rest of my life and this is the first step out of it. I'll not let you or anybody else stop me from taking it.' She went off down to the cellar to clean her shoes, slamming the door behind her. She managed to polish off some of her temper as she put a shine on the shoes. When she came back she was calmer.

Reuben was still sitting where she had left him.

'I hope you haven't forgotten that when we were married you promised to obey, Hannah,' he said quietly. 'I'm telling you I don't wish you to do this.'

At that her hackles rose again and she sat down, trembling with rage. 'How dare you remind me of my marriage vows, Reuben Bullinger,' she said, her voice low with fury. 'Have I ever reminded you of yours? Have I ever complained that you break them, night after night when you go to your own bed and leave me to go to mine?'

He flushed to the roots of his hair. 'You knew when you married me . . .'

'Yes, I did. I knew our marriage wouldn't be like other people's and I accepted that. Well, it's also not like other people's in that I shall refuse to obey you when I know you are being unreasonable; this is something you must accept. This marriage suits us both up to a point. Beyond that point you are free to do as you think right. And so am I.' She got to her feet and leaned on the table. 'Hear this, Reuben. Neither I nor my son will be stifled by your petty jealousies. You are being unreasonable, both by your attitude to Peter Jarvis and your attitude to me and my work.' Her voice dropped. 'Think what a scandal it would cause if I left you, Reuben. Folk would think they'd been right all along in what they'd thought about you, wouldn't they?'

He didn't answer but leaned his elbows on his knees and put his head in his hands in a gesture of despair.

Her eyes softened and she touched his hair, noticing that it was already thinning and liberally streaked with grey. 'I'm sorry, Reuben. That was a cruel thing to say,' she said in a gentler tone. 'You've always been good to me, and to Joseph and I'm grateful for that.' Her voice hardened. 'But I won't let this chance pass. It's not much, but it's a start, can't you see?'

He nodded almost imperceptibly.

'Trust me, Reuben.' Her mouth twisted. 'Good grief, I'm not likely to make the same mistake twice, if that's what you're afraid of.'

On Sunday morning Peter Jarvis happened to be looking out of the window when Reuben, dressed in his black Sunday best, went off to church clutching his Bible.

'I've noticed Mr Bullinger never takes his family when he goes to church, Mrs Lewis,' he remarked.

'No. Well, you couldn't take the little lad, he might disturb people. And Hannah allus uses the time he's away to finish off cleaning the house and it gives her a chance to spend a bit of time with t'little lad.' Her voice dropped. 'They're a funny pair. Never seem to go out together.'

He stroked his chin. 'Yes. They do seem an ill-matched couple.' He gave her a disarming smile. 'But it's not for

212

me to stand here discussing your neighbours. After all, it's none of my business.'

'No, but I know what you mean,' Maggie said thoughtfully. 'They've got a grand little lad, though. And they both think the world of him.'

'Yes, he's a lovely little boy. He doesn't seem to favour either of his parents much, does he? Although now and again I think I can see a likeness to his mother. When he smiles, particularly. He's got a lovely smile.'

'Well, all I hope is he won't grow up too much like his Pa. Reuben was allus a serious child and he's got worse as he's got older. Listen.' She cocked her ear. 'Can you hear Hannah singing? She allus sings about her work when he's out of the way.'

Peter Jarvis smiled at her. 'You're fond of Mrs Bullinger, aren't you?'

'Aye, and so would anybody be as knew her. She's a grand lass.' She looked at the clock. 'Time to mash. Hannah might like a cup, too. I'll give her a shout. Cup for you, Mr Jarvis?'

'No, thank you. I think I'll take a walk. Stretch my legs. I was working until very late last night. I can't get the design I'm working on quite right. The trouble is, I know it's not right but I can't quite see where. And the more I work on it the worse it gets. I guess I need to stand back from it for a while.'

'Just as you please. Well, give Hannah a knock as you go by and tell her I've mashed, will you?'

'Of course.' He picked up his hat and left.

Hannah and Joseph were still with Maggie when he returned half an hour later.

'Cleared your head, Mr Jarvis?' Maggie said cheerfully. She turned to Hannah. 'Mr Jarvis can't get his design right, can you, Mr Jarvis?'

'No. I'm having trouble with it. That's why I took a walk. I'll go and take another look at it now.'

'You ought to see some of his work, Hannah,' Maggie said enthusiastically. 'It's beautiful. Come on, show her your drawings, Mr Jarvis, I know she'd like to see them.' She was proud of her lodger's skills.

'Oh, I'm sure Mrs Bullinger isn't interested . . .'

'Oh, but I am,' Hannah said. 'My grandfather was a silver chaser, so I've been told. And he did all his own designs.'

'Very well.' He went upstairs and came down again with a sheaf of papers.

Joseph climbed on his knee and he absentmindedly put his arm round him and carried on with showing Hannah what he'd been doing.

'I can't get the shape quite right on this one,' he said pointing to a teapot with an ornate spout and handle and an intricate swag design. 'I've altered the angle of the spout but it still doesn't look right.'

'Perhaps if you angled the pouring lip just a fraction more?' Hannah suggested, sketching with her thumb what she meant, 'and tilted it, so?' She looked at him inquiringly. Then she blushed. 'It's only a suggestion. I don't really know anything about it.'

But he was nodding, his face serious. 'That might just be it,' he said. 'I knew it didn't need much adjusting. Thank you, Mrs Bullinger.' He gathered up his papers. Then he smiled as he set Joseph gently down. 'I'll know where to come if I get stuck again.'

214

She smiled back. 'Beginner's luck,' she said. She glanced at the clock. 'Goodness, I must go home. I've a lot more to do before Reuben gets back. He'll wonder what I've been up to.'

'Leave the little lad with me. You'll work faster with him out of the way,' Maggie said. And Joseph, playing happily on the rug, was quite content to stay.

'I'll fetch him before Reuben gets back. He might not be . . .' She began again, 'He likes to find him at home when he gets back on Sundays.'

Maggie gave her a deep, searching look. But, 'I understand, lass,' was all she said.

On Monday morning when she was dressed for work Reuben looked at her with something akin to admiration. 'You're looking bonny, Hannah,' he said. 'I hope all goes well with you.'

'Thank you, Reuben.' She kissed his cheek. She knew what it had cost him to say those words because she had heard him pacing back and forth in his room above hers into the small hours. This was a habit of his, she'd noticed. When he was angry or troubled he would walk back and forth, back and forth across his attic, until Hannah sometimes felt she could scream, because his footsteps had a heavy, hollow sound, as if he was walking on bare boards. Perhaps he was. Hannah didn't know. She had only ventured up the attic stairs once, when they were first married, to clean the room with the rest of the house. But she had found the door locked so she had never been again.

* * *

Hannah spent a busy and interesting day with Clara. She was fascinated with the ornate silverware displayed in the front offices of the big cutlery firms. There were soup tureens, asparagus dishes, huge canteens of cutlery destined for the big steam ships that sailed the Atlantic; sets of open razors, epergnes, salvers, all samples of the best work. She was thrown back to her days at Cutwell Hall, where the Truswell silver was displayed in huge cabinets in the hall. A lot had happened in the two years since she had been there.

At the end of the day Clara pronounced herself pleased with what they had achieved, not least because she had managed to secure work from Wolstenholmes, the large works in Wellington Street.

'I guess they've more work than they can handle,' Clara said as they left. 'Most of their work goes to America, that's why they've called the works "Washington Works". Look.' She pointed to the front of the building where the words WASHINGTON WORKS were engraved in stone. 'Done all right for themselves, haven't they? Well, maybe they'll do all right for us, too.' She paused and looked at her list.

'Truswells, that's the last call. Not that we'll get much from there, but I want to complain about the last lot they sent.'

Hannah swallowed. She could hardly refuse to accompany Clara without giving a reason. She yawned. 'It's been a long day,' she said, hoping Clara would say she could go home.

She didn't. 'Rubbish! It's not as hard as working on t'side all day and any road, you're a good many years younger than me,' was all she answered as they trudged up Fargate and turned off towards Truswell Works.

Hannah tried to hang back as Clara was shown up the stairs and into Thomas Truswell's office and she sat herself down on a chair just inside the door where the light from the gas lamp didn't quite reach. The office was furnished in expensive mahogany and plush and the scent of expensive cigars hung in the air.

While Clara was tactfully pointing out that the quality of the last lot of work had been inferior and that Mr Truswell would do well to look to some of his outworkers' methods Hannah was able to study him. Thomas had put on a little weight in the past two years and his features were definitely coarsening. Nevertheless he was still a handsome man and she could quite see why she had found him so irresistible, with his curly black hair and dark eyes – Joseph's eyes – and his charming smile. He was smiling at Clara now, disarming her, thanking her for pointing out the problem and promising that he would investigate it at the very earliest possible moment.

'You'll still do work for us, I trust?' he was asking, helping her to her feet. 'We have some rather complicated chase-work. Your silver finisher is so good . . .'

They haggled a little over price, then he suggested that she look at the work mentioned and sort it out with his manager. 'I'm sure you and he can come to an amicable arrangement, Mrs Walters.' He gave her another smile which Hannah unfairly dismissed as being totally insincere and accompanied her to the door.

Hannah stood up to follow Clara out, keeping her face averted, but Clara said, 'This is my assistant, Mrs

Bullinger. It is quite likely that you will be dealing with her in future, Mr Truswell.'

Thomas held out his hand. 'Indeed? I look forward to that. How do you do, Mrs Bullinger.' He gave her an openly admiring look. Then he frowned, as if trying to place her. 'Haven't we met somewhere before?'

She eased her hand away from his. 'I don't think so, Mr Truswell,' she replied coolly. 'Good afternoon.'

She followed Clara out.

'Oldest trick in t'book,' Clara chuckled as they went down the stairs. 'Haven't we met somewhere before. Well, I can see you made an impression there, lass. Should be good for trade.'

Hannah didn't answer.

Chapter Sixteen

Later that evening, when the Bible passage had been read and Joseph was safely tucked up in bed, Reuben asked politely, 'Well, did you have a good day with Mrs Walters, Hannah?'

Hannah stared into the fire for some time. Then she said slowly, 'I don't know, Reuben.'

'You don't know? What do you mean, you don't know?' He gave what almost passed as a smile and said smugly, 'Are you trying to tell me that I was right, Hannah, and that you should never have agreed to go in the first place?'

She looked up. 'No, I don't mean that, Reuben.' She frowned. 'I'm not sure I can explain. It was good to get out of the grease and grime of the buffing shop, that I'll not deny, but somehow it sickened me to see all that beautiful silverware displayed in the windows and front offices of the Cutlers, and the rich bosses in their smart clothes, sitting behind their great mahogany desks and smoking expensive cigars taking all the credit, while I knew where the work had all been done, by the Little Mesters, who were hardly paid enough to live on, working in filthy hulls hardly fit for rats to live in. It didn't seem right.'

'But that's the way of the world, Hannah,' Reuben said in some surprise. 'It's the rich men that give us employment. We should be thankful for that. Each man is born to his station in life, some high, some low, and it's not for us to question what that station should be.'

'Perhaps not. But you forget, I've seen how these rich people live, Reuben. I've been a servant in a house that was so big you could get lost in it – I often did – and all the rooms crammed with expensive furniture and pictures and full of silver and china even though half of the rooms were never used. Yet the Little Mesters, who've made their money for them, live crowded together in squalid back-to-backs and barely earn enough to keep their children from starving.' She shook her head, her brow creased in perplexity. 'It's still not right, Reuben, for things to be like that.'

'Ours is not to question, Hannah,' he said firmly. 'We should accept with thankfulness the station into which the Lord has seen fit to put us and look for our reward in the life to come.' He steepled his fingers. 'Nevertheless, I hope you have learned your lesson today, Hannah, and we shall have no more of this prinking and preening and dressing yourself up to go to work.'

'Oh, I've learned a lesson, all right, Reuben,' she replied with feeling. 'A lesson I shan't forget in a hurry.'

He gave a sigh of satisfaction. 'I'm very glad to hear it.'

She said no more. It was useless to argue further with

him. He simply didn't understand what she was saying. They were poles apart.

It was not until she got to bed that she allowed herself to think about the last visit of the day, to Mr Thomas Truswell, a visit she had thought it best not to mention to Reuben.

Her feelings about that visit were mixed. There was no denying that her heart had begun to thump uncomfortably when she saw him and she was relieved to find that he hadn't really recognised her as he greeted her. Yet at the same time it was something of a blow to find he had so completely forgotten her. How could it be that a relationship that had meant so much to her and that had changed – she almost said ruined, it wouldn't have been too strong a word – her life, had made so little impact on him that two years later he had quite forgotten it? Surely she hadn't altered that much?

It was another, even more cruel lesson she had learned that day.

From that day on Clara Walters leaned more and more on Hannah, deferring to her over decisions that had to be made, leaving her to deal with disputes in the buffing shop and to argue better terms from the bosses.

Yet she continued to drive herself, always there at her desk, watching what was going on, her temper increasingly uncertain.

'I don't know how you put up wi' Missus, Hannah,' Marjorie said one day when Hannah had been forced to smooth things in the buffing shop after Clara had been 'on the chunter again' as the girls put it when Clara

221

shouted at them. 'After all, we was only having a bit of a sing-song. There's no harm in that, now, is there? We allus sing at our work.'

'She's trying to work out the accounts,' Hannah said. 'She's not very good at figuring and it always makes her head ache.'

'Then she should let you do it,' Sally said unsympathetically. 'Mind you, she never used to be so bad tempered. It's only sin' her Jack died she's been so tetchy.'

'He's been gone nearly a year now so she ought to be getting over it,' Marjorie said. 'And we've all lost childer, heaven knows.'

'Aye, but you can understand it wi' t'Missus. Her Jack was all she'd got. He's allus been her pride and joy,' Sally said.

'She's not eating, neither,' Hannah said, voicing something that was worrying her.

'Aye,' Sally agreed. 'She used to be on the plump side when I first knew her but now she's as far through as a fourpenny rabbit. She'll be wasting away if she goes on this road.'

Hannah nodded. She suspected it was not simply Jack's death that was causing Clara to waste away. 'I'll go and have a word with her.'

She went into the office. 'You're not yourself, Clara, going on at the lasses that road. You know they always work better when they sing. Why don't you stay at home for a few days?'

Clara looked up, amazed. 'Stay at home? What would I want to do that for? I've nothing to stay at home for. This place is my life now my Jack's gone.'

222

'But you're not well, Clara. Have you been to see the doctor?'

'What good would that do? I've no faith in Quack's medicine.' She reached into the drawer for the bismuth and took a swig from the bottle. 'This is better than any rubbish he'd give me.' She rubbed her side. 'It helps to ease this gnawing in my guts, for a little while, any road.' She pulled a ledger towards her. 'Now, did you get that order from Dixons?'

'Aye. It's half done, too. It'll be finished by Friday.'

Clara smiled and Hannah noticed how colourless her lips were. 'You're a good lass, Hannah. I know you'll look after things.' Her expression changed and she winced with pain as there was a burst of raucous laughter from the buffing shop. 'Oh, they've started up again. Can't you shut that noise? How can they do the work properly when they're making all that row! It goes right through my head.' She put her head in her hands. She waved Hannah away. 'Go on, tell them to shut up.'

Hannah hurried through and quietened the girls again.

'But we was only having a bit of a laugh,' Marjorie said, peeved. 'Sal went to the Music Hall last night and sin' we're not allowed to sing she was telling us some of the funny bits.' She elbowed Hannah. 'Bit naughty, some of 'em was, too.'

'I know. It's hard,' Hannah said with a sigh. 'But t'Missus is really poorly today.' She patted the air. 'Just keep the noise down for five minutes while I try and persuade her to go home. Once she's out of the way you can start up again,' she promised.

She hurried back to the office. Clara was slumped over

the ledger on the table. 'Come on, it's home for you, Clara,' she said gently, going over and touching her shoulder. 'I'll get Polly to call a cab.'

'It's only a spit down the road,' Clara protested weakly. 'I can walk it.'

Nevertheless she was glad for Hannah to help her into her coat and hat and down the stairs to the waiting cab. 'I'm tired. I just need a bit of a rest. I didn't sleep much last night. But I'll be in tomorrow,' she promised. 'I've the wages to do.'

'I can do them,' Hannah said firmly.

'Aye, lass, so you can.' She gave a weak smile. 'I know I can rest easy. I've taught you well. Things'll be all right in your hands.'

Clara never came back to her buffing works. After three days at home she was taken to the Infirmary, where Hannah visited her every day for a month before she quietly died in her sleep as the bells rang in the New Year.

Reuben watched dispassionately as Hannah wept at the news.

'I don't see why you should take on so, Hannah,' he said. 'After all, you did more than your Christian duty by the woman, visiting her every day while she was in the Infirmary and neglecting your family.'

'That's not fair, Reuben. I've never neglected my family,' she said quietly. 'I always left work early in order to visit Clara.'

'And lost time for it.' He sniffed. 'It wasn't as if she paid you over the odds, neither. Any road, she was only your Missus.'

'She was much more than my Missus, Reuben,' she

replied, wiping away her tears. 'Clara took me in when nobody else cared whether I lived or died. She was my friend. I shall miss her.'

'Was she a true Member of the Faith?' he asked suddenly.

She looked up, surprised. 'I don't know. I never asked. All I know is that she was a good woman.'

'Then comfort yourself that she's gone to a Better Place,' he said loftily.

Hannah closed the buffing shop so that all the lasses could attend Clara's funeral, promising them that they wouldn't lose pay over it. She was determined that Clara Walters shouldn't go to her grave with no one but herself to mourn her for without her son she had no relatives.

A week after the funeral a letter came for Hannah, bidding her to go to Messrs. Rawlinson, Rawlinson and Crabtree, Solicitors, in Angel Street, where she would hear something to her advantage.

'I shall come with you,' Reuben announced.

She looked up at him in something approaching alarm. 'There's really no need, Reuben,' she said quickly. 'I wouldn't want you taking time off work. I don't suppose it's anything very important. I'm sure I can handle it.'

'I expect it's about Mrs Walters. I expect she's left you a bit of money,' he said. 'And if that's the case I want to make sure they don't swindle you out of it.'

'Oh, Reuben, they wouldn't do that! If they were going to swindle me they wouldn't have written in the first place.'

'It's not right for you to visit the place alone. You're a woman, remember.'

She opened her mouth, a retort on her lips, but thought

225

better of it. There was no arguing with Reuben when his mind was made up.

So, for almost the first time in the three years they had been married they went out together, walking side by side but never touching, to Angel Street.

The news was beyond what either of them had expected. Clara Walters had left everything she possessed to Hannah.

Mr Crabtree looked at her over the top of his gold-rimmed spectacles.

'Mrs Walters made this will soon after her son died,' he said. 'She told me that you were the nearest thing to a daughter she had and she wanted you to know what a high regard she had for you.' He cleared his throat. 'There can surely be no clearer way of showing it than what she has done here.' He tapped the will with a long white finger. 'There is a little money, not much, and whatever you can raise on the furnishings of the house. The house itself, of course was rented. But there also seems to be a small property on Pond Hill that Mrs Walters actually owned. I believe she used it as some kind of workshop?'

Hannah nodded dumbly, her senses still reeling from the news.

'Aye. It's a buffing shop now. My wife works there,' Reuben explained pompously.

A ghost of a smile flitted across Mr Crabtree's parchment-like face. 'Well, Mr Bullinger, your wife not only works in it, she now owns it,' he said, getting to his feet. 'And that being so, I assume you would like the deeds made over to your good self?'

'Aye, that will be . . .'

Hannah got to her feet. 'Indeed no, Mr Crabtree!' she said sharply. 'The deeds will be in *my* name, if you please. Mrs Walters left the property to *me*.'

Mr Crabtree looked a trifle flustered. 'I do realise that, Mrs Bullinger, but as the law stands your husband . . .'

'Mr Bullinger and I do not have a conventional marriage, Mr Crabtree,' Hannah said. 'I don't wish to go into details but since the property belongs to me it will be in my name.'

Mr Crabtree looked doubtfully towards Reuben, who with some embarrassment signalled his agreement.

'I must say this is most irregular,' he muttered. 'But very well, we'll have the deeds made over to you, Mrs Bullinger. It should be quite straightforward.' He turned to Reuben, studiously ignoring Hannah and said obsequiously, 'In any case, Mr Bullinger, we shall be here to advise you on any difficulties. Not that I foresee any. Mrs Walters made sure everything was done correctly.' He turned back to Hannah and pushed the papers across to her. 'Now, if you will just sign here, Madam . . .'

Hannah signed, her eyes blurred with tears at her employer's generosity. Mumbling her thanks she left the building with Reuben by her side, a smug, self-satisfied expression on his face.

He put his hand under her elbow, hustling her along. 'I don't know why you needed to make such an exhibition of yourself, Hannah,' he said irritably. 'What difference does it make who owns the deeds? We'll sell everything, of course. It'll give us a nice little nest-egg to put by for Joseph. Happen it'll be enough to send him to one of them paying schools. That man, Mr Crabtree, said he would advise us. Well, it may be as well to ask him where the best place would be to invest the money.'

She stopped in the middle of the pavement, causing chaos to the people scurrying back and forth and turned to him. 'Will you leave me alone, Reuben! Will you stop trying to make my decisions for me! I've not had time to catch my breath yet.' She blinked in the bright winter sunshine. 'And you're wrong. Those deeds are mine and the property is mine. Clara left it me and I'll not sell it, whatever else goes. There are ten lasses working there and they'll depend on me now. I'll not see them turned out into the street with no work.'

He gaped at her. 'But the place is nearly falling down. You've said so yourself.'

She gave a little secret smile and said softly, 'Well, now I'll have money to build it up again, won't I?'

It was a measure of Hannah's popularity that the girls in the buffing shop were not in the least envious of her good fortune. They had all been worried that with Mrs Walters' death the place would be sold and they would lose their jobs so they were overjoyed to hear that things would continue much the same as before.

'Except I'll get the stairs patched up and the windows mended,' Hannah promised. 'And that engine downstairs needs looking at. Ted Bishop does what he can with it but his trade is making penknives not looking after steam engines. Any road, he's getting past it, poor old chap. He must be eighty if he's a day.'

The following Saturday afternoon Hannah left Joseph

with Maggie and together with Reuben and her brother Stanley went to the house on Pond Hill.

At first, still smarting over the scene at the solicitors, Reuben had declined to accompany them. But his innate curiosity got the better of him and he changed his mind at the last minute. Neither Reuben nor Stanley claimed to know much about steam engines but Stanley had a friend who did and he was going to meet them there.

While Stanley and his friend were busy with the engine Reuben decided that he would mend the stairs, much to Hannah's surprise. Whilst this was all going on Hannah tried to make some kind of a clearance in the cellar. Ted Bishop had his work bench in the only clear space under the window with the engine to his right, a heap of coal beside it. On the wall opposite to the engine, just inside the door, the stairs led up to the floors above. The space behind where Ted worked was piled nearly to ceiling height with empty boxes, newspapers, rusty biscuit tins, old buffing wheels, discarded buff brats, in fact the detritus from years that had found its way there and then been simply left. It had been a source of worry and annoyance to Hannah ever since she'd worked there.

'It's a miracle the place hasn't gone up in flames long ago,' Hannah said to herself as she began to sort through the rubbish to see what could usefully be burnt on the fire in the buffing shop upstairs and what she would have to get the rag and bone man to cart away. Before long she had quite a heap of useless rubbish out in the yard and several boxes of newspapers and firewood neatly stacked inside.

She had also reached the back wall of the cellar, which she guessed hadn't seen daylight for a long time. To her amazement there was a door in the corner, under the stairs. The latch was rusted in but when she called Stanley he managed to free it and push the door open, expecting to find a cupboard. But it wasn't a cupboard they found, it was a room. A room that obviously hadn't been used for years. It was quite empty except for an old broken chair in the middle of the floor. What light there was came through a grimy skylight in the corner.

'Well, well, to think there's been a room here all this time and nobody knew about it! I wonder if Clara knew?' Hannah began to dance round it, kicking up clouds of dust from the floor. 'We'll have to clean it up and then we can use it, can't we?'

'It'll need bug-blindin'. I'll do that for you,' Stan said eagerly, 'them walls is filthy.'

'Not yet you won't.' Hannah gave a laugh and play-fully boxed his ears. 'You're supposed to be helping your friend with the motor out there.'

'He's nearly finished. I'll go and get some whitewash, shall I, Annie?'

'No, not yet. Have a bit of patience, lad. We've got to clean the place up before we can start on the walls. Go and fetch a broom and help me sweep some of this muck out.'

By the end of the afternoon the engine that drove the buffing wheels had been thoroughly overhauled, the stairs were mended, new glass had been put in the windows and the room behind the cellar was swept out and white-washed. Hannah had even cleaned the skylight, which now let in a reasonable amount of light.

'What are you going to do with that room you've found, Hannah?' Reuben asked as they trudged home,

230

weary but pleased with their afternoon's work. 'I suggest you let it to a family. It's dry and it's clean now. And there's water in the yard. Yes, I'm sure that's the best thing to do with it. It's not a bad-sized room.'

She didn't answer. The afternoon had been full of surprises, she was tired and she needed time to think.

The next morning, being Sunday, Reuben went to chapel, leaving Hannah behind to clean the house. She gave her bedroom a perfunctory dust; Reuben wasn't likely to go there so it didn't matter if it wasn't swept properly. She assumed Reuben kept his own room clean. The rest of the house she skimped through as quickly as she could. Then she went with Joseph for her Sunday morning chat with Maggie.

'Ah, good. I've just mashed,' Maggie greeted her with a smile. 'And you, young man, can finish colouring the picture Uncle Jarvis drew for you yesterday.' She tousled his hair. 'He reckons you'll make a good artist once day. Here's your colouring chalks.'

Obediently, Joseph stretched full length on the rug in front of the fire and began colouring, his pink tongue jutting out between his teeth.

'Well, love, did you do all you set out to do yesterday?' Maggie asked, pouring the tea.

'Oh, we did. And more!' With shining eyes Hannah told her about the room she had found. 'Reuben says I've to let it to a family but I'll not do that. I don't feel it would be safe, not with all that silverware about,' she said, sipping her tea thoughtfully. 'You never know whether people are honest, and Ted Bishop's got a lot of tools and things in his workshop, too.'

'Aye, that's right enough. But what will you do with it, then, if you don't let it?'

'I could expand,' she said slowly. 'Take on more lasses.' She shook her head. 'But I don't think I'm ready to do that. Not yet, any road.'

Peter Jarvis came down the stairs with his coat on.

'I'm just going out for a breath of fresh air, Mrs Lewis,' he said, after bidding Hannah good morning. 'I've been working since six.'

'Have a cup of tea before you go, Mr Jarvis. It'll warm the cockles of your heart. It's a bit nesh out today and looks like rain.' She poured him a cup before he could answer. 'Go on, tell Mr Jarvis about your room, Hannah,' she said.

Hannah laughed. 'Not much to tell. I've uncovered a room behind the cellar in the buffing shop and I haven't decided what to do with it. Reuben wants me to let it to a family . . .'

'You couldn't do that, could you? Not with silverware about. Not unless you could lock it away,' he said.

'That's what I think.'

'How big is the room?'

Hannah looked round Maggie's room. 'About this size, I should think. A bit smaller, perhaps.'

'It would make a good-sized workshop, then.'

'Yes. That's what I think. The cellar itself is let to a penknife maker, Ted Bishop.' She smiled at him. 'I'll have to think about it. There's no hurry to make a decision.' She looked at the clock on Maggie's mantelpiece and got to her feet. 'I'd better get back. Reuben will be home shortly and he likes his dinner on the plate when he gets in. Come on, Joseph. We're going to find Papa.'

232

'Take my picture?' He held it up. 'Show Papa?'

'Why don't you leave it for Maggie?' Hannah knew it would only annoy Reuben to know that Peter Jarvis had drawn it for Joseph. Reuben had no artistic skills.

'No! Show it to Papa.'

'Oh, very well.' She looked at Maggie and raised her eyebrows to the ceiling as she took Joseph's hand and hurried him out.

She made Joseph wait until after they had eaten their meal before showing his picture to his father, knowing the response it would receive. Reuben was still jealously complaining about the child wasting Peter Jarvis' time and paper with his scribbling when there was a knock at the door.

Hannah went to answer it and found Peter Jarvis himself standing there.

'I wonder if I might have a word with you, Mrs Bullinger?' he asked, twisting his hat in his hands nervously.

'Yes, of course. Please step inside.'

He inclined his head towards Reuben, sitting in his usual chair by the fire. 'I don't wish to intrude on your privacy, Mr Bullinger, but there's something I would like to discuss with, um, Mrs Bullinger. And yourself, of course,' he added hurriedly.

'Uncle Jarvis. Look, my picture. On the wall.' Joseph scrambled to his feet and pulled Peter Jarvis to look at it.

'*Mr* Jarvis to you, Joseph!' Reuben said sharply. His voice softened. 'Now sit down and look at your picture book, laddie, and let's hear no more from you. Remember, little children should be seen and not heard.' He waited until Joseph had settled himself back on the rug by the

233

fire, then looked up at the other man. 'And what might that be, Mr Jarvis?' he asked gravely, indicating a chair.

Peter Jarvis sat down. 'It's about this room that you've discovered,' he began.

'News travels fast, Mr Jarvis,' Reuben said, with a lift of his chin. 'How do you know about that?'

'I told Maggie when I fetched Joseph last night,' Hannah said quickly. 'I expect she told Mr Jarvis. Isn't that right, Mr Jarvis?' She willed him to agree.

He nodded. 'That's right. Mrs Lewis told me about it,' he said. He paused for a minute. 'I was wondering, could you tell me a little more about it?'

'It's just a room in a cellar,' Hannah told him. 'Like I . . .' She nearly said, like I told you but stopped herself in time. 'Like most cellars. It's a bit smaller than this room, I should say. Wouldn't you say so, Reuben?' She thought she had better include her husband in the conversation.

Reuben nodded. 'Would you be interested in renting it then, Mr Jarvis?'

'I might, if it was suitable for my purposes.'

'What's gone wrong? Aren't you happy with Maggie, then?' Hannah asked, surprised.

Peter Jarvis burst out laughing. 'Oh, I wouldn't want to *live* in the room, Mrs Bullinger. I'm more than happy lodging with Mrs Lewis. No, I'm looking for a workshop. I've been intending for some time to branch out on my own account when I could find suitable premises. I've my own ideas and I'd like to see them through from start to finish. I've learned a lot at Dixons but now I feel it's time to move on. I feel the need to spread my wings, if that's

234

the right phrase. Oh, I shall still do work for them but I'd like to feel free to take on other commissions as well.'

'Well, you're very welcome to come and take a look at the room,' Hannah said. 'See if it will suit your needs.'

'What about rent?' Reuben said quickly.

Hannah turned to face him. 'I'll discuss that with Mr Jarvis when he's decided whether the room suits his purposes, Reuben,' she said shortly.

Reuben got to his feet. 'I'll fetch my coat.'

'There's no need, Reuben. I've no intention of going to Pond Hill this afternoon. I'm sure Mr Jarvis will be happy to wait till tomorrow to see it, when I'll be at work anyway, won't you, Mr Jarvis?'

'Certainly, Mrs Bullinger.' He got to his feet. 'I'm sorry. It was wrong of me to come to discuss business on a Sunday. I should have waited until tomorrow before approaching you.'

'Oh, that's all right. It's just that it's cold and it's raining and Pond Hill's a tidy step from here. Call it laziness if you like, Mr Jarvis.' She smiled at him, willing him to understand the real reason she was unwilling to go.

'We should have gone today. It's not raining much,' Reuben said petulantly when Peter Jarvis had left.

'But as he said, it's Sunday. I didn't think you'd be very happy to discuss business on Sunday, Reuben. It should be a day of rest.'

'But I shan't be there to advise you tomorrow because I shall be at work.'

Hannah smiled. 'So you will, Reuben. Never mind, I'm sure I shall manage quite well without you.'

Chapter Seventeen

Peter Jarvis found the new cellar well suited to his purpose and took it at a rent that satisfied Hannah although she knew it was a good deal less that Reuben would have had her charge and he said so, in no uncertain terms, as soon as she came downstairs after putting Joseph to bed.

'You're a fool to yourself, Hannah. What do you think you're doing, letting the room for such a pittance? Are you intending to run a business or some kind of charity?'

She refused to be ruffled. 'If I'd never found that room I should have managed perfectly well without the rent from it, Reuben,' she answered, sitting down and picking up her sewing. 'As it is, the money I shall get from it means I can start a sick club for my lasses and I'll still have a bit over for keeping the place in good order, something Clara never bothered over much about. Remember, Mr Jarvis is just starting up, he can't afford a high rent, not yet any road. When he can afford to pay more happen I'll charge more.' She bit off a length of thread and threaded her needle.

236

'He'll not tell you,' he said with a sneer. 'I've seen his sort before.'

'I'm not greedy, Reuben,' she said quietly. 'I shall manage. And I'll still be able to contribute a bit extra to the running of the house here.'

'I don't need you to contribute more, woman!' Suddenly Reuben was furious. 'I'm not thinking about myself! That business was left to you, as you made *very* plain, and I'll not touch a penny of what extra you earn from it. I was only offering advice, which you'd do well to take.' He shuffled irritably in his chair.

'Thank you, Reuben. I know you mean well, but this is something you know nothing about. If I need advice I'll go to Mr Crabtree.'

'And pay over the odds for it,' he muttered.

'It'll be money well spent.'

His eyes blazed and he leaned forward in his chair. 'I know what you think, my lass. You think that just because I'm only a common or garden grinder who works in swarf I've got nowt but swarf in my head. But I've as good a head on my shoulders as the next man and I'm telling you if you go on the road you're set on you'll end up wi' nowt.'

'Then I'll be back where I started, won't I? And I'll have nobody to blame but myself,' she flashed back. 'But I'll not fail.' Her eyes grew dreamy. 'One day I shall have a house on a hill, away from all the grime and filth of the town, where Joseph can breathe good fresh air and I can look out on hills and trees and green fields and the sky will be a beautiful blue instead of the murky grey that's all we see between the buildings here.'

'Well, if you tek my advice . . .'

'If I need it I'll ask for it.'

He was silent for a long time, staring into the fire. Then he said, 'I didn't want to have to say this, but since you're so set on the road to ruin I've no choice, Hannah. Clara Walters may have left that property to you but in law, as Mr Crabtree pointed out, I can claim it. You're my wife. What's yours is mine.'

She went as white as the sheet she was mending and her green eyes glinted gold. 'If you dare to make any attempt to do that, Reuben, I shall divorce you,' she said quietly. 'I could, you know. I have ample grounds.'

Flushing, he lifted his chin. 'And how would you explain Joseph? *Our* son?'

'My shame in confessing my sin would be nothing compared with yours.'

He stared at her for several minutes without answering. Then he took down his Bible and opened it and began to read aloud Psalm Twenty-two, one of his favourite passages:

'My God, my God, why hast though forsaken me? Why are thou so far from helping me . . . ?'

But if Reuben was less than happy Hannah's buffer lasses were like a pack of chattering monkeys in their excitement when they saw the work that had been done over the weekend, especially the discovery of the room in the cellar, although up in the attic Grace declared grumpily that she had known about it all the time but had forgotten its existence.

'I'm sure the belts run smoother now the engine

downstairs has been overhauled,' Marjorie said fancifully as she set the spindle running again after changing her buff.

Polly picked up the coal bucket. 'I'll just go down to t'cellar and get another bucket of coal and mend t'fire.'

'You'll not!' Sally said. 'You've already been down there three times this morning and this place is like an oven. I don't know what's got into you.'

'I do.' A girl called Ellen who had not been with them long laughed. 'She's wanting to get first glimpse of the man who's renting the new room.'

Polly blushed. 'I'm not.' She tossed her carrotty locks. 'I'll go and see if t'Missus needs more coal on her fire then.'

Hannah was sitting at the table that was now her desk sorting through papers. She was trying unsuccessfully to put the quarrel with Reuben behind her. He had been silent and wooden-faced at breakfast and had gone off to work without even a word of farewell and she was wondering how best to effect some kind of reconciliation without giving in to him. She decided that the best thing might be to get some of his favourite chitterlings for tea as a peace offering. Not that she intended to back down, there was no question of that, but she was anxious to let him see she bore him no ill-will. Satisfied in her mind she turned back to the papers on the desk. She found that during the last few months Clara had let things slip alarmingly and she realised that the poor woman must have been more ill than she had ever confessed.

Polly poked her head round the door. 'Shall I bring a fresh bucket of coal up for t'fire, Missus?' she asked. 'Aw, look at that, it's nearly out. You should have shouted.'

Hannah looked up. She couldn't get used to being called Missus although the lasses had slipped quite naturally into using the title. 'Oh, yes, please.' She looked into the dying embers of the fire and gave a little shiver. 'I hadn't noticed it was so low.'

Polly went rattling down the stairs with the bucket. She was gone some time. When she came back her face was streaked with coal dust but she was beaming.

'He's arrived,' she announced in a loud stage whisper. 'Oh, he's reet handsome. I filled his coal bucket too, while I was about it, and lit his fire. He was reet grateful. He's got a lot of stuff. Tools an' all. He says he'll come up and have a word with you when he's got himself sorted out, Missus.'

'Thank you, Polly. Yes, put some coal on the fire. Then you'd better get back to work.' Hannah frowned. 'Weren't you supposed to be doing that batch of apostle spoons today?'

'Yes, Missus. I'm going back to finish them right now. But I have to keep stopping to mash the tea and keep the floor swept. And look after t'fires.'

Hannah stroked her chin. 'Perhaps it's time we took on another errand lass, then you could work on t'side all the time. You're shaping up well enough.'

'Oh, I'd like that, Missus.' Polly's face lit up.

'I'll think about it.'

She turned back to the work on her desk. There was a great deal to think about, she was discovering.

When she had time she slipped downstairs to see Peter Jarvis. He had moved his bench in under the skylight and was in the process of sorting out his pitch pots, hammers and punches. A heap of rolled up designs lay on the end of the bench and a large carpet bag stood on an old kitchen chair, waiting to be unpacked.

'I hope you'll be comfortable here, Mr Jarvis,' she said with a smile. 'I see Polly has already lit your fire for you.'

'Yes, she was very keen to do that.' He gave a boyish, almost apologetic smile and gazed round him. 'I must get myself organised and put up some shelves. You won't mind if I put up shelves, Mrs Bullinger?'

'Not at all,' she smiled. 'You can't do this old place much harm. In fact a few shelves might help to hold the walls up!'

They both burst out laughing and it struck her that she seldom had much opportunity to laugh these days. Reuben was not a man with a sense of humour.

As soon as she could find an opportunity she went to see her mother. As always she took her father a bottle of beer; he tolerated her these days although it could never be said that he welcomed her with open arms.

He was lying on the couch. It was his permanent home now because he had barely breath to walk, let alone climb the stairs and he looked shrunken and yellow. He opened his eyes when she entered and an unexpected flicker of pleasure crossed his face although he didn't speak.

Her mother busied herself with the kettle. 'I was just about to mash,' she said. 'I'll get an extra cup.'

'You're not working then, Mam?' Hannah asked, after she had sent Joseph out into the yard to play with his young aunts, her sisters Fanny and Agnes.

'No, I've had to give up to look after him.' Jane spoke

in a low voice, glancing towards her husband. 'It's hard, but at least it means I'm here to look after t'little ones, so Elsie and Maudie can get their proper schooling.' Her voice dropped even lower. 'But it'll not be for much longer,' she whispered. 'Sometimes I wonder how he's lasted this long, but there' – a ghost of a smile hovered round her mouth – 'he was allus a stubborn sod.' She nodded towards the bottle on the table. 'He'll enjoy that,' she said in her normal voice.

'Enjoy what?' A hoarse, laboured whisper came from the couch.

'Annie's brought you a bottle of beer. Will you tek a drop?'

'Aye. Whet me whistle.'

Hannah watched as Jane poured a little beer into a feeding cup and gave it to Nat. She could remember her father downing a whole quart without drawing breath but now a few short sips was all he could manage.

'I'm glad tha's come, lass,' he said when Jane had lain him back on the pillow. 'I'm not long for this world.' He closed his eyes.

'Does Mary know how bad Dad is?' Hannah asked in a low voice, when she could see that her father had fallen asleep.

Jane shook her head. 'We never see her. She's not been near for years. You know how it was with her, she couldn't wait to get away and go into service.'

'Yes, I remember. She didn't even come when Stan had his accident, she relied on me to let her know how he was.'

'There you are then. She's not likely to come back now, is she?'

Hannah frowned in the direction of her sleeping father. 'She ought to be told about Dad. She'll want to know and he'd like to see her, wouldn't he?'

Jane nodded. 'Reckon he would.'

'I'll call at the Brownings on my way home. If she's not there now likely they'll know where she's gone and I can call on her.'

Suddenly, Nat's eyes flew open. 'Is bloody Truswell still alive?' he croaked. 'Joe Truswell? Have I outlasted him?'

She went over and took his hand. 'I believe he's still alive. But he can't work any more. I heard he had a stroke a while back.'

'Serve him bloody right. I can't bloody work, neither.' There were long pauses between sentences while he struggled for breath. 'I'll bet he's got plenty o' doctors and nurses dancing round him though. Not like me, stuck on this bloody couch.' He stopped and closed his eyes, exhausted. 'Bloody Truswells,' he muttered. 'I curse the lot of 'em.'

As he spoke the words Hannah looked out of the open door and saw Joseph, playing hopscotch with the little girls. Cold fear clutched her heart. Joseph was a Truswell.

She watched him playing for several minutes. If anyone had cause to curse the Truswells she had, she reflected bitterly. Then her gaze softened as she watched her son. He was worth all the bitterness and pain; her only regret was that he had been robbed of the life to which he was entitled.

She said thoughtfully, 'I don't curse the Truswells, Dad. They've done our family wrong but I'll not waste my life cursing them like you've done.' Her eyes narrowed. 'I'm going to beat them.'

'Fat chance,' he jeered in a faint echo of his old self. 'You're nowt and allus will be. Like the rest of the Foxes. We're all nowt.'

'Oh, no, Dad, that's where you're wrong,' she said firmly. 'I'm already on my way up. That's what I've come to tell you. You know I've worked in Clara Walters' buffing shop for several years? Well, she died a while back and left me a legacy. Not a lot of money, mind, but something better. She's left me the buffing shop.' Her eyes began to shine and her words began to tumble over themselves in her excitement. 'It's in a little old house on Pond Hill. Oh, it's nothing very grand, in fact she only managed to buy it because it was condemned, but it's mine. Reuben thinks I should get rid of it but I'll not part with it. I'm running that buffing shop. I'm Missus there now and I've a good bunch of lasses working for me. They'll not let me down and I'll not let them down. It's the first step, Dad.' She grinned. 'I've already got a silver chaser renting a room in the basement, too. It all helps. Ah, you wait.' Her eyes went dreamy. 'Hannah Fox is going to be a name to be reckoned with. There's money to be made from the big steamship companies. Cutlery, tableware, they want the best and they're willing to pay for it. That's where I'm aiming. In a few years' time I'll have gathered a workforce second to none and Hannah Fox Silver will rank up with Dixons and Mappins and Wolstenholmes.' She stared down at her father and her lip curled. 'And Truswells won't even be in the picture,' she said softly.

Nat made a sound that would have been a laugh if he

could have managed it. 'I thought like that once-over,' he croaked. 'Look where it landed me.'

'Yes, but your thirst always came first,' Jane reminded him acidly. 'Your dreams all drowned in a beer glass.'

Nat ignored that. 'Any road, tha's only a woman,' he said scathingly. 'Sheffield's a man's city. Get back to tha husband. If he's got any sense he'll give thee a good thrashing, knock some sense into thee.' He spoke in short, breathless bursts.

Hannah flushed with temper. 'I may only be a woman but I shall do what I set out to do, Dad,' she answered between clenched teeth. 'The pity of it is you won't live to see it. Because I'd just like to make you eat your words.'

'Annie!' Jane's voice came like a whiplash. 'Your dad's poorly. Think on. Now's not the time to quarrel with him.'

'I'm not quarrelling with him. I'm telling him,' Hannah snapped. 'But he's not listening. It's a pity he can't give any of his children credit for having more guts than he ever had.'

'That's enough!' Jane banged her hand on the table. 'If you can't be civil then you must go.' Her eyes filled with tears. 'But for God's sake make your peace with him before you go.' Her voice dropped. 'If you don't do it now you'll never have the chance.'

Hannah bent and kissed her father. 'Maybe you don't think I'll do it, Dad, but you could at least give me credit for trying.' Her eyes filled with tears. 'And I'd like to know I had your blessing.'

He put up his hand and took hers and pressed it briefly to his lips. 'Aye, lass, you do. I wish you well. Hannah

Fox Silver . . . Now that would be one in t'eye for bloody Truswells. A pity I'll not live to see it.' His eyes closed.

On her way home Hannah called at the Brownings' house. She stood outside for several minutes debating whether to ring the front doorbell or go down the area steps to the kitchen door. Then she took a deep breath and taking Joseph firmly by the hand walked up the steps to the front door.

A mop-headed servant girl with freckles and a cap perched at a rakish angle opened the door.

'I've come to see my sister, Mary Fox,' Hannah said. 'Is she in?'

The girl shook her head. 'Nobody here of that name,' she said.

'Who is it, Lettice?' a silvery voice called from within the house. Hannah recognised Mrs Browning's artificially refined tones.

'It's me, Mrs Browning. Hannah Bul . . . Hannah Fox. Mary Fox's sister,' Hannah called.

Mrs Browning came bustling to the door. 'Oh, my dear, do come in. I remember you so well. You were such a help at the dinner party I held, weren't you? Arrived in the nick of time, as I remember. But your sister isn't here any more, my dear. She left, oh, it must be well over a year ago. She married a young man in soft furnishings at Cockagnes. In fact, my husband gave her away at her wedding.' She primped a little. 'We gave her a very nice wedding, although I say it myself.' She frowned. 'It was strange. She didn't want any of her family there. I couldn't understand it.'

'Can you tell me where she is now, Mrs Browning?'

Hannah asked, when she could get a word in. 'Our father is dying and she ought to be told.'

Mrs Browning shook her head. 'I don't think I can help you, my dear. Soon after they married the young man left Cockagnes and went to work for Cole Bros on Fargate.' She frowned. 'I've an idea he left there and went somewhere else after that, but I can't remember where.'

'Do you know where they live, Mrs Browning?' Hannah asked patiently.

'No, my dear, I don't. They had rooms, temporary, like, when they first married. I don't know what they did after that. He was quite a well set-up young man, Mr Tripper. Very neat and polite. I should say he'll go far in Trade. I'm sure they're very happy together.'

'I'm sure they are. Thank you for your help, Mrs Browning.' Hannah left, knowing she had no hope at all of finding her sister.

Three days later Nat Fox died.

In spite of her mother's protests Hannah paid for the funeral, insisting that at least Nathaniel Fox should have his own headstone and not be buried in a pauper's grave. Jane considered the money could have been better spent on a new couch and a more comfortable bed but was somewhat mollified when Hannah offered to take on her eleven-year-old sister, Elsie, as errand lass at her buffing shop. With once again being able to work herself and Elsie as well as Stanley also in employment both the bed and the couch might be attainable in the not-too-distant future. Life without Nathaniel was not without its compensations.

Hannah didn't tell Reuben she had taken Elsie on. She knew he would only complain of extravagance and anyway since their disagreement she found it best not to talk about the buffing shop to him at all. If she needed advice she found herself turning more and more to Peter Jarvis, plying his delicate craft in the cellar.

Every night, when the lasses had gone home and everywhere was quiet she would go through the house to make sure the fires were all safely dowsed, the lamps dimmed and the machinery safe. Ted Bishop, the penknife maker who had worked there and looked after the steam engine for years, was over eighty and he came in less and less now that Peter Jarvis had arrived, knowing that Peter would take care of the things he had always made himself responsible for. Peter was usually still at work when Hannah finished her rounds.

'I think it might be best if I get you a set of keys cut,' she said as she laid hers on the bench for him to lock up when he had finished. 'Then I shan't need to disturb you when I leave.'

'You don't disturb me, Mrs Bullinger,' he said in some surprise. 'It's nice to discuss what I've been doing with someone who appreciates it.' He stood back from tracing in the design on a silver communion chalice with a tool that looked like a chisel. 'There, that's nearly ready for me to work on with my punches.' He put it to one side and turned to give her his full attention. 'You look tired, Mrs Bullinger. Why don't you sit by the fire for a few minutes?'

'I've got a headache, that's all.' She squeezed the bridge of her nose with her thumb and forefinger. 'No, I mustn't sit down. I must be getting home. I'm already later than I intended because I had some paperwork I wanted to finish and Reuben gets annoyed if I'm late.' She yawned. 'Will you be working much longer tonight, Mr Jarvis?'

He grinned and ran his fingers through his thick, fair hair. 'Probably. When I've finished what I want to do on this chalice I'll get my pencils out. I've got ideas for a punch bowl that I want to work out and when I start designing I lose track of time.'

She didn't return his smile. 'You're lucky, Mr Jarvis. It must be nice not to have to account to someone for every minute,' she said wistfully.

'I'm sure your husband is only thinking of your well-being, Mrs Bullinger.' His voice was gentle and he was looking at her with concern.

She pulled herself together and said briskly, 'Yes, yes, of course he is. Reuben is very good to me. And to Joseph.'

'He's a little lad any father would be proud of,' Peter said. 'He's as bright as a button. He'll go far, that lad.'

She hesitated and then sat down on the edge of the old chair that stood by the fire and bit her lip. 'When Mrs Walters left me this place Reuben wanted me to sell it and invest the money so that I . . . that is, so that we could pay to send him away to school when the time comes. But I refused to do that.' She looked up. 'I've wondered since whether I did the right thing, Mr Jarvis. I so desperately wanted to keep the buffing shop; oh, I know it's not much but I felt it was something of a beginning for me. But now I wonder if I sacrificed my son's future to my own selfish wants?' She spread her hands. 'It's worried me ever since and there's been nobody I

249

could talk it over with. Reuben is . . .' She hesitated and began again, 'Reuben isn't . . .' She shrugged. 'There's been nobody I could talk to about it.'

He was quiet for some time. Then he said, 'Believe me, the money you could have raised on this place wouldn't have paid to see your son through school, Mrs Bullinger. It would probably only have paid for a few years and then what would you have done?' He raised his eyebrows. 'Are you anxious to send your son away to school?'

She shook her head violently, then put her fingers to her temples as her head throbbed. 'Oh, no. It was never my idea. I couldn't bear to part with him. But Reuben thought it would be better for him. Make a man of him, I think were his words.' Her mouth twisted at the irony.

'I think you're very wise, Mrs Bullinger. Enjoy your son while you're able. You never know what the future might bring.'

She looked up sharply. 'What are you saying, Mr Jarvis?'

'I'm sorry. I shouldn't have spoken like that. Forgive me.' He was silent for several minutes, then he said, 'It's just that I once had a son, very like Joseph. He died, some seven years ago, in a cholera epidemic. My wife died, too, in the same epidemic.'

'Oh, I'm so very sorry. I had no idea you were even . . .' She stopped, realising that what she had been going to say would have been rude.

He smiled at her, a small, slightly crooked smile. 'Seven years is a long time, Mrs Bullinger. And although one never forgets, it's true what they say, time is a great healer. Leaving London and coming here helped, too.' He took a deep breath. 'With any luck you'll make enough from this place to pay for his schooling and university too, if that's what you want,' he said, changing the subject abruptly.

'If he's clever enough,' she said with a smile. She looked up earnestly. 'But it's such a relief to know I haven't deprived Joseph by my selfishness.' She got to her feet. 'Thank you, Mr Jarvis, for listening to me. Now, I must hurry. Reuben will be furi . . . anxious. Goodnight, Mr Jarvis.'

'Goodnight, Mrs Bullinger.'

She went home thoughtfully. She felt privileged that Peter Jarvis had confided in her; she doubted whether he had told Maggie about his wife and child. Knowing Maggie she wouldn't have been able to keep it to herself if he had. She resolved to say nothing about it, not even to Reuben. Poor man, no wonder he was so quiet and reserved. Suddenly, she longed to comfort him in his loneliness, then pulled herself up sharply. That was no way for a married woman to think about a man she hardly knew.

For his part Peter Jarvis stood for a moment and then sat down at his bench. He had always avoided listening to Maggie's gossip but he knew how fond she was of Joseph and also of Hannah and he couldn't help realising that she had little time for Hannah's husband. A hard man, she called him. Peter could believe that and felt saddened. Hannah deserved better than that. She was a woman who needed warmth, cherishing, loving . . . With an effort he pulled himself together and got on with his work.

Chapter Eighteen

It took her several months but Hannah visited all the big cutlery companies to inform them that she had inherited Clara's business and was keen to take on work at competitive rates. Sometimes she was recognised from the times she had been there with Clara but more often she was received on her own merit. Managers sitting behind their large desks were impressed by this young, neatly dressed woman with the unusual green eyes, who stated her business calmly and confidently and refused to be intimidated or flustered. She inspired their confidence and they promised her work.

She left Truswell's until last. She had heard tales that the quality of Truswell's silver was not what it used to be and she had almost decided not to go there, but something – curiosity, perhaps, or even some sense of flirting with danger – after all, she might encounter Thomas Truswell – found her climbing the stairs to the manager's office at the Truswell Cutlery Company.

The manager was out of the office and she was asked

to wait as he wouldn't be long. She sat down and looked round her. It was a small well-appointed office but the bank of pigeon holes behind the desk was crammed with dusty-looking papers that looked as if they hadn't seen daylight for years. There was a set of fish servers carelessly wrapped in newspaper on the bench at the side and the desk was littered with letters and sheets of figures. The whole place had an unkempt air, as if life was moving too fast for it to keep up.

After about five minutes the door opened so she stood up and turned round. But it wasn't the manager that had entered, it was Thomas Truswell himself. He was still wearing his outdoor clothes and looked as if he had just entered the building. To her annoyance her heart began to thump painfully but she kept her voice calm as she held out her hand and stated her business.

Even as she spoke his eyes were searching her face and she could tell he was not really listening. It took all her efforts to hide the effect he was having on her and to keep her voice level and cool.

'I'm sure I've seen you somewhere before,' he said when she finished speaking. She could see admiration in his eyes and she felt gratified yet at the same time a little nervous.

'Yes, Mr Truswell, I've just been telling you, I came here with Mrs Walters, but she has passed on and now the business is mine. I should like to think I can count on your good will.'

'Oh, you can indeed, Miss er . . . um . . .' His eyes never left her face.

'Mrs Bullinger.' She took a deep breath and with it a

calculated risk. 'But from now on the business will be known under the name of Fox. Hannah Fox.'

'Hannah Fox!' She watched as a panorama of expressions passed over his face. A flare of unmistakable recognition, followed quickly by apprehension, fear, uncertainty and finally, as if a shutter had been pulled down, a bland smile. He went over to the door and opened it to usher her out.

'Of course, I leave all these details to my manager, Mrs . . . Miss . . . er . . . Fox,' he said, his voice a shade too hearty, 'but I see no reason why we shouldn't continue to use your business as before.'

She made no attempt to follow him to the door. 'Thank you, Mr Truswell, but it was your manager that I came to see,' she said quietly. 'I was told I wouldn't have long to wait.'

'Yes, well, yes, all right, I expect Briggs will be back in a moment. Now, if you'll excuse me.' He gave a quick nod and escaped. As he passed the frosted window in the corridor Hannah saw him take out a white handkerchief and mop his brow. She allowed herself a satisfied smile.

All over the town work flourished. Sheffield cutlery and silverware was exported the world over and a very profitable trade was in supplying tableware for the huge steamships that sailed the Atlantic. Their owners were hungry for silverware to grace the dining tables and cabins of the first-class passengers, and the Sheffield Cutlers were all too ready and willing to feed that hunger with the help and exploitation of the Little Mesters working long hours in their dingy hulls. They thought of everything; if there wasn't a need they created one, they even provided open – cut-throat – razors for the cabins of the rich, one for every day of the week, suitably inscribed.

Hannah's business also thrived. The big factors who put their names to the products, Mappins, Dixons, Wolstenholmes, made the enormous profits but Hannah's pride was in having a hard-working group of lasses who would turn their hand to whatever she asked and therefore she was never short of work for them, even though she charged slightly over the odds. She had carried on Clara's tradition of never allowing work that was less than perfect to leave the workshop and always delivering on time. Many was the 'rush job' that landed in Hannah's lap because of her reputation for reliability.

But Reuben showed no interest in what she was achieving. She was not surprised; she knew she had antagonised him by not taking his advice and the fact that she had been right to go against his wishes only fuelled his antagonism. He stubbornly continued to work at the craft he knew so well, grinding lethal-looking butchers' knives, working in his grimy hull astride a wooden horsing, bent over the big sandstone grinding wheel. The wheel was anchored to the floor by big chains and ran in a trough or 'trow' of water to keep the blades from overheating. Particles of sandstone thrown off the wheel turned the water to thick yellow swarf that coated everything, including the grinder himself.

He developed the inevitable grinder's cough. At night, lying in bed, Hannah could hear him coughing in the room above and knew there was nothing that could be done about it. Grinders all developed coughs, it was an accepted hazard of the craft, just as they suffered from time to time with what they called 'canker', a poisoning of the fingers or thumbs when the swarf got into an untreated cut. It was a fact of life. Grinder's asthma had killed her father and she had no doubt it would eventually kill Reuben.

When Joseph reached the age of six Hannah sent him to a little Dame's school in Orchard Street. Reuben approved of this and would take the little boy on his knee after tea each night and question him on what he had learned. Then he would take down the Bible and encourage him to make out the words. He was delighted when Joseph read a passage without fault, not realising that although the print was too small for him to understand Joseph had heard it so many times that he knew it off by heart.

Hannah was contented. Her business was flourishing. Her buffer lasses worked well for her because they knew she treated them fairly. In fact some of the younger ones began to look on her as a kind of mother figure although she herself was still only in her early twenties. No longer did young mothers have to struggle back to work three days after a confinement because they couldn't afford to stay away longer; Hannah's sick club provided for them to take at least a week, more if necessary, to recover. And when little Matty Porter got into debt Hannah cleared it for her, keeping a few pence back from her wages each week until she had paid it off.

It was only at night, in the privacy of her room, with Joseph making little snuffling noises in his truckle bed at the foot of her bed and Reuben either snoring or pacing up and down coughing in the room above, that a weary loneliness came over her and a sense of something important missing from her life. At those times she longed for a pair of strong arms round her, she longed to lay her head on a comforting shoulder, to know that somebody cared for her. She longed to be able to admit how weak and vulnerable she felt, how heavily her responsibilities weighed on her at times.

At those times she would remember the loving – if loving it could be called – she had known for those few brief summer weeks at Cutwell Hall, when she had been so expertly led into an awakening of emotions and passions she had never known existed and had believed it would never end. In the darkness she would relive those precious moments, the touching, the melding of flesh, and she would see above her those laughing black eyes, mocking her. And her pillow would be wet with tears.

These were her secrets. Secrets that nobody seeing Hannah Fox striding purposefully to her buffing shop on Pond Hill or making her regular rounds to the cutlers would ever have guessed.

She visited the Truswell Cutlery Company less often than the others. They were not willing to pay for work of Hannah's standard and Hannah was not willing to settle for less.

She was arguing with the manager there one afternoon when Thomas Truswell came in. She hadn't seen him for a long time and she noticed briefly that he had put on weight.

'Oh, good afternoon, er . . . Mrs Fox, isn't it?' he said politely, his face blank.

'Good afternoon, Mr Truswell,' she answered with a

smile. She was as certain as she could be that he remembered her, and she was just as certain that he would never admit it. The knowledge made her feel vaguely superior. 'I was sorry to read of your father's passing,' she added. She had seen reports of the funeral in the local paper, where much had been made of it and had been saddened. She always felt Sir Josiah to be a kind man at heart.

'Thank you. He'd been ill for a long time.'

'So I understand. My condolences to your mother.' She had been kind, too, and could never have foreseen the results of her kindness to Hannah.

'Thank you.' He turned to the manager. 'I'll come back later, Briggs. When you're free.' He went out and closed the door behind him.

Briggs shook his head. 'He'll never be the man his father was.' He leaned forward confidentially, obviously assuming from her conversation with Thomas that she was well acquainted with the family. 'Master Thomas hasn't the interest in the business his father and grandfather had. They say it's clogs to clogs in three generations and I'm afraid that might be true in this case. Mr Thomas is a sight too fond of cards and cock-fighting if you ask me, and one or other will be his downfall, you mark my words, Mrs Fox. That and the amber liquid.' He mimed lifting a glass to his lips.

'Oh dear, I hope you're wrong, Mr Briggs,' she said.

'Aye, so do I, Ma'am, for the sake of the business.' He shook his head. 'It's been a mortal blow to him that his wife's too sickly to bear him a son, too. Y'see, a man needs a son. There's no incentive for him to carry the name on if he's got no son to follow him.'

'Indeed no.' She paused for a minute. Then she said, 'Those soup tureens we did for you last week. The silver plating was so thin as to be almost unworkable, Mr Briggs. My lasses are used to working on best quality material, you know.'

'I'm having to economise where I can, Mrs Fox,' he said apologetically. 'Business isn't what it was, and you must admit your charges are higher than most.'

'That's because we're reliable. We do a good job and we get it done on time. We have no truck with "sours", work paid for before the job is done. I've even heard talk of sours not finished by Friday night being thrown in the river. That's dishonest. We don't ask for payment until the job is satisfactorily done. But if you think our charges are too high, Mr Briggs, perhaps you'd better look elsewhere for your finishing. I can assure you we are not short of work.'

'I'm glad to hear it, Mrs Fox.'

Hannah left the office. At the head of the stairs she encountered Thomas. It looked almost as if he had been waiting for her. She nodded to him and made to pass him but he didn't move. She could smell whisky on his breath. So Mr Briggs had been right.

'It was kind of you to ask after my mother, Mrs Fox,' he said, smiling at her. 'May I enquire after your family?'

She raised her eyebrows in surprise. 'Since you ask, my father died several years ago. My mother is well, thank you, Mr Truswell,' she answered gravely.

'And your husband?' he persisted. 'I notice you are not using his name. I trust he is not . . .'

'I prefer to use my own name for business purposes. But my husband is tolerably well, thank you.'

'I see. You have children?' He was watching her closely.

'I have a son. His name is Joseph.' She hesitated, then threw back her head and looked straight at him. 'He will be seven next May. Thank you for your enquiries, Mr Truswell. Now, if you will excuse me . . .'

Reluctantly, he stepped aside so that she could continue down the stairs. She knew he was watching her but she didn't look back. She was too angry. She didn't know what had got into her that she should have revealed Joseph's age. It hadn't been necessary, indeed it hadn't been wise because it would take very little working out on Thomas Truswell's part to arrive at the truth. It could only have been some perverse sense of triumph in the light of what Mr Briggs had just told her that had goaded her into such indiscretion.

Her temper was not improved when she got back to the buffing shop by the smell of burning that assailed her nostrils at the foot of the stairs. She rushed up to be greeted with the news that Elsie had upset an oil lamp and nearly set the whole place on fire. One girl was still lying on the floor half-fainting with another waving a smelling bottle under her nose.

The others crowded round Hannah.

'There was smoke and flames everywhere, Missus.'

'Yes, we was scared for our lives.'

'I ran down for Mr Jarvis afore t'stairs caught.'

'And I went up to fetch Grace before she got trapped in t'attic.'

They were all talking at once so Hannah had difficulty in discovering exactly what had happened. A quick glance round showed that not much damage appeared to have been done, despite what they said although she could believe that it had only been quick action by Peter Jarvis that had saved the whole rotting building from going up in flames.

She sent them all home. They were clearly in no fit state to continue working and anyway it was getting near time for them to knock off. When they had all gone and the place was quiet she made a pot of tea and went down to Peter's workshop to discover what had really happened.

He was sitting and trying to sketch, holding his pencil awkwardly with hands heavily wrapped in rags by Sally.

'Thank you, Peter,' she said, pouring a cup for herself and one for him. 'Goodness knows what would have happened if you hadn't been here.'

'Oh, I'm always here, Hannah,' he said without smiling. 'You can rely on that.'

'I do, Peter,' she said with a yawn. They had long since adopted the use of Christian names although neither could have said exactly when. She yawned again and began sipping her tea.

'God, I'm tired. I could have done without all this tonight,' she murmured, rubbing her forehead. She sighed and looked over to him. 'But what exactly did happen? From what I could make out from the lasses – although they were all talking at once so it was difficult to make much sense of what they said – the whole place would have gone up in flames and they'd all have been burnt alive if you hadn't gone to their rescue.'

He burst out laughing. 'That's a bit of an exaggeration. The fact was, I heard them screaming so I rushed upstairs to see what was wrong. It seems Elsie had knocked the lamp on to the floor as she lifted a pan of work on to the bench. Fortunately the lamp was nearly empty so there wasn't much oil to spill out. What did spill caught fire, of course, but I threw a couple of shovels of dry sand on to it and stamped it out. It was all over in a matter of minutes.'

'That doesn't explain your hands,' she said.

He looked down at them. 'Ah, well. No, it doesn't. And that could have been nasty because a bundle of old newspapers caught. They were already soaked in oil where the lasses had used them to wipe up grease and muck from the wheels so they flared a bit. I knew I had to get them out and as the windows won't open it was a case of getting them down the stairs and out of the door. It only took a few seconds but my hands got a bit scorched.' He held them up, grinning. 'Mind you, Sally was a bit over-zealous with the rag when she bound them up. I don't really need them bandaged quite so heavily but now it's done I can't get my fingers free to undo it.'

'It's probably best to leave them like that, for tonight, anyway.' She poured them both more tea. 'Thank you, Peter. It was a brave thing to do.'

He shrugged it off with an embarrassed laugh. 'Well, I couldn't let the place burn down, could I? I'd have had nowhere to work.'

She sat sipping her tea for several minutes, then said, 'I've been thinking.'

'What again? You're always thinking.' He grinned. 'You'll wear that brain of yours out if you're not careful.'

'No, I'm serious. These oil lamps. They're dangerous.'

'No. They're safe enough. Look how long they've been around. You've got them at home. Maggie's got them.

262

Candles, too. Oh, you hear of the odd fire, but you've never had any trouble here before, have you?'

'No, but there had to be a first time.'

'Rubbish. It was pure accident that Elsie knocked the lamp in the buffing shop over. Although I know she's your young sister, she does go at things like a bull at a gate sometimes, doesn't she?'

'Yes, she can be a bit clumsy. But of course it was an accident. She wouldn't have done it on purpose, would she, now? That doesn't make it any less dangerous.' She took a deep breath. 'I think perhaps I should have gas laid on. I've had it in mind for some time.'

'What? Here?' He made another attempt at sketching with his bandaged hand while he thought over what she had said. After a minute he threw down his pencil. 'Be realistic, Hannah. This place isn't worth it. Look at it, nearly falling down round our ears. The roof leaks, Grace has to keep a bucket up in her room to catch the drips, and I don't know how many times I've mended the windows and doors. And the stairs are becoming down-right dangerous again.'

She sighed. 'I know all that.'

'Well then, what's the point of having gas laid on?' He smiled at her. 'Have you discussed it with Reuben?'

'No. I've only just thought of it.' She drained her teacup and set it down on the saucer carefully. 'In any case, I don't discuss things like that with Reuben. He's not interested.'

He raised his eyebrows. 'Not interested? But surely . . . After all, he's your husband. I would have thought . . .'

She cut him short. 'The business is mine. I make the

263

decisions.' She grinned wickedly. 'After I've talked things over with you, that is.' She picked up his pencil and idly began to sketch the picture of the Cutler's Hall he had propped up on the bench. 'What do you think I should do, then, Peter?'

He watched her for several minutes. Then he said, 'I think you should go into designing. You're good. I didn't realise you could sketch like that.'

She shrugged. 'I've always been able to draw, ever since I can remember. Maybe I will. One day.' She threw the pencil down. 'But that's not what we're talking about. So you don't think this place is worth putting gas in?'

'No, I don't.' He spread his hands. 'I don't know your financial situation, but have you ever thought of expanding? There are several empty warehouses that could be converted to workshops down by the River Sheaf. You've got water power there, too, if you need it. Then you could take on extra hands . . .'

'Whoa, there! Hold on, Peter. You're going too fast.' She held up her hand. 'I've no ambition to become another Dixons, or Mappins.'

'I know that and I'm not suggesting you should.' He gazed round the grimy walls of his workshop. 'But surely you could do better than all this.'

She pinched her lip. 'Yes, you're probably right. Perhaps I should start looking for another house like this one. God knows there's plenty of condemned property in the city.' She laughed. 'I should be able to find one in better condition.'

'I think you could do much better than that, Hannah,' Peter said, shaking his head.

She looked at the watch hanging at her belt. 'Well, I don't have to make any decision tonight, do I? I'll just go up and check that everything's safe' – she gave another wide yawn – 'and then I'm off home to see my son.' She sighed. 'That's another decision I've got to make. Reuben thinks he's old enough and should be sent away to boarding school, but I think there are plenty of good day schools in Sheffield.'

'Why is Reuben so anxious to send him away to school?' Peter asked.

'He says it will make a man of him.' She made a face. 'He should talk,' she added under her breath.

'What do you mean by that?'

'Oh, nothing.' She got to her feet, then staggered slightly and clutched the table.

Immediately, Peter was at her side, his arm supporting her. 'What is it?'

She gave a laugh. 'I went dizzy for a second. I think I got up from the chair a bit too quickly. That and the fact that I'm tired. I've had a long day today. And hearing about the fire was the last straw.' She smiled at him. 'I'm perfectly all right now, though.'

'Are you sure?' He still had his arm round her protectively and for a second she thought how pleasant it would be to lay her head on his shoulder and forget all her worries. Then common sense prevailed and she straightened up.

'Yes. I'm sure. I'll just go upstairs . . .'

'*I'll* check that everything's in order upstairs. You go home, Hannah.'

She nodded. 'I will, then. Thanks, Peter. I must hurry,

too. I'm already late and Reuben will be cross. He doesn't like it if I'm late.'

She adjusted her hat and pulled her coat round her and hurried out into the cold night air.

He watched her go, a muscle working in his jaw. He couldn't make up his mind whether he was a saint or a fool. A saint for managing to resist the temptation to take her in his arms and kiss her the way he had longed to do ever since the day he had first met her, or a fool for letting the opportunity go.

Chapter Nineteen

For several days Hannah turned things over in her mind, trying to decide what would be the best thing to do. She knew that Peter was right and that it would be uneconomic to have gas laid on to the property on Pond Hill. As he pointed out, it was unlikely that the Gas Company would agree to it anyway. At the same time, the prospect of renting a disused warehouse and adapting it to her use was daunting, to say the least.

'You've been very quiet these past days, Hannah,' Reuben remarked as she cleared the table after the evening meal. 'Are you poorly?'

'No, I'm not poorly, Reuben. A little worried, but not poorly.'

'If you're worried about the lad's schooling . . .'

'I'm not. Joseph will do very well where he is, with Mr Shackleton, for a year or two.'

'The lad's growing. To my way of thinking . . .'

She banged the plates down on the table. 'Oh, leave it, Reuben, can't you! I've got other things on my mind. Business things.'

267

He sniffed. 'I'm not surprised. I knew you'd never make a go of that business. I said right from the start it should be sold and the money put aside for t'lad.' He went over to his chair and sat down, pulling his Bible from the shelf. 'Headstrong, as usual. You wouldn't listen. Well, now you've got yourself into a muddle . . .'

She slapped her hands down on the table and leaned on them. 'That's where you're wrong, Reuben. I haven't got myself into a muddle. Far from it. The fact is, I've to make up my mind how to expand. Whether to buy another condemned house or whether to buy up an old warehouse and have it converted.' She was gratified to see the expression of complete surprise that crossed his face before he settled it into lofty disdain.

'The Bible says, "Lay not up for thyself treasures upon earth, where moth and rust doth corrupt,"' he quoted. 'I believe that. You are becoming far too grasping, Hannah. I don't like to see it. It doesn't become you. You should be thankful for the station to which the Good Lord has called you and not try to rise above it.' He snorted. 'Buy up an old warehouse, indeed!'

She gave a sigh of exasperation. 'It's not that I'm trying to "rise above my station", as you put it.' Her voice began to rise. 'Don't you realise, Reuben, I've got ten buffer lasses working for me? They all depend on me to put bread in their children's mouths. Surely it's up to me to do the best I can for them. My God, where would they be if I gave up?'

'Please don't raise your voice to me, Hannah. And please don't blaspheme in my house. I . . .' He began to cough and it was some minutes before he could speak again. By that time Hannah had left the room and gone downstairs to vent her spleen on the washing up in the cellar.

They didn't speak again and at nine o'clock Reuben took himself off to bed.

After he had gone Hannah sat for a long time, staring into the dying embers of the fire. It was no use, she couldn't talk to him. She and Reuben had never been close; she had never expected that they would be. But in the years since Clara died and left her the business on Pond Hill a chasm seemed to have opened up between them that was impossible to bridge. They had always lived as brother and sister, now they lived like strangers.

She set her jaw. It was her own fault. She had chosen this marriage to give her child a name, knowing it could never be like a normal marriage. She had no one to blame but herself that she felt so lonely and isolated within it.

She heaved herself wearily to her feet and went upstairs to bed. By the light of the candle she stood looking down at Joseph. He was lying with one arm flung out on the pillow, dark lashes sweeping his cheeks, his mouth slightly open, totally relaxed. Totally vulnerable. She thanked God that at least this barren marriage had saved him from the shame of being born a bastard.

The next morning Reuben went off to work without even saying goodbye to her or Joseph which showed the depths of his displeasure with her. She resolved to be more patient with him in future, to talk to him more about the business. Maybe if she tried to involve him in it he would be less disapproving of everything she did.

She took Joseph to his school in Paradise Square and then went on to Pond Hill. The place was already humming with industry and she couldn't help a feeling of pride in her little business although the building it was in was now so dilapidated that it was beginning to look more and more like the little crooked house in Joseph's nursery rhyme book.

She went up the stairs and after looking in at the lasses, who were already hard at work to the accompaniment of the latest music hall songs, went on to her office and sat down. Today she would take a careful look at her financial position and decide what to do. She pulled the ledger towards her and began to make calculations, aided rather than disturbed by the familiar noises around her. She worked steadily until about ten o'clock, when she heard the sound of unfamiliar feet on the stairs and a voice she didn't recognise calling urgently.

'Mrs Bullinger. Where's Mrs Bullinger? It's Mrs Bullinger I'm wanting.'

She went to the door. 'I'm here. What is it?'

A boy of about twelve, barefoot, in ragged trousers and a coat covered in swarf stood there, panting, his eyes wide with fear. 'You'd best come quick, Ma'am. There's been an accident at Fletcher's Wheel. It's your man. T'men sent me to fetch you, before it's too late.'

Even as he was speaking she was reaching for her hat and coat and she outstripped him on the run back to Fletcher's Wheel.

Reuben was lying in the yard, on a door stretched across two trestles, a group of men round him. They stood aside as she appeared and she saw that he was completely covered with a large bloodstained sack, apart from where his boots hung out at the end.

'What is it? Have you sent for an ambulance?' she gasped, catching hold of the corner of the sack.

A horny hand covered hers and prevented her from lifting it. 'Tha'd do well not to look under there, lass,' a grinder's gravelly voice said gently. 'He's dead. If it's any comfort to thee he'll never have known what hit him. T'wheel exploded and a chunk caught him reet in t'face. Nearly knocked his bloody head off, poor bugger.'

'He's had nowt but trouble wi' that bloody wheel ever sin' he had it,' a man standing near said. 'He were allus at it wi' his hack hammer, trying to keep the damn thing true.'

She gazed down at the sack-covered figure. An arm had slipped out from under it and the hand she recognised as unmistakably Reuben's dangled uselessly. Gently, she took hold of it and tucked it under the sack at his side. It was still warm.

'I need to see,' she whispered.

The man lifted the corner of the sack. She looked, then closed her eyes and turned away. A burst wheel was one of the hazards of a grinder's life. Sandstone wheels were notorious for bursting. It could be caused by a flaw in the natural sandstone or if the stone wore unevenly and ran out of true and wasn't levelled with the hack hammer kept handy for the purpose. There was little chance of a grinder escaping without injury from an exploding grinding wheel even though the wheel, which could weigh anything up to two tons and rotated at over three hundred revolutions per minute, was chained to the floor. Hannah knew all this. She had grown up with the knowledge and she had heard of grinders being horribly injured. But she had never before seen what a grinding wheel could do. Reuben's face just wasn't there any more.

Her eyes rested on his boots, still sticking out from under the sack. They were big, heavy boots, making his legs appear too thin and stick-like to support them. As she stared at them they seemed to epitomise his life; the burden of shame he had dragged around with him too heavy to support, his almost fanatical religious fervour only adding to the burden instead of lightening it. Yet he had been a good man, a dedicated craftsman, even a kind man in his way. And she had reason to be eternally grateful that he had not only accepted Joseph but loved him as the son he could never have fathered for himself. Suddenly, tears coursed down her cheeks and she began to weep uncontrollably. She wept with pity for Reuben's sad, guilt-racked life, but even more she wept with remorse for the harsh words that had passed between them the previous night and she wept with regret that she would now never be able to keep her resolution to involve him more in her business on Pond Hill. It was too late.

She felt an arm round her shoulders. 'I'll tek thee home, Missus,' a husky voice said.

Reuben was buried with his mother and father in the shadow of the Ebenezer Chapel. The Reverend Enoch Partridge, minister at the church, conducted the funeral. He was a tall man, dressed all in black, who walked with his shoulders hunched forward and his hands behind his back, his pale face with its hooked beak-like nose almost obscured by a black, wide-brimmed hat. When he removed it he reminded Hannah of a picture she had seen of a vulture and she disliked him on sight. The way he conducted the funeral, laying almost gleeful emphasis on the sinfulness of man and the retribution that would be wreaked upon him, did nothing to improve her opinion of him. Listening to this man's fanatical outpourings it was no wonder that poor Reuben had been so obsessed with sin and guilt, she realised, hating the man even more.

She had a tombstone erected on which were engraved in large letters the words GOD IS LOVE. She truly believed this and she hoped that in some strange way the words might help Reuben to achieve the peace in death that he had never known during his life, for there was little enough evidence of God's love in the Reverend Enoch Partridge's twisted and dangerous brand of Christianity.

On the Saturday afternoon following the funeral, with work finished for the weekend, Hannah reluctantly went up to Reuben's attic bedroom. She had only been into it once before, when she went up briefly to fetch his Sunday suit for him to be buried in and even then she had felt she was violating his privacy. Now she must take stock, clear it and make it ready for Joseph. He was nearly seven years old now; it was time he had a room of his own. But going through Reuben's private possessions was a task she had no heart for.

She need hardly have worried. The room was austere in the extreme, the walls plain white and the furniture sparse: a hard iron bedstead and a chest of drawers. As she had guessed, the floor was bare except for a small rag rug beside the bed. There was a cupboard in the corner over the stairs that had held his Sunday suit. Now it was empty except for a shoe box right at the back. Hannah realised she shouldn't have been surprised. Reuben was not a man to choose comfort. But she was surprised to see his mother's file-maker's stiddy standing in the corner, with the files all carefully laid out on it, just as it had stood downstairs under the window when she had first come to the house. So this was what he had done with it when Joseph's cradle took its place. She thought he had given it away. A small rueful smile twisted her lip. She should have known Reuben better than that. She should have guessed he would never have parted with it.

She summoned up her courage and began to empty the drawers in the chest of drawers. She hated going through his personal things; she felt like a voyeur, looking at things that she had no right to. Yet she knew this was irrational since all his clean linen had been through her hands in the wash tub times out of number. The top drawer held nothing but a large Bible and a pile of religious tracts, which she resolved to give back to Mr Enoch Partridge at the earliest opportunity. Then she made a heap of all his clothes; there were plenty of men who would be glad of them. His Sunday shoes might as well go too.

She reached into the back of the cupboard for the shoe box. It was too heavy to hold shoes, and anyway Reuben's Sunday shoes stood neatly side by side under the foot of the bed. She fished it out and opened it, then sat back on her heels and stared.

The box held nothing but two leather pouches, one containing sovereigns, the other half sovereigns. When she counted them all she found that there was over two hundred and fifty pounds in the two pouches. She let the coins run through her fingers, glinting gold in the shaft of spring sunlight that came through the tiny window. She had always known that Reuben was a careful man, careful, in fact, to the point of parsimony. She knew, too, that grinders' wages were not high and so she had never begrudged paying her share – sometimes more than her share – towards household expenses. He didn't drink, like most of the other grinders, and his only recreation, if recreation it could be called, had been his church. She hadn't realised he was a miser.

Carefully, she replaced the coins in the leather pouches. What could she do with the money? What would Reuben have wanted done with it? She refused to even consider giving it to the Reverend Enoch Partridge; to her mind he had done nothing but blight Reuben's life.

She put the box back where she had found it; she needed time to consider what to do with it and turned her attention to the room itself. It wouldn't take much to make it comfortable for Joseph. Some pictures on the wall and a bigger rug on the floor and his toys and books would make it much more homely.

But first she went over to the file-maker's stiddy and gathered the files together and wrapped them in a duster and took them downstairs. Then she fetched the stiddy. Maggie was sure to know of someone who would be glad of it. Likewise Reuben's clothes.

'Don't you want to keep anything?' Maggie asked in surprise when Hannah took them over.

'No. Why should I? The clothes will do some poor soul

a bit of good and the stiddy – well, Reuben's mother was nowt to me,' Hannah said with a shrug.

'But surely you'll want to keep the stiddy, sin' Reuben set such store by it, after all it were his mam's . . .'

'Reuben's dead and gone. It's the living I've to look to now. Do you know anyone who might like it?'

'I daresay I do.'

'Good. Then you can take it and give it them.' She nodded towards the teapot in Maggie's hand. 'Come on, are you going to mash that tea or are you just showing me the teapot?'

Maggie put her head on one side and gazed at Hannah. Then she turned her attention to the kettle. 'Ee, you're a funny lass. You keep your feelings bottled up, don't you? I remember when my Wally died I wept for three days and nights. I never saw you weep but the once over your man, and that was the day the chap from Fletcher's Wheel brought you home.'

'And then I wept for all the wrong reasons,' Hannah said, turning her head and staring out of the window.

'Whatever are you on about? I don't understand.' Maggie frowned.

'No. Well, you wouldn't, would you? You don't know the truth of it.'

'I shall if you stop talking in riddles and sit down and tell me,' Maggie said sharply. She clattered the cups and saucers in her annoyance as she poured the tea. She pushed a cup over to Hannah. 'I'm sorry, love, it's none of my business,' she said more gently. 'You don't have to say anything you don't want.'

Hannah sat down and looked up at Maggie, her eyes

bleak. 'I think I do want to tell you, Maggie,' she said slowly. 'You see, I've found a lot of money upstairs in Reuben's room and I don't know what to do with it.'

Maggie grinned widely. 'But it's yours, love. Now your husband's dead everything's yours. It's the law.'

Hannah shook her head. 'I don't feel I've the right to it. You see, I have this awful feeling now that Reuben's dead that I did him a terrible wrong when I married him.'

'Whatever do you mean, lass?' Maggie said, shocked. 'I'll own you seemed a strange pair, but that's not to say . . .'

'Well, you see, he didn't really want to marry me and I only wed him to give Joseph a name.'

'You mean . . . ?'

Hannah nodded. 'Yes, Joseph isn't Reuben's child. I was already pregnant when we got wed.' She looked up. 'But you knew that already, didn't you?'

'Yes, but it never entered my head that he mightn't be Reuben's . . . I just thought, well, you know.'

'Reuben and I have never slept together, neither before nor after our marriage,' Hannah said in a flat voice. 'You see, Reuben isn't like that. He couldn't . . .' She paused, embarrassed, fishing for words. 'Reuben is . . . was not like other men. He couldn't bear a woman to touch him. It was men . . .' She looked up and added quickly, 'Not that he ever . . . at least, only the once. That was it, you see. We had an agreement. If we got married his secret would be safe because no one would ever suspect . . . and my child would have a father. It was my idea. I suppose you could say I blackmailed him . . .' Her voice trailed off.

Maggie put her hands to her face and closed her eyes

briefly. 'And to think I'd known that lad ever since he were a babe in arms and never suspected there were owt wrong with him. Well, you wouldn't think of such a thing, would you, not in a million years? Him being a grinder, and all. That's a man's job if ever there was one.' She was quiet for a long time, then she reached over and laid a hand on Hannah's arm. 'Whatever the whys and wherefores of it all I'll say is this, love. That child brought sunshine into Reuben's life. He idolised him. Surely that must count for something. And another thing. He thought the world of his mam, and he was like a lost soul after she died.' She smiled encouragingly. 'So I reckon he was glad of your company, love, even if he wanted nowt else.'

Hannah nodded, relieved. 'Yes, I suppose that must count for something. But it doesn't solve the problem of all that money.'

Maggie poured more tea, holding the teapot high to release the stream of steaming amber liquid. When it was done she pushed Hannah's cup over to her, saying, 'Well, as I see it, the money's yours to do as you like with. You were a good wife to him – well, as good as he'd let you be – and' – she gave Hannah a grin – 'it can't do him any good where he's gone, can it?'

Hannah smiled back. 'It's funny you should say that. He used to say, "Lay not up riches for thyself where moth and rust doth corrupt" and to think, he'd got all that money hidden away upstairs!'

'Aye, he was a strange man,' Maggie said.

Hannah finished her tea and got up to go. 'I'm glad I've told you, Maggie. You've no idea how much better I feel now.' She looked out of the window at Joseph, playing marbles in the yard. 'I think I might take Joseph and go and see my mother,' she said. 'It's time I went. I haven't seen her since Reuben died.'

'You do that, lass. And don't worry about keeping that money. It's yours to do what you want with.'

Half an hour later, dressed in her widow's weeds and with a black-clad Joseph by her side, Hannah left Orchard Court for the trek to the Wicker to see her mother. As they crossed Balm Green they met Peter Jarvis.

'Hullo, Uncle Jarvis. Have you just come from Papa's grave?' Joseph asked innocently.

Peter patted his head. 'No, lad. I had a piece of work I wanted to finish so I've just come from Pond Hill.'

'Have you seen Papa's grave? There were lots of flowers.'

'Yes, lad, I've seen it. Now, where are you off to, might I ask?'

'We're going to see my granny. She lives near the Wicker. And my aunts. I like playing with them.'

'My youngest sisters are nearly the same age as Joseph,' Hannah explained with a smile when she saw Peter's perplexed look.

'I see. Well, I won't keep you, then.' He doffed his hat and carried on.

When he arrived home he told Maggie he had seen Hannah.

'She looks very pale,' he said as he took off his coat.

'Aye. Well, she would. It's the black clothes. Any road she never carries much colour, does she?' Maggie was sitting by the fire, knitting.

'I suppose not.' He sat down and stretched his feet

towards the fire. Maggie liked him to sit with her and not to hide away in his room. 'It was a dreadful shock for her, losing her husband like that. I guess it'll take her a long time to get over it.'

'Hm,' Maggie said, her knitting needles clicking furiously.

He looked up quickly. 'What do you mean? Hm?'

The knitting needles didn't falter. 'She told me summat. I don't know as I should repeat it, but it makes a lot of things clearer.'

'I see. Well, whatever she told you I suspect it was in confidence and no, you shouldn't repeat it.' He lit his pipe and picked up the newspaper.

For some time there was only the sound of knitting needles clicking in the little living room. Then the clicking stopped as Maggie leaned forward and pulled down the newspaper so that she could see Peter's face.

'I'll tell you this, though. Reuben Bullinger hasn't been the only man in Hannah's life.'

He shook the creases out of the paper and raised it again, more to hide the sudden flush of quite unreasonable jealousy that swept over him than because he wanted to read it. 'She's a handsome woman. I would be surprised if she hadn't had other admirers,' he replied levelly.

'One of them was Joseph's father. The lad wasn't Reuben's child.'

Peter said nothing but Maggie noticed that his knuckles showed white as he gripped the newspaper. After a minute he said from behind the paper, 'You shouldn't have told me that, Maggie. It was told to you in confidence.'

She bridled a little. 'Well, I know you won't say anything, Peter.'

He lowered the paper, his face like thunder. 'Of course I shan't say anything. And neither should you have done. It's none of our business. I shall forget you ever spoke about it.'

But of course he knew he wouldn't forget. He knew that as he lay in his bed at night he would wonder endlessly who it might have been, if Maggie's words were true, that Hannah had so freely given her love to.

Chapter Twenty

Hannah spent an hour with her mother. The difference in Jane since the death of her husband was amazing. She looked ten years younger and when she smiled, which she often did now, there were marked traces of the pretty young girl she had once been. Now the lines of worry and half-starvation had gone from her face and she had put on a little weight she was quite a striking-looking woman.

The house, too, had undergone something of a transformation. With Stanley and Elsie working, as well as with what she could herself earn there had been enough money to buy some pretty curtains from the second-hand shop, as well as to replace the old couch and to buy a large hearthrug.

'You've even bought yourself a comfortable armchair, Mam!' Hannah said delightedly.

'Yes, well, the old stickback chair fell to pieces so I had to do summat.' Jane went to the cupboard by the side of the fireplace. 'I got this china off the market, too. I thought it was pretty.' She held up a cup. 'I needed some new. I hadn't got much of anything left after your dad died. He'd chucked most of it at me, one time or another.' She shook her head sadly. 'Not towards the end, though. He hadn't the strength.' She put the cup down on the table and picked up the old chipped teapot from the hearth. 'You'll have a cup of tea? I was just going to mash.'

'No, thanks, Mam. I had one earlier. With Maggie.'

'I'll not bother, then.' Jane sat down and reached over to Hannah. 'I was sorry to hear about your man, love.' She sighed. 'It's allus the same, that bloody grinding wheel gets 'em all in the end, one way or another. At least your man died quick. Not like your dad, poor sod.'

'You miss him, don't you, Mam?' Hannah said.

She nodded. 'Aye. I do. He were a reet bugger to me most of our married life, but all t'same I wouldn't have wished the living death he suffered the last months on anybody, least of all him.' Her gaze softened and became nostalgic. 'He were a handsome man when we wed. And he'd such plans. He weren't going to spend his life in a grinding hull, not him! He'd got plans! But I never knew quite what his plans were and when the babies started coming and the drink got a hold on him the wonderful plans got forgot and he stayed at the grinding and it got him in the end like he allus knew it would.' She pulled herself together. 'But that's enough of that. What about you, lass? How will you manage, with your man gone? And what about your place on Pond Hill? Elsie says she likes working there, but I've told her it might not last, because you won't be able to carry it on wi'out Reuben behind you, will you?'

Hannah's eyes widened and she gave an incredulous laugh. 'Oh, yes I shall, Mam. Reuben had nowt to do with Pond Hill,' she said. 'That business is mine. I'm Missus there and I run it, like Mrs Walters did. Reuben dying won't make any difference. It'll carry on like it's always done.'

'It's all very well for you to say that, Annie.' Jane looked doubtful. 'But you'll never manage, lass. Not on your own. A woman needs a man behind her. Oh, I know you've allus been headstrong and you might think . . . but now he's gone you'll find Reuben was the one who . . .'

'Reuben never had anything to do with it, Mam. He was never in the least bit interested,' Hannah explained patiently. 'In fact when Clara left it me he was all for selling it – not that we'd have got much for it, the house was already condemned. But I refused to sell so he washed his hands of it. I was glad. I didn't want him interfering.' She smiled grimly. 'He thought he'd only to sit back and watch it go down the drain. But I'd seen how Clara Walters worked and she didn't have a man behind her! Any road, I've kept it going. In fact, I've already got more lasses working for me than she had, so now I'm looking for a bigger place,' she added with a lift of her head.

'Well, I never.' Jane sat shaking her head from side to side. 'I never heard anything like it in all my born days. You, running your own business. Well, I never. I allus thought it was Reuben behind it all.'

'Well, now you know. It's my business and I'm proud of it.' Hannah smiled at her mother and got up to go. 'I'm glad you're managing all right, Mam.' She fished in her purse. 'But I think you should throw away that old chipped teapot and buy yourself a new one to go with those pretty cups. A present from me.'

'Can you afford it, lass, now Reuben's . . . ?' A look from Hannah silenced her. 'Thank you, love,' she finished instead.

'Come and say goodbye to your granny, Joseph,' Hannah called out of the door.

Dutifully, Joseph came in and kissed Jane. 'Fanny and Aggie have been teaching me a new game of marbles,' he said proudly. 'It's a good game. I won. I won all theirs from them.'

'Then you'll just give them back, Joey,' Hannah said firmly. 'You can't take all their marbles.'

'But I *won* them, Mam.'

'And now they haven't got any. How would you feel if someone had won all your marbles?'

He grinned. 'I'd make sure they didn't.'

Jane ruffled his hair. 'There's no getting across you, is there, lad? You're just like . . .' She frowned. 'Who is he like, Annie? I don't see much of Reuben in him and hair as dark as that doesn't run in our family.'

'He's like himself, aren't you, Joey?' Hannah said quickly. 'Now give at least half those marbles back, then we must be on our way.'

Reluctantly, Joseph emptied the marbles out of his pockets and counted them carefully whilst Hannah watched. He was developing into quite a striking-looking child, with his black hair and dark eyes. As her mother had noticed, no one in the Fox family had such colouring and her fear was that the older he became the more he would favour his natural father. Already she fancied she could see Tom Truswell in his cheeky smile. Then common sense prevailed. The two were never likely to be seen together so her secret was safe.

In spite of Joseph's complaints that his new shoes hurt, Hannah took the long way home so that she could look at the warehouse Peter had told her about near the River Sheaf. It was a tall, unfriendly-looking building, badly in need of a coat of paint, and when she looked through a broken window pane all she could see was a large expanse of concrete floor with iron stairs in the corner. She didn't like it. Anyway, she was sure it was too big for her purposes.

Her mind made up she bought Joseph a bag of sweets from a market stall in Fargate, which miraculously cured his sore feet and they continued on their way home.

When it came to bedtime, although he was tired from his long walk Joseph insisted on sleeping in his new bedroom, so she made up the bed, putting the feather mattress from his little truckle bed on Reuben's hard mattress to make it more comfortable, whilst he carried up all his most treasured possessions and arranged them round the room.

'Will you miss me sleeping at the foot of your bed, Mam?' he asked, snuggling happily between the sheets and cuddling his teddy.

'Oh, I shall, Joseph,' she assured him, tucking him in.

'Well, if you need me you can always call.' He looked up at her, his black eyes serious. 'Don't be afraid, Mam, I shall look after you, now Papa's gone.'

She bent and kissed him. 'Thank you, Joseph. I know you will and it's a real comfort to me,' she whispered, a lump in her throat.

Downstairs she sat for a long time gazing into the fire. Although the days were lengthening with the spring the house seemed cold, especially in the evening. It seemed empty, too, without Reuben's large, overbearing presence. She missed him.

But how much more she would have missed him if they had been loving and close, she thought with a sigh.

She remembered the money Reuben had left, still hidden away upstairs in the cupboard in Joseph's bedroom. It would go quite a long way towards buying the bigger premises she needed and, as Maggie had pointed out, now Reuben was dead it belonged to her.

But she couldn't use it. She didn't feel she had any right to it. She went upstairs to bed. Even the bedroom seemed empty and chill now that Joseph's little figure was no longer at the foot of her bed.

On Monday she returned to work. Things had gone on much the same in her absence; she had known they would; she knew she could trust Sally and her buffer lasses. Peter had kept an eye on things, too.

But she found it hard to cope with their sympathy. She felt a fraud and she kept wanting to say, 'It wasn't like that! Reuben and I weren't a normal married couple! We didn't even love each other!'

But she said nothing. It would have been too much of a betrayal.

Peter watched her, trying to help and support where he could but powerless to do more than listen when she chose to talk to him. He was disappointed that she found the warehouse by the Sheaf unsuitable. He knew that a move was urgent; the houses on Pond Hill were soon to be demolished, a fact Hannah seemed unwilling to acknowledge.

One afternoon he was thinking about this as he worked on the base of a large candlestick. It had already been set into pitch, which would be melted away when the work was done, so that he could begin chasing the design on to it with his hammer and punches without denting it or spoiling the shape. He was so engrossed in what he was doing that he wasn't aware that he was being watched until a voice said, 'I'm sorry to disturb you. I did knock but you didn't answer so I came in. I've been watching you work. I must say what you're doing looks pretty tricky. What happens if you make a mistake?'

Peter put down the punch he was using and picked up another one. 'I don't make mistakes. There's no margin for error in this work,' he said absently, examining the punch, putting it down and selecting another one. Then he looked up. A man in a smart frock-coat and checked trousers stood there, his top hat and gold-topped cane in one hand, a bunch of flowers in the other. He recognised him at once as Mr Thomas Truswell. 'Oh, I beg your pardon, Sir,' he said in surprise, getting to his feet. 'Is there something I can help you with?'

'Yes. I'm looking for Mrs Fox. Mrs Hannah Fox.' He looked round Peter's cellar with undisguised distaste. 'Have I come to the right place?'

Peter nodded. 'You have.'

'Good. Then perhaps you'd be so kind as to tell her I'm here. Thomas Truswell's the name.'

Peter didn't move. 'You'll find her in her office at the head of the stairs,' he said coolly. He was not prepared to act the lackey to this arrogant man.

'Oh. Thank you.' Tom Truswell nodded and turned to go.

'But mind those stairs. Tread near the wall. They're not safe in the middle.'

'Thank you again.'

Peter went back to his work but it wouldn't go right. He kept wondering why Tom Truswell had come bearing gifts to Hannah. It had never occurred to him to buy Hannah flowers; now he wished he had. He threw down his hammer. If the work didn't go right there was no point in carrying on. As he had told Tom Truswell there was no margin for error. He shrugged on his jacket and reached for his hat. A walk would perhaps calm his spirits.

Upstairs, Hannah was making up her accounts. She looked up as she heard the unfamiliar footsteps on the stair and she raised her eyebrows as Thomas Truswell knocked and came in at the open door.

'Mrs Fox,' he said with a disarming smile. 'I heard of the tragic death of your husband and I've come to offer my condolences.' He handed her the flowers, hothouse carnations.

'That's extremely kind of you, Mr Truswell,' she said in surprise. 'Thank you.' She laid the flowers on her desk and got to her feet. 'Will you take a seat?' She went over and removed a heap of papers from the only other chair in the room.

'Thank you.' He waited until she had re-seated herself, then sat down, resting his hands on the gold top of his cane.

There was an awkward silence between them. At last she picked up the flowers and smelled them. 'These are lovely, really lovely. But you shouldn't have, Mr Truswell. There was really no need . . .'

289

He waved his hand. 'The flowers are nothing, I assure you. The gardener picked them out of the greenhouse for me this morning. The house is full of them.' He chewed his moustache for a minute. Then he said, 'Is your business going well, Mrs Fox?'

'Yes, thank you,' she said politely. 'I have as much work as we can handle. In fact I'm thinking of moving to bigger premises shortly.' She gave a nervous laugh. 'This place is falling down round our ears.'

'Yes. Your man warned me about the stairs.'

She frowned. 'My man?'

'Yes, downstairs. Working in the cellar.'

Her lips tightened and there was sharpness in her tone as she said, 'You mean Mr Jarvis. He is not *my man*, he is a craftsman, a very fine craftsman at that, who rents space from me.'

'Oh, I see. I beg his pardon.' He obviously thought it unimportant.

There was another silence. Then he said, 'I wonder if I might be able to help you there. We have a small warehouse at the back of our premises no longer in use. I'm sure it could be easily converted to your purposes. Would you like to come and see it? I'm sure it would suit you admirably.'

'I already have other premises in mind, Mr Truswell,' she said quickly. It was not quite a lie.

He inclined his head. 'Well, if they should prove unsuitable, please let me know.'

'Thank you.' She picked up a pencil and began fiddling with it, wondering what the real purpose of Tom Truswell's visit was. She gave a surreptitious glance at him from under her lashes. Although he was a married man with the full weight of the Truswell Cutlery Company on his shoulders he still managed to preserve a kind of schoolboyish charm. It was easy to see how any woman could fall under his spell. He only had to smile that lopsided smile . . . She sat up and straightened her shoulders, dismayed at the turn her thoughts were taking. 'I'll bear it in mind. Now, if you'll excuse me . . .'

He didn't get up. He hesitated a moment then said casually, 'How is your son, Mrs Fox?'

Immediately she was on her guard. 'He is well, thank you, Mr Truswell.'

'He . . . you will both no doubt find things difficult now that your husband is dead.'

'Many widows manage perfectly well, Mr Truswell. I trust I shall be one of them.'

He inclined his head. 'I have no doubt you will, Mrs Fox. No doubt at all. Even so, I thought perhaps I might be of some assistance.'

'In what way?' she asked coldly.

He spread his hands. 'He is being educated?'

'Of course.'

'May I ask where?'

She stood up and etiquette demanded that he did the same. 'I really don't see that it's any of your business, Mr Truswell, but since you ask, he goes to school at Mr Shackleton's Academy in Paradise Square.'

'And then?'

'I haven't decided.'

'There are a number of very good schools for those

who can afford to send their boys to them,' he said, staring out of the window.

She kept her eyes on him. 'I am aware of that. When the time comes . . .'

'I believe you told me that the boy was nearly seven?'

'He is seven. His birthday was last week.'

'Then it's time these things were decided.'

With a swish of her skirt she went round the desk and opened the door. 'As I have already told you, Mr Truswell, when the time comes I shall make my decision as to the right place to send my son. Now, if you'll excuse me . . .'

He didn't move. 'Since your husband is no longer able to offer you advice or to make decisions I would like to offer my assistance, Mrs Fox,' he said smoothly.

She lifted her chin. 'And why should you presume to do that, Mr Truswell?' she asked.

He looked straight at her. 'I have no son of my own, Mrs Fox. It is a source of great sorrow to me. I felt it would be a generous gesture to educate some boy less fortunate than any child of mine would have been.'

She held his gaze. 'But why choose my son? There are any number of boys on the streets in a far less privileged position.'

He gave a hint of the lopsided smile that still had the power to send a thrill through her. 'I am not intending to set up a ragged school, Mrs Fox. I have simply offered to educate your son, since his – since your husband is no longer with you.'

Her gaze was still locked with his. Keeping her own expression blank with the utmost difficulty she searched desperately for even the tiniest hint of recognition, the merest flicker of remembrance of warm summer days on the moors by a running stream, of shared, stolen hours of love. But the black eyes that held hers were blank, totally impersonal, the eyes of a businessman hoping to make a deal. To steal back his natural son without admitting parenthood. Hannah turned away, disgusted.

'I am gratified that you should take such an interest in my son, Mr Truswell, but I think you must look elsewhere to distribute your largesse,' she said, with more than a trace of sarcasm in her voice. 'I am sure there are other, perhaps more deserving cases scattered around the town.' She was gratified to notice his expression darken, though whether from embarrassment or temper it was impossible to guess. She went on smoothly, 'I can assure you that Joseph will be perfectly well provided for. His father . . .' She laid slight emphasis on the words. '. . . His father,' she repeated, 'left money to be used for his education.' She smiled what she hoped was a cool impersonal smile and held out her hand. 'And now, if you'll excuse me, I have work to do.'

He took it and held it a fraction longer than was necessary. 'And that is your last word, Mrs Fox?' he asked, his eyes warm now with the hint of shared but unconfessed secrets.

'Absolutely, Mr Truswell.' Deliberately, she withdrew her hand.

He sighed. 'Very well. But if at any time . . .'

'Good afternoon, Mr Truswell.'

He inclined his head, picked up his hat and cane and left.

After he had gone she sat in her chair, her hands

covering her face, quivering with rage and with something else that she couldn't name but that made her feel completely drained. How dare he come and try to claim his son yet refuse to name him? How dare he come here and play havoc with her emotions? She hated him and all he stood for. She heard her father's gravelly voice from beyond the grave, 'If tha has owt to do wi' t'bloody Truswells tha'll be a traitor to tha family name.' She closed her eyes, thanking God that Nat had never known just how much of a traitor his daughter had been.

After half an hour in which she managed to compose herself she got up and reached behind the door for the buff brat and head-rag she kept for when she worked on the bench. She pinned on the layers of paper overalls to keep the worst of the grease off the buff brat and went through. A couple of hours helping the lasses on t'side, working on mustard spoons, a job they all hated because it was so fiddly, would calm her down and take her mind off this afternoon's encounter.

Downstairs in his cellar workshop Peter Jarvis was just coming back as Tom Truswell left. He was scowling. Clearly the interview with Hannah had not gone well. Peter began to whistle as he took up his punches again.

Chapter Twenty-One

The visit of Tom Truswell unsettled Hannah for several days. She was furious to think he still pretended not to know who she was. Not that she wanted recognition, she hastened to assure herself; it was simply that she was sure it was all pretence. She had never forgotten that day in Truswell's office when for a split second his guard had dropped and he had given himself away, revealing that he remembered her only too well. Worse, through her own stupid arrogance he knew about Joseph. She could have bitten her tongue out over that because now, he seemed to assume that on any old trumped-up excuse he could simply walk in and try to exert his influence over the boy! It was insufferable.

She told herself she wanted nothing to do with the man, all she wanted was for him to stay out of her life, so it was irrational that she should be so deeply hurt when he continued to act as though they were complete strangers. And the fact that she was so deeply hurt was a source of even greater irritation. She had thought she had put her infatuation with Tom Truswell firmly behind her, fully aware that he was a young man practised in the ways of seducing young girls. She had been stupid enough to fall for his wiles once, it was hardly likely she would allow it to happen a second time. She was older and wiser now. She despised the man; he had treated her despicably in the past and now had the gall to try to insinuate himself into the life of their child in the guise of a kind benefactor.

So why was it that whenever she saw him his charm melted her hatred and it took all her efforts to stand her ground against him? She even began to wonder if she had done right to refuse his offer to educate Joseph. Could he have given the boy a better start in life? There was nobody she could ask. Least of all Peter Jarvis. She didn't talk to Peter about personal matters.

Peter called to her one morning as she was wearily climbing the stairs after another almost sleepless night worrying over whether or not she had been wise in her decision.

'What's wrong with you, Hannah?' he asked. 'You look worn out and I've never heard you shout at the lasses like you've been doing these past few days.' He could pinpoint the time. It was ever since Tom Truswell's visit. He'd have given worlds to have been a little mouse at that meeting. Whatever could the man have said?

Hannah came into the workshop and he went on, before she had time to speak, 'Sally's been down here asking me what's wrong with you. She's never done that before. Never had cause to.'

She sat down, squeezing the top of her nose between her thumb and forefinger to try and ease the pain in her head.

'It's nothing, really,' she said.

'That's not true. Something's obviously bothering you very much. Is it worrying about finding new premises?'

'Yes, I am a bit concerned about that,' she admitted. 'I'm so anxious to do the right thing. I know we can't stay here and I want to expand the business, but I'm afraid of overstretching . . .'

'Are you worried about money, Hannah?'

She shook her head. 'Oh, no. At least . . .' She glanced at him, hesitated and went on, 'You see, I've never told you this, but Reuben left quite a lot of money. I found it in a shoe box in his bedroom when I was clearing it ready for Joseph.'

The first thing that registered was the fact that Hannah and Reuben must have slept in separate rooms and Peter's mind began to go off at a tangent at the implications of this. He dragged it back with difficulty and asked, 'What do you mean, quite a lot?'

'Over two hundred and fifty pounds.'

'Good heavens! What have you done with it?'

She shrugged. 'Nothing. It's still in the shoe box where I found it.'

'But that's ridiculous, Hannah. What on earth are you thinking about?' he said, shocked. 'It's not safe to leave it there. At the very least it should be in the bank, earning some interest. Good grief, you could be murdered in your bed for less.' He got up and began pacing up and down.

She watched him for several minutes. 'Well, you see, I don't feel I've got the right to it,' she said unhappily. 'I think I ought to save it for Joseph. Reuben would have liked that. He was very fond of Joseph, even though he wasn't . . . Joseph wasn't . . . He was very fond of Joseph.'

Peter sat down and leaned towards her. 'Keeping the money in a cardboard box for Joseph is the most ridiculous thing I've ever heard, Hannah. I'm amazed at you. You're usually so business-like and sensible.'

'I know.' She leaned her head on her hand. 'I just can't seem to think straight at the moment.'

'Then I'll have to think for you. Now, what I suggest is that you use the money to expand your business. Buy better property.' He waved his hand. 'You won't get a lot for this place, I know, but you'll get a few pounds. Think of it as an investment for Joseph.' He sat back. 'The money will do more good invested in bricks and mortar than it will sitting there in a cardboard box waiting to be stolen. I can't imagine what Reuben must have been thinking of to keep it there.'

She gave a ghost of a smile. 'It probably worried him stiff that he was "laying up riches" yet couldn't bring himself to part with it.'

He nodded and smiled back. 'That's better, Hannah. It's nice to see you smile again.' He returned to his theme. 'After all, everything will go to Joseph in the end, won't it? So it's as broad as it is long.'

She nodded slowly. 'Yes. I suppose you're right, Peter.'

'Now, I suggest you go and see your solicitor right away and get him to sort things out for you. What's his name?'

'Mr Crabtree.'

He gave a grim smile. 'I'm sure Mr Crabtree will be as appalled as I am that you've got all that money sitting there doing nothing.' His smile softened. 'Oh, Hannah, you are a little goose sometimes, aren't you?'

* * *

If Mr Crabtree was appalled he didn't show it. He had years of experience in clients' stupidity and he saved his energy for putting things right. In less than a month he had found Hannah suitable premises and arranged the finances for her and also found a buyer for the house on Pond Hill.

'The premises I have found are situated off Charles Street,' he said in his precise voice, shuffling papers as he spoke. 'It is a tenement building, only just on the market. In fact it was in use until very recently and one or two of the hulls are still occupied. If you would like to view it . . . ?' He glanced at her over the top of his gold-rimmed spectacles. 'Trippet's Wheel, it's called.'

She asked Peter to go with her.

'Well, the building seems sound enough,' he said when he had examined it from top to bottom. 'The steam engine probably ought to be overhauled but only as a precaution. It looks all right to me. The belts and drives all look reasonable and there's nothing wrong with the machinery in the buffing shop. There's a forge out at the back, I notice, and there's plenty of space here if you're thinking of expanding.' He pinched his lip between his thumb and forefinger. 'Or you could let out several more of these hulls.'

'Yes, I could do that, couldn't I?' Her feelings were beginning to see-saw between excitement and apprehension. It was a big step to take. 'My brother Stan is out of his time now,' she said thoughtfully. 'He was apprenticed to Sam Barker, the penknife maker on the Wicker, but Sam's taken on another lad now so Stan wants to start up on his own. He could set up here if he wanted to.'

She picked up her skirts again and ran up the three flights of stairs to the top floor. Peter followed more slowly.

'This could be a nice airy room if we cleaned it out and got rid of all the cobwebs,' she said, looking round it. 'It doesn't look as if it's ever been used for anything.' She thought for a minute as she surveyed the dusty room. 'This might be a good place for my office. It's a good size so there'd be plenty of room. You see, I'm thinking of taking on a girl to help with the paperwork to give me time to do a bit of designing. I've always wanted to do that and now's my chance. Do you think that's a good idea?' She turned to him. 'You're not saying much, Peter.'

He was leaning against the wall, watching her and thinking that she looked about sixteen, with her face flushed and her eyes bright with excitement. In a funny sort of way her black widow's weeds only served to enhance her youthful exuberance. He smiled. 'You're not giving me much chance, are you? You've hardly stopped to draw breath.'

'I'm sorry.' She laughed. 'I get carried away.'

He nodded towards the door. 'There's a little room on the other side of the stairs that you could use as your private workshop,' he said. 'Somewhere where you wouldn't be disturbed when you're working on your designs.'

'Oh, what a good idea.' Suddenly serious, she looked at him. 'Have you chosen your workshop, Peter?'

'Not yet.'

'But you will move with us, won't you? I mean, you'll have to find another workshop now the place on Pond Hill is sold and I wouldn't want you to think I'm leaving you high and dry.' She waited for him to speak. When he

300

didn't she added earnestly, 'You can take your pick, Peter.' She spread her arms. 'Choose whichever one you think would suit you best. What do you say?'

He gave an enigmatic smile. 'What can I say? I can hardly refuse such a generous offer.'

She frowned. 'You don't sound very enthusiastic, Peter.' She tugged his sleeve. 'At least here I'll be able to offer you something above ground. Something a bit more convenient than an underground cellar.'

'I suppose you're trying to tell me we're both coming up in the world,' he remarked dryly.

'That's exactly it,' she said gaily. 'We're coming up in the world.'

He went over to the window and looked down into the cobbled yard. He was glad for Hannah's sake that she was moving up in the world but he was only too keenly aware that as she progressed and became more prosperous, so the distance between them would inevitably increase. He had thought . . . hoped . . . that perhaps when her time of mourning was over and she could begin to think of marrying again she might consider . . . He stifled the thought even before it had formed. If she as much as suspected his feelings, feelings he had never expected to experience again, feelings that could only be allowed rein in the solitude of the night, it would be the end of their friendship. For friendship it was, and he valued it more highly than he could ever say.

He turned back into the room. 'Did Mr Crabtree tell you who the previous owner was?' he asked.

'No. Does it matter? Anyway, I'll see when I get the deeds.'

'You'll get a surprise.'

'How do you know?' She went over to him and looked up into his face.

'Because I've already made it my business to find out. This place was owned by Truswells Cutlery Company, although not many of their workforce worked here; it was rented out and used mainly as an investment.' He pointed to a rotting window frame. 'They obviously didn't consider the place worth spending money on. Or couldn't afford to and that's why they're selling,' he added as an afterthought.

'Tom Truswell offered me a warehouse to rent at their factory that day he came to see me,' she mused. 'And the work we've done for them lately hasn't exactly been of the highest quality. I wonder . . .' Her eyes glinted green as she turned to Peter. 'Oh, if only my father were alive to see this day! I think I should take this place, don't you, Peter?'

He nodded. 'It certainly seems very suitable to your purpose.' He frowned. 'But what was it you just said about your father, Hannah?'

'I said, if only he were alive to see this day.' She perched on the window ledge. 'Oh, it's a long story. But briefly, according to my father, when they were both young men, Tom Truswell's grandfather stole my grandfather's designs; apparently Grandfather had an eye for designing, no doubt that's where I inherit it from, and Abe showed them to Marshams the cutlers as if they were his own. Mr Marsham took Abe Truswell into the business on the strength of the designs and eventually Abe married his daughter. When old Marsham died Abe changed the name of the business to Truswells.' She shrugged. 'My father could never forget the injustice done to his father. I suppose it's understandable, really. But he developed a hatred of the Truswells that pretty well ruined his life. He blamed them for everything that went wrong in his life, instead of facing up to the fact that his misfortunes were mostly of his own making.' She gave a half smile. 'It would please him to know that I intend to buy Truswell property. Eat into the Truswell Empire, I suppose you might say.'

'Well, I don't think there's anywhere that would suit you better,' Peter said. He just hoped she wasn't taking it for all the wrong reasons.

The move went smoothly. Hannah couldn't help feeling a little sad at leaving the old Pond Hill house but her buffer lasses were all thrilled and excited at the thought of moving to newer, slightly more up-to-date premises where the steam engine was less likely to prove temperamental and waste valuable earning time.

Only Grace objected and threatened to retire. She had worked at Pond Hill for twenty-five years, it was near to her home and she didn't see the need for change. Anyway, her knees were rheumaticky and she was having difficulty with the stairs. However, when she saw the workshop that Hannah had earmarked for her, up one flight of stairs instead of two, and with a view over the yard that Hannah had already filled with pots of geraniums, she grudgingly changed her mind and said she would carrying on for a few more months. Hannah smiled to herself, confident that there would be no more talk of Grace retiring.

Peter decided to share the ground floor with a die maker who was already working there. Between these two workshops stood the forge and the steam engine that drove the power to the rest of the building. There was room for Stanley on the floor above with Grace and on this floor was also another, empty hull. The buffer girls were on the floor above this and Hannah's office and private workroom were on the top floor.

It was all very convenient and Hannah was satisfied that she had made the right move.

Rather than writing letters she visited all the firms she did work for to inform them of her change of address and express the hope that she would continue to receive their custom. She was surprised how well she was received. She was regularly complimented on the quality of work and more than one firm remarked on the fact that they would be happy to continue patronising her because they could rely on work being done to time.

'If we have a rush job it always goes to Hannah Fox because we're confident it'll be done well and come back in good time,' one manager told her. 'You'd never believe how many of these small places reckon some time next week'll do when we ask for it to be done Friday. And when we do get it back t'job's only half done. You go on this road, Mrs Fox, and you'll go far.'

She left Truswells until last.

As she climbed the stone stairs to the manager's office she noticed they had been well swept. She noticed too, that the brown linoleum along the corridor was well polished and even the brass door knob to the office gleamed.

The manager greeted her heartily as he offered her a chair and here too there was a change. The air of muddle and neglect she had detected on her last visit had gone and everything was neatly in place.

She stated her business, slightly embarrassed because she knew he couldn't fail to realise that her new premises were the ones Truswells had been forced to sell.

'Ah, yes. Charles Street.' He nodded, obviously not sharing her embarrassment. 'Good premises. Good premises. But no longer viable for us. Much better to use outworkers all the time, we've found. Saves on overheads.'

'Then I hope you will continue to do business with us, Mr Briggs,' she said with a smile.

He steppled his fingers. 'Indeed we shall, Mrs Fox. Indeed we shall. More so, in fact, now that we have cut down on our own numbers.' He leaned forward confidentially. 'You've heard our great news, of course?'

'News? No, I don't think so.' She looked puzzled.

'Ah. Well, I can tell you, Mr Thomas is taking much more interest in the business these days. We despaired of him at one time but I must say he's really pulling his socks up now. Mind you, it's understandable. He is expecting to have a son and heir in the not too distant future so naturally enough he wants to make sure his inheritance will be safe!'

'Indeed, Mr Briggs? That's good news indeed,' Hannah said warily. Surely Tom Truswell wasn't rash enough to be thinking of leaving everything to Joseph?

'Yes.' He coughed discreetly behind his hand. 'It's . . . er, a little delicate, but after all these years Mr Tom's wife is . . . er, how shall we say? enceinte. It was thought that this could never be, but' – he gave a little coy laugh – 'nature has a way of proving the most eminent doctors wrong. Naturally, everybody is very pleased.'

Hannah relaxed. 'I'm sure they are,' she said warmly.

'It's made such a difference to Mr Tom,' Mr Briggs said, looking towards the ceiling. 'He takes an interest in everything now and he's here from morning till night, keeping an eye on things. Not like he used to be.' He leaned forward confidentially again. 'I had really begun to worry, Mrs Fox.' He flapped his hands. 'He was out gambling when he should have been here and he drank far too much. Far too much.' He smiled. 'But all that's behind him now. He's a reformed character. A reformed character.'

'I'm pleased to hear it, Mr Briggs.' She got up to go. 'We shall no doubt be hearing from you soon?'

'Indeed you will, Mrs Fox. Indeed you will.' He showed her to the door with something of a flourish.

At the bend of the stairs she met Tom Truswell. He was in his shirtsleeves and he had a silver tureen in his hands.

He waited for her at the bend of the stairs and she inclined her head as he stood aside for her to pass, noticing automatically that the tureen was not well proportioned. The claw feet were too large for the size of the bowl.

'Have you found your new premises, Mrs Fox, or would you like to think again about my offer?' he asked affably. 'The rent to the property I mentioned is very reasonable. I'm sure it would suit your purposes admirably.'

'Thank you, yes. I found exactly what I was looking

for. In fact, that's why I'm here today. I came to pay something of a social call on Mr Briggs, to make sure he knew that I'd moved into my new premises.'

'I see.' He looked a little disappointed. 'And where are these new premises, may I ask?'

She raised her eyebrows. 'Didn't you know, Mr Truswell? I've bought your tenement property in Charles Street.'

His expression darkened but he gave a casual wave of his hand. 'I leave all that kind of thing to Briggs. I knew it was up for sale, of course. It was something of a white elephant as far as we're concerned. Our aim is to consolidate, to have everything under one roof. However, I wasn't aware that you had bought it, Mrs Fox.' He glanced down at the tureen in his hand and then up at her, his expression bordering on insolence. 'Do you not think you might be in danger of over-reaching yourself, perhaps?'

She stiffened, her eyes flashed green and she controlled her temper with difficulty. 'No, Mr Truswell,' she said, her voice ominously low. 'I do not. I can assure you that these days I don't embark on *anything* without first weighing the consequences very carefully. Now, if you will excuse me . . .' She swept past him and on down the stairs.

As she reached the bottom she heard him shouting at Mr Briggs.

'The assay office refused to pass this. They said the silver content was insufficient. What the bloody hell do they think they're doing?'

The door slammed before she could hear Mr Briggs' reply and she went out into the street, glad of the fresh September breeze to cool her burning cheeks.

As her temper cooled she recalled Tom Truswell's words, 'We're consolidating, having everything under one roof.' Yet only a short time ago he had offered her a small warehouse at the Truswell Works. The two statements didn't match up, unless, of course, in spite of Tom Truswell's new burst of interest in the business Truswells were in financial difficulties. She smiled to herself. It would be interesting to see.

Chapter Twenty-Two

On a cold, wintry day the following March, while blinding snow whispered down to form a thick white blanket over the grounds of Cutwell Hall, Tom Truswell's delicate wife was brought to bed and after twenty agonising hours was delivered of a stillborn daughter. The doctor in attendance congratulated himself on having saved the mother at the expense of the child and quietly told Tom that there would be no more children for the young Mrs Truswell.

Old Lady Truswell, bitterly disappointed that her only and long-awaited hope of a grandchild was now gone, comforted her wearily bereft daughter-in-law, while Tom, furious that his hopes of a son and heir had been so cruelly thwarted, got drunk.

In the town it took some days for the news to filter through. Even then, most people were too busy trying to stay alive in the bitter cold to pay much attention. In any case, stillborn children were a fact of life – sometimes, where there were already too many mouths to feed with too little bread, a welcome fact.

The snow made the contrasting existences even more marked. At Cutwell Hall and on the hills beyond the snow glistened, stretching pure and white into the distance, the branches of the trees bowing low with their heavy white burden while the sheep in the park huddled together in dirty white blobs. Inside the house great fires were kept roaring halfway up the chimneys and scurrying maids looked out from the comfort of warm rooms and thought how pretty the snow looked.

There was no pretty white snow in the town. It turned grey even as it fell through the smoke-laden atmosphere, to be churned up and mixed with the usual filth from the gutter into a disgusting slush. The frozen population, with blue noses and chapped cheeks, hurried from rooms hardly warmer than the streets outside to their daily work, and the trams and carts toiled up and down the hills, their progress precarious even with chains on their wheels and on the horses' hooves. It was a slush that froze overnight as more grey snow fell, while the people shivered in inadequate clothing and prayed for an end to the bitter weather.

Hannah's buffer lasses struggled good-humouredly to work each day, wrapped tightly in their shawls, some with chains or old socks round their clogs, their faces pinched with cold.

'We all have further to walk to get to this place but at least once we get here t'winders fit and keep out most of t'draught,' Marjorie said, taking off shawl after shawl before fastening on her layers of aprons. 'On Pond Hill t'wind used to whistle through t'casements enough to blow you across t'room. Once Elsie gets a good fire going we're nice and snug here.'

'And t'tea mashed,' Sally said. 'Elsie, get t'kettle on. We need a mug of tea to put some heat back into us before we start work. By, it's cold out there.'

In the office at the top of the building Hannah was already at work. She was looking through the accounts. Things were looking good. The rent from the hulls she was renting out plus what she made on the buffing side showed a healthy profit even though she had already put the piece rate up for the lasses by a halfpenny, as well as employing two more girls.

Peter had been quite right, she decided. Borrowing the money Reuben had left in order to buy this property had been exactly the right thing to do, because she was already making enough to begin thinking about starting a savings fund for Joseph so that she could begin to repay it. She knew she could never bring herself to regard the money as hers.

She left a pile of invoices for Ivy, her office help, to enter into the ledger and went across the landing to her own little room. There was no fire here although Elsie had lit one in the office and briefly she considered taking the drawing she was working on across to her desk in the office where it wasn't quite so chill. But Ivy had a propensity to chatter and in chattering to make mistakes. She would do her work better without distraction. And so, Hannah decided, would she, even though it was so bitterly cold.

She reached down an old shawl she kept on a peg behind the door and wrapped it round her shoulders. Then she sat down and pulled her pad towards her. She had made several rough sketches of teapots; she was working on designs for a silver teaset; the teapot, hot water jug, milk jug and sugar basin and the tray on which they would stand. She had already tried her hand at designing mustard pots and spoons and she had sold these designs quite easily, much to her surprise. So she was trying something a bit more ambitious now. She worked for nearly two hours, sketching, rubbing out and improving, oblivious of everything except the sketches in front of her. Then, suddenly, the pencil refused to go where she wanted it to. She straightened up and tried to flex her fingers. They were so cold they were numb and she couldn't feel the pencil in her hand. She moved her feet and she realised that they too were like blocks of ice. She stamped her feet and tried to rub some warmth into her hands, feeling them tingle painfully as the blood returned. Then she picked up her drawings and took them downstairs to Peter Jarvis in his workshop.

Peter's hull was warm. It had to be for the work he did. He couldn't work with his tiny punches and hammers with frozen hands. He looked up as she entered, her shawl pulled tightly round her, hugging herself with cold.

'I've brought some designs to show you, Peter,' she said, shivering her way over to the fire to warm herself by the bright blaze, her teeth chattering. 'I've been working on them this morning and suddenly realised how cold I was. I ought to have told Elsie to light a fire in my room, I suppose.'

'You mean you've been working there with no fire?' Peter asked. 'In this weather?'

She shivered again and rubbed her hands. 'Yes. Stupid of me, wasn't it? But I didn't intend to work there for

312

long. Only to finish off what I'd been doing.' She gave an apologetic smile. 'But I had an idea that I thought might be an improvement and I sort of got carried away. What do you think?' She handed him her drawings.

He studied them for a long time. Then he said, 'I think they're very good, Hannah. I like the line of the curves and I think you're right not to over-decorate. That gadrooning round the base of each piece is elegant and it's a nice touch to repeat it at the base of the spouts.' He put his head on one side. 'Would you consider repeating it on the lids? Or do you think that would be overdoing it?' He handed the drawings back to her.

She studied them, then shook her head. 'Yes, I do. I like the plain line of the lids.'

'Mm, perhaps you're right,' he said. 'But the tray certainly needs a little more ornamentation than you've given it.'

'I know. I haven't finished that yet.'

'What are you going to do with them?'

She shrugged. 'Offer them to Mappins? They bought my mustard pots.'

He was silent for several minutes. Then he said, 'Why offer them to Mappins? Why not make them yourself?'

She laughed. 'Don't be silly, Peter. I couldn't do that. I'm not a silversmith.'

'No, of course you couldn't,' he said impatiently. 'That's not what I meant. What I meant was, why don't you get them made and market them yourself? I can get you the silver.' He nodded towards the door. 'And Matt Bell across the way will make your dies and cast them for you – the same die will serve for all the lids for a start – and you'll

313

need another for all the feet. The base of the milk jug and sugar basin are the same, too. Oh, it wouldn't be any trouble to Matt. Why don't you have a word with him?'

She sat down on an old kitchen chair by the fire and held out her hands to its warmth. 'I don't know . . .'

He leaned forward. 'Think about it. You've got practically all the processes you'll need under this one roof, Hannah. Good grief, I can turn my hand to most things, if it comes to it, and you've got your buffer lasses, plus one of the finest finishers in the town in old Grace, grumpy though she is. It's a golden opportunity.'

She nodded. 'Yes, I suppose you're right, Peter.' She smiled. 'To tell you the truth it's something I've always dreamed of. Hannah Fox Silver. And to have my own Maker's Mark. HF. Sounds good, doesn't it?'

'It'll look even better when your dream is reality and your HF punch is registered at the Assay Office.' He pulled open a drawer full of blanks. 'I'll make it for you. Plain? Or would you like the letters to be a bit ornate?'

She frowned. 'Oh, plain, I think.' Then she laughed. 'Don't you think you're putting the cart before the horse, Peter? I haven't even finished the drawings yet.'

He shrugged. 'Maybe. But it doesn't matter. It'll be ready when you want it.'

By the time the snow had disappeared and signs of spring were showing in the primroses and daffodils Hannah had planted in the tubs in the yard her first tea service was under production.

She told her mother about her new venture.

Jane was less than enthusiastic. 'Remember, my lass,

314

pride comes before a fall. You'll be over-reaching yourself if you're not careful. It's not a year yet since you moved to that bigger place. Now you're starting on this. I only hope you know what you're doing, Annie.'

Hannah gave her mother a hug. 'Don't worry, Mam. I do know what I'm doing, I promise you.' She sighed. 'I only wish our Dad was alive to see. He'd be that proud!'

'Aye, happen he would. He could never see further than the end of his nose.' She eyed Hannah up and down. 'That's a smart new outfit. What's happened to your black?'

Hannah looked down at the wine-coloured coat she was wearing and then at her mother. 'Mam, it's over fifteen months now since Reuben died. I wore black for a full year. Any road, this coat's trimmed with black astrakhan and I'm still wearing a black hat. Isn't that enough?'

Jane sniffed. 'I daresay. You're lucky you can afford to buy all new.'

'Would you like a new coat, Mam?' Hannah asked gently. 'You've only got to say, if you would.'

Jane shook her head firmly. 'No. I went into black when your dad died and I'll wear black till the day I die out of respect for him. It's a pity you don't have the same respect for your man, Hannah,' she said, looking at her sadly.

'I'm still a young woman, Mam. I'm not wearing black for the rest of my life. In any case, my marriage wasn't like yours.'

'What do you mean by that? You'd got a lot to be thankful for in your man. You were lucky. He didn't tip all his money down his throat and knock you about.'

She shook her head, conscious that she'd already said too much. 'No, that's true, he didn't. Reuben was a good man. I didn't mean that.'

'I suppose you mean you'll be looking for another husband, which I never shall,' Jane said. Her voice softened. 'Well, lass, I can't blame you for that. As you say, you're still a young woman.'

Hannah shook her head again. 'No, Mam. I'll not be looking for another husband. I shall never marry again.'

'You can't say that, lass. You never know what's round the corner,' Jane said. 'If the right man was to come along . . .'

Hannah's mouth twisted into a wry smile. 'I'd tell him I was wed to my business.' She changed the subject. 'Mam, seeing as you intend to wear black for the rest of your life, would you like my weeds? We're about the same size and I shall never wear them again. I'm sick of the sight of them.'

Jane couldn't quite suppress her delight. 'But they're good quality bombazine!'

'Then you'll be able to make good use of them. I'll pack them up and Elsie can bring them home for you.'

Hannah left. Her mother was a proud woman. It was not often she accepted help of any kind so it was something of a victory that she hadn't refused the weeds.

It was getting dusk as Hannah made her way home along Fargate. Maggie would have met Joseph from school an hour ago so Hannah stopped to buy oranges for him as a treat. Joseph was very fond of oranges.

He was lying full length in front of the fire noisily sucking one after tea when he rolled over and looked up at her. 'A man came to school today. Mr Shackleton showed him round, although he didn't seem very pleased about it. Who do you reckon the man was, Mam?'

'I'm sure I don't know, love. An Inspector, perhaps. What did he look like?'

Joseph slurped a bit more of his orange. 'I dunno. Tall. Taller than Mr Shackleton. With a tall hat. When he took it off he'd got black curly hair and a black moustache. And check trousers. I liked his check trousers. Can I have check trousers, Mam?'

'One day, darling. And did this man say anything to you?'

'Yes, he asked me my name and I stood up and said, "Joseph Bullinger, Sir." And Mr Shackleton said afterwards that I'd been very polite.'

'That's good. And did the man say anything else?'

'Yes. He asked me if I knew my ABC and I said it all through without stopping and he said that was very good too and gave me sixpence.'

'And did he talk to other boys, Joseph?'

'No. At least I didn't see him. What shall I do with the sixpence, Mam? Shall I put it in my pig?'

'Yes, dear. Put it in your pig.'

After Joseph had gone to bed Hannah sat staring into the fire for a long time. Joseph's description had been brief but it was enough to convince her that the man who had visited the school had been Tom Truswell, and she was furious to think he had been spying on Joseph. Cold fear clutched her heart. Dear God, surely he wasn't thinking of kidnapping the boy!

She spent a sleepless night thinking about it. If only

there was somebody she could talk to! She thought of Maggie. Maggie was a dear friend and the salt of the earth, but Hannah felt she had already confided in her more than was perhaps wise. She wasn't sure just how good Maggie was at keeping things to herself.

Then there was Peter. Peter was invaluable where the business was concerned. His advice was always well-considered and sound and she knew she could always turn to him. But her dealings with him were strictly business. She wouldn't dream of embarrassing him – or herself – by burdening him with her personal problems. Especially this one. She could never admit to Peter that Reuben wasn't Joseph's father, let alone reveal that Tom Truswell was! It was unthinkable. Yet something must be done before Joseph was dragged into an unpleasant tug-of-war.

There was only one person she could have shared her anxieties with. Reuben. But Reuben was dead.

When she got up the next morning she felt drained and her head ached. Nevertheless she asked to speak to Mr Shackleton when she took Joseph into school.

'Joseph tells me Mr Truswell paid the school a visit yesterday,' she said, trying to keep her voice cool but interested. 'And that he singled Joseph out for attention. Was there any particular reason for this? I thought Joseph was doing well with his studies.'

'Indeed, yes, Mrs Bullinger. Mr Truswell remarked on the fact,' Mr Shackleton said earnestly. He was a tall, thin, colourless man who looked as if he slept between the pages of his books.

'Did he speak to other boys, then?'

He nodded. 'Oh, yes. He spoke to several of the boys,

318

although not at such great length as he did to Joseph.' He leaned forward confidentially. 'He was most interested in the school. I shouldn't be surprised if a bit of money was to come our way from Truswells Cutlery Company, Mrs Bullinger,' he said smugly. 'I feel sure that was why the gentleman visited.' He rubbed his knuckles on the palm of his other hand. 'Good reports of my Academy have evidently reached his ears.'

'I hope you're right, Mr Shackleton,' Hannah said. 'I sincerely hope you're right.'

But she was quite sure he wasn't.

She couldn't concentrate on her work and early in the afternoon she called for Truswell's account as an excuse and went to visit Tom Truswell.

He was sitting in his office with his feet up on the desk, reading the newspaper. He got hurriedly to his feet as she entered and gave her his most disarming smile.

'Mrs Fox! To what do I owe the pleasure of this visit? Please sit down.'

She sat down and calmly folded her hands in her lap.

'I was extremely sorry to hear of the loss of your baby daughter, Mr Truswell,' she said. 'Of course, I wrote to your wife at the time but I haven't seen you to offer my condolences.'

'Thank you. It was a most sad occurrence. As I believe you know, my wife was delicate beforehand.' A trace of bitterness crept into his voice. 'Now, unfortunately, she hardly leaves her bed.'

'I'm sorry to hear that.'

'Yes.' He stared out of the window for several minutes. 'Of course, there will be no more children for us.'

319

'No doubt that's why you are taking such an interest in Mr Shackleton's Academy in Paradise Square,' she said without raising her voice.

He shrugged. 'I thought I might be able . . .'

'And my son in particular,' she interrupted. 'Did you think Joseph wouldn't tell me, Mr Truswell?'

He spread his hands. 'He's a bright little boy. Obviously, Mr Shackleton drew my attention to the brightest boys.' He looked searchingly at her. 'Your son is a credit to you, Mrs Fox. I'm sure you're very proud of him.'

Coolly, she returned his gaze. 'I am indeed, Mr Truswell.'

'Then do you not think you could do better for him than Mr Shackleton's Academy? I'm thinking, of course of a preparatory school with a view to public school later.'

'I think that would be beyond my means, Mr Truswell.' She paused before adding, 'At the moment.' She paused again, and before she could continue Tom Truswell cut in with almost schoolboy eagerness.

'If it is beyond your means, would you accept a little help, Mrs Fox? I'm sure you want the very best for your son and I would be prepared . . .'

It was Hannah's turn to interrupt. 'My husband and I discussed the matter fully before we decided where Joseph should be sent to school, Mr Truswell. I think we made the right decision. I am quite satisfied with the education my son is receiving with Mr Shackleton.'

Tom spread his hands on the desk. 'I will come to the point, Mrs Fox. As I have already told you, my wife cannot have another child so I have no prospect of a son of my own. That being so, I . . . er, we would very much like to adopt Joseph.'

320

'What?' It was almost a scream.

'Oh, I realise you will need to think carefully about it, but please don't reject it out of hand. Joseph stands out at that school as by far the most well-set-up, intelligent lad. Given the right treatment he should go far. But what chance does he have? For a start, where do you live? Balm Green? Not exactly the lap of luxury, is it? Think what better prospects he would have coming from Cutwell Hall, Mrs Fox.' His voice lowered and became almost pleading. 'My wife is desperate for a son, as I am, and he would be quite doted on, and given every opportunity in life, I can assure you.' He looked up, straight into her eyes. 'Of course I wouldn't have dreamed of making this offer had your husband still been living, Mrs Fox. But a lad needs a father.'

She stared back at him unflinchingly. Then she stood up. The only sign of emotion was that the colour had drained from her already pale face. 'I think I'm the best judge of that, Mr Truswell,' she said, her voice ominously quiet. 'I cannot imagine how you could dare to make such an outrageous suggestion. Joseph is my only son. His upbringing was not easy and as you so rightly say we do not live in the lap of luxury. Naturally, he misses his father but we have each other and we are perfectly contented with our lot. Joseph is happy and so am I. We neither need nor want interference from you or anyone else in our lives, and I'll thank you to leave us alone.'

With that, she left the room, closing the door quietly behind her.

Tom Truswell sat staring after her. The door closing quietly like that had far more impact than if she had slammed it and he felt uneasy. Hannah Fox had changed. The elegant, self-contained woman who had just left the room was a far cry from the innocent seventeen-year-old he had fallen in love with some eight years ago. Yes, it was true, he had fallen in love with her although God knew he had treated her badly. But that hadn't really been his fault, circumstances had conspired against him, making him act the way he had. But now, she was so cool, so self-possessed and – he searched for the word – *distant* that it was impossible to know what she was thinking.

He slumped in his chair. He had handled the whole thing badly. He had intended to be more persuasive, more expansive even, but she had given him not the slightest encouragement.

Had she guessed that he suspected . . . no, dammit, *knew* Joseph was his son? If she had guessed she hadn't given herself away by so much as a flicker of an eyelid. It was infuriating and left him feeling that she had somehow got the advantage over him. He didn't like that.

Chapter Twenty-Three

Hannah strode back to Charles Street seething with rage. How dare Tom Truswell make such an outrageous suggestion to her! It wouldn't have been quite so bad if he had put his cards on the table and openly admitted he suspected Joseph might be his son – after all, he couldn't be absolutely certain of that. But even if he had, the outcome would still have been the same as far as she was concerned. All right, so she was sorry that he had lost his only child and that there would be no more for him, but that was no excuse for him to try and steal Joseph from her. And to pretend that his only motive was a desire to give a better chance to a bright little boy who had lost his father was nothing less than dishonest and shameful.

She turned into Trippet's Wheel. Even in the throes of her fury the sight of it gave her a sense of satisfaction. At her insistence the cobbles were always kept well scrubbed and the yard now was a riot of flowers in tubs. It looked prosperous and inviting although with a critical eye she registered that a coat of paint on the windows and doors wouldn't come amiss. She made a mental note to get that done as soon as funds would allow.

Her step slowed. Trippet's Wheel was doing well but the business was still in its infancy so she ploughed most of the profits back, taking as little out of it as she could to manage on for her own use. It had never occurred to her before, but was she depriving Joseph? Orchard Court, too, where they lived was small and sunless. She thought of the green park at Cutwell Hall, the trees, the blue skies, the hills where she had once walked in such awe and wonder and she remembered only too clearly when she had been pitchforked back into the grime and stench of the town, how she had missed the wide open spaces and clear air of Endcliffe. She had nearly suffocated in the smoke and stink of the town, she recalled. But it was surprising how soon she had become used to it and now she hardly noticed it at all. Joseph, bless his heart, had never known anything else.

She thought of Cutwell Hall itself. The tall, airy rooms, the beautiful furniture and silver, all of which should come to Joseph by right if only she would allow it. Was she justified in refusing to let him go there to live? Was it simply selfishness on her part, terror at the thought of losing her son that had made her reject Tom Truswell's offer so furiously? Was she depriving Joseph of his birth-right in refusing to let Tom Truswell take him?

Her thoughts were in such a turmoil she knew she would have no peace of mind until she had talked it over with someone. Peter's door stood ajar. She didn't normally discuss her private life with him but perhaps it would be easier to talk to someone to whom she wasn't too close.

She knocked on the door and went in.

He looked up with a smile, then put down his punch and hammer and flexed his fingers. 'Good. I'm glad you've come. It's time I stopped for a few minutes,' he said. 'I'm getting cramp. Come and sit down.' He noticed her thunderous expression and added hurriedly, 'Or on second thoughts, perhaps not. You look as if you might bite my head off. Have I done something wrong?'

She sat down and her shoulders sagged. 'No, of course not, Peter. I'm a bit worried, that's all.'

'Want to tell me about it?' he said casually, peering at the work on his bench, and scrutinising it from all angles, as he spoke. Obviously she did. She wouldn't have come in otherwise, but he didn't want to make it more difficult by staring at her.

Her gaze rested on his bent head, and she noticed absently that he needed a haircut. 'I certainly need to talk to somebody,' she said with a sigh. She passed her hand across her forehead. 'Oh, dear. I'm so afraid I've done the wrong thing.'

Now he did look up. 'In respect of what?'

'Joseph.' She twisted her hands in her lap. 'I'm sorry, Peter,' she said wretchedly. 'I shouldn't burden you with my private troubles, you hear enough concerning the business, but I don't know who else to turn to.'

He reddened slightly with pleasure. 'Go ahead. You know your Uncle Peter's always ready to listen.'

'Don't tease, Peter. I'm serious.'

'So am I.' He picked up a punch and examined the tip closely.

She stared out of the window. 'I've just been to

Truswells,' she began, carefully not looking at him. 'I went because Tom Truswell called at Joseph's school yesterday and was questioning him in a way that rather worried me.'

'Have you been to see Mr Shackleton?' Peter interrupted. 'Surely what happens at school is his province?'

'Oh, yes. I went to see him this morning. He was no help. He lives with his head in the clouds. He's convinced Tom Truswell's going to put his hand in his pocket and deliver large sums of money for the school. I didn't contradict him but I was pretty sure that was not what Tom Truswell had in mind at all. But I thought I'd better make sure, so I went to Truswells to see him and find out.' She paused and bit her lip, then turned and looked at Peter, her eyes tortured. 'He had the gall to tell me he'd like to adopt Joseph.'

Peter's brow furrowed as his eyebrows shot up in amazement. 'The devil he did! But why? Why on earth should he want to do that?'

'He says he's looking for a lad to adopt because he realises he'll never have a son of his own,' she said in a flat voice. 'He said he went to the school, found Joseph to be an intelligent lad, knew he'd lost his father and thought . . . well . . .' She swallowed. 'He thought he would be a suitable choice, I suppose.'

'And what did you say?' he asked carefully.

'I told him the idea was preposterous.'

'Good for you.'

She sighed. 'Yes, but, Peter, now I'm not so sure. Was it so preposterous? I mean, Joseph would have a much better chance in life coming from Cutwell Hall than coming from Orchard Court. Tom Truswell wants to send him to preparatory school and then on to public school.' She shook her head. 'You know as well as I do that I couldn't hope to do that.' Her face took on a dreamy look. 'And Cutwell Hall is such a beautiful place. It's huge, Peter. The grounds stretch for miles, it seems, and the air is so clear and pure you can see the hills in the distance. They're all purple when the heather's out. And the sunsets are like something out of fairyland.'

'How do you know all that?' Peter asked sharply.

She glanced at him briefly. 'Oh, haven't I told you? I was in service there, years ago.' She frowned again, her face agonised. 'Am I being selfish, Peter? Am I refusing even to consider his offer simply because I can't bear to part with my little lad?'

Peter was silent for a long while. Then he said, 'How do you think Joseph would feel, being uprooted and taken away from his mother to live in a big house?'

She shrugged. 'I like to think he'd miss me. For a while. But it would all be so grand, so new ...' There was a catch in her voice. 'With a new mother I guess he'd forget. In time.'

'I think you do yourself a gross injustice there, Hannah,' he said gently. 'I think it would break his heart to be parted from you. However, leaving that aside, I'm not altogether sure Tom Truswell could do all he's promising for Joseph.' He shook his head. 'I don't think Truswells Cutlery Company is in particularly good financial shape, myself.'

Her head shot up. 'Oh, I think you're wrong there, Peter. There was a time when Tom went off the rails a bit, drinking and gambling, and it showed in the business. But Mr Briggs told me some time ago that he'd turned over a new leaf and things were looking up. And it certainly looked like it when I went there.' She pinched her lip. 'That was when he had high hopes of a son to carry on the family name, of course.'

'Appearances can be deceptive, of course,' he remarked with a trace of cynicism. 'But one thing is certain. Hannah Fox Silver is up and coming, isn't it?'

She smiled for the first time. 'I certainly hope so.'

'Well, I'd put my money on Hannah Fox being here in ten years. I wouldn't bet so rashly on Truswells. For one thing, they couldn't get rid of this place fast enough, could they? You got Trippet's Wheel at a very good price because they wanted rid of it. They needed the cash. And I've heard they've sold off a warehouse since then. Another thing. I don't get work from them any more. Not that I want it, I hasten to add, because I had to wait months before I got paid for the last lot I did.' He shook his head. 'No. Tom Truswell may be making philanthropic noises but I'd be surprised if he's got the finances to back them. That's my honest opinion.' He leaned back in his chair. 'But leaving all that aside, and supposing I'm wrong and Truswells are the richest family in Sheffield, I still think you made exactly the right decision, Hannah. Your Joseph will be far happier left where he is. With you. I'm surprised you ever had any doubts.'

Her face cleared and she got up to go. 'Oh, thank you, Peter. I'm glad I talked to you. I feel better now. Especially as you said what I wanted to hear,' she added with a smile.

'I didn't say it for that reason. I meant every word,' he said seriously. Then he grinned. 'But I'm always here, ready to give you the benefit of my homespun wisdom. Any time. My door's always open.'

After she had left his smile died. Of course, Tom Truswell was Joseph's father. He should have guessed that long ago. Now he came to think about it there was a definite likeness there, especially round the eyes, both dark brown, nearly black. And the fact that Hannah had been in service at Cutwell Hall merely added to the certainty. It wasn't difficult to piece together the story although he doubted whether, in her preoccupation with Joseph's future, Hannah realised just how much of it she had given away today. But what he couldn't guess was what her feelings were for Tom Truswell. Did she still care for him? Was that why she had even considered handing her son over to him?

He clenched his teeth, his jaw working. Tom Truswell was a cool bastard, if ever there was one. He had never cared much for the man; after this little episode he positively loathed him.

At home that night Hannah couldn't resist questioning Joseph a little. He was in his favourite position, stretched full length on the hearthrug, playing with his lead soldiers and making violent battle noises as he moved them about.

'What do you think you'd like to be when you grow up, Joseph?' she asked, resting her sewing in her lap to look at him.

He rolled over and looked up at her. 'I think I'd like to drive a tram,' he said with a frown. 'But I'm not sure. I suppose I should learn all about silver so that I can help you, Mam. I should like to help you because I know you have to work very hard.' He smiled up at her. 'When I'm a man you won't have to work so hard because I shall look after you. I'll always look after you, Mam.'

She returned his smile. 'Thank you, Joey. But you won't always want to live here with me now, will you?'

'No. I shall build you a house where you can see trees and fields. You often talk about trees and fields and big blue skies, so I shall build you a house where you can see them.' With that he rolled back and continued with his battle.

She gazed out of the window. Dusk was already gathering so she could no longer see to sew. Peter had been right. Joseph belonged to her and his place was with her. Their worlds revolved round each other and nothing and nobody should part them. And one day, as Joseph predicted, they would have a house, up on a hill, where they could see the trees and the fields and the blue sky. Not a big house, but a house with a garden where Joseph could play; and he could have a swing with a seat hanging from one of the trees . . . She smiled a little at the way her thoughts were running away with her.

One thing was certain. Tom Truswell had no part in their future.

The summer wore on. Peter obtained the silver and Matt Bell made the dies for her teaset. When it was finished each piece was stamped with her maker's mark, an ornate HF, which had to be registered as her mark at the Assay Office. It had given Peter great pleasure to design and make the punch for it. Then the teaset was sent to the

Assay Office to be examined and each piece stamped three times; with the town mark, which for Sheffield was a crown, with the letter R denoting the date and with the quality mark, which was a lion passant. When it arrived back from the Assay Office Hannah set it out on her desk and everybody in the building came to look at it.

'Don't touch it!' Old Grace said. She had lovingly put the final finish on it with jeweller's rouge and a swansdown buff and she was inordinately proud of her handiwork. Grace rarely altered her sullen expression – the lasses often called her 'Old Misery' behind her back – but as she stood and admired the design and workmanship a satisfied smile hovered round her lips. 'Aye, it'll do,' she said with a nod.

'It'll do, all right,' Hannah said with a laugh. 'It's already sold to Dixons and they want another half dozen.'

'Same design?' Matt said, thinking of the dies already made.

She nodded. 'Same design.'

'It's a good design. It'll go into hundreds, I shouldn't wonder,' Peter remarked with satisfaction.

Sally came bustling up the stairs carrying a tray, Elsie right behind her with another. 'I thought we ought to celebrate, so sin' we've got nothing stronger I've mashed tea for everybody.' She looked round at the assembled company. 'Of course, it ought to be in t'silver teapot, but I didn't think t'Missus would tek too kindly to that, so it's in t'old brown betty like we allus have it.'

'And I'm sure it'll taste just as good,' Hannah said with a smile, her usually pale face flushed with excitement.

Peter lifted his blue and white striped mug, slightly chipped at the rim. 'Here's to Hannah Fox Silver,' he said. 'Long may it prosper.'

Everybody raised their mugs and nobody thought it incongruous to be standing and looking at elegant, expensive silverware whilst drinking a toast to it in thick old chipped and cracked mugs that were not two alike.

'By Gow, Sis!' Stanley, who had left his penknife-making to join in the celebration, wiped his mouth on his sleeve. 'Wouldn't our dad have been proud this day!'

'Aye, lad. Reckon he would,' Hannah said, her eyes suspiciously moist. 'It's a pity he can't be here to see it, for he never thought I'd do it.'

Coffee sets followed the teasets with only slight modifications to the design. Then others, slightly more ornate, that required Peter's expert handiwork in the decoration. Then soup tureens, vegetable dishes, asparagus dishes, candelabra; it seemed that whatever Hannah designed found favour.

'That's because we keep the lines clean and simple,' she said to Peter, as an order came in for a set of vegetable dishes with a gravy argyll to match. 'But it would be nice to venture into something a little more elaborate. Look, I've designed this wire-work fruit basket. Do you think it's possible?'

Peter frowned at it. 'It's possible, but not very practical.' He turned it this way and that. 'We could make a plain dish and apply the wire-work design afterwards. How would that suit? At least then it wouldn't distort when you put a few oranges into it. And the grapes wouldn't fall through,' he added as an afterthought, with a laugh.

'That's true.' She studied her drawing. 'Ah, that reminds me, I still owe you for that last lot of work you did.' She grinned at him. 'I realise you've got to make a living as well as me but I always have to ask you for your bill. Have you got plenty of work?'

'About as much as I can handle. I could work twenty-four hours a day and still never be finished.' He nodded into the corner. 'I've had a Communion set there waiting to be chased for the past month. But I'll get round to it. Eventually. My job's one you can't rush.'

She frowned. 'I'm afraid I've been rather demanding of your time. I'm sorry, Peter, it was selfish of me.'

'Don't be sorry. I'm glad things are going so well for you, Hannah,' he said. 'And your work always takes priority.'

She got up to go. 'Thanks, Peter. You're a good sort,' she said. 'I really don't know how I'd manage without you.'

As she closed the door behind her he gave a deep sigh. 'Oh, I'm a good sort, all right,' he said, with a trace of bitterness.

It was late that night before he laid down his tools and went home. There was a cold wind blowing and a thin drizzle made the pavements slimy. He pulled his cap down, hunched his shoulders against the wind and thrust his hands deep into his pockets. He would be glad to get home to Maggie's fireside and the stew he knew she would have waiting for him on the hob.

He passed the news stand, where the paper boy – who looked old and wizened under his muffler – was stamping his feet and shouting, '*Telegraph*! *Sheffield Telegraph*! Boss of Truswells Cutlery widowed! Read all about it!

333

Death of Mrs Clarissa Truswell!' as he tried in vain to interest the passing crowd in the local newspaper.

Peter fished in his pocket and handed the man a penny for a paper. He usually bought one each night but tonight there was an added incentive.

He scanned the front page. For all the paper boy's shouting about it there was only a small item at the foot of the page recording the death after a long illness of Mrs Clarissa Truswell, wife of Mr Thomas Truswell, head of Truswells Cutlery Company. There were brief details of the funeral and that was all.

Peter walked on, the newspaper under his arm, his hands thrust deep in his pockets. With Tom Truswell's wife now dead it would leave the field clear for him to marry again in a year or so, if for no other reason than because he still needed an heir. And he was eligible enough, goodness knows. Tall, handsome, apparently rich – although Peter still had reservations about that – and at a guess not much more than thirty. If that. The thought gave Peter no joy.

Chapter Twenty-Four

The funeral of Mrs Clarissa Truswell was a grand affair, with plumed horses and a flower-bedecked hearse draped with black crêpe, in front of which the undertaker's little mute, only recently rescued from the workhouse, walked with due solemnity.

Everybody who was anybody attended the funeral service in the parish church, all the big cutlers and their wives and all the town dignitaries. Blinds were drawn all along the route as carriage after black-draped carriage wound along the streets where hundreds of quietly respectful townspeople with bared or bowed heads waited to pay their last respects to a woman most of them had never even seen.

Of course, it was the spectacle that drew the crowds, the black, purple-plumed horses, the masses of white flowers and the ornate hearse – the corpse within it was of secondary importance – and the long-faced dignitaries, their status measured by the number of black ostrich plumes on the hats of their respective wives.

Of no less importance was the fact that a big funeral was also an excuse for an afternoon off work and, after the cortège had passed, the opportunity for an extra few hours in the beer house.

The funeral made little difference to the working day at Trippet's Wheel because there was a rush job on for Dixons. It was for tableware of a hundred place settings and servers for First Class passengers on a new trans-Atlantic steamship soon to be launched. But the lasses felt no sense of guilt at not joining the throng to pay their last respects because it wasn't from Truswells Cutlery that the bulk of their work came. Nevertheless, in order not to miss out on the spectacle, they despatched Polly to watch the procession and report back and this she did with relish and suitable embellishments.

Sitting at her desk and working on a new design Hannah wondered briefly whether she ought to have attended the funeral service in the parish church – it would not have been inappropriate since she still did a small amount of work for Truswells and Clara would most certainly have attended had she still been alive – but after some thought she was glad she had decided against it. After the episode with Tom Truswell over Joseph her feelings were that the less she had to do with the Truswell Empire the better.

A few days after the funeral Hannah visited her mother. She had heard from her sister Elsie that Jane had been ill so she took her a bunch of flowers from the flower-seller on the corner of Angel Street. As she passed Cockagnes department store she was reminded of her sister Mary. Hadn't Mrs Browning said she married a man from soft furnishings there, but he'd moved on? It was sad that she hadn't even told her family she was to be married. It was as if she had disappeared off the face of the earth as far as her family was concerned. But that had been her choice. She had made it plain long enough ago that she was ashamed of her family and wanted nothing more to do with them. It was a sad business.

She reached the house in Angel Court. It was a far cry from the home of her youth; now it was comfortable and warm, with little ornaments ranged along the mantelpiece and pictures on the walls. Her mother was sitting by the fire, a shawl round her shoulders, knitting socks while she waited for the younger girls to return from school.

'Pull t'kettle forward, lass,' she said with a smile as Hannah kissed her. 'It's good to see you.'

'I came as soon as I could, Mam.' Hannah pulled the kettle forward, then found a jam jar and arranged the flowers. 'Elsie said you were on the mend.'

'Aye, it were only a bit of a cold. I'll be back at work next week.'

'And what's this she's been telling me about Maudie starting work, Mam?'

'Oh, aye. She's off to Rotherham next week. Landed herself a job as nursemaid to a very nice family in Rotherham that her teacher knows. She's that excited . . .!' Jane laid her knitting in her lap and gazed into the fire. 'Things are so much easier now, Annie. I don't wish to speak ill of the dead, but in your dad's day I'd have had to work till I dropped, however bad I felt, or the childer would have gone hungry. But now, with Maudie ready to leave the nest, Elsie earning a good wage and Stan with

337

his own business, I can afford a few days off now and then.' She stretched her feet towards the fire. 'I never thought to see the day,' she said with a contented sigh.

'Elsie's doing well,' Hannah said as she made the tea and poured it. 'Grace – she's our finisher – is a funny, crabby old lass and I never thought she'd ever offer to teach anyone her job, but she really seems to have taken to our Elsie and she says she'll teach her all she knows. Elsie seems to love working with her, too.' She grinned. 'Doesn't get the rough edge of Grace's tongue like the rest of us.'

Jane sipped her tea. 'Aye, Elsie gets on wi' most folk. And she's allus talking about Grace and the different pieces she works on.'

'She'll be as good as Grace in a few years. She's a quick learner,' Hannah said with satisfaction. 'And silver finishing's a good trade to have at her fingertips, too.'

Jane put her cup down and studied her eldest daughter. 'You've come a long way sin' you left home, lass,' she said thoughtfully. 'Not that you haven't had your share of trouble, losing your man an' all that. But you've done well for yourself, haven't you.' She gave a satisfied nod. 'I've seen your teasets and coffee sets in t'shop winders. And t'name, Hannah Fox Silver.' She nodded again. 'By, your dad would have been proud to see that, wouldn't he?' She looked up. 'You must be worth a lot of money, Hannah.'

Hannah burst out laughing. 'I wouldn't say that, Mam. I plough most of it back into the business.' She became serious. 'But, yes, I'm doing all right. And I'm thinking I might start looking for a house up Endcliffe way for Joseph and me before long. Not a big house, mind you,

338

but a house on a hill, away from the smoke and grime of the town, where Joseph can grow up looking at green fields and blue skies.' Her face became dreamy. 'He'd like that. And so would I.'

Jane looked at her thoughtfully. 'What about if you marry again, lass?'

'Oh, I shall never do that, Mam.' Hannah shook her head vigorously. 'I told you that long enough ago. My business takes all my time and energy. Any road, I've got Joseph. He's all I need.'

'He'll grow up and want his own life one day,' Jane said sagely. 'I hope you'll not try to hold on to him then because you're left all alone.'

Hannah finished her tea and got up to go. She gave her mother a hug. 'When that happens you can come and live with me. I won't be lonely then, will I?' She fished in her bag and pulled out a half sovereign and laid it on the table. 'That's for Maudie. Give her my love and tell her I hope she'll be happy in her new job.'

Then she kissed her mother and left.

She had stayed longer than she intended and it was growing dusk, with gathering rain clouds and a chill wind blowing as she hurried along Fargate, dodging the crowds as everybody hurried to get home before the rain began.

She slipped into the cake shop and bought a gingerbread man for Joseph. She liked to take home a little treat for him. He was nine years old now, growing tall and doing well at his lessons. Reuben would have been very proud of him.

She left the cake shop and nearly fell over a small child huddled on the doorstep.

'Want a cake,' he was whimpering. 'I hungry.'

'I've got no money for cake, Alfred.' His mother, a scrawny-looking woman, held on to the handle of a dilapidated pram in which two other grubby children sat with one hand, stretching out the other to him.

He wouldn't budge. 'I hungry,' he whimpered again.

Impetuously, Hannah held out the bag with the gingerbread man in it. 'There, little lad. Share that with your brother and sister,' she said with a smile. She turned to the lad's mother. 'I hope you don't . . .' Her voice died. 'Oh, my God! Mary!'

Mary grabbed the little boy's hand. 'Come along, Alfred, quickly. We've got to go.'

'No. Wait. Mary! I know it's you, so it's no use your trying to run away. Although God knows, you don't look much like the sister I remember. Whatever's happened to you?' She laid a hand on her sister's arm.

Mary tried to shake her off, pushing a strand of lank hair away from her face at the same time. 'Nothing's happened to me. I'm perfectly all right, thank you.'

Alfred had carefully divided up the gingerbread man and given pieces to the younger children. They all gobbled their share. 'If you please, lady, could we have another one?' he asked politely.

'Be quiet, Alfred,' Mary shook his hand. 'Come along, we've got to be going.'

'Going where?' Hannah asked. Her voice hardened. 'Look here, Mary. I tried hard enough to find you after Dad died . . .'

'Dad? He's dead?' Mary broke in, her face stricken. 'I didn't know.'

'Of course you didn't.' There was a hint of impatience in Hannah's voice. 'We couldn't find you to tell you, although God knows, we tried hard enough.'

'How long has he been dead, then?' She sounded puzzled.

'Oh, must be five years now. Five years! Mary, where have you been all this time? It's been as if you'd vanished off the face of the earth.'

Mary shrugged her thin shoulders and said nothing.

'Well, now I've found you I'm coming home with you.' Hannah's voice was firm. 'I want to see where you live so I'll not lose track of you again.' Her voice softened. 'It's been so long since I saw you, Mary. There's such a lot to catch up on.'

'No. You can't come home with me, Annie. Leave us alone, can't you?' Mary tried to move off but Hannah wouldn't let go of her arm.

'Listen, Mary. I lost touch with you once, I'll not let that happen again,' she insisted. 'Let me come with you. Or at least give me your address so I can visit you.'

Mary hesitated, looking at Hannah, then she nodded and said with something of a sneer, 'Yes, all right. I'll take you home with me if that's what you want. But you won't want to come again, I can promise you that.'

'It is what I want. But wait a minute. Come with me, Alfred.' Hannah took the little boy back into the cake shop to buy three more gingerbread men, knowing that if she hadn't kept hold of him Mary would have taken him and disappeared into the crowd.

When they came out Hannah distributed the cakes between the children, then took Alfred's hand and followed Mary as she led the way, pushing the pram, an expensive model that had seen far better days. Hannah noticed that Mary's shoulders were bent under her grubby shawl, which though full of holes, was of the best cashmere. Her skirt, too, was good quality, but muddy and torn and one toe poked through her boots.

With horror, Hannah realised that the streets Mary was leading her through were streets she'd been in before, that nightmare evening nearly ten years ago when she herself was desperately looking for lodgings.

Suddenly, Mary stopped and began to pull the pram up three steps and through an open door.

'Help Mammy like you always do, Alfred,' she said, and with an expertise born of practice, the little boy steadied the back wheels as his mother bumped the pram up two flights of stairs to a room at the top of the house.

'Here we are,' she said, putting her hand to her side as she panted to regain her breath before pushing open the door.

Hannah followed her inside. The room was bare except for a bed in the corner, covered with a grubby blanket, a table with a candle stub in a candlestick on it and two chairs pushed under it.

Mary put a loaf of bread on the table. 'You won't mind if I don't offer you refreshment, will you, Hannah?' she said with more than a trace of sarcasm. 'But I'm afraid this is all I have and the children need it more than you do.' She broke off three lumps and gave it to the three children, who ate greedily and then looked for more. She fed them in this way until the loaf had gone.

Hannah watched, open-mouthed.

'Well?' Mary stared at her insolently. 'Have you seen

all you want to see? If so, you might as well leave, because as I said, I've nothing to offer you.'

Carefully, Hannah sat down on the chair just inside the door. 'I've seen more than I want, Mary,' she said quietly. 'Far more. In fact, I can hardly believe my eyes.' She looked round the squalid attic. 'What on earth's happened to you? How is it that you've come to this? If you were in need why didn't you come to me for help? Why didn't you go home to Mam?'

'And have you laugh at me? And have you say it serves me right for not wanting to come back home once I got to the Brownings? Because I didn't want to be reminded of the squalor I was brought up in? No, thank you.' Mary took the smallest child, who had begun to cry, out of the pram and cuddled him on her knee. 'I may not have much else, but I've still got my pride.'

'Oh, Mary, you ought to know us better than that,' Hannah said sadly. 'I tried to find you, you know. I went to see Mrs Browning when Dad died, because I thought you'd want to come to his funeral, but all she could tell me was that you were wed. She told me you'd married a man from Soft Furnishings at Cockagnes. Then he left and went to Cole Bros, she said. After that they'd lost track of you.'

Mary's lip curled. 'I don't suppose she told you why he left, did she? That Harold had to leave Cockagnes when they found he was consumptive?'

Hannah shook her head, her eyes never leaving Mary's face.

Mary gave a shrug and said in a flat, bitter voice, 'It was about a year after we were wed. Harold was doing really well. We'd rented a nice little house off Change Alley and got it furnished just as we wanted. We owed a bit on the furniture, but that was all right, Cockagnes did that for their employees if they bought the stuff from them, then they let them pay it off out of their wages.' She stared dreamily at the empty fireplace. 'We were really happy, and when I found out that Alfred here was on the way we were the happiest couple in the world.' She nodded towards the little boy. 'Then Harold's cough got worse and it turned out to be consumption. Oh, they said it ever so nicely, the people at Cockagnes, but the upshot was he'd have to leave because they couldn't have a consumptive working for them.' She looked up. 'I hadn't known Harold was consumptive when we wed. Well, to be fair, neither did he. We knew he'd got a bit of a cough but it was nothing much. Not that it would have made any difference, I'd still have married him. He was a lovely man. Any road, they gave him a good reference when he left Cockagnes and never mentioned anything about his health so he managed to get a job at Cole Bros. But he was only there just over six months before he got too ill and had to leave. He'd been working in the packing department so he was hidden away and it didn't matter so much that he'd got a cough. Nobody saw him, you see.'

Hannah nodded. 'What happened after that?'

'Well, when he got too ill to work I went out and did a bit of cleaning, but by that time I was up for this one' – she gave the child on her lap a squeeze – 'and I was poorly most of the time so I couldn't do much.' She sighed. 'We sold most of the furniture, what didn't have to go back to Cockagnes because it wasn't paid off, and that kept us going for a while.' She bit her lip and gazed out of the window to try and compose herself. 'But it was hard, especially with his medicine to buy as well. Not that it did any good, it was money down the drain but at least we felt we were doing something to try and make him better.' She stopped talking for several minutes, then went on, 'The worst bit was when we had to redeem his funeral club. I didn't want him to do that but we couldn't let the children starve and it put a bit of food on the table and paid the rent for a bit longer. But it meant' – she stopped, bit her lip, sniffed and went on – 'It meant he had to have a pauper's funeral.' She bowed her head. 'I was so ashamed that my Harold had to have a pauper's funeral,' she whispered. 'And after we'd done so well when we started off. He'd even talked of having his own shop one day . . .'

'You should have come to . . .' Hannah began, then stopped herself. 'Oh, Mary,' she stretched her hand out to her sister. 'I'm so very sorry.'

Mary shrugged. 'Well, things just went from bad to worse after that. Of course, we'd already left the house and gone into rooms, but now I went from room to room, each one a bit cheaper and a bit worse than the last.' She looked up. 'You see, I manage to get the odd scrubbing job but it's difficult to get work with three little ones. You see, not many houses will put up with children hanging about while you work and Alfred isn't old enough to stay at home and look after the little ones or I could leave them with him.'

'So how do you manage?'

Mary pulled a tattered purse out of her pocket and emptied it on the table. Two shillings rolled out. 'I earned that from a week's scrubbing. But I had to leave the children out in the yard. It was all right for the little ones in the pram, but Alfred didn't like being tied to the gatepost. 'Specially when it rained.'

'Oh, Mary. Why didn't you come to me? I would have helped you. Gladly,' Hannah said.

'How could I do that? After the cruel way I'd behaved towards you when you were in trouble I could hardly come crawling to you and expect any better treatment.' She shook her head and went on bitterly, 'They say your chickens eventually come home to roost; well, mine certainly have. I know now how you must have felt then, Hannah, and I'm ashamed of what I did to you.' She closed her eyes briefly and tears squeezed out. 'God, I was a toffee-nosed little prig in those days. Well, I've got my come-uppance, haven't I?' She gave a mirthless little laugh. 'Do you know, I look in the shop windows and see all that Hannah Fox Silver displayed and I wonder what passers-by would say if they knew that I was the sister of Hannah Fox. Laughable, really isn't it?' But she didn't laugh.

Hannah got up from her chair and held out her hand. 'Come with me, Alfred. We're going to the market to see what we can find.' She saw the look of distrust on Mary's face. 'Don't worry. We shall be back before long,' she said.

Alfred trotted happily along by her side, holding her hand and his eyes lit up when he saw all the good things she was buying from the market.

'Do you like apples, Alfred?' she asked.

He hunched his shoulders. 'Don't know.'

'Do you like oranges?'

The same response.

'Well, I'm sure you like hot pies.'

'Mm. I like pies.' His mouth watered at the thought.

She bought as much as she could carry and then paid a passing coal merchant to leave a bag of coal at the address she gave. It was quite a struggle to climb the two steep flights of stairs with all the baggage she was carrying. Alfred, carrying two of the lighter bags, struggled happily up behind her.

When she opened the door Mary and the other two children were still sitting where she had left then.

'Look, Mammy, look!' Alfred cried. 'Lots of nice things.'

'There, now,' Hannah said briskly. 'These things should see you through the next few days. What about the rent?'

'Oh, you don't need to worry about that. We'll be leaving shortly,' Mary said quickly.

'To go somewhere worse than this? Some rat-infested cellar?' For the first time Hannah's voice was scathing. 'Come on, how much rent do you owe?'

'Three weeks,' Mary said reluctantly.

'And have you got coal for the fire?'

'We don't feel the cold too much. We go to bed early,' Mary said.

'Well, you won't need to do that tonight. The coal man will be leaving a bag of coal shortly and there are candles in this bag.' Hannah rummaged till she found them. She put a heap of coins on the table. 'That will pay the rent you owe.' She pinched her lip thoughtfully, then added another coin. 'And that's for anything I might have forgotten.' She laid a hand gently on Mary's thin shoulder. 'I know you don't like accepting help, Mary, but just think of it as being for the children's sake.' Her voice dropped.

'It doesn't do any of us any harm to be forced to swallow our pride now and then, painful though it might be. I'm your sister, Mary, I can't see you suffer like this and do nothing. Try and accept my help with good grace. Remember, I've been there. I know what it's like.' She gathered up her bags. 'I'll come and see you again in a few days.' She looked round. 'I might even be able to find you somewhere a bit more salubrious to live.' She gave Mary's shoulders a squeeze and kissed her cheek.

After Hannah had left Mary leaned her head on her hands and wept. She wept with shame to think her plight had been discovered, but more than that she wept with relief to know she was no longer alone.

Chapter Twenty-Five

Hannah couldn't concentrate on her work during the next few days; she couldn't get the plight of her sister Mary out of her mind. Strangely, she had nothing but sympathy for Mary, the sister who had had such aspirations that she had completely rejected her humble beginnings, the sister who had found Hannah herself nothing but an irritating nuisance when she was the one who needed help. It was a cruel irony that Mary's position now was far worse than anything she had ever known as a child; and much worse than anything Hannah had had to endure.

'You're not yourself, Missus, are you?' Polly said one morning when she brought in the tea. 'Is summat wrong? T'lasses are all asking.' She frowned. 'That last lot of work went out well on time so it can't be that. And the new coffee sets you designed look a treat now they're finished.' She beamed. 'I feel reet proud when I see your mark on them pieces, Missus.'

'Yes, Polly, I must confess I do, too.' Hannah smiled up

at her. Her smile faded and she sighed. 'No, it's nowt to do with work, Polly. It's personal. To tell the truth I'm worried about my younger sister. She's a widow with three little ones and is in desperate need of somewhere better to live. I said I'd find her a place but I've not been able to find anything yet.' She frowned. 'I never thought it would be so difficult.'

Polly pinched her lip. 'Marjorie's old aunt has just died. She's taking t'day off tomorrow so that they can clear her house. I wonder if she might be able to put in a word for you wi' t'landlord. T'cottage is just off t'Moor. Shall I ask her?'

'No, it'll be best if I have a word with her myself. Ask her to come in and see me, will you?' Hannah sipped her tea. 'Thanks, Polly. Ah, this tea's good. Just what I needed.'

Hannah lost no time. Assuring Marjorie that she wouldn't lose any pay for time lost she persuaded her to take her to her aunt's cottage. It was small but clean, in a yard with a tap in the middle shared by three other cottages and it was adequately furnished. She offered Marjorie a price for everything in the cottage which she knew was far in excess of what a second-hand dealer would have paid and then went to see the landlord and paid a full month's rent.

After that she went to see Mary to tell her about her new home.

'It's all furnished, down to the last saucepan,' she told her. 'It may not be what you'd have chosen for yourself . . .'

'Beggars can't be choosers, Annie. I realise that and I

can't tell you how grateful I am for what you're doing for us,' Mary said. Then her innate pride reasserted itself and she glared at Hannah. 'But you must understand I'm only taking your charity because of the children, Hannah. I wouldn't touch a penny of your money if it wasn't for them.'

'I know that, love. And one day you can pay me back, if that's what you want. We'll call it a loan, if you like.' She put her hand on Mary's arm. 'There's no need to be touchy about it, lass.'

Mary's eyes filled with angry tears. 'The trouble is, you make me feel so bloody guilty! That's why I'm touchy. I can't forget how I treated you when you were in trouble. I was a bitch to you. A reet bloody bitch.'

Hannah nodded. 'Yes. You were. I'll not deny that. But that's no reason why I should treat you the same way. Any road, that's all in the past. And as you say, it's for the sake of the children I'm helping you now. If it was just you I'd let you rot in t'gutter.' She grinned. 'There, does that make you feel better?'

Mary gave her a hug. 'Oh, Annie, you're a brick. And I'm an ungrateful pig.' She dashed her hand across her face, leaving a grubby mark. 'No, I'm not. I'm so grateful I can't tell you. Thanks, Annie.' She hugged her again.

Hannah looked round the squalid little attic. 'Oh, come on, let's get you out of this place.' She grinned. 'Unless you've got so attached to it you want to stay here, that is.'

'God, no!' Mary picked up a small bundle of clothes from the corner and dumped it on the end of the pram. 'This is all we've got. Let's go.'

'Come on, then.' Hannah took Alfred's hand. 'But first I'd better take you home with me so you can all have a bath. I told the landlord you were a respectable widow who kept her children spotlessly clean, so I must make sure he doesn't see you in this state.'

Mary sighed. 'I know. We're filthy. But it's so hard. The tap's in the next street and then I have to carry the water up all these stairs.' She looked round in disgust. 'God, I'll be that glad to get out of this place you can't imagine!'

'Indeed I can, lass,' Hannah replied with feeling.

Later that day, when Mary and the children were all sitting round Hannah's table, their faces shining with soap, Mary said, 'Oh, Hannah, you don't know how good it was to get into a tub of hot water.' She sighed. 'I did try to keep us all clean as best I could but I was fighting a losing battle all the while.' She bit her lip at the memory.

'I know, lass. But it's all behind you now so you can forget it and make a fresh start. Maggie from across the yard found me those clothes for the children – don't ask me where from – Maggie's a marvel! – and you can keep that dress of mine you're wearing. It's a bit big at the moment but when you start to eat properly again you'll soon fill it out.'

Mary didn't reply but her eyes filled with grateful tears and Hannah knew exactly what was in her mind.

Ignoring the tears Hannah went on briskly. 'You must go and see Mam when you're settled in to your new house. You shouldn't have stayed away all these years. It nearly broke Mam's heart.'

'I know. I will go. How is she?'

'She's fine. You'll see for yourself when you go. And you will go, won't you?'

'Yes, I've said I'll go.'

Hannah wasn't convinced. 'Promise! That's all I ask, Mary. Promise you'll go and see her.'

Mary nodded. 'I promise.'

'Right.' Hannah handed her the key to her new home. 'Off you go, then. It's number two Grayson Court, down at the bottom of the Moor on the right.'

'Aren't you coming with me?' Mary said in surprise.

Hannah shook her head. 'No. You're on your own now, Mary. The rent's paid for a month and you'll find the larder stocked with groceries. That'll give you a start. After that it's up to you.'

Mary bit her lip. 'I don't know how to thank you, Annie.'

'Go and see Mam. That's all the thanks I need.'

She watched them go. Although the pram was still old and shabby, all the children were neat and clean and as Mary pushed it, with Alfred hanging on to the handle, her shoulders had lifted and she held her head high. Hannah was confident she would manage because she had no doubt that the children's grandmother would be only too happy to look after them so that Mary could find work. All it would take was for Mary to swallow her pride and ask.

After her sister had gone Hannah gazed round her own comfortable living room. Joseph was in his favourite position, stretched full length on the hearthrug, reading, the clock in the recess was ticking steadily and the firelight glinted on a small silver figure on the chiffoniere, the only piece of silver she had in the house. She offered up a silent prayer of gratitude for her own good fortune, knowing that if it hadn't been for Clara Walters befriending her that terrible night her life might have turned out so differently and she could so easily have ended up like Mary – or worse. It was a sobering thought.

Finding Mary somewhere to live caused Hannah to turn her thoughts to her own affairs over the next few days. She had lived in the little cottage on Balm Green ever since her marriage. Indeed, she had been so busy looking after her business that she had never given any serious thought to living anywhere else. But it suddenly occurred to her that perhaps now was the time for a move.

'I've thought about it long and hard,' she said to Peter as she watched him at work on his bench. She often called in at his workshop before she left Trippet's Wheel – he always worked longer hours than she did – and talked over the day's events. She had even confided Mary's plight to him, something she had not told another soul.

'Thought about what?' He put down his punch, examined what he had just done and then looked at her, smiling. 'You've said that twice, that you've thought about it long and hard, but you haven't yet said what "it" might be.'

'Oh, haven't I?' She sounded surprised. 'Well, I'm wondering if I should buy a house. Not an enormous one,' she added hurriedly. 'Just a house with a garden, somewhere up Endcliffe way perhaps, or Fulwood, where Joseph will be able to see the hills and breathe good fresh air.'

He nodded. 'I'm surprised you've never considered doing that before, Hannah,' he said. 'After all, you're doing very well in your business now so I'm sure you could afford to.' He laughed. 'You're quite a name in the town. Everywhere I go I see Hannah Fox silver glinting at me.'

'Yes, but that's only because you recognise my style,' she said. 'Most of it you've worked on, too, one way or another.'

He nodded. 'That's true.' He stroked his chin. 'But with regard to buying a house out of town, I wouldn't blame you. Most people get out the minute they can afford to.'

'You haven't,' she pointed out. 'And you must be doing quite well yourself; goodness, you've got so much work on hand you hardly have time to sleep, in fact I sometimes wonder you don't put up a bed in the corner, but you still stay with Maggie.'

'It's handy, living there.' He shrugged. 'Anyway, she looks after me well so I've seen no reason to move.'

'Neither have I, I suppose,' she said thoughtfully. 'And I'd certainly miss Maggie. She's good to Joseph. And to me.' She frowned. 'But it would be better for Joseph to live where he can see blue sky and lambs on the hills, wouldn't it, Peter? He so enjoys it when I take him up there on the tram and we go for walks.'

'Oh, yes. Far better,' he agreed. 'Have you anywhere in mind?'

She shook her head. 'No.'

He grinned. 'I suppose you're waiting for somewhere like Cutwell Hall to be up for sale, then?'

'Don't be daft!' She grinned back. 'I wouldn't want a place half as grand as that even if I could afford it, which of course I can't. Anyway, Cutwell Hall's not likely to be up for sale, is it?' She looked at him closely. 'Or have you heard something I haven't about Truswells Cutlery?'

'No, only that they've sold another property,' he said with a smile. 'I suppose it's their continuing process of "consolidation".' His smile widened. 'But I'm not sure how much further they can consolidate without disappearing altogether!'

'We do very little work for them now,' she said thoughtfully. 'But that's not really significant because they don't like paying our prices and we prefer better quality work so it suits all round. They do seem to be aiming at the cheap end of the market these days.'

'Well, we shall see, shan't we?' He selected a punch, put it down and picked up another.

'But you think I would be sensible to consider buying a house, Peter?' she persisted.

'Yes, I told you that. In fact, if you'd like me to, I'm willing to give you the benefit of my not very expert opinion when you go to view.'

'Thanks, Peter. I shall keep you up to that.' She got up from her chair. 'Now I must go. Maggie will be filling Joseph up with cakes and pastries and he won't want his tea. And I want to call and see my mother and tell her about Mary on my way home, too.'

'Has your sister settled in well?'

'I don't know. I thought it best not to visit. I don't want to appear on her doorstep like Lady Bountiful checking up to see how her gifts are being enjoyed.'

Peter burst out laughing. 'I like that. Lady Bountiful. But I must say the picture it conjures up is of an enormous dowager lady with a hat laden with cherries that nod as you speak.'

'Oh, dear. I'm not like that, Peter, am I?' she asked, slightly affronted.

'No, of course you're not, silly. You're neither enormous, nor a dowager lady.'

'I haven't got a hat with cherries, either.'

'There you are, then. In any case, you're far too down to earth to play the Lady Bountiful.'

After Hannah had left Peter resumed work. As he worked he went over their conversation. Of course Hannah should be thinking of moving to a bigger and better house, it was something she should have done a long time ago. He had been aware of this but could never bring himself to suggest it for the purely selfish reason that he couldn't bear the thought of Orchard Court without her. The knowledge that she was living and sleeping nearby had been a source of solace to him for a long time now, although he knew they would never be more than good friends; she had made that quite plain from the beginning.

It was a friendship that he valued too highly to risk losing it by letting her know how much more than friendship he would like to offer.

He examined the work he had just done. It wasn't straight. He threw down his punch. He remembered once saying to Tom Truswell that his work left no room for mistakes. Well, he'd made one now, because his mind had been far away on other things, so somehow he'd got to put it right. It served him right for being such an arrogant bastard. He was just thankful that it wasn't one of Hannah's pieces, so it wouldn't bear the mark of Hannah Fox.

After Hannah left Peter she made her way to the Wicker and Angel Court, where her mother lived. It was late afternoon on a warm spring day, and a hazy sun was trying without much success to penetrate the smoke-laden atmosphere. Everywhere she looked, people seemed to be scurrying about like rats in a run, never even noticing the filth in the gutters and on the roads, heedless of the clatter of the trams and carts, oblivious of the stink that pervaded everything and got worse near the river.

Hannah could only suppose it was because she had been thinking of Endcliffe and remembering the fresh air and green grass, the heather on the hills and the clear, open spaces that the atmosphere of the town suddenly seemed so oppressive. Either it was that, or the sight of the flower-seller on the corner selling bunches of prim-roses, reminding her of the delicate yellow clumps she had once sat by the stream to paint.

The thought of the stream brought her up with a jolt and with an effort she closed her mind to memories of warm summer days, of dark, laughing eyes, of hands that were gentle and caressing; memories that even after all these years were painful to recall.

She quickened her step as she crossed Lady's Bridge into the Wicker and the narrow streets that led to Angel Court.

The little cottage seemed to be bursting at the seams. Elsie and Stan had just come in from their day's work,

Fanny and Agnes were home from school and Mary was there with her three children. Jane sat contentedly in her chair by the side of the fireplace, nursing the youngest grandchild, who was grizzling fitfully.

'Look who's here, Annie!' she called excitedly as soon as Hannah set foot inside the door. 'Look who's come to see us! It's our Mary. She's come back!'

Hannah went and kissed Mary. 'It's good to see you, lass,' she said. 'You're looking well. The children, too.' She turned a little away from everyone else in the room and winked at her sister. 'Is everything all right?'

'Everything's lovely,' Mary said. She dropped her voice. 'Thanks, Annie.'

Hannah made a deprecating gesture. 'That's good,' was all she said.

'I knew she'd come back one day,' Jane was saying smugly to anyone who would listen. 'And look, three little ones, and all the image of their grandpa.' She rocked the baby, trying to stop his whimpering.

Hannah smiled. Jane's eyesight wasn't so good these days and imagination had done the rest. As far as she could see there was no vestige of Nat Fox in any of them.

'Poor lass has had a dreadful hard time,' Jane continued. 'With her husband dying like that. But she's fallen on her feet now, finding that little cottage and I've said I'll look after the children while she's at work if she can find herself a place.' She nodded sagely. She felt the baby's forehead. 'He's feverish, Mary. Do you think he's after more teeth?'

'He's been like that all day. He's got a bit of a rash, too.'

Jane nodded. 'I expect it's teeth, then.' She looked up at Hannah. 'I suppose you don't know where Mary could get work, Annie?'

'Hannah's done quite . . .' Mary bit her tongue at Hannah's warning glance.

'Have you tried your old place? Mrs Browning?' Hannah broke in. 'You were happy there before and it's right near, in the town.'

'I'm going to work at Cockagnes when I leave school,' Fanny said importantly. 'I want to be a shop lady and serve rich customers.'

'Mind and pay attention at school, then. Shop girls have to be able to add up very quickly,' Hannah said with a smile.

'Oh, she can already. She's very good at sums. Didn't she tell you? She's top of the class,' Jane said, looking proudly at her young daughter.

'*I'm* going to be a nursemaid, like Maudie,' Agnes said, not to be outdone. Suddenly, her face crumpled. 'When's Maudie coming back, Mam? I didn't like her going away.'

'She'll be back in a week or two to see us,' Jane said soothingly. She raised her eyebrows towards Hannah. 'She's only been gone four days.' She was silent for several minutes, then gave a business-like sniff. 'I hope she's minding her manners. She can be a little madam at times.'

Hannah gave her shoulders a squeeze. 'She'll be fine, Mam. Don't worry. And back home to see us before we know it.'

Jane patted her hand. 'Aye, lass. You're right.'

Hannah looked round the table at her family and offered up a silent prayer of thanks for Mary's return

360

before her thoughts turned to her father. What a pity he had allowed his life to be blighted by his jealousy toward the Truswells. For that was what it had been, hidden under the guise of a past injustice. The trouble was, he had allowed himself to be ruled by it instead of trying to rise above it.

She went to the door. 'I must go. Joseph will be wanting his tea. I'll come and see you, Mary. Where did you say you lived?'

Mary smiled at her conspiratorially. 'Number two Grayson Court, at the bottom of the Moor. We'll always be pleased to see you, Hannah.'

Chapter Twenty-Six

Every Saturday afternoon Hannah cleaned the house. It was what she had always done, a habit left over from when Reuben was alive. It never even occurred to her that she could easily employ someone else to do it for her now that her business was doing so well.

It was a hot day in early June and for once Joseph was not content to amuse himself while she worked. Neither was he willing to help, as he sometimes did.

'You could at least tidy your bedroom instead of just moping about the place,' Hannah said with a trace of irritation, brushing a strand of hair back from her forehead with her forearm.

'It isn't untidy,' he answered crossly, 'and neither is the rest of the house, Mam. Any road, it's too hot for tidying bedrooms.'

'I'm hot, too,' she reminded him. 'But complaining about it doesn't help. It's got to be done so I just have to get on with it.'

'Why?'

She frowned. 'Why what?'

'Why can't you leave it for once, Mam? Why can't we go out somewhere? It's much too hot to stay indoors.'

She looked round the dim little living room where there was hardly a thing out of place. Joseph was right. Why couldn't she leave it for once? She nodded and untied her overall, smiling at him.

'All right, Joey, we'll go out. Where would you like to go? For a picnic?'

His face lit up. 'Oh, yes, Mam. I'd like that. I'll help you pack the basket.'

Between them they packed a basket with a few sandwiches, a cake Maggie had made and a drink and then they set off to catch the horse bus.

'Where shall we go?' Joseph said.

She glanced down at him. He looked a bit pale but he was animated enough.

'Let's have an adventure. Let's catch the first bus that comes along and see where it takes us,' she said gaily.

'Oh, that's a good idea. Look, here comes one now.' Joseph began to jump up and down. 'It says it's going to the Fulwood Road.'

They climbed up the stairs to the open top. Now Hannah wished she hadn't been so rash as to suggest they should catch the first bus that came along. True, this bus would take them within walking distance of open country, but to get there they would have to pass Cutwell Hall and she didn't particularly want to do this. But Joseph, oblivious of her misgivings, was chattering happily as the bus clattered along.

'What shall we do, Mam? Go as far as the bus takes us

and then walk out on to the hills till we find a good picnic place?'

She smiled at him. 'That's the general idea.'

They left the bus at its terminus and started to walk. The houses were thinning out as they climbed the hill and before long they passed the great wrought-iron gates of Cutwell Hall. Hannah tried to hurry past but Joseph went up and pressed his face against the bars.

'Look, Mam, there's a big house down here,' he called. 'Is that where the Queen lives?'

'No, love, the Queen lives in a palace.'

'Isn't that a palace?'

'No. That's just a very big house.'

'Well, it looks like a palace to me. It must have about a hundred rooms. I should think you'd get lost finding your way about.'

'Indeed you could,' Hannah said with a nostalgic sigh.

He turned away, frowning. 'I don't think I should like to live in such a big house. I expect it's got ghosts.'

'Nonsense.' She caught his hand. 'Come on, let's see if we can find a stream where we can paddle our feet. Would you like that?'

'Yes. It's very hot, isn't it?' He looked up at her. 'But how do you know there is a stream?'

'Oh, there's always a stream somewhere on the hills,' she told him vaguely.

'As long as we don't have to walk too far. I'm getting tired, Mam.'

She looked down at him. His face was flushed now, but that could simply be the heat of the day. 'You can't be tired, we've only walked a mile,' she said. 'Loosen your collar, it'll help to cool you.'

The sun shone in a cloudless sky and there was a gentle cooling breeze. Hannah enjoyed tramping through the heather and over the soft warm grass and she took off her hat so that she could feel the wind in her hair. As she walked and gazed about her, the once familiar countryside revived memories; memories of a seventeen-year-old girl on her afternoon off, clutching her sketch pad; memories of horses' hooves muffled by the mossy ground, sounds that quickened the heartbeat; memories that were best forgotten. She gave herself a mental shake and looked to where Joseph was running ahead, jumping over tussocks of heather, leading the way. The open country seemed to have revived him; he was no longer complaining of feeling tired. She smiled to herself, glad they had come.

Suddenly, he shouted, 'I've found it, Mam! I've found the stream!' He was already untying his shoes and taking them off. 'Can I paddle in it?' His eyes were bright with excitement.

'Yes, love, of course you can. But you'll find it's very cold, even on a hot day like this.' She sat down with her back to a tree and watched him ease his feet, one at a time, into the water, snatching them out again and again until, used to the temperature, he was soon splashing about happily. She closed her eyes. It was serendipity, happy accident, that he should have chosen this spot, the very place she had been to so many times before, and on afternoons such as this. Why had he come here? she asked herself. What had drawn him here, almost to the very spot where he had been conceived on a summer's day much like this one? As she watched him her eyes glazed and she saw in his place a young girl holding her skirts above her knees, paddling in the water and a young man watching from the very spot where she was now sitting. She almost expected to turn and see the young man watching now . . . To hear muffled hoof beats . . .

Then sanity prevailed. There was nothing magical in Joseph discovering this place. He could hardly fail to reach the stream from the direction he had taken and this was the most sheltered spot. Deliberately, she turned her head. There was no one there. She had never expected there would be.

She turned back and watched Joseph playing happily in the stream and her heart swelled. She loved him, desperately. How could she ever regret the folly that had given him to her, even though it could so easily have ruined her life. She pulled her thoughts back to the present.

'Come along, darling, come and dry your feet. We'll find another spot for our picnic.'

'But I like it here, Mam.' He continued splashing. 'Any road, I'm not hungry.'

'Another five minutes, then.'

Ten minutes later she managed to coax him out of the water and back into his shoes and stockings.

He stretched out on the grassy bank. 'Oh, let's picnic here, Mam, it's nice here,' he said. 'Then we can go home. I don't want to walk any further. I'm tired.'

'You weren't tired splashing about in the stream,' she reminded him with a smile.

'Well, I am now.' He rummaged in the picnic basket and found a sandwich but he only ate half of it and didn't

366

want any cake. He lay on the grass looking up through the tree at the blue sky while she repacked the basket.

'Come on, then,' she said, getting to her feet. 'You were anxious to go home a minute ago.'

'I've got a headache.'

'Put your cap back on, then. I expect it's the heat from the sun.'

As they started the long walk back to pick up the horse bus Hannah filled her lungs with the fresh, clear air and gazed into the distance, where the heat shimmered in the sunlight.

'Oh, wouldn't it be wonderful to live up here, away from the town,' she said, speaking her thoughts aloud.

He looked up at her. 'What, out here on this hill, Mam? In a hut? Or are there caves? I wouldn't mind living in a cave.'

'You would when the weather got cold,' she laughed and gave him a playful push. 'No, silly. In a house. A house like the ones we passed when we first got off the bus, maybe. Then we'd be really handy to come on walks like this.'

'Mm?' He made a doubtful noise. 'It's a long way from school.'

'Well, you'd have to be very grown up and catch a horse bus or a tram.'

'The bus made me feel sick today.'

She looked at him with concern. 'You've never complained of that before.'

'It's never done it before. I expect it's because my throat is a bit sore. How much further have we got to go before we catch the bus back?'

'A little way yet. We've only just passed Cutwell Hall.'

They walked for nearly another mile, getting slower and slower in spite of Hannah trying to urge Joseph on.

'But I told you, I don't feel well, Mam,' he said at last. 'I've got a most awful headache. Can we stop and rest for a bit?'

'What here? There's nowhere ...' Suddenly, Hannah spotted an empty house. It stood only a few feet from the road behind a laurel hedge and had a flat, Georgian façade. 'Well, I suppose you could sit on the steps of that house for a few minutes. It's nice and shady and cool there.'

He sat down and closed his eyes. 'My head aches dreadfully and my throat's sore,' he complained.

'Well, it's not much further to the bus.' She was craning her neck to see in at the windows as she spoke but they were too high. 'You sit there and rest a bit. I'm just going to see if I can get round to the back of the house.'

'Why?'

'Because this could be the very house we're looking for,' she said excitedly.

'I didn't know we were looking for a house. Any road, if you do get round the back you won't be able to get inside it,' Joseph said irritably.

'No, but I can look through the windows.' She left him and disappeared through the wooden gate at the side of the house.

The walled garden was not very big but after being used to nothing more than a shared yard it looked enormous. There was a lawn bordered with flower beds rioting with carnations, red-hot-pokers, delphiniums, phlox, and geraniums, as well as roses that climbed and rambled over the walls. Through a gap in the hedge at the bottom of the garden could be glimpsed a small orchard with fruit trees. Already the birds were busy with the cherries.

Cupping her hands to keep out the sunlight Hannah peered through the window to a stone-flagged kitchen with a black range. On the other side of the back door was another room with a marble fireplace and glass doors out into the garden. This room stretched right through to the front; she could see the laurel bushes through the end window from where she stood.

She looked up at the house. From what she could see it was perfect for her needs. And somehow it *felt* right. The moment she had set foot inside the front gate it had seemed welcoming and she had had the strangest feeling that she had somehow 'come home'.

She went back to where Joseph was still sitting on the step.

'Come and have a look round at the back garden, Joey,' she urged. 'There are cherry trees. I'm sure no one would mind if you ate one or two. The birds seem to be having a feast.'

Reluctantly, he followed her down to the orchard and ate a couple of cherries.

'Well, what do you think, Joey?' she said, turning to gaze back at the house.

He shrugged. 'Can we go home, Mam? My throat is getting worse,' he said.

She looked down at him. His face was indeed very flushed. 'Yes,' she said, beginning to be alarmed. 'I think perhaps we should. I didn't realise you felt quite so ill, darling.'

'Well, I kept telling you,' he grumbled.

'I thought it was just the sun.'

By the time they reached home Joseph could hardly speak and a dull rash had spread over his forehead.

She put him to bed and called Maggie.

'I took him for a picnic because he said he was hot, but he's plainly quite ill so I'm afraid I may have done him more harm than good,' she said anxiously.

Maggie took one look at him, then picked up his hand and looked at his wrists, where there were already tell-tale signs of the rash spreading.

'Have any of the boys at school complained of feeling ill, Joey?' she asked, watching him closely.

He nodded, then winced because it hurt his head. 'Nash Major was ill with a sore throat and his brother, Nash Minor, was sick the other day,' he mumbled.

'Anyone else?'

'A couple of boys have had bad headaches. Mr Shackleton let them put their heads down on their desks.' He closed his eyes. 'Mr Shackleton said he thought they might be sickening for the chickenpox. Have I got the chickenpox, Maggie?'

'I shouldn't be surprised, love.' Maggie went to the door, motioning Hannah to do the same. 'I don't think it's the chickenpox, Hannah,' she said quietly, shaking her head. 'I think it's much worse than that. I think it's the smallpox he's got.'

Hannah covered her mouth with her hands in horror. 'No, Maggie! You must be mistaken. It's the heat. I shouldn't have taken him out this afternoon. It was too much for him.' She went back to the bed. 'Look, it's just a heat rash, that's all it is.' She brushed the hair away from his forehead to reveal the spreading rash.

Maggie pulled her hand away gently and shook her head. 'No, love, it isn't,' she said in a low voice. 'I've seen this before. I've nursed folk through it, too. Heaven knows why I've never caught it myself, but I never have, thank God. I've allus reckoned it's because my mother had the cow pox before I was born.' She put her hand on Hannah's arm. 'Don't worry, love. I know what to do. I'll look after t'lad. But you'd better keep out of t'road if you don't want to tek it yourself.'

'I can't do that! I can't keep away. He's my son! I have to nurse him myself,' Hannah cried.

'Not if you've got any sense,' Maggie said sternly, pushing her towards the door. 'You don't want to catch it, do you? You've got a business to run, remember. You can't afford to risk taking it to your lasses now, can you? You could lose three parts of your work-force. Not that you'll be able to go to work for the next three weeks. It can take that long to find out whether or not you've already teken it.'

'You mean I might have caught it already?' Hannah said.

Maggie shrugged. 'Can't tell.' Her expression softened. 'Now, go downstairs and get me some warm water and a cloth so I can bathe t'lad's poor aching head. Oh, and another thing,' she said as Hannah turned to go, 'tell Peter he'll have to fend for himself for a few days. But speak to him through t'window, don't go too near. We don't want him teking it. Tell him I'll not risk going back home, not now I've been where it is.'

Hannah went downstairs and put a kettle on to boil. Then she went across the yard and called to Peter.

'Don't come near.' She held up her hand and took a step back as he opened the door.

He listened to what she had to say, his face creased with concern. When she had finished telling him, tears were running freely down her cheeks and she brushed them away with the palm of her hand. 'And Maggie says I mustn't go into work, either,' she said. 'Not that I could leave Joseph, any road, even though Maggie won't let me into his room,' she added.

'Don't worry about work, Hannah,' he said. 'You know your lasses will carry on as if you were there. They won't slack.'

'I know that,' she sniffed. 'They're good lasses.'

'And if anything goes wrong they can always come to me. I'll make sure things run smoothly, don't worry.'

She nodded. 'Yes, I know you'll take care of things, Peter. You're a good friend.'

She went back into her own house. He stood and watched her go. Nobody would ever know what it had cost him to stand four feet away from her, seeing her distress, when all he had wanted to do was to take her in his arms and kiss away her tears and tell her that all would be well. But all wouldn't be well. If Joseph had contracted smallpox there was more than a chance that he would die. Worse even than that to his mind, Hannah might take the disfiguring disease herself. That she too might die he refused to even contemplate.

Maggie was tireless in looking after Joseph. She bathed his fevered body and put salve on the horrible eruptions as they spread until they covered him from head to foot.

Hannah could only provide food for Maggie – she herself had no appetite – and watch helplessly from the doorway. Maggie wouldn't let her near the sick bed,

372

reminding her with perfect truth that in his delirium the lad neither knew nor cared whether she was there or not.

Each day there was a little gift left on the doorstep. A few grapes, a couple of apples, a posy of flowers, always wrapped in the day's newspaper. Peter knew that she needed to be kept in touch with the outside world and this was his way of showing his concern. She realised this and was grateful.

Joseph had been ill for nearly a fortnight. Maggie assured Hannah that he was holding his own and if he could get through the next twenty-four hours he would be out of immediate danger.

She was sitting on the doorstep, nibbling a biscuit and reading the newspaper Peter had left the previous evening. She felt vaguely out of sorts, probably because she hadn't eaten properly for several days. It was reported that the smallpox epidemic seemed to have been confined to a small area and doctors were confident they had it under control. She gave a mirthless smile when she read this. The doctor had come to see Joseph, taken one look at him and backed away, saying Maggie was doing exactly the right thing and to let him know if the lad got any worse. He hadn't been near since.

On the inside page there was an article about Queen Victoria's Silver Jubilee, which would take place the year after next, 1887. There was an idea being floated at Cutler's Hall about whether a gift of silver should be sent to Her Majesty from the Sheffield cutlers. She screwed her eyes up, trying to read the small print, but it all seemed to run together, making her head ache. And it was hot, so very hot. She leaned against the door post, fanning herself with the newspaper. A gift of silver. She wondered idly what they had in mind and imagined the quarrelling and ill-feeling that would certainly take place as they tried to decide what the gift should be and who should make it. She sighed. It didn't matter to her. It was nothing she was likely to be involved with.

'Hannah!' It was Maggie's voice from the top of the stairs.

Hurriedly, she got to her feet, clutching the door post as the world swung round like a Catherine wheel. She closed her eyes and steadied herself. She'd got up too quickly. She regained her balance and hurried through to the stairfoot door.

Maggie beamed down at her. 'Joseph thinks he'd like a few pobs.' Bread soaked in milk was the staple food of invalids.

She sank to her knees. 'You mean . . . ?'

Maggie nodded, still beaming. 'He's past the worst.'

Tears streamed down Hannah's face. 'Oh, thank God. Thank God. I'll get some for him right away and bring them up to him.' She got to her feet, took two steps, then sank down in a dead faint.

Maggie came slowly down the stairs, shaking her head. It was no more than she had expected in spite of all her precautions. Twelve days. That was the time it took. She sat on the bottom stair and stroked Hannah's brow where the first signs of the dreaded disease were already beginning to appear.

She bowed her head. Thank God, Joseph would live, he was young and strong, although he would always bear the marks of the disease. She could only pray that Hannah would have the same resilience.

374

Chapter Twenty-Seven

Hannah didn't remember much about the next few days except that she felt so ill she was ready to die. It was only the touch of a cooling cloth on her brow or the blessed relief of soothing salve that brought her back from the edge of the welcoming abyss, albeit at times reluctantly, reminding her of her duty, reminding her that she couldn't die, Joseph was ill, she couldn't leave him orphaned. But Joey would be all right, Maggie would care for him. Relieved, she began to sink again. The cooling cloth brought her back once more; this time it was Trippet's Wheel that needed her. There was so much work to do there, she had so many plans. What would her lasses do without her? She couldn't let them down. But she couldn't fight . . .

Sometimes, in the see-saw between life and death she saw Peter's face floating above hers and she felt comforted. Peter would look after everything. He was a good friend. At other times she saw the handsome face of Tom Truswell, laughing, claiming his son. At that she became distressed, calling out in a croaking voice that didn't belong to her, 'Tom! Please, Tom . . .' but her voice gave out before she could complete the sentence begging him not to take her lad away.

Maggie was tired and her legs were beginning to swell. She had nursed Joseph, now he was mending and being fretful and demanding even though, or perhaps partly because his mother lay at death's door. She carried on because she must but she didn't know how much longer she could keep going.

'Keep out! I don't want you teking it, too.' Frantically, she waved Peter away as he appeared in the doorway of Hannah's bedroom.

He took no notice but came into the room. 'I reckon it's too late to worry about that, Maggie,' he said wryly. 'You had to call me in to carry Hannah up to bed so there's no point in trying to keep me out now. Anyway, I've been thinking about it. I seem to remember I was vaccinated when I was at school in London. I couldn't have been more than about eight years old. Whole classes were done. It caused a great fuss at the time as I recall because parents thought the doctors were giving us smallpox, not protecting us against it.' He gazed down at Hannah's face, ugly with the marks of the disease. 'Poor love,' he said under his breath, watching Maggie moisten her lips as she croaked Tom Truswell's name in her delirium.

Maggie looked up at him. Although they never spoke about it she knew his secret. 'With luck she'll not be too badly marked,' she whispered. 'I've this salve. I had it from an old country woman years ago. I used it on the lad and his marks are fading nicely. There'll be one or two, mind you, where he would keep scratching.' She looked up at the ceiling where Joseph was calling her name. 'Aw, is there no peace?'

'I'll go up to him. I'll read to him for a while, that'll keep him amused,' Peter said. He gave an apologetic grin. 'I've put a stew on to cook, Maggie. I think I've done it the way you do, I've watched you enough times. I hope it'll be all right. It smells good, anyway.'

Maggie smiled wearily back at him. 'It'll be fine, lad. Just make sure it doesn't burn.' She nodded and patted his arm. 'Ee, I'm glad of your help, Peter, I'll not deny that.'

That night Maggie despaired of saving Hannah. It seemed that all her considerable nursing skills were to no avail as Hannah tossed restlessly in her delirium and the fever was at its height.

Downstairs, Peter paced up and down. Refusing to go home to bed he was supposed to be sleeping in the chair, but there was no rest for him. Over and over he relived the night his wife Sally had died. It *couldn't* be happening to him again. Dear God, it *couldn't*. He had thought that losing Sally had meant the end of the world but he had survived. He wasn't sure he could survive losing Hannah. At last, when he could stand it no longer he tiptoed up the stairs to see if there was any change.

Maggie shook her head. 'I've tried everything,' she whispered. 'If she goes on this road she'll not last while morning.'

Peter said nothing. He went up to the floor above and woke Joseph.

'I want you to come and sit with your mam, Joseph,' he said to the sleepy little lad. 'She's very ill, like you were. You know that, don't you?'

Joseph nodded, knuckling his eyes. Suddenly, he realised how grave the situation must be for him to be woken up in the middle of the night. 'She's not going to die, is she, Uncle Peter?' he asked, alarmed.

Peter wrapped him in a blanket. 'Not if you ask her not to, lad,' he said, his voice not quite steady. 'That's why I've come to fetch you.' He carried the boy down the stairs. 'Now, don't be afraid,' he whispered as they reached the door. 'The scabs on her face will fade and she'll be the mam you know and love in a few days.' He sat the boy on Maggie's knee and gave him Hannah's hand to hold.

Joseph stared at her, his face a mask of fear. 'You mustn't die, Mam,' he cried desperately, stroking it. 'Please, you mustn't die. You've got to live. Please, you've got to live.' He looked up desperately at Peter.

Peter nodded. 'That's right,' he whispered. 'Talk to her, let her know you're here.'

Joseph licked his lips and swallowed. 'You've got to get better, Mam, so that we can go and find that stream up on the hills again. We had a lovely time there, didn't we?' There was no flicker of response.

Peter put his arm round his shoulders. 'Go on, lad,' he said encouragingly. 'Keep going.'

Maggie shook her head. 'Aw, I don't know, Peter . . .'

He held his hand up. 'Let him be, Maggie. Go on, lad, keep talking to your mam.'

Joseph bit his lip. He didn't like his mam not responding when he talked to her. 'I don't know what else to say,' he said wretchedly.

'It doesn't matter. Say anything. Just let her know you're here,' Peter urged. 'Tell her you're getting better.

Tell her what you want to do when she's better. Just talk to her.'

Joseph took a deep breath. 'I was ill like you, Mam, but I'm better now. You've got to get better, too. Please, get better.' He paused, then on a sudden inspiration, 'You've got to get better so we can go and live in that house we found. You liked that house, didn't you, Mam? The one we found after the picnic. I sat on the step because I felt ill and you gave me cherries to eat. It's a nice house, Mam, and it's got such a pretty garden. I want us to go and live there.' He started to cry. 'I don't think she's listening to me, Uncle Peter,' he said.

'Yes, she is. Look.' Peter pointed to where Hannah's eyelids were fluttering. Suddenly, she opened her eyes and looked at Joseph. 'Our house, Joey,' she murmured and closed them again, settling into a calm, peaceful sleep.

'Oh, thank God,' Maggie said, wiping her eyes with a corner of her apron. She gave Joseph a quick hug then held him away from her. 'Take him back to bed, Peter. He needs his sleep.'

'Will she be all right now?' Joseph asked anxiously as Peter lifted him off her lap.

'Yes, lad, I think perhaps she might be,' Peter answered, surprised to find his own eyes a bit moist too.

Hannah's recovery was slow. In spite of the nourishing broth that Maggie made, which she ate obediently even though she had no appetite for it, she was weak and tired easily. Worse than that, she had no interest in anything. She moped about the house, frequently simply sitting and staring into space. When Joseph tried to talk to her about the house in which she had shown such interest she simply smiled and said sadly, 'One day, dear. Perhaps we shall live there one day.' She never even showed any concern about her business at Trippet's Wheel.

'Do you think she's worried about the scars on her face?' Peter asked Maggie, his face creased with worry.

Maggie shook her head. 'I don't think she'd care if she was ugly with pock marks,' she said, 'which she isn't, of course. That salve of mine worked wonders, she'll only have the odd blemish, and that mostly under the hairline.' She sighed. 'No. What she needs is something to jolt her out of this black mood. But I don't know what, I'm sure.'

Peter rubbed his temples and sighed. 'Neither do I, Maggie. Neither do I.'

Maggie looked at him sharply. 'Have you got a headache, lad?'

He looked up in surprise. 'A bit. Nothing much. It's lack of sleep. I was working late last night.'

'Are you sure? You haven't got a sore throat?'

He laughed. 'No, I'm perfectly all right. Really, I am.'

She relaxed. 'It's three weeks now since Hannah took it. If you've no sign of it you should be all right. Though how you've managed to escape it beats me.'

'I told you, Maggie, I was vaccinated against it when I was a boy.'

'Yes, I know all about that. I've no faith in such new-fangled ideas, myself.'

'Well, I'm living proof that it works.'

She sniffed. 'I hope you're right.'

He didn't tell her, it was not something he could admit to anyone, that his nights were haunted by the sound of

Hannah's delirious calling for Tom Truswell, the father of her child. He waited with trepidation for the widower's year of mourning to be up.

Every day Peter brought Hannah a newspaper when he went in to tell her how things were going at work. She always listened as he told her how Sally had taken charge of the buffing shop and was acting as Little Missus, handing out the work and collecting it in, and making sure the lasses were paid at the end of each week.

'Sally thinks it'll soon be time to take in another errand lass so that your sister Elsie can spend all her time with Grace,' he told her. 'Grace says she's shaping up well. That's praise indeed.'

'That's nice,' Hannah nodded.

'The lasses all want to know when you'll be back, Hannah,' he said gently.

She smiled, a distant, sad little smile. 'Why? You've just told me how well they're managing. And I know you keep an eye on things, so they don't really need me, do they?'

'Don't talk nonsense. Of course they do,' he said, his voice sharp. 'It's your business, remember. It's up to you to make sure it runs smoothly. Oh, they'll manage for a few weeks, months, even, but eventually things will start to fall apart if you're not there to show an interest.'

'Maybe next week.'

'I'll tell them.'

'No, don't tell them. I might not feel well enough.'

He sighed, exasperated. 'Oh, Hannah! Whatever's the matter with you? You're not a bit like the Hannah I know and . . .' He bit his lip before he finished the sentence.

'I don't feel like the old Hannah,' she said sadly. 'I only wish I did.'

The thought flashed into his mind that perhaps a visit from her lover, Tom Truswell, might help but he couldn't bring himself to suggest it.

A few days later Hannah was sitting out in the yard in a shaft of afternoon sunshine drinking a cup of tea that Maggie had brought her when her mother appeared.

'Oh, love, I'm sorry I've not been to see you before,' she said as she kissed her. 'I did come when you were really bad but Maggie said it was best I shouldn't come in.'

'I'm sure she was right, Mam.' Hannah squeezed her hand. 'I wouldn't want you taking it because of me. But what about the rest of the family?'

'We escaped it, thank the Lord. But Mary took it. She lost the two little ones and Alfred's badly marked.'

'Oh, Mam!' Hannah's eyes filled with tears. 'Poor Mary. Wouldn't you think she'd suffered enough? Is she all right now?'

'Yes, she's back at work now, although she's marked. And young Alfred's quite a sight. But he's young, with luck it'll fade in time.' She studied Hannah. 'You've been lucky, lass. You've hardly a mark on your face.'

'Maggie says my back's a sight though,' Hannah said ruefully.

'Well, that's no odds. Nobody's to see that. What about Joseph?'

'Maggie says his marks should fade eventually. She had some special salve she bathed us with.'

Maggie came bustling out with a cup of tea and a chair for Jane.

'Thanks, Maggie. And thanks for the way you've looked after Hannah. She's got a real good friend in you,' Jane said gratefully. She couldn't help feeling guilty that it had been Maggie and not herself that had nursed Hannah.

'Aye, well, she's looking a lot better now,' Maggie said, sitting herself down on the step beside them. 'We'll have her back at work before long.'

Jane looked shocked. 'Work! I should think not!' She turned to Hannah. 'I should think it's time you thought of giving up work, my lass. You've been real poorly and you can't be short of brass so I can't see the need for you to carry on working yourself to death at that place. You could sell it and live on what you get for it.'

'Trippet's Wheel needs her,' Maggie said firmly. 'Peter says so.'

'They're managing very well without me,' Hannah said. 'I don't really need to be there.' She smoothed her dress. Her hands were beginning to lose the transparent claw-like look they'd had and were smooth and white. Lady's hands. She was quite enjoying being a lady and had no wish to return to the grime and bustle of Trippet's Wheel.

After her mother had gone she closed her eyes and considered the idea of getting rid of her business. She could sell it and as her mother had suggested, there would probably be enough for her and Joseph to live on. If she did that she would have no need to work, no need to pay placating visits to the cutlers, no need to involve herself in the day to day worries and anxieties of her buffer lasses, no need to make sure the building was in good repair, no need to make sure the empty hulls were let to people who would fit in with the rest of the workers and not cause trouble. It was a tempting thought.

Maggie was furious with Jane.

When Peter arrived home she was banging about laying the table for tea.

'What's gone wrong, Mags?' he asked cheerfully. 'I can see something's got your dander up.'

Maggie sat down, brandishing a wooden spoon. 'Hannah's mother came to see her today and the stupid balm cake suggested to the lass that she should sell her business. I could have throttled her! There's you and me trying to get her interested in something and we both know the best way to do that is to persuade her back to work, then along comes her mother and says she should sell up and live like a lady. I never heard such a load of codswallop in all my born days. Can you see our Hannah being happy living the life of a lady and never getting her hands mucky?' She didn't wait for him to answer. 'No, neither can I.' She got up and began to attack the cloth tying up the steak and kidney pudding she'd made.

'Is there some of that for Hannah and Joseph?' he asked mildly. 'It looks big enough to feed an army.'

She sat down and burst out laughing. 'Aye, lad. I made it big enough to share. Not that she'll eat much,' she added soberly. 'She's got no appetite. But Joseph will. He's got the appetite of a small horse now he's back at school.'

Although he had made no comment on Maggie's outburst Peter agreed with her and he wracked his brain for some way to rekindle Hannah's interest in life. By a

384

stroke of good fortune he was helped by an article in the local newspaper the following day.

He took it home to show Hannah. She was sitting on the doorstep with an untouched basket of mending at her side.

He moved the basket and sat down beside her. 'You're looking very much better, Hannah. Have you taken your sketch pad out lately?'

She shook her head. 'I've thought about it once or twice. But I'm not even sure where I've put it.'

'Well, I think you should find it and sharpen your pencil.' He smoothed out the newspaper. 'Look. The cutlers have decided to give the Queen a present of silver for her Silver Jubilee. A piece of Sheffield silver.'

She frowned. 'Oh, yes. I seem to remember reading something about that a few weeks ago. Have they decided what it's to be?'

'No. That's just it. They can't decide. In fact, there was so much argument about it that they decided the only thing to do would be to hold a competition. Any firm – in fact, anybody – can submit a piece of silver, but it must be specially designed as a present to Her Majesty for the occasion. The piece considered the best, or the most suitable, will be given to Her Majesty when she pays a visit to Sheffield during Silver Jubilee year. The rest will be put on show in Cutler's Hall.'

'That seems to be quite a good idea,' she said with a yawn.

'Here, read it for yourself.' Peter pointed out the article.

She read it without much interest. 'It will save a lot of

'ill-feeling between the big firms, I should think,' she said when she'd read it.

'I think you should submit something,' Peter said.

'Me!' She stared at him and her eyebrows shot up nearly into her hair. 'Don't be ridiculous, Peter. I couldn't possibly do that!'

'Why not? Hannah Fox silver is in all the shop windows.'

'But I only design silver. I don't make things.'

He sighed, a deep sigh of exasperation. 'For goodness' sake, Hannah, pull yourself together and take a little interest. Why do you think I've suggested this? If you design it I'll make it. I make almost everything else you design, don't I? I've thought it all out. There's very little I can't turn my hand to, Hannah, as you very well know. And anything I can't do, any dies that need to be made and cast, Matt Bell would do for us.' He beamed at her and gave her arm a little shake. 'What do you think? Shall we give it a try?'

She stared at the ground for some time, then she looked up, nodding slowly. 'I suppose we could,' she said thoughtfully. 'After all, we needn't submit it if we don't think it's good enough.'

'It'll be good enough. There's no question of that,' Peter said, relieved that at last he had discovered something to arouse Hannah's interest.

She smiled at him. 'If this is only a ruse to get me back to work, Peter . . .'

He spread his hands. 'Would I do such a thing?' he asked innocently.

'Well, whatever your motive, I'll give it a try.' She

frowned. 'I wish I could remember where I've left my sketch pad . . .'

'I can tell you that. All your drawing things are in your little office at Trippet's Wheel, waiting for you to go back to them.' He looked at her for a moment and then took a gamble. 'Would you like me to bring them home to you?'

She hesitated, then said, 'No. I'll come to the office. That's where I work best.'

He relaxed visibly. 'I'll order a cab to fetch you tomorrow. It's too far for you to walk. What time?'

She smiled at him, a real smile, not the sad little apology of a smile he was becoming used to. 'You're a rogue, Peter Jarvis,' she said. She straightened her shoulders and said deliberately, 'Ten o'clock. Send it for ten o'clock.'

She was not prepared for the welcome she received when she walked into the yard of Trippet's Wheel. The lasses had hung flags and streamers from all the windows and there were flowers in her office.

'By, we've missed you, Missus,' Sally said, escorting her up the stairs. 'But we didn't want you to come back too soon. Mr Jarvis told us how ill you've been. Polly's auntie died from . . .' she nodded her head, unable to bring herself to say the dreaded word, 'from what you've had. Oh, thank God you got better.'

Polly came bustling in with the teatray neatly laid with a delicate china cup and saucer and matching milk jug and sugar basin.

'What's all this? What pretty china,' Hannah exclaimed.

'T'lasses all clubbed together. We wanted to buy you summat to show how glad we are you're back with us,' Polly explained importantly. 'We thought you deserved summat better than a mug for your tea.' She leaned forward. 'We've had it in t'cupboard for three weeks, waiting for you to come back.'

Hannah blew her nose, overwhelmed by the affection of her lasses, who had all crowded into the little office still in their buff brats and head-rags, their faces, filthy with what they called 'buffing muck,' creased into wide grins.

'I don't know what to say,' she said, wiping away a tear. 'I didn't expect such a welcome. It's so kind of you all. Oh, thank you. Thank you very much.'

'Just don't do it again,' Old Grace said fiercely. She had left her room to come and welcome Hannah without even being asked. 'I dunna what tha's heered, but this place has been like a ship wi'out a rudder wi' tha not here.'

'Oh, I'm quite sure that's not true,' Hannah protested. 'Mr Jarvis told me everything was under control.'

'Well, he would, wouldn't he? He wouldn't want to worry tha.' Grace went to the door. 'I can't stand here nattering all day. I've work to do.' She went off.

Sally waited until she'd gone, then said, 'Don't tek any notice of Grace. It's just her way of saying she's glad you're back. We've managed all right, although I think Ivy's got in a bit of a muddle with the accounts, haven't you, lass?'

Ivy blushed. 'The books won't balance, Missus. They're nineteen shillings out.'

'Don't worry, Ivy, I'll look at them. I expect you've put a pound instead of a shilling somewhere, that would put you out nineteen shillings.' She sipped her tea from the new china cup and looked round at all the smiling faces. Oh, it was good to be back.

Chapter Twenty-Eight

It was indeed good to be back and each day Hannah felt stronger and more eager to take up the reins of Trippet's Wheel again. She found that, as Peter had assured her, Sally was keeping the buffing shop running smoothly, but there wasn't too much work on hand and Hannah could see that a visit to some of the big cutlers wouldn't come amiss. She had always made a point of keeping in touch with them and it was obvious they appreciated her attention. Her mouth twisted cynically. There was no sentiment in business and the fact that she had been so ill would cut no ice with firms looking for work done at the cheapest prices.

The accounts too needed attention. Young Ivy was willing and she was a neat worker, but it was clear she couldn't get the hang of book-keeping. She was always putting things in the wrong column, or subtracting when she should be adding. When Hannah first examined the ledger she was appalled to discover that the business appeared to be on the edge of bankruptcy, although Ivy was quite oblivious to this. Hannah knew this was not possible and on closer scrutiny and a bit of judicious combing through and moving things into the right columns she found that in fact they were making a healthy profit. It was clear that Ivy needed a few more lessons in book-keeping.

Hannah drew a pad towards her and added this to her growing list of things to be done. She made a face. Working on a design for the Queen's Silver Jubilee seemed to be getting pushed further and further down to the bottom of the page.

It was nearly three weeks before she dropped into Peter's workshop on her way home one night to show him her ideas.

'I thought perhaps we could make a silver epergne, for the Queen's Jubilee, Peter,' she said, a sheaf of hastily drawn sketches in her hand. 'I'm not particularly happy with these drawings, I've been up to my eyes in getting things back to normal, but at least it's a start. What do you think?' She put the drawings down on his work bench, a frown creasing her brow. 'I'm afraid they're very ordinary. There's so much else to think about I seem to be quite devoid of inspiration,' she said with a sigh.

Peter stopped what he was doing and laid down his punch to pick up the drawings. 'You've got to give yourself time, Hannah,' he said. 'You've been very ill. It's bound to take a while for you to get back to normal.' He leafed through them till he came to one that caught his eye. 'This one's not bad. The proportions are good and it's a nice touch to have a cherub holding up the middle section.'

'Yes, but it's very *ordinary*, Peter. Everyone is going to think of something like that. I'd like us to find something really . . . well, *different*.' She sat down on a backless chair opposite to him. 'Can't you think of anything original, Peter?'

He shook his head. 'No. I'm leaving that to you, Hannah. I've said I'll make whatever you design. I'm not designing it, too. It wouldn't be a Hannah Fox product if I did.' He smiled at her. 'There's no hurry. You've got plenty of time. You'll think of something,' he said encouragingly.

She sighed. 'Sometimes I think I shall never again design anything worth making.'

'Don't be daft. Of course you will.'

Wearily she got up from the chair. 'The trouble is, there's so much else to do. I must find time next week to go and visit Dixons and Wolstenholmes. Oh, and Truswells.' She ticked off on her fingers. 'I've been to Mappins and Trickets already.' She gave a wry smile. 'It's amazing what a personal visit and a bit of buttering up can do, isn't it?'

Peter didn't return her smile. 'You should be spending time on your own work, not buttering up patronising old cutlers,' he said, with more than a trace of bitterness.

'I've fourteen lasses to keep in work, Peter,' she reminded him gently. 'If buttering up a few old cutlers keeps them and their children fed and clothed then it's a small price to pay.' She yawned and gathered up her sheaf of designs. 'Well, I'm off home. I'm sorry I'm not a bit more inspired, Peter. Perhaps we should forget the whole idea.'

'No,' he said firmly, taking the papers and looking at them again. 'We can work on this epergne. The centrepiece is well balanced, it's just the branches that need more thought.' He frowned. 'Keep the theme of the cherub in mind, maybe support these outer bowls on little wings . . .' He gave them back to her. 'Give it a bit more thought, Hannah. You'll come up with something.'

He watched her leave. Her design wasn't really much good but he wasn't prepared to tell her so. If it came to nothing it didn't really matter. The important thing was that it had been the means of getting her back to work and taking an interest in life. Already she had put on a little weight and there was more colour in her cheeks. Satisfied, he turned back to the work on his bench.

The next day Hannah dressed even more carefully than usual in a green dress with a creamy lace collar and a matching green coat trimmed with black braid. She completed her outfit with a small feathered hat perched on top of her upswept hair and tilted jauntily over one eye. She knew that her appearance was important when visiting the big cutlery firms and that it was vital to appear prosperous and confident, even if she didn't feel it.

It was the middle of the afternoon before she reached Truswells. It had been a difficult day. She had already visited four firms and been in turn flirted with, subjected to lecherous glances down her cleavage, left for hours in cold waiting rooms, and insulted, but had ultimately received enough promises of work to last well into the winter, which had made it all worthwhile.

She wasn't sure why she had left Truswells until last. She had already passed it once on her way to Dixons so it would have been easy enough to call earlier, but she hadn't done so, which meant that now she had to retrace her steps and walk at least an extra half mile.

She made her way up the stairs of the Truswell Cutlery Company, her heart fluttering a little, due, she told herself, to the steepness of the stairs. It was several months since she had last seen Tom Truswell and it was unlikely that she would see him today. Not that it mattered. Anyway, her business dealings were usually with Mr Briggs, the manager.

But Mr Briggs was not there. His place had been taken by a fresh-faced, eager young man who told her he had only been with the firm a fortnight. No, he didn't know where Mr Briggs had gone but he didn't think he would be coming back to Truswells and could he be of assistance to Madam? As he spoke he was continually grinning and washing his hands with invisible soap.

Hannah stated her business as succinctly as she could, apologising for not visiting earlier but explaining that she and her son had both been very ill, then left, whilst the young man hung over the banister apologising that he couldn't be of more help and assured her repeatedly as she went down the stairs that he would pass her message on to Mr Truswell immediately if not sooner.

She was glad to get out into the fresh air and away from the creepy young man. She walked home briskly. It had been a good day, she told herself and she wasn't in the least disappointed that she hadn't seen Tom Truswell.

The next morning she sent Elsie to get the first batch of work from Dixons.

'There's a big new hotel being built in Manchester,' she told Sally, 'and Dixons have got the contract for the table-ware. It's everything from soup ladles to mustard spoons. All good quality. I've fixed a price and said we'll have them done to time so think on and tell the lasses to make sure they are.'

'Ee, it's grand to have you back, Missus,' Sally said with a broad smile. 'Them masters don't tek no notice of the likes of me. We was getting all the rough stuff while you was away.'

'Well, you'll not be getting the rough stuff from now on,' Hannah assured her grimly. 'I'll see to that. Now, I'll be in my little office for an hour. I've got a bit of work to do there.'

She went to what had become known as her 'little office' and sat down. She owed it to Peter to give a bit more thought to the design for the Queen's Jubilee but she felt totally bereft of ideas. She made a few rough sketches, but everything seemed to be either a copy of something she had already done or something somebody else had done. She studied the picture of the cherub epergne. It was designed with a large centre fruit bowl held up by the cherub and with five smaller bowls for nuts or sweetmeats held on spiralling branches. She sketched a few leaves at intervals down the branches, then threw down her pencil. It was no good. Now it looked like a glorified apple tree. It would never be any good.

There was a knock at the door and Polly poked her head in.

'There's a man to see you, Missus. Shall I show him up?'

Hannah frowned. 'Who is it?'

'It's Thomas Truswell, Mrs Fox,' a deep voice said. 'I hope I'm not intruding by following the young lady up the stairs.'

Polly blushed at being called a young lady by this handsome man and also at the thought that he might have seen her ankles as he followed her up the stairs and she backed away in confusion.

Hannah stood up. 'Good afternoon, Mr Truswell,' she said, trying to keep the pleasure out of her voice. 'To what do I owe . . . ?'

'You paid a visit to us yesterday, I understand,' he said with a smile.

'Yes, I really came to see Mr Briggs, but I was told by a young man . . .'

'Yes. Young Foster. He's taken Mr Briggs' place.'

'Oh dear, I hope Mr Briggs isn't ill.'

'No, not at all. Just a little elderly. I felt we needed a bit of new blood in the place, that's all.' With a wave of his hand he dismissed the subject and laid a large bouquet of flowers on her desk. 'But I didn't come here to talk about Briggs, Mrs Fox. Nor Foster. I came to apologise for not being there when you called and to express my concern. Young Foster tells me you have been very ill. I do hope you're fully recovered. I had no idea, Mrs Fox. Your son, too, I understand, took the dreadful disease.' His face was a mask of concern.

She nodded. 'I think it's true to say that we're both very lucky to be alive, Mr Truswell. In fact, if it had not been for my dear friend, Mrs Lewis, I think the outcome might have been very different. For us both.' She picked up the flowers. 'With your permission I shall give Maggie some of these flowers.'

'Of course you may. They're yours to do as you like with.' He gave the crooked little smile that she remembered from years ago. 'But not the roses, please. They are for you.'

She buried her head in them to hide the flush she knew had spread across her face. 'You're very kind, Mr Truswell.'

'Not at all.' He paused. 'Is your son quite recovered, Mrs Fox?'

'Yes, thank you. He's back at school.'

'I wondered . . . As he has been so ill, perhaps a little treat wouldn't come amiss?'

She was immediately wary. 'What sort of treat, Mr Truswell?'

'I thought perhaps a visit to the Botanical Gardens? The fresh air would do him good, I'm sure. And you, too, Mrs Fox. Naturally, I wouldn't dream of taking your son without you.'

'I'm not sure . . .' Confusing thoughts were whirling round in her brain. He couldn't be asking her out; his wife hadn't yet been dead a full year so he was still in mourning for her. But it was Joseph he was thinking of, Joseph he wanted to take to the Botanical Gardens. Wasn't it? Was it Joseph? Or was Joseph just an excuse to get her to go with him? In that case, could she go? Would it be right? Would she be compromising herself?

'I really don't know,' she said at last.

Tom raised his eyebrows. 'Don't you think he would enjoy it?'

'Oh, I'm sure he would,' she said quickly. 'It's just that . . .'

'Ah, I see.' He nodded understandingly. 'Well, perhaps your friend, Mrs Lewis did you say her name was? Perhaps she would like to come, too. There couldn't possibly be any harm in that, could there?' He smiled at her disarmingly.

She smiled back. 'No, I'm sure that would be all right.'

'Good. Then I'll have a carriage sent round at two o'clock on Saturday for the three of you and I'll meet you at the gate of the Botanical Gardens. How will that suit?'

'Oh. Yes. That would be very kind of you, Mr Truswell.'

After he had gone Hannah sat staring into space for a long time. She couldn't help a little surge of excitement at the proposed excursion, yet at the same time she wasn't sure that she was doing the right thing in letting Joseph come into such close contact with his natural father. Especially as Tom Truswell seemed in no hurry to admit the relationship. She felt as if her mind was going round in circles and she picked up the designs for the epergne to try and calm her spirits. It was rubbish. Completely out of proportion and totally unsuitable to hold fruit or anything else. She ripped the drawings in half and then into tiny pieces and threw them in the fireplace.

Then she put on her coat and hat and went home.

Saturday dawned a warm, golden autumn day. Joseph was excited at the prospect of a journey in a proper carriage rather than a horse bus and didn't even object when his mother insisted on him wearing his Sunday suit.

Tom Truswell was waiting for them at the gate of the Botanical Gardens as they alighted from the carriage, Maggie wearing her best black bombazine and Hannah in dark blue silk. Hannah was a bit disconcerted at the crowds of people milling about.

'What more did you expect, Mrs Fox?' Tom asked, with a quizzical lift of one eyebrow. 'This is a perfect day, one of the last before winter sets in, I shouldn't wonder, and this is a beautiful garden, a perfect place to be. And with perfect company,' he added under his breath so that only she heard the last words. He raised his voice. 'Now, young man, since it's mainly for your benefit that we're here today, what would you like to see?'

'The bear pit, please, Sir,' Joseph answered, without hesitation.

Tom sighed theatrically. 'I might have known,' he said with a grin. 'Very well, come along, then. But there are no bears there now, you understand.'

'I know that, Sir. But I'd like to see where they used to be. Mr Shackleton told us they used to climb a pole and beg for buns. Is the pole still there, Sir?'

'Yes, I believe it is. Come along then, this way.'

It was a thoroughly enjoyable afternoon. They strolled in the warm sunshine, they stopped and listened to the band playing in the bandstand, they walked through the huge conservatories and admired all the exotic plants and flowers there.

'Ee, it don't look real, does it?' Maggie remarked as they stood looking at an enormous creamy pink water lily with leaves that were nearly six feet across. She was having a wonderful time, Mr Truswell was treating her just like a lady. Now and again she was so overcome with the heat and the excitement of the day that she had to stop and mop her pink face with a spotless white handkerchief.

Hannah was enjoying herself, too, but underneath there was a nagging unease. What was Tom Truswell's real motive for asking them out? He was behaving impeccably, giving most of his attention to Joseph, for whose benefit he had planned the afternoon. Or so he had said. Yet now and again, a lingering glance, a hand behind her elbow exerting a little more pressure than was strictly necessary, made her wonder if this was more than a simple act of kindness to a boy who had been poorly. Or was she letting her imagination run away with her? Were these tiny acts no more than wishful thinking on her part?

Soon it was time for tea and they sat at a table under a large walnut tree watching the peacocks strutting on the lawn, dragging their long plumes behind them.

'They're very colourful, aren't they?' Hannah remarked, watching them as she stirred her tea.

'Even more so when they spread their tails,' Tom answered. 'That really is quite a sight.'

Suddenly, as if it had overheard the conversation, the peacock nearest to them gave its hindquarters a little rustling shake and spread its tail, strutting first this way and then that to display the amazing sight.

'Ee!' Maggie mopped her face once more. 'I've never seen the like o' that before, have you, Joey, lad?'

'No, but Mr Shackleton showed us some pictures of peacocks on a magic lantern once. The colours weren't as bright as that one, though.'

'That's because this one's real,' Tom said. He turned and leaned a little towards Hannah. 'You're very quiet, Mrs Fox,' he said quietly. 'Aren't you impressed by the peacock's display?'

She nodded thoughtfully. 'Oh, yes, Mr Truswell. Indeed, I am.'

'Well now, have you enjoyed your afternoon, young man?' Tom asked later, as he escorted them back to the carriage.

'Oh, yes, Sir. Thank you,' Joseph said enthusiastically.

'And would you like to come again? Or perhaps do something different? A visit to the zoo, maybe?'

'Oh, yes, Sir, I should like that very much.'

'Very well, we'll see what we can do. With your mother's permission, of course.' He turned and inclined his head in Hannah's direction. She was sure he winked as their eyes met and she felt herself blushing like a schoolgirl.

It was preposterous, she told herself as she lay thinking over the day in bed that night. Tom Truswell was only being kind to Joseph. Nothing more. But why? Why would he pay so much attention to her son . . . unless it was not really Joseph he was interested in at all. At that thought her heartbeat quickened. Could it be true? Could it be that Tom Truswell still found her attractive? Still wanted her? After all these years, could all her dreams come true? Was there still a chance that she might be mistress of Cutwell Hall and her son take his rightful place as its heir? The thought was almost too heady to contemplate.

As for Maggie, when she got home she took off the black bombazine and loosened her stays before she prepared Peter's supper. She'd had a good afternoon, and Mr Truswell couldn't have treated her better if she'd been the Queen herself. A very polite, thoughtful man, he was. It was plain he liked Hannah, too. Maggie smiled to herself. Time would tell whether it was really the boy Mr Truswell was interested in, or whether it was the boy's mother that had taken his eye. Hannah was still an attractive woman. Time she was wed again. And Tom Truswell would be quite a catch.

She heard her lodger's step in the yard. Best not say too much about her suspicions to Peter. If there was anything to it he'd find out soon enough. So she confined herself to telling him of the sights she'd seen and the fact that her feet were killing her from all that walking about. When he asked about Mr Truswell she simply said he'd given them all a pleasant afternoon and seemed to get on well with Joseph.

Of course he would get on well with Joseph, Peter thought miserably as he tossed in bed that night. After all, he was the boy's father, wasn't he? Only Maggie didn't know that. Eaten up with frustration and jealousy, he spent a sleepless night. The next day he went for a long walk on the hills, arriving home exhausted. But he had decided what he was going to do. He would go back to London. He had been in Sheffield quite long enough. It was time to make a fresh start and set up his own business in the capital. He set about composing a letter to some of his former contacts, but letter writing always made him cross and bad tempered. He knew what he wanted to say but it never looked right on paper. He went to bed with the letters only half written and a heap of screwed up paper on the floor beside his table.

The next morning he reviewed the half-written letters and then screwed them up to join the rest then went to work. He knew the best way to calm his spirits was to lose himself in the job in hand; at the moment he was working on a Christening cup that Hannah had designed, with a complicated design of vine leaves and grapes adorning the foot.

His temper wasn't improved when he heard Hannah arrive, running lightly up the stairs and humming happily to herself in a way he had not heard since before she was ill. Obviously, her afternoon with Tom Truswell had been an unqualified success, he thought savagely.

Two hours later she burst into his hull, beaming and waving a drawing pad.

'I've done it, Peter! I've got a design!' She thrust the pad in front of him.

'What . . . ?' He took the pad and examined it for several minutes. 'Well, at least it's something different,' he said carefully. 'A silver peacock. Yes, that's a wonderful idea.' He looked up at her. 'But which way do you want it made? With the tail trailing or spread? I see you've drawn it both ways.'

She bit her lip. 'Would it be too difficult to make it so that the tail could be either way?' she asked tentatively. 'It would need some kind of clockwork mechanism, I suppose, but would it be quite impossible?' She took the pad and made a quick sketch. 'If each of the tail feathers was made individually . . . like so . . . well, a bit more elaborate than that, of course, but so that they could be opened and fan out . . .' She looked at him, her eyes alight with enthusiasm. 'I saw the peacocks at the Botanical Gardens on Saturday and that's what gave me the idea. I was working on it all day yesterday and I finished it off this morning. What do you think, Peter? Will it work?'

He took the pad from her again. 'I see what you mean,

Hannah. But it would not only have to fan out, it would have to lift as well, otherwise it would simply spread across the floor, wouldn't it?'

She frowned. 'Oh, yes, I suppose it would.' She sighed. 'And I thought it was such a good idea.'

He laughed. 'It is a good idea, Hannah. In fact, it's a wonderful idea. It just needs a bit more working out, that's all.' He studied the drawing for several minutes. 'It would have to have some kind of a twisting mechanism inside the bird's body that would lift the whole tail when it was wound up,' he said thoughtfully. He tore off the page and gave her the pad back. 'You go back to your den and get to work on the details and I'll take this across and have a word with Matt. His brother-in-law is a clock-maker. Ted might have some ideas as to how it can be done. I'm sure we can come up with something between us.' He grinned at her. 'It'll be good, Hannah. It'll be the talk of the town.'

'You really think so, Peter?'

'If we can get it right I'm sure of it.'

He was glad he hadn't managed to get the letters to London written. They would have to wait until the peacock was finished. And that wouldn't be for some time.

Chapter Twenty-Nine

Hannah was happy. She was happy because Peter was enthusiastic about the idea of a silver peacock so she could set to work on its design. And she was even happier because Tom Truswell had sent her a note, thanking her for her company, hoping the day hadn't been too tiring for Joseph, and best of all, looking forward to another outing in due course. The days sped past and she sang as she worked.

Early in the New Year she had the design for the bird finished but without its gorgeous tail. Each feather on its wings would be individually chased and the comb on top of the head was to be of silver wire topped with a tiny silver ball.

'Is it possible, Peter?' she asked as she showed him the final sketches.

He studied them. 'Anything's possible, Hannah,' he said with a smile. 'Yes, I can do this. But you haven't specified a size. How big is this peacock to be? Life size?' He grinned. 'A bit expensive, but it could be done.'

'You're teasing me.' She smiled back at him, then became serious. 'No, I thought something quite small. Say about twelve inches high?'

'With the tail to spread?'

She nodded. 'I haven't worked on the tail yet, but it would be nice if we could make each feather move separately when the tail fans. In a kind of graceful movement, like the real thing.' She moved her hands to demonstrate. 'Would that be possible, Peter?'

He smiled again. 'Anything's possible, Hannah,' he repeated.

'What about the mechanism to make it all happen?'

'Ted's still working on it. He's hit a bit of a snag, but he thinks he can get over it. We said we'd discuss it further when I knew exactly what you had in mind.' He waved her away. 'Now I've got some idea you just go away and work on the design and leave the mechanism of making it work to Ted and me. I have other work to do besides your peacock, you know.'

She shuffled her papers together. Then she frowned and said seriously. 'I never think of it as *my* peacock, Peter. It's a joint effort, yours as much as mine. With a bit of help from Matt as well, of course.'

'Well, it will be entered in the competition under Hannah Fox Silver.'

'I doesn't make it any less your project.'

'We'll see.'

She took her drawings and went back upstairs, poking her head in at the buffing shop on the way. The lasses didn't even see her. They were all working happily and singing at the tops of their voices, their buffing wheels whirring, their faces, arms and paper aprons black from the buffing muck that sprayed over everything, in spite of the brown paper shields they had placed over the wheels to catch the worst of it.

She carried on up the stairs. She had a good business going here now; the buffing shop was showing a good profit even though she paid the lasses well over the going rate and ran a sick club in case of accidents or illness. The club also covered a decent lying-in period after confinements, which she knew the lasses appreciated more than anything. It paid off. She would never be short of workers; lasses queued up when they suspected there might be a vacancy at Fox's Buffing Shop, even though they knew the rules on drink and punctuality were strict.

She passed Grace's hull. Nearly eighty now, she still worked.

'Well, I've nowt else to do, have I? I've no family and I can't read nor write so what would I do wi' myse'n if I didn't keep working?' she had said some years ago.

Elsie worked beside her now and Grace had taught her all she knew. Soon Elsie would be as good at the job as Grace.

'She's a feel for it,' Grace had said, somewhat grudgingly. This was praise indeed from Grace.

For her part, Elsie alternately loved and hated Grace. They had many a quarrel, shouting at each other over the swansdown buffs but afterwards Elsie always apologised, whether or not she was in the wrong, and would buy Grace a box of Turkish Delight, which she knew the old lady loved. Then harmony would reign for a few weeks.

Occasionally Hannah would intervene and chastise her sister for upsetting Grace.

'We can't afford to upset her, Elsie,' she would say. 'There's not a better silver finisher in Sheffield.'

'Don't worry, Annie. She'll not leave us. She loves a good barney, does Grace.' She winked. 'I know how to handle her. And a box of Turkish Delight works wonders. We get on all right together, Grace and me. She's learned me a lot. You just leave us be.'

Back in her office Hannah stood looking out of the window. The first flakes of snow were falling and being blown by eddies of wind into the corner of the yard. She pulled the old shawl she wore at work more closely round her. The sky, what she could see of it between the tall buildings, was a dull, leaden colour. There was a lot of snow up there. She shuddered.

But it would please Joseph. Tom had bought him a sledge for Christmas and had promised him that they would go sledging on the hills when the snow came. She had remonstrated with Tom about buying the lad such an expensive gift but he had only smiled and told her he was pleased to do it since he had no children of his own to buy presents for.

He had bought no present for her, which left her relieved on the one hand and just the tiniest bit disappointed on the other.

It was an odd situation. There had been several more expeditions with Tom, each one carefully designed to please Joseph. Of course she had always been included although Maggie was not usually invited to join them now. She gazed into the falling snow without registering that it was already beginning to blanket the yard. What could Tom Truswell's motive be in paying so much attention to Joseph? Was his objective to claim his son and heir away from her once he had secured his affection? He had never, ever given her any hint that he was even aware of the relationship, apart from that one day in Mr Briggs' office when he had inadvertently given himself away, mopping his brow when he thought he couldn't be seen. She bit her lip. Maybe she had been wrong, that day. Maybe she had only imagined his reaction. Maybe he had simply been blowing his nose. Yet why else should he have shown such interest in the lad? She recalled that he had even asked to adopt Joseph once, when his wife was still alive and they thought they couldn't have children of their own.

Soon Clarissa Truswell would have been dead a full year. Then what? He was an attractive man; surely it would only be a question of time before he took another wife? Could it be that he was paying attention to Joseph as the quickest way to her own heart? She blushed at the thought. His behaviour towards her was always impeccable, although she had several times found his eyes resting on her in a way that had made her heartbeat quicken. She closed her eyes, imagining a lifetime filled with moments like those she had once shared with him, that summer nearly twelve years ago and she knew that if he asked her to marry him she wouldn't refuse.

The snow continued to fall for three days, turning to dirty brown slush on the streets and lying like a sparkling shawl on the hills beyond the town.

As good as his word, on the Saturday after the snow

had fallen Tom Truswell sent a carriage, the wheels and horse's hooves chained against slipping on the icy streets, to carry Joseph and his mother up to the hills behind Cutwell Hall, the sledge firmly tied on to its roof.

Joseph, wrapped in his warmest clothes and with a thick muffler wound several times round his neck, was beside himself with excitement as Tom joined them outside the gates of the Hall.

'Will you be riding on the sledge with us, Mrs Fox?' Tom asked mischievously as the carriage drew to a halt.

'I think not, thank you all the same, Mr Truswell,' she answered with a smile. 'I think I shall remain here and watch you both from a safe distance.'

'I thought that might be so. That's why I've taken the liberty of bringing a couple of hot bricks for you to put at your feet and an extra blanket.' He followed Joseph down from the carriage. Then he turned back to her and tucked the blanket round her, looking into her eyes and saying with a warm smile, 'It can be very cold simply sitting and watching and I should hate you to take cold, my dear.'

He had called her 'my dear' and the look in his eyes had been unmistakable. She sat back, cocooned in the warmth of the blanket and watched the two people she could now admit she loved most in the whole world enjoying themselves in the snow.

It was an hour before they returned, red-cheeked, red-nosed and laughing.

'Oh, Mam, it was wonderful!' Joseph said as he flopped down on to his seat in the carriage and unwound his muffler. 'And I'm as warm as toast. You feel my fingers.'

He held out his hand. It was indeed warm.

'That's more than mine are. My hands are frozen.' Suddenly, Tom put his hand over Hannah's. She looked up quickly and found his eyes warm on her.

'Goodness, yes, you should have had gloves on, Mr Truswell.' She hardly knew what she was saying.

'You know what they say, Mrs Fox? Cold hands mean a warm heart. Have you heard that saying?' He gave her hand a little squeeze and then released it.

'No, I don't believe I have, Mr Truswell.'

Hannah was so bemused that she didn't notice the carriage turn into the drive of Cutwell Hall and it wasn't until it drew up outside the front door that she realised where they were.

'It's my surprise. Tea and crumpets round the fire with my mother,' he said, seeing her amazement.

'Oh, but we couldn't. I mean, it wouldn't be right . . .'

'Nonsense.' He cut her short. 'Mama's expecting us. As far as Mama expects anything these days,' he added under his breath.

He helped her and Joseph down from the carriage and they went in through the front door.

She glanced round briefly. Everything looked just as it had twelve years ago, the silver in the big cabinets, the huge sweeping staircase. For a moment Hannah was transported back to the day she left, slamming the door behind her and vowing to wreak vengeance on the Truswells.

I was young then, she told herself, things are different now.

She followed Tom up the stairs to his mother's sitting room, although she could easily have found her own

410

way there, blindfolded. Joseph followed behind, his eyes like saucers. He had never seen such a grand house before.

At the door to the sitting room Tom paused. 'I think perhaps I should tell you my mother is not . . . not quite herself, if you understand me.' He tapped the side of his head. 'Her mind . . . not as clear as it was.'

He pushed open the door and said a little too heartily, 'Here we are, Mama. I told you I would be bringing guests for tea and crumpets, didn't I?'

Lady Truswell was sitting in an armchair beside a roaring fire. A fireguard had been placed round it and there was a teatray on a low table in front of her. She looked tiny in the large chair but her face had hardly changed. She was still quite beautiful, Hannah thought, her complexion still pink and white, with hardly a wrinkle. Only her hair had changed. It was still luxurious, but quite white.

She went over to her.

'This is Mrs Fox, Mama,' Tom said in the hearty voice which he apparently now used towards his mother. 'Mrs Hannah Fox. Come to see you with her son, Joseph. Joseph and I have been sledging, haven't we, my boy?'

'Yes, Sir,' Joseph whispered, so overwhelmed by everything that he could hardly get the words out.

'Hannah Fox?' Lady Truswell held out a transparent hand and Hannah took it. Her rings had gone; obviously her hands were too weak to sustain them. Only her plain gold wedding band remained. The old lady smiled at her, a smile of genuine recognition. 'Oh, Hannah, I'm so pleased you've come back. You should never have gone,

411

you know. It was such an injustice.' Her eyes clouded over and she frowned. 'I don't remember why you went. We missed you, didn't we, Tom?'

'I don't know what you're talking about, Mama,' Tom said briskly. 'Now, how about some crumpets? Will you be mother, Mrs Fox? Or shall I?'

'You do it, Tom. Hannah is going to sit by me and sew, like we used to. We did sit and sew, didn't we, Hannah?' she asked plaintively.

'Say yes,' Tom murmured from behind the silver teapot. 'It's best to humour her.'

'Yes, of course we did,' Hannah said.

'And we went riding?'

'Yes, we went riding.'

Suddenly, Lady Truswell glared at her. 'You fell off and broke your back. You should be lying down. Go and lie down this instant.'

'Take no notice,' Tom whispered. In a louder voice he said, 'Hannah will go and lie down when she's had her tea. She must have her tea first, Mama.'

'Very well.' Lady Truswell took a bite out of a crumpet and suddenly noticed Joseph. 'Who is that boy? Is that Tom? Tom, you are a naughty boy for stealing all those plums. You deserve a good thrashing . . .'

'No, Mama, of course it isn't Tom,' Tom said, a trifle impatiently. '*I'm* Tom. Joseph is Hannah . . . er, Mrs Fox's son.'

'Hmph. Looks like you did as a boy.' She glared at Hannah again. 'Is he a good boy?'

'Yes, he is,' Hannah answered.

'Tom was never good. He was rotten, through and

412

through. His father spoiled him.' She attacked her crumpet again. 'He's no better now he's a man.'

'Oh, come, Mama,' Tom said with an embarrassed laugh. 'You mustn't slander me in front of company.'

'Hannah's not company. She belongs here. Sophie will be glad you're back.' She nodded contentedly.

Tom flushed angrily. 'Sophie's not here, Mama. She's married to George Boulton in Chesterfield.'

'Oh, yes.' She nodded. She waved her hand. 'Send these people away, Thomas. I'm tired.' She closed her eyes and immediately fell asleep.

Tom turned to Hannah and said apologetically, 'I'm sorry, Mrs Fox. But I must tell you that this is one of her more lucid days. Some days we can get no sense out of her at all.' He turned to Joseph. 'Have you finished your crumpets, Joseph?'

'Yes, thank you, Sir.'

'Then perhaps I shouldn't keep you any longer. It's getting quite dark outside.'

He rang a bell and in a few minutes a young girl appeared. 'Have the carriage sent round to the front, Trimble.'

'Yes, Sir. Right away, Sir.' The girl gave a curtsey that somehow bordered on insolence. Hannah disliked her on sight.

Joseph couldn't stop chattering about the excursion. All the way home in the carriage and up till the time he went to bed he talked about the wonderful day and about the great house they had visited.

'Should you like to live there, Joey?' Hannah asked rashly.

He grinned. 'I should like to slide down the banisters,' he said. 'I've never been in a house with banisters you could slide down before.'

The snow melted and turned to rain. The March winds blew and then April came and with it the first primroses in the woods at Endcliffe.

Tom Truswell had never invited Hannah and Joseph to Cutwell Hall again but there had been other outings, carriage rides, visits to the zoo and once to an art gallery which didn't interest Joseph one bit.

Twice Tom came to Trippet's Wheel when Hannah was at work. He showed great interest in everything and was impressed at the way she treated her buffer lasses.

'Not many people have such a good employer, Mrs Fox. Are you able to sustain all these benefits and still make a profit?'

'Oh, yes. I find if I treat my lasses well they'll work well for me, Mr Truswell.'

'And you rent out the hulls you don't need for yourself?'

'Yes. I rent out four hulls now.'

He smiled at her, the crooked smile that always made her heart turn over. 'No one would ever guess the shrewd business brain behind that lovely face, Hannah. May I call you Hannah? I feel we've known each other long enough to dispense with formalities, don't you?'

A few weeks later she received a letter. It was from Tom, inviting her to a concert at the Albert Hall. It made no mention of Joseph.

'. . . I have procured a box which should afford us an

excellent view of the stage. In case you are worried about the propriety of accompanying me unchaperoned perhaps it would put your mind at rest to know that the anniversary of my dear wife's death occurred a fortnight ago . . .'

Hannah read and re-read this paragraph. The implication was unmistakable and not unexpected. Soon Tom would ask her to marry him and then perhaps they would share a joke about the fact that she was to live at Cutwell Hall not as a servant but as its mistress, something that had still never been mentioned between them. It was something that must be discussed if Joseph was to be able to claim his birthright as heir to the Truswell empire. But for the moment it was not important. She stretched luxuriously. Oh, if only her father could have seen this day!

The design for the peacock's tail had not been going well, her mind was too full of Tom. She had in mind a dainty, filigree pattern that would move gently in the air when the tail was fanned, but each time she showed it to Peter he would point out something or other that was impractical, or out of proportion and she would have to return to her drawing board again.

'Will you *never* be satisfied, Peter?' she said at last, throwing down her pencil.

'Yes. When you get it right,' he said impatiently. 'You can see for yourself that this wouldn't work. Look, you're asking for too much weight at the tip of the tail feather. It'll never hold up. You need the weight nearer to the body of the bird. It's elementary, Hannah. I can't imagine how you can't see that.'

She snatched up the drawing. 'Maybe we should have

stuck to making an epergne,' she snapped. 'It would have been far less trouble.'

'Yes, you're right, it would,' he snapped back. 'Less trouble for me, too. I've had a hell of a job with the bird's head. I'm not even sure I've got the proportions right, even now.' He uncovered an object standing on the end of his bench.

'Oh, Peter, it's just right,' she breathed, her face lighting up, her temper forgotten. 'You've even caught that arrogant, proud look that peacocks have when they open their tails.'

'Well, if you go on at this rate this one won't have a tail to open,' he remarked, covering the bird up again. 'You don't seem to have your heart in it these days, Hannah.'

'Oh, I have, Peter,' she said, a little too quickly because she knew it was true. Her thoughts were always on Tom Truswell and tonight was the night of the concert.

She dressed carefully in the new gown of pale blue slipper satin she had bought for the occasion. Maggie was going to give an ear to Joseph and as she watched Hannah leave she remarked to Peter, 'We shall hear wedding bells before long, I shouldn't wonder.'

'Yes, Maggie, I rather think you may be right,' he answered, carefully keeping his voice neutral. He wished that damn peacock was finished so that he could pack up and return to London. If Hannah was going to marry Tom Truswell he didn't want to be around to see it.

'You look quite beautiful, Hannah,' Tom said admiringly as they mounted the red plush staircase. 'Do you see all the heads turning? The other chaps think I'm the luckiest man here, to be escorting such a lovely lady.'

416

He bought her chocolates and a Chinese fan in case the atmosphere became too oppressive from the heat of the candles. During the concert he held her hand under the tasselled programme. She was so happy, so conscious of his presence that she hardly knew what the orchestra was playing.

Going home in the carriage he took her in his arms.

'You know I love you, Hannah,' he said as he kissed her. 'Do you think you could learn to love me a little, too?'

'Yes, Tom, I do,' she answered and would have said, I've always loved you, ever since I was a servant in your father's house, but he began to cover her face with kisses and there was no room for words.

'I think it would be prudent to wait a few more weeks before we announce our engagement, Hannah,' he said when he at last pulled away from her. 'It wouldn't be seemly on my part to show undue haste in remarrying.'

She agreed. She knew Tom loved her. That was the important thing.

Chapter Thirty

It was difficult not to share her precious secret, especially with Joseph. She couldn't resist asking him what he thought of Mr Truswell.

Joseph thought for several minutes. Then he said, 'He's very nice, Mam. He buys me nice things. But I wish he wouldn't try to make me call you Mam*a*.' He exaggerated the last syllable. 'You're my Mam, not my Mam*a*.'

'Does he do that? I hadn't noticed.' She ruffled her son's hair. 'Well, if that's all you've got against him you must like him a bit.'

'Yes, I do. A bit. Oh, dash! I can't get this bit right.' He was struggling with the funnel of the model steamship Tom had bought him.

'Watch your language, darling.' Hannah went back to her sewing. Soon Joseph would find out that Tom was his father. It would be nice if Tom was the one to tell him. She frowned. So far she had felt unable to broach the subject of their former relationship. Tom had given her no encouragement, it was as if he had wiped it from his memory. No doubt he had had other liaisons, she was not so naive as to imagine otherwise, but had there been so many other women that he had completely forgotten their relationship? She stared out of the window. There was no denying he had treated her very badly all those years ago; perhaps that was why he refused to be reminded of their love affair. In that case maybe it was better that it should lie buried in the past. Rattling old skeletons in the cupboard was no way to begin a new life together.

At Trippet's Wheel the design for the peacock's tail feathers had at last passed Peter's critical eye. As Hannah left work late one night she called in at his workshop to see if he had begun work on them.

'I've done one,' he said, uncovering it as it lay on a tray.

'Oh, Peter, it's beautiful,' she breathed. 'So delicate. Can I . . . may I pick it up?'

'Yes, but support it with your other hand. I'm afraid I may have to strengthen the wire or it will be too fragile. It needs to have a certain amount of strength to stand up to the movement of the tail.'

'How many more will you have to make? Can you get away with less than I specified? You'll never manage fifty, will you?'

'No, but it won't need that many. Probably about three dozen will do it. We'll see, anyway.' He grinned at her. 'Ted's cracked the problem of the mechanism. He's worked it with a corkscrew, I can't explain exactly how but he assures me it'll do exactly what we want. And of course it'll all be hidden inside the body of the bird, so you won't see it.' He rubbed his hands together. 'Your peacock's going to be good, Hannah. Queen Victoria will be thrilled to bits with it.'

'It's not *my* peacock, Peter,' she said with a trace of irritation. 'It's yours as much as it is mine. I only designed the thing. Look at all the work you've put into it.'

'Well, we won't argue about it. Let's just get it finished. It's hanging about too long and I've got other fish to fry.'

She frowned. 'What other fish?'

'Oh,' he shrugged, 'I've got plans.'

'What plans?'

He turned back to his work. 'Nothing you'd be interested in.'

She left, feeling vaguely disgruntled. It was not like Peter to be secretive.

On her way home she went to the baker's in Fargate that made gingerbread men in a special way that Joseph particularly liked. The evenings were lighter now and she was going for a drive with Tom tonight so she wanted to take her son a little treat to compensate for being left behind.

'A yesterday's loaf, if you please.' A shabby-looking man was being served in front of her. 'Or even the day before yesterday's, if you have one.'

She frowned, trying to recall where she had heard that voice before.

'Here you are, Mr Briggs. You can have this one for a ha'penny,' the woman behind the counter said.

He paid and turned to leave.

'Mr Briggs!' Hannah laid her hand on his arm. As he looked up at her she saw that his face had lost its round chubby look and looked drawn and lined. 'Wait a minute,

Mr Briggs. I want to talk to you.' Hurriedly, she bought her gingerbread man and followed him out into the street.

He was trying to hurry away so that he wouldn't have to speak to her but she caught up with him without much trouble and took his arm. 'You don't look at all well, Mr Briggs,' she said. 'Are you ill? Is that why you left Truswells?'

He turned to look at her. 'Oh, no, my dear. I wasn't ill when I left Truswells,' he said sadly.

'Then why did you leave? I don't understand. You'd been there such a long time. I always thought you were happy there.'

He shook his head. 'Oh, I was, Mrs Fox. I didn't want to leave, believe me.' He tried to shake her hand off his arm and walk away but she held on.

'What happened then?' she asked.

He gave a great sigh. 'If you must know, Mrs Fox, I was told to go by Mr Tom. He said I'd been dipping my hand in the till. I hadn't, of course, but there was no way I could prove it.'

Hannah drew him to a seat by the side of the road. 'Oh, Mr Briggs. Surely, there must be some misunderstanding? I'm quite sure Tom . . . er, Mr Truswell would never want to lose you. You were his right-hand man. Perhaps if I were to put in a word for you . . .'

He held up his hand. 'I don't think *you* quite understand, Mrs Fox. Mr Tom knew perfectly well what he was doing when he sacked me. The truth of the matter was, he needed to be rid of me so that he could employ a young chap in my place, a young chap too wet behind the ears to understand what was going on.' His mouth twisted. 'You see, Mrs Fox, I knew too much.'

She frowned. 'Too much about what?'

'Too much about the money Tom Truswell was taking from the business for his gambling; his cock fighting, cards, horses. The silly little fool will gamble on anything, from whether it'll rain on Tuesday to whether a fly will reach the top of the window before it flies away.' His voice was bitter.

She was silent, hardly able to take in what he was saying. She had always had a high regard for Mr Briggs, she couldn't believe he was simply being vindictive, yet what he was saying was beyond belief.

'That business is nowt more than an empty shell, Mrs Fox,' he went on, shaking his head. 'Young Tom's gambling it away from the inside. It's been going on for years. Oh, it did stop for a while when his wife was alive but it didn't last. I knew it wouldn't. His poor father would turn in his grave if he knew half what was going on. I've warned and warned but the silly young pup wouldn't listen. That's why he got rid of me, because I was too much of a conscience to him. He's in debt up to his ears, Mrs Fox, and Cutwell Hall is mortgaged to the hilt. God knows what'll happen if he doesn't get some money from somewhere soon.' He chuckled, but it was a hollow laugh that held no mirth. 'I reckon the only thing that'll save Tom Truswell now is to marry a rich wife.'

Hannah continued on her way home, Mr Briggs' words still ringing in her ears. 'The only thing that'll save Tom Truswell is to marry a rich wife.' It couldn't be true that Tom was only interested in her for the sake of her money. She wasn't *that* rich. Well, she supposed she was quite rich if she counted up all her assets, she realised with something

422

of a shock. Her bank balance was extremely healthy and Hannah Fox Silver always sold well. It had never really registered in her mind before just how prosperous she must appear. Just how prosperous she in fact was.

As she got ready for her evening drive she thought about the day Tom had taken her to Cutwell Hall. As far as she could remember it had looked no different to when she had worked there all those years ago. The silver cabinets still stood in the hall . . . She frowned. Didn't there used to be a silver replica of the Cutler's Hall in pride of place opposite the front door? She couldn't remember seeing that. She made a rueful face. The truth of the matter was, the stars in her eyes that night had blinded her to everything else.

That evening, when Tom asked her where she would like to drive to she surprised him by asking him to take her to see his mother again.

'No point in that. She'll probably be in bed. She retires quite early,' he replied carelessly. 'Wouldn't you rather go to Endcliffe Woods?'

She laid her hand on his arm. 'No, Tom. I'd like to visit your mother. After all, if we're going to become engaged she should be the first to know.' She glanced at the little watch hanging from her waist that he had given her. 'And she can't go to bed this early, it's only just gone seven o'clock.'

'Oh, there's plenty of time to break the news to Mama.' He tried to take her in his arms.

She leaned back from him. 'Please, Tom.' She put on her most beguiling look.

'Oh, very well.' He called to the coachman to drive to Cutwell Hall.

This time she took much more careful note as she stepped into the big marble-slabbed hall. The silver cabinets were still there but they held only a few insignificant pieces of silver and these were spread very thinly between them. There was no sign of the model of the Cutler's Hall. She noticed too that most of the pictures had gone from the walls, leaving blank, unfaded spaces on the wallpaper.

Hannah followed Tom up the stairs, where the carpet was dirty and dust gathered in the corners and along the corridor to his mother's sitting room. She was amazed she hadn't noticed last time how dusty and ill-cared for the place was. He knocked at the door and walked in.

'I expect she'll be in bed,' he said over his shoulder.

'No, I'm not in bed,' Hannah heard her say. 'I'm waiting for that stupid girl to come and help me.'

She was sitting in her armchair drinking chocolate. Her face lit up when she saw Hannah.

'Ah, Hannah, have you come instead of that stupid Betty? I'm so glad. You can help me to bed.' Lady Truswell held out her hand and smiled in welcome. 'That stupid maid isn't nice to me at all.'

'Have you had your pills, Mama?' Tom asked.

'No. They make me all confused. I don't like them.'

'You must take them. They're good for you. They help you to sleep.'

'Oh, very well. I'll take them when I'm in bed. Help me up, Hannah, I'll finish my chocolate in bed, too.'

Hannah helped the frail old lady to her feet and through to her bedroom. As she settled her in bed she noticed that a film of dust lay over everything. Even the bedclothes were grubby.

'He makes me take those horrid pills so I shouldn't hear what goes on in the night,' the old lady whispered in Hannah's ear. 'He and that Betty . . .' She rolled her eyes. 'It's disgusting. But what can I do? I'm old. The pills make me confused and forgetful. Soon I shall die.' She sighed. 'I wish I'd died years ago so I didn't have to witness . . . Thank God my Joe didn't live to see what things have come to.' She clutched Hannah's arm. 'Have you come back, Hannah? Are you going to stay here? I don't know where all the other servants are. They never come near me. I think they must all have gone. I only see that dreadful girl, Betty. I don't like her at all. She's insolent and lazy.' She lay back on her pillows. 'I always liked you, Hannah. I should never have allowed Joe to dismiss you the way he did. I knew you would never steal my ring, but Joe could never see any wrong in Tom . . .'

Before Hannah could reply Tom came into the room. 'Come along, Mama, here are your pills. Now take them like a good girl.' As he leaned over his mother Hannah glanced round the room. The ring tree on the dressing table was bare and so were Lady Truswell's fingers. So where were her rings now? And where was the rest of her jewellery? There was no sign of a jewel box and even the monogrammed silver-backed brushes Lady Truswell had been so proud of, gifts from her husband on their wedding day, were gone.

The pills worked very quickly.

'Are they really necessary, Tom?' Hannah asked as they left the room. 'Your mother hates taking them. She says they make her confused.'

He laughed. 'She has to take them because she *is* so confused. Without them she's completely gaga.'

425

Hannah didn't believe him but she didn't argue.

'You simply don't understand, do you, darling?' he said, stroking her hand in a way that made it difficult for her to concentrate on what he was saying. 'You're much too soft, too sensitive. It's the same with your business. Far be it from me to dictate to you how you should run it, Hannah, but don't you think you rather molly-coddle your buffer lasses? After all, they're a rough, tough breed. As long as you pay them a living wage they can look after themselves. There's no need for you to waste your money on sick clubs for them.'

She drew her hand away. 'Thank you for your advice, Tom, but I'll run my business the way I think fit.'

'Of course you will, darling. I would never suggest otherwise.' He leaned over and kissed her, full on the lips.

For once his kiss left her quite unmoved. With cold clarity she could see for herself that everything Mr Briggs had said about Tom Truswell was true. The treasures of Cutwell Hall had gone, the place was in a sad state of repair, just as the old man had told her. And she, Hannah Fox, was to be the rich wife that would be Tom Truswell's salvation.

They went down the stairs together. In the hall she stopped.

'Where is your father's silver model of the Cutler's Hall, Tom?' she asked. 'It used to stand right there, opposite the front door.'

She watched him as she spoke and was gratified to see the expressions that flitted across his face; surprise, guilt, anger, before his features settled into suave confidence. He tried to take her arm. 'Come now, darling. You're tired . . .'

She shook herself free. 'I don't know how much longer you intend to keep up this pretence,' she said coldly.

'Pretence? What pretence?' He raised his eyebrows.

'Pretence that you don't realise I am the same Hannah Fox you seduced all those years ago, with promises you had no intention of keeping.'

He tried to take her in his arms. 'Of course I realised, my darling. How could I ever have forgotten? But I was too much of a gentleman to remind you of your youthful . . .' he searched for the word, '. . . wantonness.'

Her mouth dropped open as she struggled free. 'My *what!*' she almost screamed the word.

He ignored her and went on smoothly. 'But, darling, why else do you think I've taken such an interest in your – in *our* son?'

Her face was a mask of fury. 'And what makes you so sure that Joseph is *your* son, Mr Truswell?' she asked through gritted teeth. 'When you contrived to have me thrown out because in my innocence I had succumbed to your attentions and listened to your lying promises, how do you know what dire straits I found myself in? How do you know I didn't end up in some rat-infested cellar? Or even the gutter?' She glared at him. 'How do you know I didn't miscarry your child? How do you know Joseph isn't simply the product of being forced to sell my body for a crust?' She paused, her breast heaving. 'And if I hadn't dragged myself up out of the gutter and made good – if I hadn't become Hannah Fox Silver, *would you have cared?*'

He couldn't have looked more shocked if she had struck him. 'But I was sure . . .'

'You can be sure of *nothing* concerning me, Mr

Truswell, except that Joseph is the son of Reuben Bullinger, a good man who took me in when I was in trouble. My son is nothing to do with you, Mr Truswell, and for that I thank God from the bottom of my heart. And if you imagine that you can dig yourself out of the hole your gambling has forced you into by marrying me you are very much mistaken. You can rot in hell for all I care, Mr Truswell. I and my son want nothing further to do with you and if you try to force your attentions on me, or my son, I shall have the law on you.'

For the second time in her life Hannah let herself out of Cutwell Hall and slammed the door behind her. But this time it was with a feeling of triumph.

She was glad of the long walk home to cool her temper. Even so, that night she hardly slept. She thumped her pillow. How could she have been such a blind, stupid fool as to be taken in by Tom Truswell? And for a second time, too! She was filled with self-disgust at her own gullibility and she thanked God from the bottom of her heart that Mr Briggs, however unwittingly, had opened her eyes to the true situation before it was too late.

The next day she got up early and parcelled up all the presents Tom Truswell had given her and Joseph.

'What are you doing, Mam?' Joseph said, coming downstairs and rubbing his eyes sleepily.

She told him.

'Does that mean Mr Truswell won't be taking us out any more, Mam?' he asked.

'I'm afraid so, darling.'

'Oh, that's good.' He sighed with relief and came leaned against her. 'I never liked him, Mam.'

She raised her eyebrows. 'Didn't you, Joey? Why ever didn't you say so, then?'

He shrugged. 'Well, you seemed to like him. And he bought us nice things. But I didn't like him. Not really. I'm glad we won't have to see him any more.'

She pulled him to her and gave him a hug. 'So am I, darling.'

She left the parcel of presents at the Truswell Cutlery Company and continued on her way to Trippet's Wheel. She felt as if a great weight had been taken off her shoulders.

As she passed along Fargate she again saw Mr Briggs and she called to him.

'I must thank you, Mr Briggs,' she said when she caught up with him.

'Thank me for what, Mrs Fox?' He was clearly mystified.

'Thank you for preventing me from doing something I should have regretted for the rest of my life, namely marrying Tom Truswell.'

'Good grief! Were you contemplating that?' His eyes widened.

She nodded. 'I'm afraid so. But hearing what you had to say opened my eyes to the true situation. I shall be eternally grateful to you for that.' She laid a hand on his arm. 'Are you in work, Mr Briggs?'

'Not exactly. I earn the odd crust writing letters for people.' He smiled wryly. 'Mostly for people too poor to pay me much.'

'Then may I do something to repay you a little? Would you be prepared to work for me for a few hours a week?'

He drew himself up. 'There's no need for that, Mrs Fox. You don't owe me a favour for pointing out Tom Truswell's failings. It was not an honourable thing for me to have done so it would hardly be right for me to make capital out of it.'

Hannah smiled. 'In truth it would be as much to my benefit as yours, Mr Briggs. I have a girl in my office who's willing enough but she isn't very good with accounts. She keeps putting things in the wrong columns and her adding up is atrocious. Could you teach her?'

'In that case . . .' His face cleared and he nodded. 'There's not much about numbers I don't know. I guess I'd enjoy that, Mrs Fox.'

'I thought you might. Well, come to Trippet's Wheel tomorrow at ten. I'll tell Ivy you're coming.'

He doffed his hat. 'Thank you, Mrs Fox. I shall be there.'

She went on. At the gate of Trippet's Wheel she paused for a moment. It looked prosperous; the yard was well swept, and brightened with large tubs of geraniums. The paintwork was fresh and the windows glazed and sparkling. Any pane of glass that got broken was immediately replaced, Hannah insisted on it, saying that bits of cardboard or brown paper pasted over broken windows gave the whole place a run-down appearance. There was nothing run-down about Trippet's Wheel. No wonder Tom Truswell had set his sights on it.

Chapter Thirty-One

Hannah saw that as usual Peter was at his bench. She went in and watched him at work for several minutes before he looked up from the snuff-box lid he was chasing.

'I've done another three feathers,' he grinned. 'They're tricky. If I was charging you for my time that peacock would be worth its weight in gold, let alone silver.'

'How long have you spent on it, then?'

'I don't know. I daren't keep track of my hours!' He looked up at her. 'You look a bit pale, Hannah. Are you all right?'

'Yes, thanks. I didn't sleep well, that's all.' She picked up one of his punches and examined it. 'Peter, I'm thinking of buying a house.'

His eyebrows shot up. 'But I thought . . .'

'You were mistaken, Peter,' she said sadly. 'And so was I. There's nothing between me and Tom Truswell.'

'I'm sorry if you're upset.' He couldn't say he was sorry the affair was at an end because he wasn't. He'd never liked Tom Truswell. Never trusted him.

'The only reason I'm upset is that I was foolish enough to allow myself to be taken in by his charm. For the second time, too.' She hesitated, blushing. 'I've never told anyone this, but Tom Truswell is Joseph's father. Of course Joseph has no idea . . .'

He flushed too, but with pleasure that she had confided in him. 'I'd guessed that, Hannah,' he said gently. 'Your secret is safe with me. You must have been very young at the time.'

'I was sixteen,' she said, adding bitterly, 'But I'm twenty-eight now. Old enough to have known better.'

She was silent for several minutes, then she put down the punch she had been toying with and looked up.

'As I was saying, Peter, I'm thinking of buying a house. I saw it before Joseph and I were both ill and I thought it would have been sold by now, but I see it's still on the market. Will you come and look at it with me? See if it's all right?'

He smiled at her. 'Don't you trust your own judgement, Hannah?'

'Not any more,' she replied, making a face.

'When do you want to go?'

'Now?'

'Give me three-quarters of an hour and I'll have finished this.'

Hannah collected the key from the agents and hired a cab to take them to the house on the Fulwood Road. It was just as she had remembered it except that the garden had become overgrown with daffodils rioting among the weeds and long grass and instead of cherries in the orchard there was a mass of white cherry blossom.

With a thumping heart she unlocked the door. It

smelled fusty and unlived in and a mouse scuttled away as they walked into the kitchen, yet in spite of the chill atmosphere the house seemed to envelope her in a welcoming warmth.

'It's uncanny,' she whispered to Peter as they walked through the rooms. 'It's as if the house has been waiting for me, as if it wants me to come and live in it. I had this feeling before, when I could only peer in through the windows.'

'Then it must be right for you,' Peter said. 'I've been all over it. I can't find any damp patches or rotten wood. As far as I can see it's as sound as a bell.'

'Then you think I should buy it, Peter?'

'As I said, I can't see any structural reason why you shouldn't.' He kept his voice deliberately non-committal.

'You don't sound very enthusiastic.'

He shrugged. 'What do you want me to do, Hannah? Leap about like a demented dervish, mad with excitement? It's not my house. I'm not going to live in it. If you want it, go and make an offer. I've said there's nothing wrong with it that I can see.'

'Thank you for your advice, Peter.' For some reason she felt flat. Disappointed that he hadn't shown more interest. Yet why should he? As he'd said, he wasn't going to live there.

They travelled back in the cab in silence, each busy with their own thoughts.

For his part, although Peter was more relieved than he could say that Hannah wasn't going to marry Tom Truswell, he realised that if she bought this house it would widen the gulf between them to a point where it would be impossible to bridge. He was by no means a poor man, but Hannah had become a rich woman, and whether she realised it or not, in moving to the Fulwood Road she was moving into wealthy circles. The sooner the silver peacock was finished and he could leave Sheffield for ever and go back to London the happier he would be.

Hannah moved into her new house, number 189 Fulwood Road, in early July. It was a sunny house, with big, airy rooms that made the few sticks of furniture she had brought with her from Orchard Yard look lost and she had a wonderful time combing the furniture stores for comfortable chairs and a bedroom suite, as well as other knick-knacks, small tables, foot stools and a what-not to stand in the corner. She even bought a piano and arranged for Joseph to have piano lessons.

Joseph was happy. He caught the horse bus to school every day and felt quite grown up. Hannah too caught the horse bus – a different one – to work. But she was less happy. She couldn't understand it. She had everything she wanted, a wonderful son, a good business and a beautiful house. She was independent, she was respected. What more could she possibly want? Yet still there was an empty, gnawing feeling nagging inside her and she didn't know what to fill it with.

She even wondered if she had been too hasty in breaking off her relationship with Tom Truswell. But calling to mind her last scene with him left her in no doubt.

She had heard later that he had gone abroad and that his sister had taken Lady Truswell to live with her in Chesterfield. She was glad about that and she hoped the old lady would spend her last days happily there.

When she was settled in the new house she invited her family to a party. Stan brought his wife, pregnant and happy with their fourth child and Jane came too, looking too young to be the grandmother of six. Mary, still pock-marked by the disease that had robbed her of two of her children, was again working for the Browning family and now walking out with their groom, a widower with three children of his own. Hannah's other sisters came too. Elsie, now a silver finisher in her own right, had been married just a year and was expecting her first child soon and Maudie was engaged to the gardener where she was employed. Fanny and Agnes were both apprenticed to the milliner at Cockagnes Departmental Store and were still far too young to do more than enjoy mild flirtations with the young salesmen there.

'You're a lucky lass, Annie,' Jane said, looking round the large, airy drawing room, 'but you've worked hard for all this and you deserve it.' She turned to Hannah and smiled. 'Ee, your dad'ud be reet set up to see you now, lass. You'll be having your own carriage next, I shouldn't wonder.'

After they had all gone and Joseph had gone to bed Hannah sat in the small, comfortable sitting room, watching the sun go down, sending its last golden rays over the garden and wondering why she felt so flat. She was where she'd always wanted to be, she had a successful business and the house of her dreams. Maybe that was it, she decided. When you've got all you've ever wanted there's nothing left to strive for. It seemed a hollow victory.

Because there was nothing else to do she threw herself with even more vigour into her work at Trippet's Wheel, turning out more designs for teasets, condiment sets, tankards, chalices, epergnes, cake stands; it seemed that she had the Midas touch. Everything she did was successful and turned, if not to gold, to silver. But it gave her no pleasure.

At the end of September Peter sent a message up to her office telling her he had something to show her.

She hurried down to his hull. Matt's brother-in-law, Ted, was there with him and as she went in they uncovered the object on the bench.

It was the silver peacock.

It stood there, on a silver base, its head cocked proudly, its tail feathers lying along the base like a silver sea.

Ted leaned forward and gently turned a silver key in its side. After several turns he stood back as with a gentle whirring sound the tail began to lift, then gently he touched a lever and the tail spread, standing up behind the bird like a silver fan.

Hannah's eyes filled with tears. 'Oh, it's beautiful, Peter,' she breathed. 'I didn't realise it would be so perfect.'

It was exquisitely made, the tips of the fan so fine that they moved gently in the air.

'I only followed your design,' Peter said, obviously delighted with the result. 'And Ted made it all work.'

'Aye,' Ted said laconically, 'it's not a bad job.' He wiped his hands on his apron. 'Well, I must be getting back. I've work to do.'

'Let me have your bill, Ted,' Hannah called, still unable to take her eyes off the peacock.

'Pete's already got it. I hope you'll be as quick to pay it, an' all.' He went off, laughing, well pleased with his efforts.

'Well, do you think it'll be good enough to give to the

436

Queen, Hannah?' Peter asked as he gently touch the lever and the fan closed, then after a few seconds rustled down to rest.

She bit her lip. 'I don't know.' Suddenly, she looked at Peter, her face agonised. 'We can't do it, Peter! We can't part with it. We can't put it in for the competition. It might win!'

He looked at her in amazement. 'But, Hannah, that's why we've done it! And think of the boost it'll give to Hannah Fox Silver, even if it doesn't!'

'Hannah Fox Silver's doing all right. It doesn't need a boost.' She shook her head. 'No, Peter, it's no use, we can't part with it. Look at the hours we've both spent on it. We *can't* let it go. At least, *I* can't.'

'What are you going to do with it, then?'

'I don't know.' She looked at him unhappily. 'It's yours as much as mine, Peter. What do you think?'

He wound it up again and together they watched as the peacock went slowly through its little ritual.

'I think,' he said at last, 'I think I'd like to make you a present of my part, Hannah. You can put it in your new house and think of me sometimes when I'm gone.'

She looked at him and said sharply, 'Gone? Gone where?'

'Back to London.'

She sat down on the old backless chair. 'Why, Peter?' she asked, shocked. 'Aren't you happy here in Sheffield?'

'Oh, yes, I've been very happy here,' he said without looking at her. 'But I don't feel there's anything to keep me here now.'

'You could buy up Truswells Cutlery Company. It's on

437

the market. I saw it in the paper today,' she said eagerly. 'I'm sure you could afford it.'

'Oh, yes, I could afford it,' he said, 'but I don't think I want it, thanks all the same.'

'No. No, of course you don't.' She bit her lip again and tasted blood. She hadn't realised how hard she had been chewing it. 'Well, if that's what you want I hope you'll be happy and successful in London, Peter.' She hesitated. 'I shall miss you.'

'I shall miss you, too, Hannah.'

She went to the door. 'I should like to have the peacock at my house. Will you do me a favour and bring it, Peter? I wouldn't trust anyone else with it.'

'Yes, of course. I'll bring it tonight.'

She went back to her office and sat staring into space. She couldn't believe Peter was going to leave Trippet's Wheel, he seemed as much a part of it as the very bricks it was built with, and was as solidly dependable, too. He had been her rock ever since she started here. She couldn't imagine how she would manage without him. A tear fell on the desk and she brushed it away impatiently and tried to settle down to some work.

That evening she put on a new dress, determined to make something of the occasion. She had thought long and hard, trying to find the best place to put the peacock and in the end had decided to put it on a small table in what she was beginning to regard as her own little sitting room. The dress she had chosen was a soft pink watered silk, with a lacy collar and cuffs, but even though she knew she looked nice in it, it did nothing to lift the terrible depression that seemed to sit on her shoulders these days like a squat, ugly toad.

438

But she put on a bright smile when she went to answer Peter's knock at the door.

'Come in,' she called with forced gaiety. 'I've even got the sherry out to drink to your happiness and success in London.'

'That sounds good,' he said, smiling back at her. She noticed that he too had dressed for the occasion, in a grey suit and with a pearl stud in his cravat. She had never seen him looking so smart; usually when she saw him he was wearing his old working clothes and she suddenly felt unaccountably shy in his presence.

To cover her confusion she poured the sherry and handed him a glass. 'What shall we drink to first? Our peacock?' She nodded towards the box where the peacock was still carefully shrouded.

He raised his glass. 'To the peacock.'

'No. To *our* peacock, Peter,' she insisted.

'Very well. To our peacock.'

Solemnly, they both raised their glasses. Then, suddenly, Hannah crumpled into a chair, dropping her glass, the sherry spilling unheeded down her skirt. 'Oh, Peter, please don't go to London. I can't bear it if you go away,' she sobbed.

He said nothing, but stood looking down at her and after a minute she pulled herself together and stood up. 'I'm sorry,' she hiccupped, trying to dry her tears with the palm of her hand. 'I shouldn't have said that. It was selfish of me. It's just that I've been feeling a bit depressed lately and you going away seemed to be the last straw.'

'I don't know why you should feel depressed, Hannah,'

439

he said, perplexed. 'Surely, you've got everything to be happy about, a successful business, a beautiful house . . .'

She shook her head. 'I know. But strangely enough, it was moving into this house that made me realise how empty my life was. Suddenly, even with Joseph here, I realised that I was lonely. So dreadfully lonely.'

He took her hands in his. 'Is it still Tom Truswell, Hannah? Are you miserable because he's gone away?'

She looked at him, genuinely surprised. 'Good heavens, no. Why on earth should you think that? I told you, Tom Truswell means nothing to me. Nothing at all.'

He frowned. 'Then what?'

She turned away from him. 'It's nothing. I was just being stupid, that's all. Go to London, Peter, if that's what you want, and be happy.'

He came and stood behind her. 'It's not what I want, Hannah. I'm not going to London to be happy,' he said gently. 'I'm leaving Sheffield because I love you. I've loved you almost from the first time I saw you, only then you were Reuben Bullinger's wife. Since then I've watched you, helped you even, to grow further and further out of my reach. I can't ask you to marry me, you must realise that. You're Hannah Fox, the most successful silver manufacturer in Sheffield, whilst I'm a mere silver chaser renting my hull from you. It's the wrong way round, Hannah, people would think I'm marrying you for your money and I've too much pride for that. So the only thing left is for me to leave Sheffield and go right away. Goodbye, Hannah.' She felt his lips on her neck as he kissed her softly.

She spun round and wound her arms round his neck

and he gathered her to him and kissed her over and over again, their tears mingling as they clung together.

At long last he released her gently. 'It doesn't solve anything, Hannah,' he said seriously.

'But I love you, Peter, and you love me,' she said, 'surely nothing else matters.'

'My pride matters to me, dearest. I can't – I won't be Mr Hannah Fox. I'm sorry.'

She sat down. She knew he was right and she respected him for it.

After a long time she looked up at him. 'My achievements are as much yours as mine, Peter. Everything I've done has been with your help, your advice. It's only the name that makes it mine. Without you I should still be the Little Missus of a buffing shop on Pond Hill' – she grinned ruefully – 'if it hadn't fallen down round our ears by now. Could we not make it a proper partnership, Peter?'

'What do you mean?'

'You're not a poor man, Peter. If I was to sell Trippet's Wheel we could buy Truswells Cutlery between us. We'd alter the name to Jarvis and you could run it as you saw fit.' She shrugged. 'I could still do a bit of designing if and when I felt like it. Would that be enough to salve your pride?'

He stared at her in disbelief. 'You would do that?'

'I'd do anything to keep you by my side, Peter,' she said quietly.

'Oh, Hannah,' he said, shaking his head. 'What can I say?'

She gave a crooked little smile. 'You could say, Hannah, will you marry me?'